Dry Dock

MARINA
DE NADOUS

Matador
9 Priory Business Park
Kibworth Beauchamp
Leicester LE8 0RX, UK
Tel: (+44) 116 279 2299
Fax: (+44) 116 279 2277
Email: books@troubador.co.uk
Web: www.troubador.co.uk/matador

ISBN 978 1783060 184

British Library Cataloguing in Publication Data.
A catalogue record for this book is available from the British Library.

Typeset by Troubador Publishing Ltd, Leicester, UK

Matador is an imprint of Troubador Publishing Ltd

Dedicated to Little Arthur

The Celestial Sea Voyages

Book 1 The Celestial Sea
Book 2 Dry Dock

THE COPPER BAND

He found it when he found me.
For months he wore the homemade
Metal band upon his wedding finger,
Thinking it was for another;
The perfect decoy.
She wondered; The Copper Band?
He mislaid it for a while,
But then it was found and back on his finger.
When asked, he could in all honesty say:
"It is for another."
But she knew he was beginning to wonder
If it had a significance for them.
She liked to see him wearing it; The Copper Band,
Interesting and mysterious upon his slim hand,
Lending dignity in manhood.
The Copper Band; intrinsic denting and organic waver,
Matching their unlikely union in solid possibility.
And at their sad, unwanted parting
He placed it with ceremony upon her little finger.
How strange, and yet prophetic
When it slipped from her hand just hours later.
"Perhaps this is meant to be;" they wondered.
Alone and grieving, it reappears in the bottom of her bag;
Old friend returning; constant companion
On their extraordinary journey.
She is bold. This cannot be taken from them; old friend.
She slides it upon her wedding finger.
She likes it there, The Copper Band;
Associated with healing, joy and the sacred number **7.**

Prologue

"Unfurl the second Jib, My Lady," Lord Swallow calls loudly from the helm. "We're into a close haul; the Main Course needs more tension; we're heading out; away from the coast."

They are off, sailing upwind with controlled risk. The adventure is totally thrilling; all consuming. Wind and water dance irresistibly, sharing their knowledge with the sailors. The World's Soul lies before them, a truth they recognize. The full potential of The Boat is harnessed and The Craftsman shares their joy. He watches the windswept couple. They are glowing——so capable. They have time to put The Boat through her paces; to sail for uninterrupted months where they bond with their vessel, intimately embracing every nuance. They waste not a single moment.

The Ocean swell takes them far off land. They feel safe on board and trust the seaworthiness of The Boat with a faith of steel. They take her to the very edge, at times heeling at dangerous angles, at others loosening the sails for less risk. They have never been happier. They know these are blessed, glorious times and they enjoy them to the full. Big swells, foaming wave crests, threatening storms and blue skies with solitary, accompanying gull greet them with variety and challenge every morning. Days of effortless tacking are followed by near disastrous gybing. The exploring of uncharted seas offers fulfillment of the highest quality. Sweet elixir of celestial joy and boundless freedom sweep over the deck and fill the sails——until the day they venture back towards the coast and a patrol boat unexpectedly pulls up alongside.

"Lower your sails and follow us back to the Marina, please. You are voyaging without a Registered Sailing License." The loudspeaker shocks the crew of two and stops the Boat dead in her wake, causing a lethal tear in the Main Course. The Craftsman winces at the devastation, yet bows to the path of the Quest. Three Marine officials stand by with authority and paperwork; a red clipboard keeping the papers from blowing away. With an audible tremor in his voice one of the officials declares: "This Boat is to be confiscated for the foreseeable future. You will follow us to the Dry Dock bay in the Marina——without delay."

Part One Under Bare Poles

She is manhandled. Those involved are efficient and well-meaning but they misunderstand the nature of the thwarted vessel. Lord Swallow and his Lady are helpless in the face of the Marine Officials who drag their beloved Boat into dry-dock. Her claret paintwork is badly scratched and an ugly gash lacerates her deck. She hangs at a forlorn angle as the dockworkers wrestle her into place. The webbing straps cut into her sleek underbelly; the risk of seeping ulcer and permanent damage frighten her stricken crew. The iron cradle greets her like a cold slab in a morgue. The Craftsman hears the dockworkers' bawdy remarks; their jovial speculation and suggestions as to why a fine vessel should be brought into yard when obviously brand new—and at the start of the prime season; "must be a legal case, eh bro?"

The industrial yard is messy. Vessels of The Celestial Sea's calibre take up residence during the winter months only; not when the summer winds offer perfect sailing conditions. Piles of old rope and wire lie about in rusting neglect like ironic mind-talk metaphors. The smell of tar and oil fill the air. The atmosphere is one of cold mechanic and black-streaked toil. How can her crew leave her here, alone? She looks horribly misplaced. She is a Queen amongst the unkempt who paw her hull, grasping her velvet gown in unkind leer and undignified demand. A seagull already resides on the middle mast. Will they cover her to keep off the worst?

She is sitting straight at last; the crooked angle had been the final insult. There is pride in her bearing still, despite the cruel affront. Lord Swallow and his Lady are slow to leave her side, vowing to make regular checks on her well-being. They overhear the remarks of those at work with trestles, chains and blocks: "What are we meant to do with her, Boss?" the dockworkers ask the remaining Marine Official. "Just keep an eye on her—don't let anyone near her; especially those two." He jerks his head in their direction. "Why, what have they done? Go on, you can tell us. We wouldn't let on."

The official gathers up his papers with a grunt; "you wouldn't understand," he tells them. "It's a complicated matter. Treat that vessel with respect." They shrug their shoulders and watch the man and the woman who appear so distressed beside The Boat. Their hands are linked and their heads lean against the slender keel. The waterline mark is barely visible. She can't have been at sea long.

Chapter 1 Ulcer

Saturday 1st December 2006

P.m. Mouse {Unsent}: And so, Lord Swallow, the deed is done and we were brave to the very last. I am weeping useless tears, thinking of you alone with your report-writing, lesson planning and packing—but without our regular contact. We have become dependant on the joy we share. We have supported and sustained each other on every level for many months. To be deprived of our Boat is devastating, for our Love is TRUE and we both know it.

Yes, we managed to cry in the end, holding each other one last time as we had agreed. I hope you will cry a lot. I hope you will allow yourself the belonging as we accept this painful treasure. A gaping wound—a warrior wound that we gift to others—a peace offering to maintain general harmony. At what cost? At the cost of our personal homecoming; our fulfilment as man and wife. Here I am, alone again on our Mountain, domestic tasks piled up around me as I write. I am a fishing widow once more. The tears course down my face as I think of our abandoned Boat; my face that you have held and kissed and cried into with such tenderness. I will meet you at ten tonight amongst the stars, as we have agreed, to cry together; to pluck the Angel harps and caress each other tenderly. This is so hard—so cruel. I shall weep for many days. The prospect of a barren Christmas holiday too; a holiday we were so looking forward to sharing. Oh My Love, My Sweetheart, My Friend, why do we have to go through this? I suppose we have brought it upon ourselves. Or have we?

I cannot leave our precious Boat just yet. I am standing by her side in the dry-dock, running my hand along her beloved keel in thanks and love and blessing. I feel you there too your hand in mine, your lips upon my brow, your body asking to be loved. I am listening to the C.D you gave me; the song, 'Andy', is playing, flooding my heart with memories of rolling wave and sandy shore as we sat in my van while you sang to me one last time; prompting the tears at long last.

My Love—this is too hard, your Lady X

The lunch party at the beach had gone well I suppose; a strangely surreal affair. I was welcomed lovingly by the family. All the staff was present, including The Board of Trustees and their offspring. We sat together in the sun, the conversation turning to Christmas holiday festivity. Martha's husband, Matthew, was busy at the barbecue beside the upturned kayaks and drying swimming towels. Christmas cards with snowy scenes and winter cheer adorned the mantelpiece in the main room. I asked those gathered if they had ever experienced a winter Christmas, and if they had, did it feel strange. "Oh no," replied several, "it felt right—definitely."

Martha handed around a dish of some sticky concoction—"Go on, try it; a favourite of ours made by a relation. She always delivers a generous box-full before Christmas." It certainly was good; nutty, with chocolate and caramel pieces. Big J. was friendly. Martini's baby daughter sat on her lap, dressed in natural fibres and pretty florals. She wore a fine woollen cap tied under her chin with silk ribbons. I chatted happily enough; semi-buoyed-up by my night away with Adrian. Martha's house sits above the shore—a large, comfortable rental. The family enjoys the coastal position having lived inland for many years. Martha took over Adrian's class last February. She has been at school a year.

The children played on the beach for the majority of the afternoon. I opened the broken gate at the end of the garden and stepped onto the shore to join them. A weathered bench leaning into the sand dunes was waiting for me. Pretty, coastal flowers provided a carpet for my sad feet; I recently discovered the creeping, succulent plant with its yellow flower is called 'Kokihi'; or 'New Zealand Spinach'. The leaves can be eaten as a vegetable. Kokihi grows all along this coastline. I spent a while sitting on the bench looking out across the sea, sensing another beside me. Adrian and I have agreed to no contact over the next three weeks—not even a friendly conversation. It was Adrian's suggestion; a clean break as the teachers demand until the 22nd December when we can speak as friends.

I like the way Martha's garden wanders onto the shore. I untangled a piece of old wire sticking out of the sand and put it aside, resigning it to a bin at the end of the day. The children had fun playing in the waves with their friends. The Laird and I joined them for a while, taking off our shoes and paddling in the water.

P.m. Mouse: {Unsent} Goodnight, My Darling. I am so sad I cannot send this message. I find comfort in writing upon the small screen—there is a grain of life in that. It will fly to you through our telepathic airwaves, coming to rest in your heart at ten tonight as we have agreed. I pray that you will grieve long and deep. I hope this can be a healing for all the hurt and damage one small boy had to bear. Cry for young Adrian my Love; cry for Little Arthur and for 'us' over the next three weeks before school ends. Don't distract yourself from learning this important lesson—the final one.

Sunday 2nd December 2006

A.m. Mouse {Unsent}: Grey, featureless dawn greets the gaping wound in this Warrior's soul, the sword beside her no comfort. Her Spirit is dying and she has no inclination to fight for its survival. "We had no choice," she tells The Laird; her long time Earth companion who shows concern. "We dived into the waves together." "But it **is** your choice," he replies. "You can

4

do what you like." "Perhaps," she answers. He is quiet, adding: "Thank-you for coming home."

She knows full well this is not what they would choose. Oh no. Their enormous sacrifice is made under the pressure of others' opinions and peace of mind. What business is it of theirs anyway? A love story rich and rare—a private world that should never have been intruded upon. At times she is angry with them all. Those around her have their desires fulfilled. They take their pleasure whenever they feel so inclined. Yet this, their perfect, God-given joy is harshly ripped from them both. Untimely, unjust raid—just weeks before the Christmas break. The bleak horizon of the coming weeks looms sad and solitary before her. She cries again.

I work in the garden all afternoon, tackling the long grass behind the cabins. We like to maintain a zigzag path up to the Pa Site. I need a solo job today. A Sunday of tears and non-life—wishing I were in Adrian's arms. I manage to cook. We eat outside. It is the second day of proper summer. I try to keep going, feeling terrible—lifeless—flattened like the path I tend. There is a fresh breeze today. The sky is blue but I am completely wrecked. In all honesty I thought I had more stamina. I am proved wrong.

P.m. Mouse {Unsent}: *Second night without you. A day of empty Spirit. I am light upon the Earth—so light I may not return completely. I am afraid of this wound; a lethal gash without the hope of healing. I am afraid of leaving our beautiful Boat alone for so long—deathly scared that her magic will never return and that I will lose you to dry land. I know I have little to offer.*

My Lord Swallow, I am afraid of the empty space inside me. I want to cry for longer but already sense a blank nothing infiltrating every cell of my body. How do I return to the half-life when the other half is banished? Today I found your Copper Band; it had fallen off my finger when we packed up the van. I wondered if it was meant to go, leaving me totally bereft. But no, there it was this morning, waiting in the bottom of my bag—a small piece of you. I shall be bold and place it beside The Laird's gold wedding ring. I like it there.

Monday 3rd December 2006

I wake this morning, strong in my conviction that I belong with Adrian. Maybe I feel less empty; defiant even. How dare others intrude upon our private life? How dare they confiscate our Boat? We spend our lives giving out to our community. This gift we request is large and unconventional, I know. The life-giving potential will not subside. The potential is not of a selfish nature either—so much could come of it. Last night the telephone rang. Adrian's father was asking after the Fijian family; had I heard how the little boy's operation had gone? He has never telephoned before but I wasn't surprised to hear his voice. I felt it was Adrian reaching out to me without breaking our agreement. Yes, the operation had been a success and the family is being looked after in Auckland. We chatted like old friends although he didn't mention his son.

I want to burn our agreement—yes I do. I want to see flames devour the flimsy paper; so binding despite the wretched nature of the imposed sentence. The words on the paper glare at me. We do not agree with them in our depth of soul. They are insults. Every stroke of the pen is an insult. Tonight I held a dying chick, trying in vain to keep it alive. I thought I might feel a sense of relief, walking back into an uncomplicated life. Stepping through the family door after Martha's party I was aware that my old life has little meaning without the balance of the new.

A.m. Mouse {Unsent}: You asked our Guardian Angel, Cordelia, to telephone-to ask how I am and to say I don't need to be in class tomorrow. Thank-you, Sir. I wonder if you ask out of guilt, or care? Would you find it too hard to have me there, working beside you? I pray you are over the eternal feelings of guilt; the non-perishable residue of childhood. I pray you don't turn away from the grief—that you will allow the healing. Dare I hope that your wound matches mine? That our Love is equally important? At times I am sure, but sometimes I sense confusion. Our relationship has been based on rich communication but now these questions remain unanswered. The loss is so painful.

My week begins as usual, but it is empty and dull. Am I blowing everything out of proportion? Am I indulging in self-pity; a Drama Queen in the Mind Play Kingdom? Am I bored? Do I need this saga? I drive, I shop, I cook and I care for my family. I exist.

I glance at my desk before the children wake. My horoscope stares at me; one I cut out of a magazine in the dentist's waiting room. I don't usually bother with them. This one made me stop and wonder; that's why I brought it home.

'Sagittarius-the month begins with the only full moon in your sign this year. Thus you may find yourself considering the pluses and minuses of a relationship. It is both a time of union and separation. It is also a time when your personal energy is at a premium, by which I mean your insights are more profound and your ability to affect the course of a situation, especially a relationship, is more powerful than ever.'

That's rather apt isn't it? Better keep it for the story. I file it away.

P.m. Mouse {Unsent}: You walked across the playground ahead of me today, Lord Swallow. You almost danced. Did you know I watched? Light and free—do you feel relief, my Lover? Had everything become too much for you? I wish I knew. I can only guess. If you felt relief I would be better able to harden my heart. *Perhaps the entire episode was a creation of my imaginative mind-play, provoked through boredom and homesick malady unacknowledged. Has our bond been a curiosity for you? A novelty with some comfort thrown in? Have we, in fact, used each other? Have you steered our Boat towards the harbour on purpose—perhaps subconsciously? I wish I knew if we are worth the wretchedness. I could move on faster if you had just been humouring me. Hmm—*

These doubts and unhappy sentiment lap quietly at the fringes of my ache. They claw at me in a friendly kind of way. They test me. The fuel for self-indulgent introspection and inward life brews in me. And yet I find a sliver of comfort in the familiarity of my own plateau. At least it isn't boring.

Late P.m. Mouse {Unsent}: *Goodnight, My Beautiful Swallow Man. I am feeling lighter this evening. The dark maelstrom of doubt has been chased away by our companion sun. Thank goodness for the light; its strength outshines any dark. I have always liked the exercise of making a room as black as possible—how difficult it is to seal every nook and cranny; every window and door surround. Class 6 carry out the experiment at school every winter, don't they? What a lengthy procedure to black out the classroom. And then—just one tiny match is lit and the black is defeated entirely.*

The Laird is being kind and accepting. "My sails are slashed and ripped," I admit. "Well, that's the consequence of such frightening intensity. It is unsustainable. You have to realize that." The Laird is very keen on the whole, *'learn through consequence',* module. I must be providing him with the perfect, fallen pupil material. "You don't understand", I try to explain; "it isn't the intensity that has ripped the sails; that couldn't be further from the truth. It is the abrupt, unwelcome halt that has done the damage. The intensity is not a negative force. We have had authority and paperwork thrown at us and we have stalled unnaturally. You see; there is a beautiful balance of intensity and gentle, everyday rhythm in the love—"

I don't say more—it is not fair—The Laird so wishes the whole affair to be over; proved negative, unworthy and hopeless. Of course he does. I want to add: *'And do you know; I am feeling pretty angry that we have been cornered as we have. Oh no, it is certainly not our choice to have halted the creative and beautiful flow of our love. In truth, it is an enormous sacrifice'.*

But I don't needle him further. Another small chick was dying today. I cared for it a while. When I checked later it had disappeared. Big J. has asked me to bake for a music recital taking place later on this week. Her afternoon request made me resentful and cross. Why can't others see beyond conventional barriers to our creative sharing? The life-giving nature of our love overflows; surely they have felt it over the past months? Of course not. I can't possibly hope for any such idyll. So, I have said "no" to the baking—a firm and definite "no". I cannot cook for the school any more. If they won't entertain the possible credence of my relationship with one of their star players, well, they will not benefit from my gifts either. They are linked with Adrian in a symphony of pure, unselfish joy. Even my husband allows this relationship to a certain extent, so why cannot they? I know; unprofessional; others' opinions—how might the children be affected? However, the school will be less rich as a result. There.

I am not a vindictive person but it feels good to air these feelings; to show that I won't be taken advantage of. I hope I might feel better soon.

Late P.m. Mouse {Unsent}: *Hello, My Friend. I wonder how your night wraps herself around our hurt. This is an unnatural sorrow. Surely the negative vibes; the deep pain, is more detrimental to the children's well-being than the delight and positive nature of our love. They are acutely aware on a level we cannot see. Why—isn't this the foundation of the special education they receive? That they absorb the hidden vibe; the truth? I would like to air that more. I need to discuss the thoughts and feelings filling my mind. My Darling, I imagine your 'mind-talk' might be telling you that I am rejecting you; blaming you. I know you well—you will feel I might accuse you, especially as I am trying to keep out of your way. Please understand that I sense beyond the obvious and that I cannot face you now because of the pain. I wonder how you will react to the free time after so many months. You will have more of the precious commodity. I know you will easily fill the hours. There is so much to do at this time of year.*

I am slow to mend myself but I am making headway. I imagine you arrived there more quickly than I. Have you been more able to put 'us' behind you? Hmm—an element of distraction there I suspect. What do you hear when you question the nagging mind-talk? Does our Love stand up in its truth? Your violent outburst in the van frightened me. What lies buried, Sir? Your reaction to my tears—yes, I felt your slight irritation despite the concern—has left me questioning your ability to love another. Your endless need to tackle the mind-talk in every situation, which always leads to issues of self-concern, makes me question the completion of your course. Have you found a way to truly love the young Adrian? You see, until that happens you cannot love another.

Go gently, My Friend Adrian. Know that I am beside you—confusion or not. M—X

The darkness hits. My chest infection deepens; a sign of grief, Cordelia tells me. I am cold towards the caring Laird. He has cooked supper and come to bed for some comfort from his wife and I cannot turn to him. Torrential rain dashes the wooden cabin in recognition of my sad loss. The Laird is cross. I wake in the night; the pain in my chest sears red hot and real. Anxiety for my health wakes me fully and I sit up. *"Come on; try harder—take control. This connection with Lord Swallow is more powerful than even you imagined; come on."* Adrian has suggested some karmic link between us all; is he right? What challenge are we working through? A black cat keeps crossing my path at the top of the driveway. I have never seen it before. And today I burnt my fingers as I baked for the family. Dear Angels, what is going on? And how is he faring? My Beautiful Prince, cast back into the freezing waters. Does his wound bleed as much as mine?

Tuesday 4th December 2006

Today we meet—the first contact for three days; a lifetime of silence between us on these sad, separate voyages. Why does it have to be this way? We are both nervous, avoiding our soul connection by averting eyes. I wonder if others in our Festival Group sense the strange vibe. We sit so close; knees almost touching in this bizarre human ritual. I wonder if Adrian notices The Copper Band; the bold display alongside my wedding ring. There is a moment when we might have had a private word, but that is snatched away by another's presence. My Love, this is unbearable. I am breaking up inside with ripping, depleting grief. I am unhappy.

P.m. Mouse {Unsent}: The ache is ever present—infiltrating; steel edged—acidic; hopeless beside non-stop, worldly task. The intense grief is physical as well as mental, taking her by surprise. It lies beyond her control. She feels the sadness in her eyes. They are heavy and clouded; perpetual tears on stand-by. For what does she grieve? A question asked over and over. Does she weep for herself? For him? For Little Arthur and the breath he is denied? For the future of their precious Boat; deserted and unloved? Or is this a past life issue? Perhaps they never got to say goodbye last time around—never had the chance to grieve properly.

Wednesday 5th December

Today is my brother's birthday. I have two brothers. Jonathon is two years younger than me. A successful London banker he is the eldest son in the family. The Laird and I send a birthday message by e-mail. I busy myself with Cordelia and Lois at school; working on the Advent Festival together. I haven't been able to contribute much recently. The new festival should be spectacular. The original idea of spinning globe, class tableaux and storytelling looks promising, accompanied by the music Adrian and I have composed. We have asked Mitch to be our Festival Narrator. He was one of the performance cast members who entertained our school in October. He has accepted our invitation. The pressure is on. We really need a second melody to break the scenes, but Adrian is too busy and we are keeping apart, so that is not to be.

The Go-Getter's class is away on camp in Hamilton this week. The Laird and I pay them a visit after lunch. My husband tries to make light of our situation but I am too sad to respond. His intolerance kicks in before long. We spend time with Martha and the parents helping out with the busy class. I walk the Bog-Brush away from the Adventure Park; another 'No Dogs Allowed' sign glaring at me. There are very few dog-walking places in New

Zealand. The Reserves offer a canine welcome, and some parts of the beach, but compared with home there is an unfriendly attitude. I suppose many animals are kept on the large sheep farms and lifestyle blocks as working/guard dogs, and then there are the pig-hunting dogs that are vicious and to be avoided. The latter must have a good dose of Pit Bull Terrier in their breeding, although they have longer legs. They often have mottled coats in black and tan; definitely a *'Bill Sykes dog'* with their ugly leer and menacing expression. I have seen them tied up in back yards, thankful that the chains are strong, and I have seen packs of them in the back of open Utes; presumably 'en route' to hunting forays.

I remember The Laird returning from College one day last year, expressing surprise over a conversation with a student: "One of my Year Ten boys told me he couldn't be in school on Friday," he recounted. "When I asked why, he replied: *'I'm going pig-hunting with my uncle.'* I asked him more. What do you use—a rifle? Do you know what he answered? *'Oh no, we go in with knives and 'stick' em. The dogs bring em to bay and grab hold of their ears. That's when we go in with a knife to slit their throats.'* And then he rolled up his trouser legs to show me his collection of horrific scars—*'from the boars' tusks, Sir; they're big buggers!"*

Having digested that shocking piece of pioneering information we regularly spot pig-hunting magazines in the Dairies and Service Stations; magazines with gory pictures of children as young as **7** with blooded foreheads kneeling beside their grizzly trophies; and teenage lads carrying boars out of the Bush on their backs. This is the only way to carry your pig. I suddenly realize the origin of the term 'piggy-back' must hail from exactly this scenario. Even the keen huntsman in The Laird is a little shocked. Such blatant display of the sport would have The English up in arms. The Animal Rights activists would have a field day. Things are certainly different in New Zealand. The pioneer spirit is alive and kicking; 'trotting', I should say-*'trotting through the Bush after them buggers!'*

Once the dog has been exercised we drive to a Hamilton suburb and collect The Laird's now completed kilt. Mr. McNish, a quiet, older man—more Scottish than the Scots—has converted a large shed in his backyard into a smart retail outlet. The building is painted a burgundy colour and a pair of antlers above the door tells the visitor they have arrived. Mr. McNish makes all the kilts himself; even fashioning chrome belt buckles to complete the Highland attire. We ordered our own fabric through one of my fabric warehouse accounts at home. The Wallace Hunting Tartan sports a rich brown background with claret and black lines marking the check. The tone contrasts well with The Laird's auburn colouring. The shop is full of the accessories a budding Laird needs to adorn his impressive figure. I help choose a kilt pin, a pair of claret stockings and of course, a sporran. My husband looks rather splendid in his outfit, I have to say. I like to see him happy. While he chooses a suitable belt buckle I flick through the albums that sit on the coffee table alongside the tartan swatches. Photos of Mr.

McNish's Piper Band, and books on Celtic history, reveal him to be quite an authority on his subject. What a treat to spend time in his den.

The Laird takes a surprising detour on our way home to collect two Kune Kune piglets—my late birthday and Christmas present. My husband presumes I will feel better with a diverting gift. He is kind, but misunderstands. My 'love language' is not that of receiving gifts. He is so like his mother; a gift means everything. The piggies are very sweet but I am not in the mood right now. They travel in a cardboard box in the back of the van. The male is creamy in colouring and the female ginger. I presume he hopes they might keep me occupied and away from Adrian during his Christmas break in England. We certainly haven't given the piglet matter any thought. I expect The Laird imagines they will just settle under the house or something, or that his wife will 'snap to' and magic a pigpen. Anyway, we end up shutting them in 'Alcatraz' for the night; the little-used hen-house.

P.m. Mouse {Unsent}: My Darling, I have missed our ten p.m. meeting. I have been distracting myself with the mending pile while The Laird noisily plans his U.K Christmas trip over the telephone. At last I snuggle up—wrapped in your arms. Today we fetched The Laird's new kilt. How he adores shopping for himself. He gets more like his mother every day! He did look very smart in the completed article at the Scottish outfitters in Hamilton. He plans to wear the kilt at his brother's wedding in Scotland. I tried to get excited with him, cutting a dash in his new attire, but it is not the reality I have grown accustomed to in recent months. I am not ready to leave my Swallow Man. Sleep well, My Love—M—X.
P.s we collected two piglets on our way home.

Thursday 6ᵗʰ December 2006
A.m. Mouse {Unsent}: No particular feelings this morning—accept perhaps one that asks: "you don't know how deeply he loves you, so what is all the fuss about anyway?" I hope your 'mind-talk' is abating, My Friend, and that you can go about life more easily than I. Go gently—X

Unfortunately the piglets escaped from the makeshift hen-house overnight. They were off, roaming the cold hills all night and the male is missing. We bring the female back to the garden and give up our hunt for the other. A neighbour telephones at lunchtime, having found a dead piglet in her paddock-"Was it yours?" She asked. "I think it died of exposure. We buried it on the farm." We thank her and feel sad. I was not attentive enough. The Laird always leaves the loose ends to his wife and his wife is not in good form right now; she is undone. Sorry little piggy.

P.m. Mouse {Unsent}: We travelled through Cambridge on our way to Hamilton yesterday. I liked the pretty wooden houses and avenues of trees.

Everything looked polished; lavish somehow with exuberant planting bordering the road intersections and roundabouts. Happy people milled about, welcoming summer and the glorious, Kiwi sunshine.

Hamilton brought back memories of our lunchtime stop there when you left for Europe. We held hands in public for the first time, feeling strange but exhilarated. I wondered if I should tell The Laird of our trip but decided not to. I did some decorating and gardening work in the sun for Sarah today. Thank-you for coming up to the car as we were leaving school. It was kind of you. Your eyes found mine and you asked how I was doing. I replied honestly—"So, so." You mentioned several times how busy you are; reports, assessments etc—"You must be getting a lot done then?" I asked. Your eyes were soft and caring. You gave the impression of enjoying the heavy workload. As you walked home I followed you in the van down the drive. I didn't turn and wave. X

The man I love walked ahead gracefully, parting the long grasses down the side of the school drive as he moved. I swear he stands straighter at school. At other times he can be a little cowed. I imagine his state of mind must determine how solid his bearing. He must be feeling in control today, or was he putting on a show for his Lady who followed him sadly on her grey stead at pick-up time?

P.m. Mouse {Unsent}: *My thought today is that we couldn't have gone on as we were; with you getting more anxious and loaded with guilt while your 'mind-talk' took control. Something tells me you manifested this harsh climax—oh, unconsciously I'm sure. Did your deeper self cry out for a let-up from the growing intensity? I can see truth there. Were we too intense in our self-scrutiny? Was the very nature of our perfect bond a death nail in itself? Too perfect? If we ever share a future we must remember that. Do you in fact need less time to brood on self rather than more time as we have previously wondered?*

There are so many questions to ask you, My Darling. Will we write this second Book together or will I write alone? I don't think I have ever felt so alone. I find myself wondering about your comment on starting another relationship—"I'm not sure I can face having to go through all that 'will you, wont you, could you cope with me' stuff." My Love—your mind-talk is such hard work, I know; the endless picking through the bones. The next time we hold each other, and there will be a next time, we will sweep away the pile with one, final stroke. I shall be firm with you. We shall not revisit any of it. I have noticed recently that this is what you like; someone to take a controlling stand—providing the boundaries. Am I right? At times you like me to take command. Is this why you feel slight irritation at my tears? If I am weak those boundaries collapse and you feel unsafe. Hmm; all speculation of course. I may be quite wrong.

Did you tell me about your busy life to let me know there's been little time to miss me or grieve for us? In this instance I envy you your single, male focus. I love you Sir, despite all questions and concerns. Step carefully, knowing I am by your side—M-X

Very late P.m. Mouse {Unsent}: Dear Friend—I am in your arms but I cannot feel you with me; I think you are on your course tonight. Last week you worked on closing our relationship. Will you tell them this week how it went? Will you say you feel so much clearer; that you are glad it is over? Or will you say you find it hard; that you are grieving? I imagine you will say you haven't had time to think about it but that you saw me and I appeared okay. Will you tell them I am tough; that I can cope?

Goodnight, Fine Sir. I pray you sleep well. M.X

Chapter 2 Undone

Friday 8ᵗʰ December 2006

A.m. Adrian: *Hi, sorry to break the agreement. A request only; I'm sorry. Little wooden house? Little green chest? Class 3 today? Smoking pipes? Clogs? Brown broom? Oak barrel? Are you still 'She who provides all'?*

Mouse: *Hi, Friend. Green chest okay, wooden house okay, no broom, no clogs, no smoking pipes, no oak barrel. Sorry. Still 'She who provides all'—or some of, anyway.*

Adrian: *Thanks. Busy, but still thinking of you a lot—-*

Mouse: *—X*

"Come on boys, we have a couple of errands to make before your trip home. We have time to shop before your hair appointments." The Laird is taking both boys to England for Christmas. They fly tomorrow. Simon the hairdresser is a touch gay, with henna highlights and eyebrow piercings. My lads like his fashionable haircutting. I am nervous. It is five-thirty and Adrian is meeting The Laird in town, as agreed. My two men have chosen a bar for their difficult mission. "Does it have to be a bar?" I asked The Laird earlier; "wouldn't the park be better?" "I don't want anywhere secluded; certainly not anywhere you have sneaked off together for your secret rendezvous," he replied. "I might be tempted to punch him if we were alone. A bar is fine." I waved him off; thankful that he isn't aware of the full state of our relationship. He doesn't know we are complete lovers. He has a swimming lesson followed by a whisky evening. Between swimming and whisky he is meeting Adrian; non-stop action as usual. He tentatively takes the prepared envelope containing a poem written months ago. Is now the right time? Oh, I am unsure.

"Here is something for you and Adrian; two copies, but you must read it at the same time, okay? Don't open it unless the opportunity presents itself." I know they will follow the same lines nervously, especially The Laird. He departs the Southern Hemisphere tomorrow for nearly three weeks, leaving me close to the man I love. It had been good to see Adrian earlier. I delivered his requested items, hearing in his message a small plea for some recognition. Our love is alive and well.

EARTHMATE, SOULMATE

Earthmate, Soulmate, Laird and Prince,
So this is how it is, so right and yet so — —
Now I know why I have always felt incomplete,
Like a missing jigsaw piece.

Earthmate, Soulmate, Laird and Prince,
I cannot believe the joy, the sense of well being — —
I need you both, left and right.
Steady and grounding, Laird on my right,
Protector, provider, long-time friend and companion,
Past and future; solid, unbending.
Vital and liberating, Prince on my left,
Recently met, yet veiled for years in my soul,
Friend and instant playmate; vitality matched,
Sailing free in joy with me,
Maybe for a short time, maybe for longer.

Earthmate, Soulmate, Laird and Prince,
Loosen my bonds, carry me high.
I know I ask for an extraordinary gift.
Please hold me — —
For now — — -X

I include a separate slip of paper, asking them to build me a private sanctuary; somewhere close to the house where I can be still—where I can write. Is this too much? Have I gone too far? Can I really expect The Laird to take such a massive leap of faith? I return home with the children, wondering what's happening between the two men. Will my husband wonder if he can leave me alone on The Mountain for Christmas? Should he give his permission for me to be with Adrian? As these thoughts swirl around my head a sudden, wild rainstorm hits the cabin with force and at the same time a nosebleed overtakes me and does not abate. The Laird will not return until much later.

I am already in bed when he climbs the stairs and I cannot bring myself to ask about the meeting. We talk about the whisky instead. Eventually my husband is brave enough to mention the unavoidable—"well, I saw him. I didn't punch him." "Was it okay?" I hesitantly ask. "Yes, bizarre but okay." "How was he?" I ask again; "fine." The Laird is tired and grumpy. The last night before his departure is packed to bursting, as always. With school reports to complete, lessons to plan/delegate and packing to finalize he also has to deal with a straying wife and her lover. Poor man; I am taxing him sore.

P.m. Mouse {Unsent}: *The sweetest kisses move across her lips as she finds him under the stars. Such tenderness—fragile flutter as they meet* *at last. It has been a long day. She senses him so close tonight. She feels his eyes on hers; the connection he demands aligned and perfect. Dare they hope their exquisite union might be allowed? My Lord Swallow, tonight we move as one again. I desire you more than words can express.*

"Come lie with me, where waves of passion wash over our own, private shore; where we linger on the sugar-coated rim of a pink champagne glass"-

Saturday 9th December 2006

The Laird is less grumpy this morning. We hold each other close for a long time. He takes the succour he needs and I love him as I have always loved him. When men are comforted they become much lighter and more content. Women are different. Our loins don't rule us to the same extent. Although I have read that fact countless times it is revelatory to experience. Apparently women need to be 'in love' to really desire lovemaking, while men need to make love to be 'in love'. Well, that is certainly true. So, my husband seems to be happy today, stating: "Strange day I had yesterday—awful weather to match the subject, but I didn't punch him. We read your papers. Happy Christmas!" He doesn't say more. I don't like to ask. What does he mean by; "Happy Christmas?" He went to the bar wearing The Kilt. My poor Swallow Man must have had a shock when he walked in. I hope he didn't think I had laid it on—purposefully. In an awful way it's quite funny.

I leave Rinky with a school chum at nine a.m. and drive my boys to Auckland. We have time to meet whisky friends of The Laird's before 'check in'. Tony and Sheryl own a wine bar in Ponsonby and treat us to a selection of fine beverages and yummy eats. The Bog-Brush stays in the car and I check on her regularly. The sun is hot today and we can't find a shady parking space. I really like Auckland, especially the pretty residential streets in Ponsonby and Devonport. We have been here a few times and always feel comfortable.

The dog and I enjoy a quiet stroll while The Laird is talking whisky to his cronies. I pause opposite a three-storied, white-painted villa. Bougainvillea tumbles over the veranda. The windows are a pleasing, soft lilac. I feel at home in the narrow streets and quiet parks; I like the established gardens that remind me of home—the established bit that is. The exotic plants are quite different. The boys are reading in the car. It is time to fetch The Laird who is still partying; we mustn't be late for the flight. We manage a fleeting visit to the Fijian family on the way—just. {The Laird is prone to organizing the maximum sociable engagements into any outing.} The family is staying with contacts nearby and doing well. By three o'clock it is raining hard and we make a dash for the airport. I don't like waving my boys goodbye; Cedric hugs me especially tightly. With warm kisses and best wishes I leave my trio at the airport entrance. I need to return home before nightfall if possible.

P.m. Mistress to Laird: *On my way now. Several wrong turnings.*

Missing you already—not looking forward to the loneliness. Have a wonderful time. I love you all so much—tears in my eyes—X

Laird: *All's well here. Hope you are still awake? It's your sleepy time. You are with me at the very core of my being. Your holding my heart allows me to love as God wills. Give Rinky the magical Christmas memories you had as a child. Think of me when you scratch the pig's tummy. Your Weary Warrior—X*

Mistress: *Will do, My Brave Warrior. Sorry to send you into battle. Thank-you for your shining valiance. I don't deserve my Celtic War Lord—*

Laird: *Just boarding. Sleep well. Kiss the piggy for me.*

I have a tearful drive home. The swishing windscreen wipers accompany me. Thank goodness for my strong faith—and the dog. I would be bereft as well as sad if I didn't have either.

I turn out the light at eleven p.m. Rinky is tucked up, fast asleep. It has been a long day. I reach for my phone and send Adrian a blank text—just a kiss, that's all. Not allowed, I know, but I need to feel him close.

Late P.m. Mouse: *—X*

Sunday 10th December 2006

The morning starts bright. I send golden wings and prayers of protection to my boys in the air—and then I lie, entwined with him; the man I love in the deepest sense. Does he think of me this moment? Does he lie with me right now? I wish I knew what happened at the bar meeting yesterday. What was agreed? What was left unsaid? If my Lord Swallow doesn't call for an early meeting then I will. I feel so sad today. What a dreadful waste of our precious time together. I am aching for Adrian. Does he ache for me? Perhaps this is a female thing. The Laird's loving text, telling me I am at the core of his being, makes me realize that although we are close he is not at the core of mine and he doesn't really know what it means. I need to be joined at the core of my being with another—truly joined. Without emotional passion and perfect chemistry the union is a half-baked affair.

So, the lonely vigil begins. I am powerless to oppose its cruel subjection. How I wish Lord Swallow would roar up the drive and stride in through the cabin doors and into my waiting arms. He would be masterful; the decision taken to break the agreement in the face of our truth. We would hold each other gently beside the wood-burning stove for a long, long time. Nothing else would matter. It never does. The Minx and I go to church and then to the market. We traipse around the usual toy stalls—why are the plastic horrors so appealing to children? Luckily Rinky rarely wastes her money on

18

the nine-minute-wonders. She is mature like that. The morning is a repetition of last Sunday—an intensity of grief; so heavy. There go those Sundays again. We stay at home for the rest of the day, playing with our piggy. We have named her Molly.

Monday 11th December 2006

A.m. Mouse {Unsent}: Lord Swallow, did you come to me last night? As I fell into deep sleep I felt you enter my room. You stood beside the bed. I got up and you held me against your linen shirt. We kissed; the intensity of our union surprising us. We kissed long and deep—reaching The Garden Gate instantly—boldly forging ahead down familiar paths. Our delight at such homecoming was obvious in every breath we dared share.

And then you were gone and I woke alone. Was it just a dream or did you really come to me? On waking I lay in your arms again for over half an hour, knowing I hadn't imagined your presence. We played; teasing and rolling as we always do; undressing each other slowly. I felt the soft, downy hair on your arms and the touch of your lips all over me like silk treats. We laughed together; you were so firm inside me—and so deep. We were powerless in the face of the ancient law. The woman in me held the inevitability tightly. I coaxed you eagerly to plant your seed as high as possible. And when you climaxed my whole body pulsed and dipped; consuming the holy magic and taking it home—X

It is a day of lonely reflection. I paint and garden for Sarah; I accomplish some pressing town errands and then settle down at the computer to write our Workshop Agenda; the final one. The boys have arrived safely in my parents' home. They appear on the 'Skype' screen; how strange to see them against the familiar background. Our childhood portraits hang opposite the camera. The family is well and excited. I miss them, but it is Adrian for whom I long. The stillness is comforting; the house so quiet. Oh, how I ache for my Man. It feels so wrong to be banished from our togetherness.

P.m. Mouse {Unsent}: My Darling Friend, I am sorry to break our sad agreement but our beautiful Boat needs some attention. I have been unable to leave the dry-dock; visiting several times each day to run a loving hand along her keel. The last few days show she is not fairing as well as we had hoped. Signs of damage and general disrepair are obvious. Peeling paintwork, seagull mess and foul weather have already taken their toll. I'm doing what I can to keep off the worst; yesterday I wrestled with a huge piece of plastic but the wind kept snatching it away and I gave up. I have reached a point where I need your skill and manly strength, if only to have some assistance in holding down the plastic while I secure it with ropes. I cannot care for her alone. This total abandonment is too harsh. After all, she is not used to it and even the Harbour Master is away; left for a European Christmas apparently. I only contact you now out of deep concern for our precious vessel—knowing that she cannot wait for the end of term on the 22nd, as we have agreed. Can we have an earlier meeting? Or at least a phone call? Sorry to have to ask. Your Lady.

And this is the message I send for real:

P.m. Mouse: *Fine Sir—do you feel the need, as I do, for an interim catch-up? This total cut-off is proving negative rather than positive for your Lady. There are things we need to discuss before the 22nd. Perhaps a phone call? Or come and visit and I will try to behave as you would wish. M—X*

Tuesday 12th December 2006

A.m. Mouse {Unsent}: *Tuesday morning of my lonely vigil. You haven't replied to my message—unlike you, My Friend. I need to know your thoughts; need to hear how your meeting went with The Laird. Can we make any plans at all over this gifted time before it is snatched away? I am physically bleeding from this wound; nosebleeds and constant taste of blood in my mouth from my aching lungs. Perhaps if you could tell me it means little I could stop grieving—perhaps.*

I continue my gardening work for Sarah this morning. Her elderly tenant, Bill, is not too keen on weeding. He is scared of her huge dogs at the back of the section. I don't blame him; they sound so fierce—massive Rottweilers behind a high fence that shakes when they hurl themselves against it. Rinky took Adrian's other wooden house into school earlier— apparently I had sent the wrong one down The Mountain on Friday. He sent a lovely message while I was gardening. A short text, but it meant a lot.

A.m. Adrian: *Thank-you, My Lady.*

This afternoon we have an Advent Festival practise; the first with the whole school. I have to say it is a shambles. Once complete the spectacle should be good. How strange and lovely to hear the children singing our song—sad and poignant. I catch My Minstrel's eye several times, as he does mine. He helps me load up the car afterwards. "How are you, My Friend?" He asks kindly. "Not good," I reply——"definitely not good." I speak of the grief— yes, he can see that. He says his lesson has been one of shame. He's feeling okay really; he wants me to know he is still my Man. He mentions the photograph that he took of me on the beach. "It's on my screen—I often look at you. Oh, and I opened the envelope Big J. gave me from that woman, Julie, remember? No spark there!" Adrian is kind and caring, saying he's worried I have no support. He understands how everything has been taken from me. He wants me to know he is here. I lean into the van door, feeling waves of sadness. It's so hard not to be held by him. "I wonder what the grief is about," Adrian asks. "Something to do with having played in The Garden of Heaven but now The Gate is locked against us," I reply.

Adrian mentions Christmas. Perhaps I would like to join his family in

Auckland; as a Friend, of course. "Thank you. I'll think about your kind suggestion. And we need to discuss the final Workshop day. Cordelia thinks it important you join us; after all, the families have been there for all three of us." "Okay, I can be there," he answers. "I haven't had a minute to think—work is taking over completely. I keep missing our ten o'clock rendezvous. Can we make it eleven? I shall be more present then. I was with you last night; did you sense me?"

I drive home, pleased that we managed a brief meeting. Adrian told me he'd mislaid his phone. Had I sent a message? He spoke a little of the meeting with The Laird; "two men facing each other, trying to speak of their feelings—hmm; not easy. I promised I would stick to the agreement. I have such strong people around me at the moment; The Laird, Big J. Martha, Martini—all insisting I stop. I cannot ignore such a clear message." I told Adrian how I am feeling the opposite; "it's as if I am on the edge of freedom," I said. "I am alone and yet not. The Laird's *'Happy Christmas'* message is still ringing in my ears. Is that the optimist in me? Oh—I found The Copper Band; it was in the bottom of my bag. I have it next to my wedding ring. Do you mind if I wear it?" "You decide," he said; "it's fine by me, although do you think it should stay on your wedding finger?" I admitted that our shared adventure was more important to me than I realized. The strength of our magnets is overpowering. I don't want to fight them. Yes, it is right for the ring to rest there. "Perhaps take it off when The Laird returns, eh?" He suggested.

P.m. Adrian: Can I call you tonight once Rinky is in bed?

Mouse: Hi Friend. You found my message then? Thanks for the offer. Let's stick with the agreement; it is important for you. Our catch-up today will suffice for a while. Thank you for your lovely words. I'm feeling easier this evening. Still lots of work ahead for the Workshop tomorrow. Are my three benches still at school? Also missing the wide rake. Can you bring them when you come tomorrow? That would be grand. Keep clear for school. I'm still your Lady; a paler version anyway. I don't like being pale. Maybe my lesson? -X

Adrian: Hmm—I was all set to give you a call. Now not sure if I should. Maybe I should do a process. Feels like a clean break has had its time and shown up what needs highlighting: not knowing how the other fairs; sensing the gulf, or in my case, not feeling so much, but aware. Maybe just cautiously reconnect? One text a day? Or is this too much even? Is **this** text too much? Will I flare up again—will you fill my mind? And you? How will it be for you to reconnect?

Mouse: Oh Fine Sir—My Beautiful Lord Swallow—I'm not sure we can fight the strength of our magnets; not sure either of us wants to enough. Perhaps we should keep things as they are until the week is over. Then have a phone chat or text conversation at the weekend. M—X

How would it be for me to reconnect? Have we ever disconnected? I have a frantic evening getting sorted for tomorrow; our final Workshop session. Endings all around, or are they beginnings? I wonder what might be coming next.

P.m. Mouse {unsent}: *Impossible task—the magnets have been joined for a while now. How can they be forced apart? The pull of their attraction is powerful and real. This forced repel is causing her untold damage. She feels the life being dragged out of her; literally. She fears for her health. The weakening is tangible. Dear Angels, you hold us safely; do we really have to wade through this agony?*

Wednesday 13ᵗʰ December 2006
Dear Whanau, {Maori term for extended family}
The final Workshop session is fast approaching and we would like as many of you as possible to join us on our Mountain. We have had a fun & busy year with beautiful exchanges on many levels. Wednesday will certainly be a day of festivity, thanks giving & the closing of a special chapter. Every closing has an opening, so as well as finishing we will be preparing for something new, remembering our interconnectedness in life's intricate web as we go our separate ways. The day will begin promptly at 9.30 a.m. ——can we ask you to get here by 9.15? You will have to wait & see what we have planned! We have Pita Bread, which will need filling for lunch. Can we ask you to bring fillers for this? Just a potluck selection. Wednesday is the 13th—considered by modern society to be unlucky. However, in ancient times the number 13 was held as a magical number. Here's to a magical day for us all. We are looking forward to seeing you.

I am organized by the time our magical day begins. Deep blessing enfolds The Mountain; I can feel it. Cordelia arrives early and I make her chuckle when I introduce The Laird's Christmas present-"A pig to keep me out of mischief." "That's hilarious!" She laughs. "What's her name?" "Molly," I say, picking up the adorable bundle. "You know, you should write a book," she adds. "Hmm—now that you mention it, I am writing a story." I have time to tell her a little of the content; of course she is central to all that has happened over the past **17** months.

Last week we planned our surprise day for the Workshop families. "Wouldn't it be wonderful to have a *live* 'Woods Person' in the den? I suggested. Who could we ask? Cordelia telephoned a special friend of hers; a local, Maori Lady called Anita Hine Te Rio. Anita is a storyteller and knows the area well. She has jumped at the opportunity to be our Mystery Woods Person. We shepherd her into position before the families arrive. She stands beside the fire in the Woodsman's Den wearing a flowing, velvet gown in earthy tones. She looks as if she has materialized out of the Bush as a mystical elder, dripping with magic from her velvet folds. The kettle is full and the Den looks inhabited. The children are brimming with excited questions as they spill out of the vehicles; "who is the Lady in the Den? What is she doing there?" We express surprise and after our formal greeting we head down the drive to investigate.

The day is a resounding success. After the event Krista sends us a beautiful e-mail with a commentary on our final gathering alongside some poignant photographs:

E-mail from Krista:
We followed the clues to the Woodsman's Den where we were held, spellbound, by local author Anita Hine Te Rio who told us of her childhood years over the hills of this Mountain, listening to her Grandma telling stories—"Grandma, Grandma, tell me another story"—-as she went to sleep beside her in the big bed every night. Out of all her siblings, *she* was the one chosen to sleep with her Grandma. Now she is a Grandma herself and enthrals her own 'mokopuna', {grandchildren}, with the stories of her people. Anita told us the story of our volcanic Mount in the harbour; how he earnt his name—'Mauao'—'caught by the light of the sun.' 'As a child, my siblings and I explored every inch of this Mountain on our ponies— this particular area was called 'Tuku Tuku' which means; 'where the pigeons drink'. My people were Woods People—for generations that is what they were, here on this very Mountain. Thank-you for asking me here today to tell you my stories.'

There is so much magnificence, in the ocean

Kia Ora Anita, {goodbye for now}, you are inspiring. Thank-you.

At last the sun came out and wow, fresh spring has overtaken the Twealm Realm since we were last here. Things have definitely changed——new flowers and new plants everywhere. There was much lighting of the fire and swinging on the tree swings while the mammas chatted and laughed together. Trisha and Matthew played together in the grasses, whispering secrets and finding insects.

There is so much tranquillity, in the forest

Molly, the Kune Kune piglet, was invited inside—'Kune Kune' in Maori means 'round and fat', well, she is certainly that! Rowena got more than her fair share of cuddles.
We made paper by shredding old paper and pulping it with water. Then we sieved the lot and patted it dry with towels. We dried it by the wood-burning stove. European, December weather was invited to the Mountain today and it was lovely to have the fire lit.

We made Baby Jesus walnut cradles with wool and beads to hang on the Christmas tree. The finished babes looked so snug and warm in their fleece-lined beds. And another fantastic lunch around the wooden tables—pitas filled with dips and salad bits. Our children have been converted to herbal tea drinking.

At last the sun came out. Little Annie played happily in the sun with her ribbon dancing and swirling in the breeze.

Thanks a million for everything: A Pohutukawa for the Lady of the house, which will flower bright and red each Christmas time. And an Aloe Vera plant for Adrian and Cordelia each—a plant of healing. Did you notice the babies sprouting from the Aloes?? The sparkler on the cake didn't go all the way—hinting at more to come.

There is so much hot energy, in the fire

What a year we have had.

Vigour shine through me,
Shine and sing,
Through legs and arms,
Sing and shine through hands and feet,
So I will grow strong,
In heart and head,
Vigorous and strong,
In breath and speech.
{Rudolf Steiner}

Well—I am blown away by the families; their kind appreciation and this delightful account of our final day together fills me with gratitude. Krista's e-mail is a poignant and clever piece of writing with snatches of our 'Ocean' song punctuating each paragraph. I have read it several times already. Yes, the magic has been with us all, 'to be sure', as the Irish would say. As I forward Krista's e-mail to Cordelia and Adrian I realize these special families have played a big part in the mystery that holds Adrian and me; they are fellow sailors on 'The Celestial Sea'—she has always been open to a larger crew, 'for sure'. Krista even hints at something magical underlying the whole, another one of those unexpected surprises comes to me from the screen. Have the women felt an undercurrent of something other? I wonder if Anita Hine Te Rio felt anything. She was truly amazing; and to think that her people really were *Woods people'* on this, our beautiful Mountain! What an amazing way to finish our year, with a surprising twist at the end. Well, something other is directing this antipodean show, without a doubt. The things that keep happening cannot be pure coincidence alone.

After our final group photograph the three of us dash away for the end of school. Another festival practise awaits our direction. Everything continues to be on the disorganized side and we are slightly frantic, to put it mildly. Adrian and I find a quick moment to chat at the end of the afternoon. He had been a little off colour during our mountain day. "I had a really awful morning—Big J. gave a poor assessment of my teaching skills. I'm feeling grim." My heart goes out to my lovely friend and I can't even gather him up in a big hug which is what he needs right now; wavering our agreement would confuse him more. His perpetual torment boils and struggles. I feel for him. Rinky and I stop for a quick supper with Felicia and her two children before we go home. Bernard is away.

Home at last—Phew! What a day.

P.m. Mouse: Darling Friend—I don't like seeing you upset. I'd like to share the day. Please call later if you need to talk. I'm here for you still. Rinky and I had tea with Felicia. M—X

Adrian: Hi, Dear Friend. I won't ring you tonight. Feeling back on track after my knock today. Had a very friendly tea with Jocelyn's gang and then went visiting children's home gardens for the award ceremony next week. Busy as hell. Still more report writing to do. One and a bit to go, plus clean-ups and re-wording; final edit. Children's verses for next year to choose— one each—this weekend's task. You seemed in better spirits today. Well done. Shame I missed the beginning of the Workshop day. Anita Hine sounded quite something. Sleep well tonight; I sure will-X

Mouse: —X—X

I sleep soundly. Adrian and I meet at eleven p.m. for our etheric rendezvous under the stars. I know he is there.

Late P.m. Mouse {Unsent}: The children came. They came once more for him; for her-"You must be present, however hard," their Guardian Angel advised. "After all, it was for you both that we have danced together this year." Yes, they came, bringing gifts and smiles. We heard stories; discovered that Anita Hine Te Rio, a local storyteller and author, has been our 'Woods Person' all along. We crafted together one more time; advent decorations and hand-made paper. We ate our final lunch; a cosy, cabin celebration. And he was there, and they were at ease with each other, secure in the light of their beautiful love. Their eyes met across the wooden tables; tired and jaded after their heart-wrenching ordeal. A year to remember. As the day closed the children sang again, the mothers were tearful; and she wondered if any of them noticed she was wearing his ring.

Chapter 3 Undercurrent

Thursday 14ᵗʰ December 2006

A.m. Mouse: Good morning, My Friend—business only. Could we sing our festival song in a round? Sudden thought in the early hours.

The Mountain is calm today. Peace descends after an unprecedented year of boundary crossing and realignment. We have sailed oceans of set tides and unpredictable weather patterns. We have crossed frontiers to a new horizon. Months of optimistic vision and blind faith have led us to this reality. Our Boat has been undaunted by storms and unknown destination. Despite the seagull mess her Spirit is undeterred, even now. The iron cradle holding her hostage cannot rest easy. The wind has changed; the battering of the last twelve days is over and the crew is left drained but alive. She saw him earlier today, a sun-kissed glow upon his countenance; the man she loves still. He acknowledged her morning message about singing in a round. And then he was off, bounding away with enthusiasm, secure in the love they share.

The washing flaps in the manageable breeze on the whirly-gig line. I lie, flat out in the sunshine, listening to the chickens mumbling their daily mumble and the pig chomping in the grass beside me. The daily communion— to stop a while and 'be'. The bleating of a sheep makes me think of my boys on the far side of the world; a family wedding and Christmas looming near. I wonder how they fare. I expect they'll phone later. I lie on damp grass, not missing them too badly. All I want is sleep. Yesterday I found my packet of new socks that went missing; they were in the freezer, along with a surprised lettuce and a red-faced bag of tomatoes. A good indication of how bewildering, yet beautifully unexpected, the past few months have been.

The day concludes with another festival practise in the sun. Cordelia, Little J. and I co-ordinate the groups that wait patiently on the playing field. We are making progress. Adrian is busy mending one of his gazebos; we need them for the last day of term in case it rains. "Our festival days are always dry," says Big J. "There's no need to worry." Nevertheless, the group has decided to play safe. We have ordered five new gazebos; with Adrian's two we will have enough for each class. "One of the legs broke in the gale last night," my Swallow Man swears under his breath. "Shall I give you a hand?" I ask. "No thanks—I'll deal with it." I watch as he bundles the unwieldy structure into the back of his car. He is taking it to a friend's workshop to use some welding equipment, I presume. I wave him off.

The boys are having fun in England; keeping up with The Laird's crazy timetable. They seem to be dashing between art exhibitions in London, sociable rendezvous on various pheasant shoots, the trip to Scotland for the wedding and parties in Sussex. My bemused parents try to keep up as they meet planes and lend cars, providing endless support and nourishment. The rich tapestry of friends and connections is the same as ever, waiting with open arms for The Laird's perpetual hunger for entertainment and interaction. I sometimes wonder if his manic habits are quite normal. The Go-Getter has succumbed to his bad chest; not really surprising. I send them motherly love as I dash about on the other side of the world; busy but calmly busy in comparison.

The Bog-Brush actually caught Blossom the rabbit today! Luckily they were only playing. Blossom makes mad dashes across the cabin floor-right past the dog's nose on purpose. I miss our eleven o'clock lovers' rendezvous. I wonder how Adrian's course went tonight. I hope he has finished his reports.

Friday 15th December 2006

A.m. Mouse {Unsent}: Good morning, Lord Swallow. How was your evening course? And how go the reports? I hope this break has allowed you to really concentrate on School. I love to see you standing proud in your profession. You have a straighter bearing when you are vocationally at work. I sense you embrace your natural dignity. You permit some self-love. This is why teaching plays an important role in your life. The true 'you' can be alive.

Friday morning—mmm—another lovely day. I had a telephone evening; three calls from home. I almost feel I am there. I even dreamt about the wedding—something about a fridge door not closing in the church sacristy. One of my peculiar dreams; a regular feature I'm afraid to admit, although when it's a real howler a nomadic beast usually features! Must be that overactive imagination of mine! It's that time of the month again—no complicated surprises you'll be pleased to hear.

I am missing you, although feeling better; more normal I suppose. A part of me is anxious that our magic might get lost; that we stamp out our flame with each passing day. Will the spark remain? Will it provide a clearer way after the 22nd? I don't want to lose the magic; apart from holding the key to The Garden Gate it allows me to write—and I love to write. Without that I am an emptier vessel.

I see how it can be—for me anyway. This will be your decision, My Friend. After all, my life's journey is mostly set. The magic we share lies at my very core but on a practical level it will always remain an 'extra'—I suppose. Except of course when the Senior Males are away which will begin to happen more and more. But for you, a mature man in your prime, this may not be enough. I cannot promise the arrival of Little Arthur and if we are so wrapped up in each other you may not be open to other opportunities. Who knows? Do you think we can be together in a more measured way? Allowing space between us, yet remaining Lovers?

Could we tell the world that we are involved creatively; that we communicate through our text prose and a certain time spent together? We allow ourselves the creative sharing—writing, music, invention. The creative form remains our personal domain. We have come out of hiding. We are clear and have stood up in front of all—and now it is private; our business.

Our relationship is life-giving and beautiful—that's all anyone needs know. We are involved together in artistic endeavour. We have laid our cards on the table and been blessed by a certain understanding from others. But we have been hurt and weakened—probably necessarily, but that is enough. The Love between us is a positive, not a negative entity. We can develop it in whichever way we choose.

I think the decoys across your path have, in fact, been permit tickets. I looked up the relevance of the names: Jules and Julie—'related to Jove—King of Gods—God of the skies-belonging to Julius, {from Roman times} —or belonging to another.' Also a name associated with taking a Lover while pregnant; under cover, veiled; making lovers safe. In a way The Laird has given his permission. He doesn't need the details, just no sneaking behind his back. We can be open about our creative times. The artistry takes many shapes and privately we allow ourselves the glory of our swan moments. A new Leafy Glade beckons—somewhere private for our creativity to flourish— somewhere we find together; where we don't have to keep looking over our shoulders.

I want to make your home with you; to plant roses and vegetables; to apply my decorative skills to your space. Somewhere warm and homely, uplifting and inspiring; somewhere to nurture The Small One and all the other children who come under your roof. When next we meet, let's think on this—it feels so possible to me. Is it just my over optimistic mind-set? This impacts much more on you than on me, My Friend, so the decision is yours, to be taken slowly and with deep consideration. These thoughts mark a massive life change. Will we make it? A gift like this comes once in a lifetime but it carries a hefty price tag. X

My spare time is filled with logging our precious texts, even those I never send. I like to use the small screen of the mobile phone. The limited space curtails my tendency towards frothy language and long sentences. With my phone by my side I can write whenever I am inspired. I might be waiting in a car park or watching a sports match—anything—a private world offering escape and freedom. I spend an hour gardening for Bill this morning. He is away on holiday. The fierce dogs are quieter today. I put the weeds in the chicken coop; passing the back of the dog enclosure each time I have a full bag. Rinky's class is giving a concert this afternoon and I must organize cards and end of year gifts for Little J. We have further festival practises too—the end of term is only a week away. At last the routines are coming together.

The Class 2 tableau requires thirteen, floral headdresses. Mary's tears make the thorn bushes bloom—the harsh spikes replaced by colourful display. I have volunteered to make the headdresses. A hasty trip to the Two-Dollar Shop sees me returning with a heap of fabric roses and some broad, black elastic. Guess what my weekend task will be? Lord Swallow walks with me as we pack up for the afternoon. "I have a free evening," he declares. So, we shall meet at last. He will come up to The Mountain and we will allow ourselves a 'catch-up' and try to find the road ahead, as friends of course; nothing more. Relief—some light shines at the end of the dark tunnel. Rinky and I drive home quietly.

P.m Adrian: Hi Friend. Shall I come up for tea after touch rugby? Shall I bring something?

Mouse: Yes, do—you don't need to bring anything. M—X

Later, Adrian: Hi Friend—heading up now. Could very nearly be in for a kip. Think I'd be a lot more fun to be with—

Mouse: I'll tuck you up somewhere then. Promise I won't join you. I'm sorting out the tool shed. Loads of dust so I need a bath anyway. Come snooze away—

My Lord Swallow sleeps long and late; the weary Elf-Prince, home at last from troubled forays. I read to the Minx and put her to bed. She is always well-behaved at bedtime and drops off quickly. I do join Adrian eventually, slipping between the covers of his cosy nest in the caravan. No touching, mind; just platonic friendship. I am impressed by our self-discipline. This is a strange time for us both. Adrian reaches for his diary when he wakes. I am pleased he's kept up his writing over the past two weeks. Beautiful words soothe my anxious ear. Yes, I am important to him. {I wish I had a copy. I'd like to include his writing here.} I am very touched.

I read him my convoluted, unsent messages. There is a multitude of emotion and mind-talk to discuss. Some of my paragraphs upset him; "I don't agree that I manifested our Boat's dry-dock sentence. That sounds too cold; lacking any Angel holding." I am more than happy to bow to his opinion. I don't like that thought either. I love reading to Adrian—but oh—it's hard not to curl around each other. I place a pillow between us. There, that makes for less temptation—sort of. We smile at each other; endlessly smile. Nobody can steal *that* gift. I catch a glimpse of the impressive King; he speaks with reverence about loyalty and choice; the difference between being cowed into submission and standing up for one's truth. My goodness, the dark places he has travelled this past fortnight! You can imagine. My wretched Prince—the self-torture continues. Our quandary only adds to his turmoil. We cannot turn our backs on each other now. "My feelings are unchanged; I see how it could be," I tell him. "Hmm—but I have promised The Laird," he replies. "His side of the story is very different from yours. I have the teachers to consider too. I would have to choose."

This is Adrian's choice but he cannot reach a conclusion. I kiss him lightly on the brow and slip away to my own bed at one a.m. The hours slip away all too easily. We are thwarted Lovers; the need to be close with each other makes me frustrated and restless in my lonely bed.

Saturday 16th December 2006

How lovely to wake, knowing Adrian is here. We are calmer today, maintaining our distance despite our matched desire. Oh—how we long for each other's touch; the accustomed sanctuary is tantalizingly close. The knowledge of the man in him, his tender stroking as he takes ownership of me, sets every love juice flowing. I am ripe for him. I have never experienced the strength of a man's potent protection and claim. I desire him more than words can say. I only have to close my eyes to feel his hands running up my back, then slowly down my thighs. I sense him lingering where he longs to ease himself; his long limbs pressing hard against mine as our Rhythmic Dance begins. The fiery mystery we know is ours will not abate.

I let him sleep late again, delivering a cup of tea to the caravan and beginning the day with a 'process' session. He makes us breakfast later on— a banana omelette, no less! A new one on us. Rinky and I are not convinced but enjoy the taste-bud challenge. We potter in the garden until lunchtime. Lord Swallow tackles the collapsing gorse fence, stripping off his shirt and applying himself with his usual zeal. Rinky and I leave him in peace. He is like a young boy at play; intent on his creative task.

"Have you got the present?" I call from upstairs. The Minx has been invited to a party in town at midday; we had better get a move on. I am dog-tired after such a late night but I manage a second foray to the Two-Dollar Shop for extra fabric roses; I underestimated the first time around. I pass Adrian heading down the hill as I return home. He has gardens to visit for the competition judging—one all the way out in Maketu. "Why don't you come with me?" He suggested earlier. We shall see. Right now I just need my bed. I sleep for most of the afternoon.

P.m Adrian: *What time are you collecting Rinky? I'm heading out to Maketu around 5p.m.*

Mouse: *Hi Friend—how go the gardens? I've been snoozing all afternoon; more tired than I realized. I'm collecting Rinky at 4.30p.m. She may be too tired to do more. We'll see. What da plan? M—X*

Adrian: *Hmm—might be easier to do our own thing. I would like to talk to you some more but without 'Mrs. Flappy Ears', although I could do the* *kiddie thing too. Might be more in the mood by then. Haven't stopped yet and still feeling a bit wobbly. Any inspirations?*

Mouse: *Can I phone you? Oh platonic Lover of mine.*

Adrian doesn't answer my message. He must be busy. I begin the headdress stitching, my thoughts never leaving him.

Later, Mouse: *Are you home, My Friend? I'm almost down the hill. Shall I drop by? Or is Big J there? Perhaps you are in the shower? —X*

Adrian: *What's the story? Getting keener to see you—maybe that's the time not to? Hmm—cruise on round, My Dear. Big J's home but let's open it up; if you're keen?*

I don't get to Big J's in the end; a cuppa at the birthday party keeps me longer than I thought, and I don't think Adrian and I should be seen together; platonic friendship or not. Rinky and I go home and he telephones instead. "I'll head off to Makatu now, and then come up to the Mountain later, if I may?"

P.m. Mouse: *Hi, Friend-I'm really excited; I forgot to say earlier. There are two sections of land for sale just bordering the Everglades. $150—165,000 each. Just having a moment of daydreaming. Promise I'll behave when you get home. Loving you—platonically of course—M-X*

P.s my over-riding sense today, My Love? I want you to establish your bombproof, quiet pride and dignity above anything else. Because you ARE worthwhile. I don't think you realize how impressive you are when the King tips the scales. You can be anything you choose. All it takes is the flick of a switch in the mind-set panel to tame the mind-talk—perhaps accepting the constant, verbal presence but quelling it before it knocks you. Although the lessons on self-questioning are important I think the time has come to take control of them, rather than let them control you.

I desire this for you, My Love, more than I desire you in my bed—and that is a LOT. I want you to breathe life into your potential. Without it the future lies wasted. You are SO special. Your strengths, placed inside measured reality, will yield untold riches. And I am not thinking of myself in this picture. I hope you will stride this path of humble dignity. Your friendships, career and interests will solidify when this mantle lies about you. Your gaze will turn more outward. Your intentions will bear weight and the respect you command will be extraordinary.

I know you can be that man, for I already know him well. And your Lady? She will watch you with quiet pride and be happy to see you walk your path in life, either beside her or waving from a distance. Yes, My Love—this is today's lesson—M-X

Adrian arrives home at **7**.30 p.m. and we eat together before The Minx goes to bed. We sit in comfortable companionship once she is asleep, sinking into the cosy cushions of the open-doored caravan. Adrian works on the children's verses for next year while I tackle the rose headdresses. Each child is given a special verse by their teacher, often hand-crafted. The pupils learn their verses by heart and treasure them like precious, lettered jewels. We are like an old married couple as we work, the pillow between us anchoring our passion. Will it become a memory? A comfortable memory as we sit in the sun and turn to domestic toil. Hmm—even this is extremely pleasant, we both agree.

"You know, I've only just realized the huge impact our relationship has on my life," Adrian admits quietly. "I told Big J. that without you I feel less solid; less strong. I have been really wobbly recently. She asked how you were. I told her you have been grieving but you are through the worst. My lack of Ego is the real problem. Big J. has given me some exercises. She suggests I hold an object in my mind and repeat the same movement every day at the same time. I feel shallow. If we can't be together I'll have to join a church group or something."

"I think you should stop there, My Friend," I interrupt him. "You have an amazing wealth of knowledge and skill; now is the time to mature into those gifts." I kiss him lightly before heading to my own bed; hoping he might come to me. And he does—shyly—knocking on my bedroom door. "Can I come in a minute? I'd like to say goodnight properly." I welcome him and he lies on top of the covers for a short while. We have never been together in my bedroom. He kisses me lightly on the lips and massages my neck. I stroke the back of his head. "Would you like to sleep here?" I tentatively ask; "platonically." He declines—"this is enough for now."

My sleep is filled with dreams of my gallant Prince. I am deeply in love with Adrian. I cannot and will not deny that I am.

Sunday 17ᵗʰ December 2006

Sunday, and what will today bring? I am up early; ready for Adrian should he call. The vision comes quickly to me this morning; a continuation of my dreams where my Prince is crowned King. The picture portrays my Lover wielding his magnificent sword with Angel strength and royal determination. His mighty strokes clear a path through a forest of thorns that reach above his head. A turreted castle stands in the background—and suddenly he is through the impassable tangle and finds himself in a clearing. Before him stands a small boy; a trusting child whose eyes are filled with tears. Something troubles him. He is waiting to be rescued and holds up his arms to the King; "At last—you have come for me."

I send Adrian a message, asking if he feels like breakfast in bed:

A.m. From the caravan, Adrian: *Hi. Actually, breakfast in bed would be fantastic. What's cooking? Third week of Advent today. I have a lovely wreath at home. Shall we make one? Oh, and a warm flannel for my eyes if I* *can be so demanding.*

So, we continue with our work, enjoying the platonic creativity and playing with The Minx in between times. I lend an ear to the Maestro report writer, adding a few comments here and there. Adrian writes the most perceptive and nourishing accounts of his year with each child; a two-page essay for each of his precious charges. Once again I feel privileged to be spending sacred time with the Class 3 teacher.

The sun shines and shines. Adrian talks about adding music therapy to his teaching skills; what do I think of that? Amiable chatter and intimate sharing—the stuff of perfect friendship. The crystal clear views from our Mountain Eyrie keep the gates of possibility wide open. By late afternoon he departs for more pupil garden viewing and Rinky and I go to School to join a group of willing parents cleaning classrooms. Before climbing The Mountain road back home we deliver the school keys to Big J's house. In fact, we meet Adrian in the lane at the end of her street. "I'm in trouble for handing in reports late," he tells me through the car window. "Big. J. wasn't impressed that you've been working on the reports with me—unprofessional again— oops. So, is it back on?" he asks. I am confused. "What's back on?" I ask with a large question mark. "What's back on?" I repeat. "I'll speak to you later," he replies, taking the keys.

P.m. Adrian: No, silly. Big J. asked if it was back on between us. I didn't want to hide anything so I told her I was with you platonically; that you had been helping me with reports. Put my foot in it one more time. Oh well, my Nemesis strikes again. Stand up and be counted. Don't know if she believed me and although with potential to be problematic I feel fine. My lesson is not to take her reactions too personally—just be quiet for a while. I did that today. Have to admit I hadn't considered the professional angle—

Mouse: Oops—but there again, I **have** been working in class, and with the Festival Group, and on the school lunches—so—might she accept my credence? Also had the thought; perhaps this is our chance to stand up for our truth? A positive, creative partnership; accepted by my husband—and our creative form is private; our business—based on integrity. They can trust us, or what? No, My Friend, not silly. Use your sword. No mind-talk. Speak later? M—X
P.s Big J. won't be able to dispute the wonderful quality of the reports.

Monday 18ᵗʰ December 2006

I hear nothing more from Adrian. Perhaps he is worried about Big J's suspicions. The last week of term requires his full attention and the holiday atmosphere of the weekend is over. All I receive is a brief message that leaves me unsure.

A.m. Adrian: Good morning. Did I leave the garden certificates in the caravan?

34

Well, two can play at unemotional, non-attachment word-play. Perhaps he is too busy to consider the impact of a cold message. I send Adrian an equally unemotional response, wondering if he will notice.

Mouse: *Good morning. Yes, you did. I shall bring them down.*

P.m. Mouse {Unsent}: *Thought today, My Friend? Well, I'm not sure what you are thinking. Did I confuse you at the weekend? Was it too much when I read my diary? The vixen enticing her prey into the lair of cosy quandary and undeniable homecoming. How was it for you, having me so close but without our longed-for touch? I relished the closeness we shared, your tenderness speaking to me through every move you made. I enjoyed our joint creativity although I have to admit to frustration.*

Oh freedom and natural conclusion, you tease us with vain moral and high-standing intention, denying the bud of him her comfort and caress. The female and the male—physical constraint banishing the natural rhythm of his form inside her. She yearns for the coupling; for the Angel in the boy as his lithe body welcomes hers; the core of his manhood vulnerable and helpless in her woman's velvet secret. His woman—yet not his.

I suppose it is a beautiful frustration; the frustration of an expectant mother who waits for the arrival of a longed-for child. She knows the child will arrive—but when? The due date is past and time marches on. Every day the weight in her womb increases. Yes, the inevitability is nigh as she carries her gift to the world, preparing to give birth and deliver unto the stream of Earthly life. Perhaps I will move through the frustration. Perhaps I will learn to live with the womb weight. "My Love—I need your tender lips brushing mine, lingering with me in my Garden; with delicate tongue-tip-whispers and dewy caress. I long for the sensuality of you; of us. I want to kiss your neck, stroking the curls that rest easy upon your collar. Mmm-is it all or nothing for us?

I keep thinking how important for you the decision is; the decision to strike out for what you really want in your career and your life; to identify and develop your key strengths. I think you are discovering one-to-one or small group teaching might be more natural—am I right? You can leave the large group teaching to others. Have you ever thought of teaching adults? I wonder how you are today. You didn't telephone last night or say anything personal to me this afternoon—except when I asked if you were still in trouble: "That will need a conversation." But you haven't phoned or been in touch. Perhaps you are waiting for the end of term. Has Big J. threatened you with losing your job? Or maybe you need time to think through the many life-changing decisions we spoke about. Well, whatever happens I am here for you. If you don't see things the way I do, then what is there to fret over anyway? Let's just leave things finished, as they are."

ALL OR NOTHING

Stamp out the spark, Sir?
All or nothing.
Daily encounter,
Shoulders brush with dull connection,
All or nothing.
We will not fan the flame.
Return it to mundane waver,
Death of a new life.
Pull the curtain over trembling 'might be.'
All or nothing, Sir,
All or nothing.

Tuesday 19th December 2006

P.m. Mouse {Unsent}: I am sitting in the Woodsman's Den wearing the long coat. I need protection from the rain and bouncy dog this evening. It was a long day out wasn't it? Soaking, excited children and tolerant adults at Saturn Springs for our School Triathlon day. All were present; happy and dripping. Noisy, digging machinery improving the drainage, {an unwelcome addition}, chatting mums sharing sandwiches under the basic shelter where bodies mustered like sheep and soggy trainers waited for owners' rescue. Competitors biking, swimming and running, despite the rain. My Lord Swallow in white T-Shirt, dark waistcoat and rain-drenched smile busy in the middle of the action—the school's voice of rally and command.

I couldn't stand by your side. I couldn't ask you to come in my car. Teachers and others alert; watching and aware, I'm sure. I could hold my head up high in front of all, even now; could you, My Friend? I could tell them we are together in our own, special way. They couldn't take that from us.

But then we packed and left. Flat spirit—okay—but only a fraction of its potential. I wonder.

STAMP OUT THE SPARK?

Stamp out the spark?
Not I, Good Sir,
'Tis central to the glory and truth of us.
Knife-edged keel, perfect love; unconditional,
Dripping in steady, clear-eyed peace.
You know and I know.
Stamp out the spark, Good Sir?
'Tis not possible——I see you.

The Bush foliage drips steadily. The baby ferns coil in the iconic 'Koru' shape. They look like young snakes in their nest; so cosy in the middle of the Punga Fern under which I sit. Their parents shelter them from above, reaching for the light and protecting their young. The babies are alive, watching me from hairy coats that cover them in dark fuzz. I turn the metal bands that bare witness to lovers' vows, both official and unofficial. Two rings on my finger; two husbands. The rings are friends, happy together on the same digit. Copper and gold beside each other. I like them. The 'Koru'—a popular shape symbolizing renewal and rebirth—another circle. I have seen it often in greenstone and whalebone carving; an easily recognisable, national symbol.

THE COPPER BAND

He found it when he found me.
For months he wore the homemade
Metal band upon his wedding finger,
Thinking it was for another;
The perfect decoy.
She wondered; The Copper Band?
He mislaid it for a while,
But then it was found and back on his finger.
When asked, he could in all honesty say:
"It is for another."
But she knew he was beginning to wonder
If it had a significance for them.
She liked to see him wearing it; The Copper Band,
Interesting and mysterious upon his slim hand,
Lending dignity in manhood.
The Copper Band; intrinsic denting and organic waver,
Matching their unlikely union in solid possibility.
And at their sad, unwanted parting
He placed it with ceremony upon her little finger.
How strange, and yet prophetic
When it slipped from her hand just hours later.
"Perhaps this is meant to be;" they wondered.
Alone and grieving, it reappears in the bottom of her bag;
Old friend returning; constant companion
On their extraordinary journey.
She is bold. This cannot be taken from them; old friend.
She slides it upon her wedding finger.
She likes it there, The Copper Band;
Associated with healing, joy and the sacred number 7.

P.m. Mouse: {Unsent}: *Tuesday evening and my lungs ache. You* *haven't been in touch. We were on the point of reaching some conclusion, either way, and now total silence—except for a friendly wink today. Are you keeping clear until the end of term? I wish I knew. I can handle two days of silence, but not more. The longing—the grief—tears at me incessantly. Why such intense attachment? I know your spirit recognizes mine as partner, albeit it in a more subconscious fashion than mine. What would happen if that recognition became more conscious for you? When I imagine that— well—the recognition is overwhelming. I imagine often. I have seen you realize it sometimes. Your Spirit stands unashamed; your head held high; a noble glance in my direction, my sharp intake of breath—and it is present.*

I have been with you this evening, Lord Swallow. Did you feel the heat of your Greenstone as I placed my hand upon your chest? The connection is so strong today; undeniable. Do you feel the same magnetic pull? I sometimes wonder if the feeling is really strong when we think of each other simultaneously. I think we might be surprised if we recorded time. Are we synchronized? I wish I knew. I love you, My Darling Friend—deeply. Sleep well tonight. I pray we can talk again soon. I miss you more than words can say—X

GOLDEN RAIN

Will he come to me?
Does he ache to dance with me?
Does he sense our lips meeting?
Will he taste the golden rain with me?

Late P.m. Adrian: *Good feedback on our work, My Love. Apparently I write the nicest reports of all the staff—*

38

Chapter 4 Undeniable

Wednesday 20th December 2006, Advent Festival

A.m. Mouse: Well done on the reports, My Lovely Friend. Are we forgiven then? Rain lashes The Mountain. I can't even see the pine trees. And what of our Festival? Might it clear? Or do the Angels express upset at the turn of events? Hmm—she wonders. She is tired; missing him—

Adrian: He has been learning about The King. He has begun to plan a chamber from where The King will rule; fair, wise, gracious and playful. All is well in the Kingdom when The King is at home. The King was at home yesterday and the neighbouring Queen above, sometimes The Ice-Queen, {Big J.}, welcomed him back with a hug! Keeping The King in his Palace is very important right now. And the Festival? Still hopeful. We practise without gazebos and see. Gentle and easy day; maybe squash—{Wonder what he was going to say?}

Mouse: He takes up his reign—in wisdom and intuition, as priest and counsel, listening to the community and building on his strengths. She is pleased. One-to-one; Master of Ceremonies, Voice of the School. No need to be a front-line troop leader. Others can apply their skills there—X

Adrian: Do you have a white shirt I could wear?

Mouse: I'll bring one down. The only suitable one belongs to The Laird— Peruvian with a strong blue trim at the collarless neckline. See you shortly.

Adrian: Not to worry—rather not wear one of The Laird's.

Mouse: Might tip you off your throne, My Love. I understand.

The intermittent rain allows a successful festival practise. Our professional narrator is full of enthusiasm and good ideas. Thanks to the clever direction of Lois, Cordelia and Adrian the performance comes together. Drama and theatre are not my forte, unless they make up a live story of course. I provide background support. We are pleased with the result, albeit it very under-practised. Good—hopefully the sun will shine this afternoon and everything will go well.

Adrian spends the early morning fashioning a simple bamboo arch through which the Kindergarten Leavers will begin their Primary School journey. I love the oval shape; he has even plaited a flax threshold. The arch stands at the top end of the large circle of gazebos. Chairs for the audience are placed in between each class shelter. I hope everyone brings umbrellas. Parents arrive throughout the morning with carloads of fresh flowers. We decorate the gazebos and the arch. My friend Sammy spends a long time on the arch; the result is spectacular. A mass of blue hydrangea adorns the bamboo structure while pretty camellia and gladioli frolic amongst the greenery. The sky is overcast and we make sure there is adequate cover for the musicians if the heavens open during the performance.

They do—a torrential downpour—but not before the kindergarten children walk the petal path through the arch. The white clad children follow the path laid by myself, Cordelia and Lois. This is a sacred moment; our stage as we open the festival, scattering the petals from our baskets to the accompaniment of the harp. There isn't a dry eye amongst the community as the six-year-old Angels follow the petals, each presenting their Class 1 teacher with a white lilly before joining their classmates on a rug inside a gazebo.

Once the youngest children are settled, Mitch strides into the centre of the circle stage. He makes everyone laugh as he calls for the donkey—"Has anyone seen the donkey? We need the donkey!" Mary and Joseph wait for the faithful beast. Two children from Class 3 wearing a donkey suit are pulled from one of the gazebos—reluctantly. Mitch has to coax the creature out and pulls hard on the long rope. Everyone laughs; a light moment after the reverent Petal Path ritual. And now the various scenes unfold with our song between each. Mitch tells the story that accompanies every tableau, following the Holy Family's journey to Bethlehem as they overcome the elements in the way of rock, thorn, wind and dark night. Class 1 hides under a long, grey cloth as Joseph leads Mary and the donkey through the stony path. Their elbows and knees stick out; sharp rocks that make the going rough until the Angel Gabriel asks them to soften and they become rounded and less harmful to tired feet.

The rain sets in seriously as Class 2 begins, but we continue anyway. Hmm—The Angels are upset. Adrian and I glance at each other, our imposed separation keeping us at different sides of the circle. The musicians play our melody and The Heavens open more. I notice our names are together at the top of the music sheets—'Composed by': —

ADVENT FESTIVAL SONG 2006
Candle, in the night, though your light be small and slight,
Shine you now with strength and might. For whom do you wait here tonight?
Wind they feel you, harsh and cold, spider, weave a blanket bold.
Warmth you'll give to those within, to Mary and her sacred kin.
Dew, fall, tame the thorns, donkey's coat is pierced and torn.
Dull the thorns to let them through, for the child, roses bloom.
Stones, gathered, sharp and rough, making Mary's journey tough.
Smooth your edges, soften now, Gabriel will show us how.

We complete the scenes without faltering, although the families hurry away at the Festival close. The rain is heavy and home beckons. We ask the community not to applaud; the children and staff offer The Festival as a reverent gift; a treasure to be shared rather than a piece of drama. Applause is reserved for the Class Concerts that took place earlier in the week.

We pack the gazebos away quickly. Adrian and I spend minimum time together; our spark subdued by the rain and tasks-in-hand. We are both aware of others' eyes and opinions. I hate the dulling of our passion although I know it is a temporary state. The abundant flower stems are piled in the centre of the playing field. I hesitate to dismantle the bamboo arch; I know it waits for something. Will Adrian and I walk under the magical frame? It is left intact. I am pleased. As I reverse the van off the back field Adrian says he will be in touch. I hope he might come to me tonight. I need him.

P.m. Adrian: *Hello, My Dear. Nearly free. Oh boy. Would like to do some planning with you. Beautiful work on the festival from you team of sturdy, creative women.*

Mouse: *Fine Sir—I'd like to do some planning, some talking, and some stilling with you. Would you like to come up here? The sun is out, The Minx is in bed and the menagerie vaguely under control.*

Adrian: *Probably not this evening, My Good Friend. Will complete reports and catch up with Mitch who's staying here tonight. Just dropped Keegan's shoes off at his house. {One of the home-schooled children from the Workshop.} Strongly suggested they think of sending him to our School. Love to see him join us—the Go-Getter's class, eh? So, how about tomorrow night? Something special; roast lamb and presents, candles and a tree.*

I don't reply immediately. I was looking forward to seeing Adrian tonight. There are questions that need answering. What decisions do we make now? I feel sad and flat—alone. Does he still want me? Oh well, it's probably better this way. I shall stay silent tonight. I don't feel like writing much either. I'm glad I didn't manage to deliver Keegan's shoes; it would be wonderful if the wee chap joined our School. Adrian would have done a great job on selling the idea. He would have been more direct than I might have been. I imagine they couldn't afford the fees though, even though they aren't expensive. Families struggle to keep their heads above water in New Zealand and the Government provide yearly, educational funding for each home-schooled child. I heard the amount falls in the region of eight hundred dollars. Many home-schooled families have lots of children. I have met several with eight or nine offspring.

I head to bed with my man, together in my mind but in a still space. I don't want to think about tomorrow or any tomorrows. I just need to lie quietly in his arms.

Late P.m. Adrian: *Are you awake?*

Mouse: *Mmm—Just.*

Adrian: *I'm standing at the Festival arch—about to follow The Petal Path; really, I am. What does this mean? Connection with the children's destiny; our destiny? Earth, sky, wind, stars, moon, clouds; a good life. My handiwork—your handiwork—crafting for others. What is our learning; our fate? The answers are not coming yet. Wait—wait is all they say. Wrestle, ponder—yes, but wait—*

Mouse: *Strange; I imagined us walking through the arch together—a Gate—in the dark; some sort of private ritual. That's why I didn't strip away the flowers—*

Adrian: *Nice to know we're still connected and Angel-dusted. I went down to set the school alarm. Decided to walk after a late meal. Feel the urge to come see you; snuggle up. But—big but—this is waking the Private Passion I would have to say. The school year has finished. Now what? More information please, Good Angels.*

Mouse: *Stamp out the spark? Not I Good Sir-'tis central to the glory and truth of us. Knife-edge keel—perfect love; unconditional; dripping in clear-eyed peace. You know and I know. Stamp out the spark, Good Sir? 'Tis not possible—I see you.*

Adrian: *Ah yes, but my word, the word of a King—not to be given or broken lightly. Clear must the sign be—and the children—honouring—no confusion for them; clear adults, clear in their boundaries. The King must be in residence to make decisions around these matters, otherwise his impulsive brother will make wild decisions in his place, especially at this out-breath time. So, this King will bid his Queen goodnight—his, but not his. Until tomorrow closes. Lamb roast?*

Very late, Mouse: *She is kneeling by his side. They have made a vow-the content is hidden. They held hands and walked through the arch in the dark—solemn—afraid—no lips brushing assurance. They have walked The Petal Path and are kneeling where it ends—in thin air now the gazebo has gone. Their swords are beside them. She does not want to knock him from his throne. A new King kneels beside her and she is awed by his strength. She bows her head in humble subdue—waiting—a sense of ominous dark around them. Tomorrow then.*

Adrian: *Not only Queen—Fellow Warrior—Elven; he too. Longbows and quivers—the far-reaching arrows of? Wisdom? Thought? Love? But there in the thin air of the deserted gazebo space, they agreed. Friends—up and joyous.*

Mouse: These Elven Warriors-side-by-side at the end of the Petal Path; laid by his Queen and by Lois; {he knew she was to play a part.} Two small Copper Boxes lie waiting for them—perfect cubes—intricate, woven mesh. You can see straight through them. They fit in the palm of their hands perfectly. One each. She takes her sword and splits their red-hot spark in two. She places each half inside a separate box. He seals each with his sword. No word is spoken.

I sleep fitfully; disturbed by the darkness; the image of our solemn ritual so powerful. I experience a fleeting vision of a wholehearted return to The Laird, but it is weak and quickly replaced by the thoughts I record before eventually falling sleep. I shall send them to Lord Swallow in the morning.

Thursday 21ˢᵗ December 2006

A.m. Mouse: The sealed gift is not a parting token. The gift brings ownership in a new consciousness. It is only as a King that he can accept The Copper Box. And as he looks more closely at the woven detail he spies intricate trees, rivers, ocean and a Boat. This is a precious jewel—unequalled. The metal is solid, despite its woven construction. A heat-resistant ingredient prevents their fingers burning as they handle the treasure. They can do whatever they please with their caged sparks. The fire is contained, measured and sealed in a mesh of integrity, transporting them to the next level of pure, considered Love. She can be physically close in this knowledge, as cheeks brush traces of Celestial Union and tongues taste Angel Nectar. To make love on this plateau is her natural medium; a separate, yet integral place that can rightly be named 'Paradise'. She senses no judgement in her entry there—even if only in the ether with him—X

Adrian: It is a problem. I don't want to box it yet—don't even want to separate it. The Kingly draw to honour is a new force only and do I want to let go of The Boy? The one who goes behind? Who acts a little deceitfully? He wants her bad—and the honour is a distant ideal. He wants her comfort, her touch, her listening, her adoration and her reassurance. The warm mother— The Boy held. But she offers him Kingship instead. She frees him; cuts her own longing—

Mouse: Oh no, Sir—my longing is not cut—it is intensifying. She wants him bad too, but as a King—yes, as a King; for only a King can handle this force in measured nobility. X

Adrian: Points to the stars—to the higher places—the heightened life— The Warrior Priest King. These are new ideas. How does he walk as King? How does he bear his crown and mantle and wield his sword? Not ready yet to give her up—oh, longing of my loins—yes, I would have you again and again—not give this up. But to have this is to stay in the shade; to shun the sun—to hide Love—to be discreet. There is no other way. My word has been given. I have spoken.

Mouse: *She is asking if he could join her on this high plateau. She would show him how. He would maintain his word and his honour. It is a lot to ask. She is hesitant. She needs him so much. Perhaps it is not possible. It requires concentration and vulnerable opening.*

Adrian: *I stand in the sun from now on. I open my actions. My love is honourable and Kingly. The darkness is opened to the light of the citizens; to The Children of the Kingdom—to The People. The King is not weakened. But Lady, when I need you, when the Little Boy Prince who was wounded is present, you are a mother to him. Does The King need to let him go now? And how does 'The Wild Man in the Pond' come out? Where does The King keep his Copper Box with the halved spark?*

We will speak of these things when we next meet. New heights; a ritual leaving—a coronation; two coronations—receiving the mandate, the mantle and the crown. The sceptre and the thrown too. Yes, we must take our places on the thrones, restoring the fallen King and Queen. The Kingdoms; the prosperous Kingdoms. Great rejoicing. Far easier is the burden of desire when such a solemn oath is taken and the light that enlightens the wise heads of Kings shines forth.

Mouse: *Let's dwell on these ideals during the day. A fire is lit; her passion trying to gain control. The washing load is on—Class 1 curtains to be washed in the normal rounds of Earthly duties. Am away to shop in an hour. I'll get the lamb and trimmings. The Queen and young Princess might even go to the Hot Pools. And the King? Reports still to complete? And a clear head for Kingly matters of State? See you later, Lord Swallow. A Coronation, a new chapter, a wise counsel. Go gently. Your Lady——X*

Mouse {Unsent}: *Thwarted love; intense—so beautiful. The power of it drags the very life force from her. Even her ears are hurting today. Her whole body is sluggish and overwhelmed by desire and longing—light breathing, heavy chest, little appetite. She suspects these emotions are the result of their synchronized thought patterns. Are they telepathic signals? Soul to Soul—so strong. Oh my, oh my. Do you feel me beside you, Lord Swallow? My hand is covering your Greenstone. I picture you feeling the warmth as you stand in Big J's kitchen.*

Did you know, Sir, my longbow skills have finite accuracy? I can shoot an arrow swift and sure, and as it flies it takes on a golden hue; the pure reflections of an impassioned sun. Let's have some fun on dry land—let's run and play in the forest together, fine-tuning our marksman skills. I would have you take me again and again, My Liege—I am not ready to give you up either. But our time has come to find a way and we will find a way. We have not been led this distance without a reason. We have not ridden impossible storms and high seas for nothing. We have to find a life-giving outlet for our growing passion; for ourselves and for others, otherwise I fear it may consume us entirely. Have we not aired our bond amongst friends and family? They have seen as much as is necessary; as much as they can cope with. They have tasted a small piece of the fruits of our creativity. And now we need to work on our major creation—our writing; and for this we need our passion; oh yes, fine edged and oiled—our pens are dependent upon it, but in contained form. Can we manage that? Our adulthood raising it to new levels with lots of fun thrown in. Can we do this?

I love you more than words can say—X

The Minx and I attend to domestic chores. We shop, we cook and we play with the animals. Molly the piglet loves coming inside. She finds piggy tucker under the kitchen table, although she is learning about the delights of the larder cupboard, which isn't quite so good. She sits in front of the fire every evening. Although the summer has arrived, mornings and evenings are chilly on The Mountain. The Bog-Brush has gone humping mad—bonkers in fact! Rinky and I laugh so much as we try to contain her behaviour. Why do female dogs do that? Unfortunately she has discovered a way to escape The Mountain's ten-acre stronghold. Luckily she hasn't strayed beyond the pond—yet.

We visit The Twealm Realm after lunch, playing on the seesaw and swing, dodging the showers and eventually heading back inside to wrap Christmas presents. I feel a fraud trying to be Christmassy—without family and cold weather the festival is irrelevant. My thoughts and emotions couldn't be further away. Poor Rinky—she must sense her Mother's preoccupation although I am trying hard to make the holiday fun. The Laird has telephoned three times since yesterday but I keep missing him. He left a message. Am I meant to keep missing his calls? Cordelia also phoned, giving me the details of a 'Love and Forgiveness' website. She says that true love is an initiation.

P.m. Adrian: *I am coming. Sorry I am late. I want to finish the reports completely before I head up, so I don't have to come back down too early tomorrow. What are you up to?*

Mouse: *Hi Friend. What am I up to? Dealing with food, animals, washing and a longing that I am steadily getting under control. T'will be safe by the time you get here. Am just about to feed The Minx—then pop her into bed with a cosy story. Lamb is cooked. Do finish reports—good to be clear and still on this roller coaster of an adventure.*

Later, Adrian: *Lovely Lady, I am alone—fully. On my way.*

Mouse: The fire is lit; supper awaits my Lord. And his Lady? She is ready for him.

He comes to her at last—Kingly and tired, hungry and hers. He holds her in his nobility; they embrace with tenderness and love as Lord Swallow and his Lady. A free man; his school burden over for the year. They turn naturally to each other, to relax, to catch up on their marathon week and to sleep deeply together. They share a late meal of roast lamb; The King blesses the meal with his priestly reverence. They pray for guidance and clarity as this new chapter begins. He gives thanks for the bounty spread before them both. His prayerful words bless this new story, unfolding as each day passes. They smile; relieved to be here at last.

The candle winks in company with the mumbling fire and the night is theirs—theirs on this new, platonic plateau; neither of them feeling the slightest bit platonic. The King's reign is determined; resigned even. There really is no other choice. With wistful eyes and beseeching smiles they lie, fully clad, in their fireside bed reading dairies and text messages to each other; trying to find a way forward and enjoying being together.

We are so tired. I don't stay all night beside Adrian. I leave The King eventually; kissing him behind his left ear and whispering with a wry smile; "I shall go upstairs now and make love to you."

Friday 22nd December 2006

What a blessed morning. I descend early into Adrian's waiting arms—a natural welcome under the covers fully dressed; totally wrapped up in each other yet maintaining the boundaries we have agreed upon. We wake slowly; there is so much to discuss. "We will stay here for Christmas," I tell him. "It feels right somehow. Thank-you for your kind invitation." We share a bottle of warm Supergreens and I massage his sore gut, knowing he desires my touch to extend further. I can feel his manhood waiting for my loving caress, my fingers restrained and disciplined beside his masculinity. The agony is tantalizing and delicious.

The hours tick past and The Minx wakes. I leave our fireside nest before she comes downstairs. We are all dressed and join Adrian on the bed for breakfast. Lord Swallow is playful and cheeky with her-"Will you marry me, Rinky?" He jests. "No, of course not silly—you are already married to Mummy!" She replies without batting an eye-lid. "No I'm not," he answers hastily—"Mummy is already married!" We laugh and read stories together. One book is particularly apt; depicting an Irish lass who refuses the hand of the local teacher for the love of the Elfish Prince who teaches her to dance in The Fairy Kingdom.

We get up and tidy the cabin. We discuss holiday plans. My parents arrive for a month on January 10th. We are excited. After a while Adrian becomes quiet and takes the dogs out for some 'thinking time.' "Thoughts in my head—need to process some of this stuff," he explains. When he returns we spend time writing and talking through our final commitments. Rinky is engrossed in a game upstairs and we allow her a dose of holiday video. Adrian and I have an important, final task. "Come, My Lady, time to climb to the Pa Site; let's weave grass coronets and crown each other in our separate Kingdoms—a parting ceremony." We gather string, scissors and a rug before heading out into the immensity of our Mountain landscape. The sun is glorious although not warm enough to remove jumpers on the mountaintop. We reach the Pa site quickly—"oh—we've forgotten the swords." The Elf Prince bounds away down the hill like a young gazelle, swiftly returning with the precious swords. It is a stiff climb to the top and we collapse on the rug together; laughing and so happy.

The visibility is crystal clear this morning. We are quiet as we gather the long grasses. Two crowns are quickly fashioned; we decorate them with the yellow buttercups that grow on The Mountain, adding the blue hydrangea sprigs that I rescued from the festival. We smile. We are madly in love and cannot hide the fact. This is glorious fun, and within our boundaries; we hope. "There, all done. Let me place this crown upon your noble head, Sir."

We stand, this is a serious moment. Taking up our swords we knight each other with gracious, spirit-filled reverence. We vow to keep to our own Kingdoms; to take up our appointed reign; Lord Swallow and his Lady; alone with the ancestors, The Angels and the blue, blue sky; our bond as sure as the return of the morning light. The vow we make laughs in the face of the truth, but we make it for the greater good. Our loving gaze is alight with every mystery wrapping the potential of humankind. "I want to take a picture; wait a minute;" Adrian places a little pocket camera on a nearby post and sets the timer. The skies are bright blue, the green of the surrounding valleys sumptuous as a velvet gown and the focus perfect. Several photos are taken. Afterwards we look at them with interest; how strange—the one where we face each other is unlike the others. The background blue and green is replaced by a magical, white light; our figures appear veiled, almost as silhouettes. We don't know what to say. I am aware of Adrian's sharp intake of breath that matches mine; the picture is simply beautiful; a magic token from Heaven. I don't think we are alone on the Pa Site.

We head back to the house, aware that Rinky might worry if we are outside for too long. I climb the stairs to check on her-"Can I finish watching the video, Mummy? It's almost at the end." Adrian needs to leave in an hour. Our serious conversation continues beside the warm fire.

He stands apart from her, yet close in the way that matters. He leans upon his sword with a dynamic, Kingly stance. She is proud of her beautiful Elf Prince. He speaks of his need for the sun from now on, in everything he undertakes. "How would a King rule; how would he wear his crown? How would he rule his subjects? What union would be right for his subjects? This one? And what of heirs? No? And yet, even The King needs a private world; might a yearly retreat for us both be allowed? The moon time with my Queen is now over. Any future must be honourable and Kingly. I realize that Big J. represents '*the axe of my stepmother*'; every fairytale has to have a tricky stepmother. Hmm—I worry about heading back down the hill and facing her at home. She is my Landlady, my Principal and my friend. But she does represent my stepmother. I am a young boy always in the wrong; a sneak. No—I am a King now. I shall go back and face her," he declares. "*I expect you are wondering where I have been? If I have been with my Lady?'* I shall say. '*Well, I will exercise my right as a grown adult and not tell you! There, that's my secret.'*

"Good, I feel strong now. Yes, The King is on his throne." She watches him and smiles, loving him so much. She speaks of her ability to reach the Heavenly Realm through tantric touch but understands it might be unfair to suggest he accompany her. "It is unkind of me to even ask."

"You are someone else's wife; a mother; how do you feel about that? And the children?" He asks directly. She explains again about her private side; how she can be close with him and still face The Laird with integrity. In her eyes the purity of their bond raises it above anything sullied. Hmm— more of her idealistic dream time? They agree then to be together, but on this new, higher plateau. No touching but cuddles allowed and she may kiss the back of his neck as she passes. They will allow work meetings, yes, and a retreat once a year. Perhaps. Messaging every day? Definitely—neither wants to reduce their literary contact. Do they allow themselves romance and passion in prose? Yes, their story is dependent upon that ingredient. So, out in the sun from now on. Planned times of meeting—open in front of The Laird, {if he agrees}, but no physical touch. Lord Swallow admits that he desires his Lady too much; his physical needs move in quickly. The waves of attraction and longing overtake him instantly, he tells her. Why, he only has to picture her in her white cotton and he is undone. And yet the denial; the resisting of these temptations provides a rich slice of exquisite emotion. "Bring it on, My Love," he teases. "You can parade in front of me any time; lure me." "Am I allowed to touch you at all?" She asks—"NO"! —He replies. "You know, I think our private passion is far from extinguished," she continues; "if anything, we are fuelling it by trying to impose these boundaries."

Adrian speaks of alchemy; perhaps we will transform our passion into something else. Is this the result of intense emotion and synchronized longing? Perhaps we are being pulled to a higher plateau by something other. Will I have a partner to accompany me to these levels after all? I wonder. Is this what we are about; have been all along? The culmination of our daring, Ocean Voyage brings a personal centring. I can relax. We have arrived in our beautiful Garden. I sense a veil lifting. My Lord Swallow suddenly grasps the entire meaning of our dialogue. "The only thing we have, in fact, disengaged from is the physical and you don't need that as the main focus to step through The Garden Gate." He states. "Am I right?" "Yes," I reply quietly; "I only require minute doses; a 'knife-edge', to reach the plateau. If you read back through all the poetry and messages you will find a common thread."

My gaze falls to Adrian's Copper Band upon my finger; "Your ring—do you like me wearing it or should you take it back?" "Has The Laird seen it?" He asks hesitatingly. "Yes," I reply, "he has." "Hmm—perhaps I will have it back—when we meet after Christmas. Let's go away somewhere; we could take your van. We can keep our integrity intact. Could Rinky stay with a friend?" "Yes, I'm sure I can arrange something. Oh-and let's keep the ring really safe. We could melt it and make two rings one day if The Angels smile upon us," I add hopefully. "We mustn't lose it. The Copper Band is too precious now."

Domestic life kicks back in and I sit Adrian down in the kitchen and give him a haircut. He needs a woman's touch to curtail The Wild Man in the Pond. "I never use soap or shampoo," he admits when I offer to wash his wavy locks-"It's much better to simply use water." I manage to persuade him otherwise, although I know there is some truth in what he says. "This is a natural shampoo; it will give your hair a healthy shine." We seem perfectly able to switch from the celestial to the mundane and The King allows his Queen the benefit of the doubt. I smile with genuine happiness and send him on his way, delivering The Minx to a friend at the bottom of the hill 'en route'. I need to complete the Christmas shopping without 'Mrs Flappy Ears/Beady Eyes'. She plays for a couple of hours with Sonya the potter's children; the family who gave us Monty the kitten earlier in the year.

Midday, Adrian: *Help. Need some advice. Lady in Black is on heat—since last Thursday—maybe earlier. Just about shagged by a dog at Sarah's shop. Maybe was! Vet could give her a pill to halt the process. $70 and would take several days to work. Would mean she wouldn't get pregnant. Got to make a choice now—*

I telephone Adrian straight away to chat through the options. In the end he decides against taking any action. His dog had a surprise litter last year and the whole process had been a great success. Would it really matter if it happened again? As I replace the receiver a sardonic grin creases my face—glad it's the dog and not me!

Early P.m. Mouse: *Hello, My Gallant King. Did I tell you how attractive you are in your new reign? Well, you are. Your Lady is calm and proud—proud to walk beside you, if only from afar. How goes the clearing up at home? And were you Kingly with Big J? I won't come out to the party this evening; too late for Rinky. Our English guests, Sam and Emma, arrive very late—after 11p.m. I need to organize the top cabin for them. Will leave the lights on so they can go straight to bed. Enjoy the party. Maybe see you later? X*

* * * * * * *

Late P.m. Adrian: *All over the place is The King; might be drunk. Big realizations today have stirred up the demons; life-shocks everywhere. "Great," he says half-heartedly. Not started cleaning up his Palace yet, but car is tidy with a small repair accomplished. Poor old chariot needs care and a tune-up. I'll do that tomorrow. Will probably stay here tonight and nurse my sorry heart. All is well. Just about to go to Heather's party; fashionably late. Will come up early tomorrow. Need—*

Mouse: *She is sleeping long and sound—sleeping in their fireside bed—supper uneaten, guest cabin still to prepare. She nestles into the memory of him lying beside her. And then his message wings its way—he is in distress—what can have happened in the short time he has been gone? Why is he drunk? His Palace still to clear? He must have been partying; Christmas cheer; and now she cannot look into his eyes and help him through the life-shock. X*

Mouse: *Sorry if my last message sounded like a nagging wife. You are a free man. I was feeling protective-"Who dares hurt my Love", or something along those lines. I will miss you tonight though. Well done for fixing the car; must have taken quite a time. Sorry I can't help clean the Palace. Go gently on the new King. His Queen is holding him—X*

Our guests arrive very late and I rise to greet them. Sam is an old school friend of my younger brother and was a regular cottage guest in Dorset many moons ago. An effervescent character, he is embarking on a professional singing career. His leggy girlfriend is the complete opposite—an intellectual, classical beauty on her way to actress success. She seems reserved. We chat for a while and I return to bed after one p.m.

Saturday 23rd December 2006

Adrian: *He wakes and thinks of his white-clad, soft-bodied woman—her embraces—her graces—her charming, sweet faces. Maybe just as well he kept his distance last night or full into her arms he'd have fallen. For The King was not strong—with all that's gone on; that too tempting would have been the comforts calling.*

Now resting and drifting through the events of yesterday: The Crowning; of swords and wreaths of hay; and the touch of The Angels in the trick of the light; a treasure to hold; a gift from the heights. A slow and easy morning start, new energy—Christmas ideas for nephews and nieces; arrows and together we make a bow. I'll take all my tools with me to Auckland. Somehow feel cleared of heaviness today. A purge. Late music making at the expense of my voice and weariness. Mmm—clear heart; new resolves. Had work to do around making mistakes and staying connected with others. Humble apology for one and clear headed choice for another, but learning from both.

50

Yesterday I learnt about the alchemy of lust. This is important and amazing for you fill me with longing my white-clad, light-bathed Lady of grace and comfort and provision. Oho! What a challenge before us—galvanising—transformational—excruciatingly so. Let's take it slow. Instead of undressing and caressing we'll be breathing and expressing. Steady as a flagpole—strong as a bull—graceful as a swan—humble as a servant—honest—

Mouse: *My Darling King, I am sorry you have had to go into battle, and on the day of your crowning too. I wanted to hold you last night; to help you find The King again. If you had found being with me too tempting I would have spun away. You see, I have been held by The King and although I adore The Prince, only The King can lure me into deep rapture-X*

P.s I have a thought. The alchemy is an old friend of mine; the transforming of lust into something higher; that exquisite entrance through The Garden Gate. I know there is a link. And from the celestial perfection we are personally nourished and can truly give of ourselves to others in humble service. Welcome home, My King—my soul is weeping—with joy. I never dared believe I would be accompanied through The Gate—X

Rinky and I deal with animals and clear up the cabin. The morning drags by slowly. Sam and Emma stay in bed until midday! Emma is keener to maintain her fitness programme than chat. She downs a bowl of muesli and heads out for a run. I wish her stamina in this mountain terrain. Sam would like to linger but I sense Emma is anxious to keep moving. I don't find her particularly warm or friendly; she doesn't know us from Adam.

Midday, Adrian: *I'm on my way, stopping off at Cordelia's first.*

Mouse: *Lovely, My Friend—we are just cooking bacon and eggs; very late brunch.*

We share a pleasant meal together. I wonder what Sam thinks, seeing me with another man. The Laird and I have been together for so long. Sam was a schoolboy when he first visited our rural West Country retreat. I introduce Adrian as a friend; nothing more. Sam is a singer, specializing in a particular technique. He gives Adrian an impromptu singing lesson and we listen with interest to his tales of a London Gospel Choir and other aspects of his career to date. The King is slightly thrown by the whole episode but he manages to perform. We produce guitars and try out our song; *'Soldiers of Fire'*. Rinky gets bored and after a while our guests depart. {Unbeknown to any of us at the time, Sam goes on to become a leading Star in one of Andrew Lloyd Webber's musical talent contests in the U.K. His career is made. He must have found our amateur music making a touch naïve. Never mind; it was lovely seeing him again. Adrian gave him with a songbook when he left. "Thanks," he was grateful. "Now I will *have* to learn the guitar. I promised myself I would master the art during our holiday."}

Adrian and I attend to The Minx and then we unwind with foot massages and cups of tea. Adrian needs to relax and share his thoughts. He is restless until he clears the air around himself and around us. We snuggle and doze together while Rinky plays upstairs. An unsuccessful disc loading to back-up The Book writing leaves Adrian questioning our integrity. "Is there a level of deception in our writing? Nothing should be hidden from The Laird. We must ask his permission to record the story. But how do we protect our intimacy? Is it possible?" The same questions go round and round. "I love you," I tell him. "This story is asking to be written, that's all I know." The King stands with his sword again, asking me questions that I cannot answer: "Perhaps you should look at the route of your actions. Could there be something at fault there?"

He packs his car with the tools and drives away for Christmas, leaving his Lady with a nagging sadness. Why do I continue to sense such positivity about our relationship? Surely feelings of guilt and uncertainty should be colouring my optimism by now. "And how will things be in several years time?" Hmm; questions, questions.

My ears are hurting again this evening. I suppose I am not hearing the message. Rinky has a disturbed sleep. Is she picking up the troubled vibe? She is slightly feverish and wakes me several times in the night. The lesson today? That everything must be up for scrutiny—even our Book. Nothing hidden. But haven't we had our fingers burnt enough? Do we really need to reveal all? Perhaps. I feel more content when I think of our story as a gift to others. We have no cause for shame. If we ever get to publish, anonymity would be a pre-requisite. All names and places would be disguised. The intimacy is too personal. And what of Little Arthur? He is keeping a low profile while we wrangle with words and swords, verse and coronets.

Sunday 24th December 2006 Christmas Eve

A.m. Adrian: "Dear Laird—I want to write a book about our adventure in coming to New Zealand and especially about my affair with Adrian. It is quite a story and I think could be of interest to others. I am committed to our family and I am not trying to restart my relationship with Adrian. I have a sense our story might be important. We write to each other a lot by text messaging and I have kept a record of our correspondence. The pages of prose hold a record of the unfolding events and because we both enjoy the creativity of the written word a poetic slant to the story makes it into something interesting.

How would you feel if I turned it into a novel/autobiography? I would work on some parts with Adrian—with openness to our meetings. I would ask you to respect the privacy, because of its sensitivity. I know that you have been hurt by our actions in the past. I cannot see any other way of turning something beautiful into something life-giving. It needs to go somewhere and although preferring to keep the content private I would agree to you reading what is being written. I am sorry to maintain a life apart from you. I honestly do not know of another way. I want to respect you and honour myself at the same time.

This fling with Adrian has revealed and touched a part of me that I never imagined could be brought up, into the light. Could you stand by me still? While I write this anonymous tale of romance? If you say no I will respect your decision. I will not go behind your back. However, I would not let the idea disappear. I would ask you again at a later date."

Mouse: *Yes, I have had the same conversation in my mind. I would exchange the word 'affair' with 'connection' though. What we hold in our hearts is way above the murky connotation of that term. I would say: "We have raised our love to something that can bathe in the sun. We are upholding our agreement. There will be no secrets from now on. Our written word would not be hidden from you, although we would suggest you don't read the story from cover to cover, especially if it is ever published. I know you would respect the delicate nature of the content and although you feature heavily throughout your identity is anonymous. The trust and love in our marriage allows us our independence. I know I ask for an extraordinary gift; one that is not in accord with a conventional marriage. Might I be so bold as to suggest the level of your vocational work is also not in line with a conventional marriage? I ask this out of an intuitive sense that this is the right path to tread. I will always love you. Thank-you."*

Good morning, My Love. Thank-you for your clear thoughts and beautiful words—matches my thinking; as always. I don't like the word 'fling' though— men's talk perhaps? I have got the computer disc working. I have sent you the beginning of The Book. Let me know if you received it okay. I hope you are well? X

Adrian: *How much do you love The Laird? This is the crux. Answer it straight up—in a man's way. Do you want to grow and deepen with him? Where do you see your marriage in 5 years time? Do you really want to separate? Face it. Answer it. Do you want to be with this man? How much?*

Mouse: *My Darling—you are my True Love. I cannot answer these questions yet. I know they have to be faced. I shall be clearer once the family returns. Thank-you for your valiant Kingship; your patience. You know how much I love you. I wish it could be easier. I would not wind back the clock though; oh no, I certainly would not.*

Adrian's strong questions are important. I wish I could answer him straight. I should turn him away and resign myself to the long haul; and yet, I cannot. The Mountain is exceptionally quiet this morning. Rinky is sleeping long and late. We potter at home while I chew over our quandary in all its tantalizing beauty and chaos. Adrian is in Auckland with his family.

* * * * * * *

Later, Mouse: He cannot see the whole of me. He knows something other lies central to his wife but he cannot engage with its essence. I think he is afraid of what he would find there. We dance to a different rhythm. He does not cherish me, although he is always caring. I have come to know a complete union in another's arms. Every day the longing for that connection overwhelms me in its certainty. I cannot ignore the truth.

Adrian: Aching for sunlight to cast away shadows and veils. Longing for strength and authority to flow freely; the Kingly way. Yes, clear light of truth. Sorry to be— {Missing text; bother.}

Our small group of presents are wrapped and ready for tomorrow. Rinky is so excited; bless her. I couldn't feel less festive.

Midday, Adrian: Church in Auckland; stayed for clean up afterwards. Scrubbed the stairs. Ate a big bowl of ice cream—oops—and a scone. Wasn't allowed to keep in contact with you as much as I had hoped; credit and battery ran out at the same time. Had to leave you with the questions I'd posed. Did you go to church? I'm back in bed, digesting ice cream before gardening and making Christmas presents. See you in my dreams—

Mouse: My Love—Rinky is under the weather and we haven't been out yet. May not even make our Christmas Eve invite to Bernard and Felicia if she doesn't pick up. We'll see. I continue to be stripped bare. Thanks for keeping in touch. Missing you—rather a lonely Mountain. I would like to have come to church and eaten ice cream and scones with you. The upshot is that a good chunk of The Book is recorded. I'll try to send you more later on. Still finding my way around it all. I'll certainly join you in your dreams. We can be as free as we like there. X

Midday, Adrian: Why is Rinky sick? Post-school come down? And you— lonely; regretting choice to stay behind instead of going to the U.K to be with the family? Maybe it is your Ashes time? I wonder if women have one. Delphine could be interesting to talk to if you wanted company. I'm studying 'Iron John' in bed. Yum. Missing you too; not with strong longing right now; a bit of floating debris on my pool today. I can't see clearly right now. Want to be clearer after a snooze. Go well. Use the space as 'Deep Goods Time'. The ultimate Christmas really. Seek the joy in the low and the lonely-peace.

Mouse: He will only stand in the sun from now on. He cannot work on The Book if there is secrecy; he will surely not be free to make love with her on their new plateau. She is not addressing the real issues—she is expecting the impossible—unfair, damaging even to both these fine men. She must send him away. She must attend to her duties; the duties of her own Kingdom. Their Kingdoms are not the same. Her mind is a giant pipe dream—unkind to the new King who struggles with the ordinary world, let *alone this high plateau of celestial intuition. The rain and wind lashes the cabin again. He is gone. The guests have gone. The family are on the other side of the world. It is Christmas. She is stripped completely bare; even the comfort of her private world is brought into question. All is gone. And Blossom, the loved pet rabbit, is found dead on the grass by the water tank. No feelings of any longing right now either—empty—flat—okay—ish. Strange times-peace.*

Adrian: *My Love—it is the time for play. When all else is gone create something new—walk—cut—knit—sew-cook—use—the body—dig—paint Alcatraz—landscape. Out of the head and into the hands. Work-make another gorse fence—start digging the trampoline into the ground as we have discussed; stop it blowing away on windy nights. Plant the Pohutukawa tree the Workshop families gave us. Fill the driveway holes—action—to quell the pain; to air the wound. Breathe!*

Early P.m Mouse: *Cooking, writing, sewing—can't leave the house; Rinky asleep and she might wake, needing me close by. A woman's world rather than a man's, though I can imagine you tackling a bereft state in that way. Thanks for the suggestions and kind thoughts. X*

The Minx picks up enough to spend the evening with Bernard and Felicia's family. We enjoy a delicious roast meal, sharing presents under the Christmas tree beforehand. The Wood-burning stove adds a merry crackle and Felicia's festive Dutch traditions create an authentic atmosphere. Bernard is a perfectionist and tends to be the kitchen maestro. He isn't a typical Kiwi man—he could be Swiss or German perhaps, with his delicate hands, lean frame and eye for detail. He wears gold-rimmed spectacles. Felicia is tall and skinny. She crops her hair short and is a deep thinker with pretty, pixie-like features. She has a strong interest in all things spiritual while Bernard tends to 'pooh pooh' any such nonsense. I sometimes wonder how she persuaded him to adopt the alternative schooling that has brought us all together. I always enjoy walking back into their comfortable home—the home where our antipodean adventure began in July 2005.

We listen to carols outside the Wesleyan Chapel in the centre of town after our Christmas meal. The town is made up of a series of wide, leafy avenues and we duly find a piece of grass and sit on a picnic rug together. The temperature drops as the sun sets. I'm glad we dressed warmly. Rinky wears her red Christmas coat with the velvet collar. The chapel is decorated with Christmas icons in garish lighting along the top of the building. The brass band rallies the carol singers and various speakers stand up at a microphone and tell Yuletide tales from years gone by. A Christmassy atmosphere envelops those gathered and one of the parishioners distributes candles. My heart softens, inviting a longing for Adrian's hand in mine as we welcome this Holy Night.

Late P.m. Mouse: Happy Christmas, My Darling. As Christmas Carols fill the night and one small girl hangs up her stocking with heart-warming excitement I cannot abandon the truth of our love. It is your arms I long for; your smile and belonging that accompanies me this Holy Night. I know I should face reality, and of course you are a free man. But the Pa site photo—that is reality too—X

Adrian: Hello, My Darling. I cut my finger just as your message came through. I was thinking of you and about to text you myself. I'm sitting at my Mum's table, making presents from shells and sticks and flax—thinking of you. Can you help me set up a workshop? A really productive one that makes money; near the school. Let's get business-y. Yes, Merry Christmas. I'm on a wild burn—love being creative. A term's worth of stored up invention—rush. Going to midnight mass tonight I think.

Mouse: Wish I were with you. Rinky and I have been making felt stars— yes, let's get going. My little festive companion picked up and we managed to get out this evening. Too long at home can be negative. We went to a candle-lit carol service in town. It was special; the first taste of proper Christmas. I so wanted your hand in mine. I felt you loving me with tender kisses as I sat with my little candle on the grass. Thank-you. Take me to church with you.

Monday 25th December 2006 Christmas Day

A.m. Adrian: Good morning and good wishes, My Lady. The King has risen early after a late night mass. He will also attend the 8 a.m service. A slight gloom hangs over him. Where is the sun? He had life-shocks I suppose—church service after a hell-for-leather creative binge. My mind accuses me of selfishness and indulgence, not so good for a Kingly stance before The Lord. He wonders how his Lady fairs, alone on the bare Mountain. He needs—he chooses to attend to the tasks of the morning; to honour his commitment to his church community—clear—not rushed—ready; not running from tasks pushed to the last minute. But he loves to get to the bottom of things; loves to find his Kingship. He wonders what the lesson today will be. He must focus. He wants to enjoy being able to give freely of himself in joy and love. He wants to share this with his family; to be light and generous. Is this possible today? He is tired—life-shocky. And how is she? Mmm. He hugs her close and kisses the top of her head.

Mouse: Good morning, My Liege—My Lord Swallow. Was that you in my bed at 2.45 a.m? If not, it must have been Father Christmas. Well; I would never have credited him with passion of that calibre! The Rainbows are still rippling through your Lady on The Mountain. Happy Christmas again. One very excited Little Lady was up before dawn to open her stocking. Luckily she went back to sleep when I growled at her. We will go to church at 9a.m. The service is primarily for the children. They are invited to dress up and join the nativity scene at the front of the church.

Later, Mouse: She has had an important thought; the key to The Garden Gate is alchemy—she has known it all along. He has found a way to understand it—to put it into words. She longs to take it to its very limit; longs to take him with her. But maybe this is too dangerous. Their caged sparks might burst out of their boxes and scorch them badly. Angel territory only? X

Rinky and I drive down the hill to the parish we prefer near the coast. We like the family atmosphere as opposed to the formal church in the centre of town. Lots of children have dressed up. Various Angels and shepherds make their way to the front of the church. One little boy walks down the red-carpeted aisle wearing a sheepskin cloak. He clutches a toy lamb in one hand and his father's hand in the other. Rinky didn't want to make a spectacle of herself and sits beside me quietly. She is rather taken by a glittering little girl who has come dressed as a star.

I always enjoy this service. The light, informal gathering celebrates the essence of family. The priest addresses the service to the children who sit on the wide altar steps beside the Nativity Scene. A friendly German lady sits next to me; she must be in her seventies. "This is my best friend;" she introduces an older man who comes in late. They make me laugh during Holy Communion. "Show off," she says to him when he heads for the central aisle instead of waiting with us for the nearest Eucharist Minister.

When we get home we unwrap a few of the parcels that wait under the pale branches of the little tree. I couldn't lay my hands on a regular fir tree. A couple of days ago Rinky and I followed signs to a Christmas tree plantation in the hills behind Waikite Bay. A whole field of bushy firs, lined symmetrically beside a bungalow, found us selecting a small specimen. The trees remind me of the type you see growing in tubs at London hotel entrances. It was duly chopped down for us and loaded into the back of the car. We haven't many decorations but Rinky and I have adorned it nicely. It is strange to be so alone on Christmas Day.

Of course the family phones from England—how wonderful—everyone is there and the party spirit flies down the telephone wires. The Minx and I treat ourselves to pancakes filled with mince and cheese sauce. Rinky plays with her new toys and I manage to log texts and get more of The Book down. What is my lesson today? My ears are hurting again—am I not hearing the message? The grief is replaced by longing. What have I learnt since yesterday's place of empty ashes and sadness? It is my pride, my determination not to succumb to a strong Earthly association; yes—that has been highlighted. I don't want to let go of Heaven; refuse to in fact. I am stubborn and will stop at nothing to keep the key to The Gate. To discard the key would mean entering the human realm of emotion and lack of control. I would cry a lot more and become vulnerable. Is this my lesson? Hmm—I am unsure.

This morning in church I felt Little Arthur in my womb—tangibly. I sensed the whole family on the pew beside me; including Adrian of course. Little Arthur; as I watched the children at the altar my mind turned to the unborn child. This is a special child—ancient links—mystical event directing a storyline—linking hemispheres and nationalities—unconventional arrival—legend in the making. Who is he, or she? The reason behind our soul longing? The questions resume; the strong visionary sense at church continues to surprise. At the moment of consecration a cascade of Rainbows overwhelmed me and the sense of being held in Christ's Christmas Light of unconditional love was very real. Will I carry this child one day? Our prayerful verse before lunch echoes my sentiment:

> The Light-filled beauty all around me everywhere,
> Calling me to leave my Earthly dwelling———-

P.m. Mouse: *Gentle candle, greet this Christmas dusk with soft focus, allowing streams of kind kinship on our short Earth journey together. I hope you are having a truly blessed day with your family, My Darling. I hope you managed to find your Royal standing. I have had some interesting insights over the past two days; I'll tell you later. The second part of today's verse is beautiful; I enclose it here for you: 'My Angel calls—his love I shall not shun, with joy we fly together and are truly one.' Perhaps we are each other's Angels—X—t'would explain a lot.*

Mouse {unsent}: *The Small One has been with me all day—deep inside my womb longing. Little Arthur came in a rush of Rainbows at the consecration during the morning service.*

I sleep early on the sofa by the fire. I wake in the middle of the night and continue to write up The Book. I can't wait for Adrian to see the finished pages and add his magic touch.

Very Late, Adrian: *Don't expect you to be awake—just acknowledging your earlier message. So tired, but family rich. Talk soon.*

Mouse: *I'm awake. Been asleep but now working late on The Book; it's coming together nicely. So pleased your day was good. Speak in the morning-X*

I am really enjoying my writing. How exciting to see the story taking shape upon the screen. It is a record of events really; I don't think I could invent a storyline like this. I always wonder where writers get their inspiration for fictional novel writing. This story is a matter of jogging my memory where diary record is lacking and copying down the precious text messages. Of course, the first three parts are written from memory; I didn't have a mobile phone when we first arrived in New Zealand. In fact, my sharp memory surprises me. I have recalled a number of small details, confirming my realization that observation comes naturally to me.

Adrian has a long holiday ahead of him. Will he rise to the challenge and help me with the writing? I can tell he is unsure of our integrity, so he might not respond. How I long for him to run with the story.

Tuesday 26th December 2006 Boxing Day

My sister Mizzie has sent Rinky her latest published collection of children's books; the perfect Christmas present. We read them together when she wakes. Rinky is thrilled with her generous present of all six stories. A new puzzle keeps her busy after that and I doze again on the sofa. I wake to a gentle sensuality that fills me from top to toe. I don't hear a word from Adrian this morning, but he is certainly close by. I hope he is sleeping long and sound.

Midday, Mouse: *Good morning, My Love. Hope you have had a long, lazy time in bed. I woke early. Passion a little more under control—unlike yesterday when I could have sliced the altar cloth with it. Managed to get more of The Book done before Rinky woke.*

Late, big breakfast followed by another little snooze on the sofa. Feeling very relaxed today; more even-paced. Wonder if my painful ears have something to do with the computer? Rather like the mobile phone; I seem to attract radiation. The sensation is more of a pressure than a pain and it seems to come on when I am stressed. This is a new state in which to find myself. My mood is never disturbed.

Anyway, I have just resurfaced in your arms—neither of us wearing much. A gorgeous hour of gentle lovemaking with you makes me float off The Mountain. My Darling, your hands are stroking me repeatedly in easy, comfortable caress. I am kissing your bare chest; revelling in your ownership and manly claim. I feel your breath in my ear and your waking loins seeking my female comfort. We keep dropping off to sleep, the bliss of sensuality drugging us into slow-motion intimacy. We aren't riding the waves with a knife-edged keel this morning; too soft and sleepy for our usual intensity— more human perhaps. I think I'll stay here a while longer and run my hand up your long thighs—Mmm—X

Mouse {Unsent}: *She could be intensely intimate with him when they are not sleepy though. This is their newfound plateau where the slowest of movements; the most graceful of swan muzzling—necks and backs—limbs and loins; fingers and hands lead them in their Rhythmic Dance. The passion is excruciating in its checked ardour. The Garden Gate swings wide open for them and they glide through without a sound. She could go there without breaking her vow for this is sacred ground; most Holy; and they have the key. She can separate her worlds like this and run them side-by-side. She knows she cannot ask him to join her in this way. The route is only clear in her mind, and perhaps it is delusional and should be questioned. She can* *taste the divine elixir whenever she chooses. She loves to take him there; watching him 'alight upon shores of a beloved, known land.' One day-X*

Rinky and I potter at home with the animals and Christmas presents. We craft and I write. I answer Adrian's direct questions, not *'straight up in a man's way'*, but as honestly as I am able. I don't send the long message—just store it in the phone's archive file. Perhaps I might read it to Adrian when we are next together.

Mouse {Unsent}: *And so to address the questions.* **How much do I love The Laird?** *This is an Earth bond of a quarter century—of children, family, and friends; past, present, future. I cannot undo or alter this. The joy a man and his wife should share in deep intimacy has been half-present for many years; she now wonders if it was ever actually present? They were so young—her imagination so vivid; she could orchestrate anything and make it real. Now she knows differently. True love hits you unexpectedly; a synchronicity and chemistry that defies all reason; that scales all surface matters and boundaries. Could she replace one with the other? Even if Lord Swallow had the stamina of an ox it would be difficult to step into every facet of the husband role. And what of his taste for hectic family life? There is little time for stillness—for reflection—for daytime rest. And on top of all that the financial demands of earning a good income to support such a life.*

The relationship shared by Lord Swallow and his Lady is based on their natural inclination—to be still—to go deeper—to work side-by-side in gentle rhythm. A monastic attitude permeates their union. They might feel stifled with the constant presence of children, even though they are at ease with regular domestic involvement. Perhaps they might manage with one child— and a generous income to relieve any pressure. And so, the question; 'How much do I love The Laird?' Not as deeply as I should but probably more than I realize after all these years. If I had to make a choice, one way or the other, right now, I could not abandon my duties and my strong ties.

The celestial bond we share, you and I, is perfect the way it is. We are Angels upon Earth and we have stumbled upon a Secret Gate through which we can play in the Garden of Heaven. Should it remain hidden? A secret shared by those Angels who choose not to walk Earth's land? Is it, in fact, a mistake that between us we gain entry? The way things are now means there is little worldly pressure—save that of integrity. There are no demands calling you away from your need for contemplation. We find time for delightful companionship and levels of exquisite touch and truth. We share invention and creativity—and our writing—every day. The Garden is there whenever we feel like running out to play. If our relationship was more regular it could lose its edge in the hurly burly of domestic fracas.

And this suits her so beautifully too—a private life of such beauty and tingling excitement, wrapped up in the joyful warmth of familiarity. She loves the stillness they achieve, as well as the passion. He provides the perfect antidote to her spinning role as wife, mother, hostess, and comforter.

She could even imagine bearing his child in the heart of her family. She would need his help and input, but perhaps from next door as a close friend and neighbour; a measured input to suit his stamina and means. A blessed, adored child who chooses two fine men as father and a large, family embrace. A child bearing an important mission? An unconventional idea, I know. However, the image will not fade; if anything it grows stronger.

And so to the second question: **'Do you want to deepen with the Laird?'** And this has to be the deciding factor, for marriage is dependant upon it.

For years I have tried to take him deeper without any joy. Something blocks his letting go of fear. Have I given up too early? Have I become unenthusiastic due to the lack of strong chemistry? I expect so. I have tasted the real thing—why should I be interested in the half measure? Our marriage has always been about going out to others. This is The Laird's natural calling; his soul food, but not mine to the same extent. He says he would like to be still; to go deeper—but I don't think we share the same language to achieve that ideal. And his eyes—he does not look deeply into me. He does not challenge or match me at my core. He is a different kind of spirit. Our journeys have come a certain way together but are they now over? Does The Laird need to find a more appropriate richness himself? I mustn't forget there are two people here who need something new. Having tasted the ownership of a spiritual authority I do not want anything less. The desire for this level of spiritual communion is overwhelming. The Laird could never replace Lord Swallow. I do not miss The Laird when he is away. I ache for Adrian when we are apart even for two days.

However, I wonder if I am more attached to The Laird than I realize. Surely some yearning should kick in soon? I am surprised I can let go so easily. Perhaps his constant short temper with me over the last few years has distanced my dependence, despite his regular care.

The third question: **'Where do I see myself in five years time?'** Do I **still wish to be living my life with The Laird?** Or do I long for Lord Swallow to be my permanent partner?

I see us as a strong family unit, but living fairly separate lives in five years time. The Laird might be running his own schooling venture, moving regularly between N.Z and the U.K. He will expect me to hold the fort; to be a business partner and back-up support. I shall be happy to do so if I am granted my own, private life. I see us having two homes; perhaps the main one being here, in New Zealand. I see myself spending a certain time in each hemisphere every year. The children will be growing up. They will spend a lot of time with The Laird on his educational programmes; as long as they can take his belligerent manner. I imagine they may choose their own, independent path rather like their mother! A little of The Laird goes a long way; bless him.

I suppose I see us as a creative, on-the-move learning experience, with regular stops to refuel. I see myself as a free woman; if The Laird will relinquish his solo claim as he pursues his vocational calling. Of course in doing so he might need to find his own, personal companion, although I have recently wondered if the Monastic tradition wouldn't suit him better. He doesn't really like women and now he mistrusts them even more. I know I have exacerbated that issue. I can only see myself supporting his level of dynamism and vocation with some support myself—yes, from Adrian of course.

But who really knows what five years might bring? How do you make God laugh? Tell him your plans. Hmm. And what of your life desires and needs, My Lord Swallow? Do any of these mad, unconventional ideas fit into your dreams? Could we really make it work? The Boat's Quest—to change the accepted norm and birth a new code of practise—are these just the ramblings of a deluded, tired housewife who doesn't have enough to fill her wild imagination?

Let's offer these questions up. Let's air them and pray over them, for they are the 'denouement'—the conclusion of this story that seems to be writing itself.

There—I hope that answers Adrian's reasonable questions. The answers don't point to any new direction. Perhaps I'll get a chance to show him the paragraphs and he'll make sense of my thoughts. The unconventional picture doesn't fade in written form, although the idyll would only be possible if The Laird felt safe with a freer status.

P.m. Adrian: Hello, My Darling. I am currently up a tree. Big out-breath after heavy process with my stepbrother Rory. Plans? When might you come up to Auckland?

Mouse: So, my Swallow is up a tree; of course he is. Take care of your beautiful wings, My Love. Just on our way home after supper with Louise and Andrew. Rinky and I have been to the Hot Pools this afternoon. We had fun diving for a shiny sticker that we found. I can come up tomorrow, arriving early afternoon. Does that suit you? Rinky will stay the night with Sammy's gang. My boys fly into Auckland at 11.45 a.m on Thursday. Speak later? M X

Rinky and I had a delightful evening with Louise and Andrew's family. I expect I chatted too much; a nice change after solitude and intense writing. They are always keen listeners, or perhaps they were being polite. I think we represent a very different world with our wide experiences and opinions. Being relatively new to the school they are interested in my knowledge of the philosophy that underpins the education. Having been involved for fifteen years I have learnt a certain amount, although as one door opens a hundred others appear.

Wednesday 27th December 2006

A.m. Mouse: Good morning, My Lovely One. I am up early—working at the computer again. Just sent you more chapters. I might not get another chance until I have cleared it with The Laird. Can you let me know your plans? Do you want to meet up? If so, I need directions etc. Hope I'm not phoning too early. M—X

Adrian: So, My Love, we plan a rendezvous. How do we keep this in the sunlight? I need to work to find The King, that's for sure. Around family The Prince tends to surface. But good work has been achieved. I have just arrived at Dad's place and he is keen to spend the day with me. What say we meet up in the late afternoon? I'm thinking of a spot that's not far from the airport—maybe 4ish. I will meet you at a BP service station on Great North Rd at 4.30p.m.

Mouse: Sounds good, My Love. Do we sleep in the van? Can we do that and stay in the sun? Passion is under control at the moment. Will try hard to keep it there. Could be a big test for us. How do I know which service station? Will have the Bog-Brush I'm afraid—but not the pig, you will be pleased to hear. M—X

Adrian: Take the motorway right into the city and follow signs for North Western Motorway. Go past St. Luke. Then turn off at Pt. Chevalier until you get to the Great North Road turn off. Go up there for about 1km and the station is there. Sound all right? Let's consider how to stay Kingly. It's tough cos we're both longing and horny and know the opportunity here. Could we tell The Laird about this trip? Because that's the line—the acid test.

Hmm—Adrian tells it as it is—straight up in a man's way. 'Horny and longing!' His Kiwi manner sometimes takes me by surprise because it is the complete opposite of our regular, romantic expression. I love the way he constantly surprises. Adrian is far from predictable.

Later, Adrian: I need your help. You are coming up to collect your husband and it will be a pleasant extra to see me. That's the take. You are not like a bitch on heat—panting to see your Lover; or are you? And me? Yep, a dog sniffing out a bitch—at the moment that is, before clearing a life-shock. Off to the notebook—

*Mouse: I can tell The Laird; a trip keeping to our agreement. He should be okay with that, but I **am** hungry for you. Hmm—just talking to you raises the Rainbow levels. Perhaps I should bring a little tent in case we can't keep clear?*

Adrian: Good idea. Thanks for acknowledging the truth of it. Tricky times—yum. This is where powerful alchemy can happen.

Mouse: *Alchemy indeed, My Lord Swallow. X*

I copy down Adrian's travel instructions and pack a small bag. I mustn't forget the dog food. My hairy companion will be thrilled to see Lord Swallow. Her Mistress is definitely excited at the prospect. What else might we need? A thermos of tea, some crackers and fruit—and my current diary—

Midday, Adrian: *Well, I just organized with Mum and Dad and Jenny for our connection. I told Dad what we're doing; alchemy. He got that but said it was a hard thing to do. So now it is in the light. I have made myself accountable—damn! Now I can't have you again and again; boo hoo. Lust is on the run-transformation is the one—lead to gold; overcome the longing to hold. Soft-bodied woman, you shall not be mine. Your mind however will do fine; raising it up into the sun.*

Mouse: *Other Christmas learning? She has learnt that under her physical layers; when all is laid bare—she is a stubborn, proud Angel. She will not relinquish her hold on Heaven to join wholeheartedly in the dance on Earth. She has looked for a way to let go but is unable to do so. This is who she is— at her very core—her strength and her reason. Should she make herself let go? Her ears have been aching badly all day; her longing for him; for Heaven, so intense. Does she not hear the message? Or perhaps she does but won't take any action. Why the aching and the longing? Her hold on everything is slipping. Should she just let go completely? Don't know. She still has a house, a family and animals to care for. She cannot let go.*

Adrian: *Just like entering that cold water on the beach at our 'Eight Dollar Finale'. Standing strong—iron forces—Sun and Mars forces. Not Venus; out of her realm and into Mars energy. Strength. Noble strength. Zeus— Artemis. Who is Artemis' man? Apollo? I have a gift for you, oh Hunter bold. Time to move camp—change the energy into activity—into movement—drive— arrow flight—focus. No languishing or lingering; time to move. You up for it?*

Mouse: *Sounds noble and grand. I may have trouble totally disengaging from 'us' though. I might feel too sad and heavy to be creative. We'll see. Maybe I can fall in love with The Laird again; maybe. Whatever works best for you, My Friend. Well done for telling the family. Nothing like cornering ourselves completely—X*

P.s Sorry to bother you while you are with family but I need some help with the computer. Can I phone you? Just text me when a clear moment appears. My mantra for this week is: "I do not desire My Lord Swallow. I will not entertain thoughts of unbuttoning him from top to toe, curling my swan- longing around him."—Hmm—X

Later, Adrian: *Sorry to miss calling you. Just got back. Did you sort out the computer problem?*

Early P.m., Mouse: Hi there, My Friend—just delivered Rinky to Sammy's house. Sammy and I get on really well—similar 'go-getting' minds. She showed me around their lifestyle block. They looked at ours when it was first on the market but decided against the steep gradients! Sensible people. They are very enthusiastic about everything. I enjoyed seeing the catering kitchen—organic cookies in the pipeline—impressive machinery. Wish we lived over the fence; we would get really stuck in together. I didn't get the computer sorted. Will ask you when I see you. Really looking forward to that—platonically if I get my head sorted. Am just leaving Sammy's now. Will text as I get closer to Auckland. M—X

Adrian: Oh good chariot—-carry My Love with care. God speed and safety; clear head—warm heart; bridled loins—strong body.

Mouse: -X x

* * * * * * *

The roads are empty until I reach the outskirts of Auckland. I relish the sense of freedom and adventure. I can't wait to see my man, despite our hopeless situation. The Bo-brush keeps me company; sitting on the front seat beside me I notice others smiling as we pass. She takes everything very seriously from under her shaggy eyebrows, especially clandestine adventures!

Early P.m. Adrian: How are you doing, My Love? Can you text? Not sure how far I am from meeting you—depends on traffic. See you very soon.

Mouse: Just joined Waikato Expressway—X

Adrian: You should be here—I am. Where are you now?

Mouse: Still heading towards city; Manakau coming up. Have I gone too far? Will wait instructions at the sports stadium.

Adrian: No, roll on. I thought you were on the North Western Motorway. How's the traffic? You're on the Northern. Keep going til you see a sign heading to either West, or North West Motorway; miles on. If traffic is bad text and tell me where you are and we'll plan a diversion.

Mouse: Traffic bad but moving. Just passing Green Lane East. Heading North into Auckland. Am I on track? Sorry to keep you waiting, My Love—X

Adrian: I'm cutting more bow staves. Doggie just killed two Pukeko chicks and ate them!

Mouse: *Only you—still loving my Woodsman—X Here I am.*

We meet in the rain, my Woodsman and I. He appears from behind the service station with a bundle of long sticks on his shoulder, Pukeko Hunter at his side. He wraps me up in a big hug. He smells lovely; windblown and mossy. "Come on, My Lady—follow me; Mum's expecting us." I follow Adrian to his mother's house, which is relatively close by. I have met Jenny before and she gives me a warm welcome. Thank-you Angels. Adrian's family understands. We are blessed—yet again. Jenny's little house is neat and airy. Pretty china and interesting books catch my eye, as well as a piano opposite the front door in the main room. She has prepared a salad and ordered fish and chips for supper. Adrian and I offer to collect the food. It isn't too wet; the walk will do me good after three hours driving. So—off we go—walking the dogs under dripping umbrellas. The meal includes some deep fried kumara, {Maori sweet potato}; a novel extra at the fish and chip counter. Oh, how wonderful to be together again. It honestly wouldn't matter where we were; our instant chemistry is infectious. We practically bounce along the peaceful streets of Blockhouse Bay.

Strolling beside the Park with our supper wrapped in newspaper, Adrian discloses his plan for the evening. Has he arranged for us to stay with his Father and Stepmother for the night, I wonder? Or with Jenny? "We *could* stay with Jenny," he says; "she wouldn't mind if we had the same room. We really need time alone, My Friend—do you agree?" Of course I do. I have been longing for some privacy with the man I love—forbidden or not. "How about we take the dogs and drive over to Western Auckland? There's a beautiful beach with a D.O.C campsite, {Department of Conservation}. We used to visit as a family. I know it's wet but that wouldn't matter if we took your van. It would be a lovely place to spend the night. Did you bring the bedding? Good. We'll set off after tea."

The fish and chips are delicious and we share a pleasant meal together in Jenny's kitchen. We chat about all sorts of different things—"I don't know how I'm going to afford the dentistry work I need," Jenny tells us, continuing the conversation about the high cost of dental treatment in New Zealand. "I suppose I could take in a lodger, although I don't want to; I've done it before." We discuss her friends at work, the imminent birth of her first grandchild in Australia and the work Adrian plans to do in her small garden. "Who's having the last kumara chip?" He asks hopefully.

We say goodnight at **7**.30, and together with the two dogs Adrian and I drive away into the wild night, heading for the Western Bays. We are off on another thrilling adventure. Beyond the residential avenues of Titirangi the roads become narrow and bendy as we take to the hills. The wind picks up and driving rain makes the windscreen wipers work overtime. Our nighttime escape is clad in anticipation. No matter the rules and boundaries the chemistry is as potent as ever. Native Bush on both sides of the narrow road accompanies us as we climb up over the Waitakere Ranges before dropping down to the coast. The headlights startle the foliage into sharp focus—shiny with the wet—enticing us further and further; no turning back. The Punga ferns with their dark trunks are eerie and familiar, both. We are in the middle of nowhere. Surely we can't be on the edge of a major city? The taller Mamacou ferns catch my eye as well as the solid trunks of the Kahikatea and Kauri trees. The Bush deepens. I feel safe beside Lord Swallow. I would follow him anywhere.

Eventually we arrive at Whatipu Beach; a beautiful cove surrounded by individual, volcanic hills that reach to quite a height. "This was a favourite beach when I was a child," Adrian tells me. "Let's stop and walk the dogs before we get to the camp ground." We clamber out of the van into the dusk and stroll through a gully between the dunes. The grass is short and clumps of Pampas Grass make for an interesting, evening jaunt. The rain has stopped and the evening is ours. The dogs are very excited and we let them dash ahead beside the dunes. There are two types of Pampas Grass here in New Zealand; the common fluffy kind from South America and the native variety, which is less fluffy and more golden; commonly known as 'Toitoi.' There is an abundance of both growing on this coastline. I am pleased when Adrian puts his arm around my waist as we follow the hounds. We can be close without stepping over any boundary. We love each other and allow ourselves the pleasure of holding hands and being intimate. No kissing though. Oh no—that would be far too dangerous. But this is perfect and lovely. The familiar glow of emotional homecoming fills me from top to toe, making me feel so alive.

Whatipu beach lies at the northern head of the entrance to Manakau harbour. Powerful currents cross the sand bars to greet the Ocean—a renowned area for shipwrecks, so the guidebook tells me. A forest walk leads along the ancient range of hills that rise steeply from the Tasman Sea and end at this beach. The dunes are hill-sized and sun-dried driftwood lies in heaps. Apparently a cave here was once used as a ballroom. River valleys ending in long beaches interrupt the cliffs along this coast. The sand is black. Whatipu holds several 'Wachi Tapu', {sacred sites}, of particular relevance to the Te Kawerau Iwi, {tribe}. It was also used as a seasonal fishing ground and was well known for shellfish and shark.

Once we have parked up for the night we shut the dogs in the van and walk down to the water. Dusk is on the run and a narrow path leads us through waist-high dune grass. We walk in single file. "This is your Christmas present, My Huntress." Lord Swallow hands me his latest work of art; "a bow and set of arrows that I have made you. I've had a thought these past few days—about Apollo and Artimis. They were twins—brother and sister. Is that you and I? Could that explain why we have forged such a strong bond? I like the mythology; the mystical connotation. What do you reckon? You are a Sagittarian too; a Huntress—part horse with a strong, stubborn nature."

Adrian's enthusiasm is infectious. I consider his words while swatting the mosquitoes that have found an easy, nighttime feast. "Mmm—'Myths and Mosquitoes'—I'll think on that, although I don't feel very sisterly." Adrian pulls me to him and wraps his arms protectively around me as we stand at the water's edge in the dark. He kisses the top of my head. "This is just perfect;" his words echo my thoughts. Our leather boots are chased by the gentle aftermath of the bigger waves and we step back to avoid getting wet. One of the towering rocks behind us provides shelter from the wind. The solo giant has crept up to offer protection. I turn to look up at the enormous shape, ancient and eternal, here on the shore. Despite the restrictions Adrian and I are content with just being together. I relax into his claim as if we have always been one. We both know that we belong.

"To be a permanent couple would be wonderful, wouldn't it? To make love time and again with the intimacy we share and invite a child to join us— mmm—I can taste the joy," he sighs. "I could imagine us spending days wrapped up together like that; couldn't you, My Love?" There is no need for me to answer. As we pick our way back towards the camp ground a group of fisherman passes by with torches and buckets—off to catch lobster, my knowledgeable companion informs me. Their lights bob about in the dark as they locate the waterline. For a fleeting moment I imagine them as water sprites, dancing out of the sea to steal some time on the beach when nobody is watching; nobody that is except us—a couple of sprites ourselves.

I make up our bed in the van and we take off a few clothes. How lovely to be snugly and close again. A pillow division helps us resist the passion that refuses to abate. We score ten out of ten for restraint, although Lord Swallow admits to excruciating desire and physical longing—even my baggy underwear, purposefully chosen this morning, doesn't deter him. We distract ourselves by reading diaries and text messages and Adrian takes me through a 'process' to unearth The Stubborn Angel and sort out my sore ears. "I want more of you to be seen," he declares-"You have so much more to share. I want the world to see the mature woman I know."

We continue to have such fun. I adore Adrian's light spirit; his sense of adventure and permanent optimism. How perfect we are for each other. I return the Copper Band before we rest; he slides it on to his little finger. As we bless each other for the night I find myself wondering about the ring; its presence in our story is becoming a central feature. We manage a little sleep and in the morning we head back into the Waitakere hills to go harvesting. Of course The Woodsman has his eye on some perfect timber. The sun is glorious—how we wish the whole day could be ours. Adrian leads me to a point in the Bush where a viewing platform offers spectacular views over the rainforest. He climbs a Totara tree and finds a broken limb that he pulls away. We begin to run out of time; the single focus of the artist just needs one more branch. "You won't be late for the airport will you?"

* * * * * * *

I *am* late-a detour sends me on a lengthy excursion and my boys are waiting outside the airport by the time I drive in. How lovely to see everyone. "Sorry I wasn't here when you arrived—a traffic detour kept me." I explain. "It's tricky to gauge the journey time when you drive straight from home," says The Laird. I decide to be honest—as we have agreed; everything in the sun from now on. "I drove up last night," I admit. "I've been staying with Adrian and his family; just as good friends."

Part Two Pontoons and Paint

Of course, The Craftsman keeps watch over the boat-yard; he would never leave anything to chance—they needn't worry. The Celestial Sea has settled into her new position. She surrenders to her fate. The plastic shelter is tightly secured and those pesky seagulls have lost interest. A tugboat bobbing alongside the nearest pontoon is offering greater pickings as two men clean the decks and bag up their rubbish. The raucous cries of the birds fill the air as the dockworkers go about their daily business. Nobody gives the covered vessel a second glance. Unfortunately she has become part of the debris and residential hulk that litter the yard. If the Marine Officials bothered to look closely they might be surprised to find she has shifted within the iron cradle; that the binding chains are loose.

The beautiful weather continues. From her shrouded position she spies other boats, free and gracious upon the ocean. Colourful spinnakers and billowing white sails fill her with longing. The thwarted potential saddens her. She will be brave. If kindness and understanding wash over her deck the chance to sail may return. She will take imaginary voyages until then; she will enjoy that. There—even thinking about where she might travel heralds a little joy. They will never steal her dreams.

"Hey, check this; that Pommy boat's shifted hasn't she? Do you see?" A short fellow, repainting a vessel close to The Celestial Sea, has noticed her loose chains and brings a pause to his work. He calls to his mate. Drat—now they will tie her down again; she might lose her view of the wider ocean with its summer activity. "Best call the boss, eh?" Suggests the man whose dripping paintbrush is making a small, green pool around his feet.

The Harbour Master is furious. He slams the office door shut and strides towards The Boat. The fellow who made the report is startled by the Boss' reaction. He moves quickly, inadvertently walking through the pool of paint. What is this vessel about? There appears to be some hidden agenda known only to The Marine Officials. The Harbour Master is a thick set, authoritative man with a commanding manner. Few dare cross him. He reaches for his phone and moves out of earshot. Those watching assume disinterest while overhearing his furious tirade. Heading back inside, the Harbour Master turns suddenly and hurls a heavy stone against The Boat's hull.

Chapter 1 Pause

Thursday 28ᵗʰ December 2006

"What!? I can't believe you went against my wishes and spent the night with Adrian; that's why you were late collecting us, isn't it?"

Oh dear, I am in trouble again. Any argument with The Laird explaining our position and maintained agreement falls on stony ground. "Aren't I allowed one night of fun?" I ask plaintively. "You have had over two weeks of party time while I have been alone. Can't you allow me that? I promise we kept to our agreement." Apparently not. In many ways I wish I hadn't even mentioned my exciting excursion. "How can I trust anything you tell me?" He replies. The atmosphere is tense as we drive home.

P.m. Adrian: *Wonderful news. My sister Angie just had a 6 lb baby boy called Philip. Red hair, blue eyes like his Dad. Really quick delivery. No drugs. First baby—fantastic. She read so much about it and it really paid off. Love to the family and welcome home.*

Mouse: *Congratulations! Uncle Adrian. Amazing that it went so easily. I got stuck in traffic on the way to the airport; touch late but all's well. Another dead bunny found on the grass. Thank-you for such a special time—missing you already—ears very fuzzy although feeling buoyed up by my Apollo. X*

Last month the neighbouring farmer informed me he was going to deal with the rabbits on his land. We keep finding dead bunnies at home—Blossom's offspring no doubt, as well as poor Blossom herself. Have the poisons spread up here? Did they spray from the air? I suspect they spotted our bunnies and 'accidently included our land'. Kiwi's have little tolerance for vermin. As I chuck the body into the gorse I think of Adrian and his parting words——*"Don't compromise your time with the family. Give them all of yourself."* I will certainly try. It was hard to say goodbye to him for the summer holidays.

Adrian's father sent me a text message early this evening, asking for the Fijian family's Auckland address. I relayed the information, adding: *"I'd like to take this opportunity to say how much I value your lovely son's friendship. Adrian is a very special man—truly. We share a connection of the richest kind.'*

Well—that was an unexpected communication; unexpected and nice.

P.m. Mouse: Supper's on the table—travelers almost abed. A few grumbles—"Dog's too big—too much stuff in the car—why did you need a ten minute kip on the journey? Did you go to bed late? Why are you texting?" {I sent your Pa the Fijian family details.} Nothing hidden—all out in the open. 'Bugger you lot, I have a life too'. Learning to put my foot down. You would be proud of me, My Darling. Loving you so much—M—X.

Late P.m. Mouse: The House is her's—they slumber, all. Artimis takes control and reaches for her Apollo. How is he? How has his day been? He will be pleased to hear she is feeling clear. She has not compromised the quality of her time with the Castle Inmates. But now, as the night greets The Mountain she is beside him—her hand belonging in his—her lips awaiting his touch—X

Adrian: Well done. I have gardened, dozed, watched movies and hassled my mother. She had a big dump about a phone conversation with my step mum about the impending birth. Straight into it I went—mind-talk busters are go. Sadly I got cross with her victim drama. Still useful, but my button is people—her—taking responsibility for self-blaming. Could have been more compassionate on my part. I went and gardened for a couple of hours. Nice. Lots of admiring thoughts for you.

Friday 29th December 2006

A.m. Mouse: Good morning, My Darling. Have been in your arms—covering you all over in Angel balm—mmm. Interrupted by the Bog-Brush who wasn't happy about staying out on the deck all night; Laird's strict orders. I'd like to climb back into bed with you really—mmm again. Household will sleep for hours I expect. Might get more of The Book down. Cedric gave me a computer lesson last night. Hopefully I've sorted out the disc. The time will arrive when I can tell The Laird about our writing. See you in bed—it will be your Artemis teasing you—X

I don't hear from Adrian today. Is he keeping out of the picture? He'll be concerned about The Laird's reaction to our nighttime adventure. He'll want me to think of the family, without any interruptions or daydreaming.

P.m. Mouse: Goodnight, Fine Sir. I hope you had a good day? We had an interesting one here. Big conversation just now with The Laird; told him everything, pretty much. He says we owe it to our marriage to go deeper; to try and find what I need. I suppose he's right. Don't feel like it though. Just wanting to keep you in the picture. All abed here. Lots of special love, M X

74

Saturday 30th December 2006

A.m. Mouse: Tricky times as The Laird comes to terms with the importance of this new relationship in her life. She will keep her Lover posted. Please don't keep your distance; she needs you close in these turbulent waters. Can you write something for our 'Myths and Mosquitoes' adventure at Whatipu? While it's still fresh in the mind.

Adrian: Glorious sun shards stream, dazzling through the blinds; the day beyond calling. Use me well; my glory is here and now. He feels the warm lemon in his throat and belly—fiery—slightly unpleasant. Greens soon to ease that. He considers her recent messages. What has it been like? Is it an angry husband who asks this? Has a change taken place? Perhaps our good Swallow should offer to keep his distance while The Laird and Lady work out their standing. He wants her to be present to the family; not distracted by a double life. Yes, he wants to halt contact for 3 days; integration air lock; what say you? For are we not back where we were before? Let us give time to establish truer relationships with those ones. Rise up, oh Artemis—honour them completely—open the privacy; the rusted door of the inner world. Let some of that strength and magic come out to bathe the whole family—a balm—more of you seen than ever before.

He wants that for her; for them. He wants this new growth with The Laird to develop. Give him something new to fall in love with. Call it from him. Swallow knows not what it means but senses the honour of others as very important. He catches glimpses of the family new—with Mother Artemis taking a stronger, more commanding position—the double that she is; powerful and nurturing. Come Artemis; flex your bow, loose your stubborn hooves, shake your mane—wild.

P.m. Mouse: Oh Apollo—my challenger—my deep sea Lover—3 days it is then. I take my lead from thee; my stubborn hooves reluctant to budge. I fear the dampening of my Spirit. Maybe if I know you hold me still I can be noble and strong. She bows to him and reaches for her beautiful, hand-crafted bow-X

Adrian: Yes my Artemis—as your twin brother—who watches and feels and waits. There are new foundations to establish here, I think, and then I will return. No, you are not alone, but he is quiet as he holds her.

Mouse: -X

I hope Adrian might continue to write—write but not 'send'. I hope he might divert his passion into the written word. The desire to record this tale across the waiting pages of our Book grows daily. I can see the finished copy. But The Laird has refused his permission. I may not work on The Book with Adrian, although he says he can't stop me writing in my own time—just not when he, The Laird, is present in the house. He doesn't see our agonizing disengagement as enough. "You saw each other—you spent the night together—what does that tell me?" He will not entertain the idea of our closeness without the physical. The lack of black and white clarity annoys his hard-edged perception. This narrow side of his character is increasing; something I have noticed in men of a certain age. His attitude lies at odds with many conversations we have had over the past months. Any soft-edged nuance is suddenly 'woolly nonsense.'

My mind takes me back to Whatipu Beach:

MYTHS AND MOSQUITOES

Black sand, intermittent rain; friendly hands desiring more.
A stroll amongst fisher-folk; torches moving on the beach,
Spirit rocks; impressive, volcanic mass and Toi Toi grass.
A fable from Greek Mythology; he is high with inspiration.
Artemis and Apollo; twins. Artemis strides across the water;
Her twin brother born a day later.
Artemis—huntress; protector of mothers and children.
She takes off The Copper Band.
He places it upon his little finger;
"I like it there—Kingly"-says he.
She is an Archer; Sagittarian, and he a Bull; Taurus.
He asks that she open up and share herself with family;
He tells her this is where potential lies.
She considers the sister role, unsure and excited both.
Meanwhile the mosquitoes feast upon the quandary.

We stop communicating. I continue with the usual rounds of family life. My ears ache continually and I feel flat. Every time I mention Adrian The Laird erupts—understandably. I cannot be open and share my feelings; my thoughts. He would rather bury his head in the sand and forget the episode. No, he is definitely not happy about my writing; the nature of the script exacerbates the whole affair. I can see where he is coming from. But I love my writing, a pleasure I can turn to when he is away—watching rugby—working—playing hockey—giving whisky talks or socializing on the scale he demands. I will not deny myself this pleasure. I have no idea where we will end up. I will take one day at a time. The only certain agenda is my connection with Adrian. I have never been more certain of anything in my life. Where am I meant to take it? Write about it—yes, for now I can write about it.

I put down my pen and apply myself to the impending New Year's Coromandel trip. Our Kiwi friend Chris and his wife are over from the U.K for the Christmas holidays. They have invited us to stay for a couple of nights. We are looking forward to spending time with them. The drive is pleasant, although my spirits are low. The Laird is cross—he thinks I should just *'get over it'*; sort myself out and wake up to reality.

Sunday 1st January 2007 New Year's Day

A.m. Adrian: Gentle sun stirs strong and vibrant—stilling the mind—asking to be breathed. It is steadying and readying—a blessing with its beautiful blaze.

Last night—New Year's Eve: he watched, sometimes as though from a rooftop, unable to enter the stream of high, alcohol-fuelled energy and boisterous, back-clapping oneness. The teenage years revisited. Sigh—so much wasted. The Earth needs love and all she gets is thoughtless action. Desperate eyes seek meaning; something sure. They strive for a pose, an answer, a clear sign. Nothing. Just powerful music. Maybe the cynic, the sad one, has missed some of the goodness in this? People close—sharing—singing—focused. And the band; all the trappings of a grungy rock machine but actually older men playing the role. It is somehow false, laying out the old favourites although not too bad I suppose. And was that a Christian reference? And the drunkenness was intense. Very well—high police presence—maybe that was okay.

But he longed for more—his companions—his broken-hearted stepbrother, his nephew, niece and boyfriend were somewhere different to him. He wanted the stars and the sea—and connection. He wants deep companionship most of all; an ear that understands. He realizes that he doesn't want to waste this friendship. There is so much potential. He has been sitting with a low-lying life-shock over the past few days. It was almost unnoticed; growing like a boil. It hit him strongly on his journey down. Not belonging; the King fallen. But today—the New Year—he is restored. A seeing eye and a resolution.

He wishes for a house—he longs for land—but he is not ready to be tied up to the hitching rail of massive debt—not ready to railroad himself into career decisions. No. His resolution is to simply be right where he is—await The Angels call to grow; trust that the life forces will guide. Live as a man who knows that he is whole and complete exactly as he is right now, not with the underlying nag that he should have a house, a career, a wife and children. Not that he is missing out; missing his opportunity. No! He turns to his Angels—fully and completely placing his faith in them. He acknowledges their wisdom and their love. He gives them the mandate to guide his life. He releases the steering wheel, placing his faith onto his helpers. "May the peace be with you." Yes, into battle he would go, to battle against the gripping illusion of control. I am your humble servant—my actions follow your promptings. My Kingship turns to you with wholehearted adoration. May your sheltering and uplifting powers stream into my life——into my raised hands. To you I turn my questioning gaze—with every action I seek your touch, your nod, your approval. Not others, only you. I step forward and ask to be selected as representative of your will; in faith; in trust—in service— guide me.

This is my New Year's resolution. Deepen me. Sharpen my hearing. Fire my courage.

Mouse: *A beautiful cove in sunny James Cook Bay. A peaceful morning. Young friends over from the U.K with their small children. Silent walks on the beach where she seeks his hand. He is with her, she knows, yet far away. A quick check of her phone—perhaps he has left her a message? It is a new year; might he wave the 3-day ban for today? She very nearly sent a message with an X last night.*

Relationship between The Laird and The Lady is in a state of limbo. She had an emotional outburst yesterday; most unlike her. She threw something across the room: "I'm an f'ing, reluctant Angel—I don't want to be here. My time is spent; a quarter of a century; another needs me now. How can I turn my back on a connection like this? I never knew such depth was possible this side of Heaven."

You would have been impressed, My Love. Not sure where it puts us but The Laird is serious and pensive. Big life-shock for him, poor Laird. I must be hard-hearted or something; my mind-set remains unchanged. I am loving you, My Lord Swallow. I cannot promise anything—but my passion—X

And so, we welcome in 2007, wondering what it will bring. Can we work on these huge life questions with The Angels? The number 7 is sacred; associated with copper, so I read recently. Might this be our year? And in what way, My Apollo? I send you deep blessing and love at the start of this New Year; in our time of waiting and trusting. Dear Christ in us; hold us close in your radiance—X

Adrian: *Well-phew! That's news. Goodness me. Intense times— catalystic. Keep breathing. Maybe this is the lid coming off a lifetime of bottled contents. And what is coming out? Truth? Watch it; check it. Maybe just what is needed? A bit scary however, particularly for The Laird. And for me? A little. I support you coming out; fully. Unsure about my part though. My vision is you and The Laird deeper, closer—more real. And me? Creative friend. Keeping a respectful distance.*

Mouse: *Yes, stand proud and slightly apart in the sure knowledge of our bond, My Love. Join me there. I have always been an onlooker in the same way. Let's stand side-by-side as friends, as lovers, as whatever we want to be. I need to see you soon; talk through ideas. M. X*

Hot Water Beach on the Coromandel peninsula is an iconic, Kiwi experience. Follow the surprisingly large number of people with garden spades—you can hire one at the beachside shop if you haven't brought your own. Find a steaming spot in the sand at low tide and dig yourself a hole—

the hole fills with hot water. This geothermal activity is a legacy from an active, volcanic past. We all have a go, although I'm certainly not in the mood for removing any clothing and wallowing. I have to laugh—large ladies and gentleman of every age with their rear ends firmly wedged in their chosen beach location; satisfied smirks and assorted family gathered, despite the sudden rainstorm.

Some volcanoes develop large reservoirs of underground water; eventually emerging at the surface. The boiling liquid cools as it ascends. There are two fissures on Hot Water Beach. The mineral water is salty, although not seawater. Calcium, silica, bromine, potassium and magnesium are among the trace elements that can reach temperatures of over sixty degrees centigrade.

The day starts fine. I walk the dog along a quiet road above the beach while the others 'wallow' in the hot water. I am looking forward to some quiet time in the van too; I have several messages to log. The quantity of script calls for daily attention. I always enjoy a quiet stroll in the residential areas. We are parked on a steep hill and the Bog-Brush and I get our daily workout reaching the top. Very few footpaths traverse landowners' property. Extensive sheep farming means dog walkers are *not* welcome. The residential roads climb sharply from the beach. Like much of New Zealand the houses are a mixed bag; colourful modern buildings boasting generous decks and sea views sit alongside 1970's bungalows with white painted, stucco garden walls and wrought iron gates. I am always surprised at how tightly packed the Kiwis build their homes. The gardens are often small although the views and plentiful outdoor living areas are wonderful. With a natural playground at the bottom of the driveway, who needs a large garden anyway?

Many cul-de-sacs back onto the ever-present, wild country. England is tame in comparison. The house at the top of this particular cul-de-sac owns a small Tangelo orchard. I notice a collection of old motorbikes parked beneath the nearest tree, covered by a blue tarpaulin. Tangelos are the juiciest of the citrus fruit; a cross between the mandarin and the grapefruit. They are commonplace in this part of the North Island. As I head back to the beach the raindrops increase, followed by a heavy downpour. "Why were you away so long?" The Laird asks accusingly. I retaliate—again unlike me— "can't you get off my case?" We don't stay more than a couple of hours. The children and I shelter inside a beach tent while the chaps take surfboards into the waves. I don't feel present to anyone at the moment.

We leave The Coromandel in the late afternoon. The Laird grips the wheel, muttering under his breath; "I'm finding it hard to love you right now." I suppose I should make more effort and return to a place of peaceful submission. He keeps telling me I am in the wrong—"I will get really cross with you before long, you know. We should wait six months to see if this '*infatuation*' is anything serious." I don't say very much. What is there to say? I know we are meant to be treading this difficult path.

We return to The Mountain; to the usual routines of domestic life and the endless T.V sport in the top cabin. The separate cabin is a bad idea. The Laird is always up there. I don't like it. Bloto, boring dullness—I don't want it any more. I resent his endless distraction techniques. Yes, that is what they are. He is unhappy without permanent distraction. If the T.V isn't blaring a book is always in hand; or an excursion being planned—or people being met. What is he running from? Life offers so much more. I know my husband is capable of more. I know he would rise to a new horizon if I showed him the way. He relies on me for innovative thought and direction. Will he ever follow me across this unconventional frontier? His reversion to immature habits surprises me. His 'talk' always points to deeper possibilities. Is he unable to 'walk his talk' when the chips are down? Do his occasional bouts of depression reveal issues he needs to address? I am unable to help him release the fear I sense underlies his unease. Perhaps the situation I place him in is, in fact, my way of making him face the demons he tries to avoid. Perhaps this is our pre-planned, Earthly challenge together.

Monday 2nd January 2007

A.m Mouse: *How is the King? And where is the King? The Queen needs to know; she feels incomplete without knowing. She rises early from a morning of entwined, etheric passion with him; his strong hands upon her still. She turns to her Lover—X*

Adrian: *He wakes blinkingly—the waves of 3 others' sleepy breathing resonant in the small room. Whangatama with his stepsister Rosie, her children and friends. Spent the day yesterday with my nephew, 16-year-old Ned. Got stuck on the wrong side of the estuary when the tide came in—had to swim back and send a passing kayaker to rescue the dog and my clothes. Freezing. I've been eating chocolate—dark and delicious. Edge of a sore throat; oops.*
But how am I? Hmm. The King has lost his throne. Why? No quiet time yesterday? Playing the 'fitting in' game? Television—a certain level of numbness—completely disaffected by adventures of the day; a bit of an embarrassed feeling. Process time, or breathe—reclaim; remember my resolution, which is total trust. But what if I have done something stupid? I'll just go do some writing. Be back in 20 mins. How are you?

Mouse: *Hello, My Beautiful Friend. So, we were quite close to you then; think we drove through Whangamata on our way to James Cook Bay. Amazing scenery. What have you done that was silly? Getting stuck on the wrong side of the estuary? Sounds a real adventure.*
How am I? I'm sitting on a log in glorious sunshine. I went back to bed earlier but wasn't allowed to rest long; the Bog-Brush was desperate for a

walk. That's why I am down the drive while the Castle Inmates slumber on. I am feeling flat, resigned and quiet. Nothing I can do at the moment to move or change anything. The Laird thinks I am living in a giant bubble; that I will come to my senses soon. He says we need to get life back on track and that 6 months will tell us if it's just infatuation. He doesn't believe I can keep to my household duties. Any mention of our friendship or joint projects makes him cross. In being open I am always slammed; understandably really. So, I have no choice; I am cornered. I don't know what to do. I only know that what we breathe between us is very special, and real, and true; that we have something important to do together, whatever that might be, and that I am missing you a lot—X

Adrian: *Go, Girl; come Artemis—dig deep. What is the mind's interpretation? What leads to feelings like this? Remember that events are ours—for us—to learn and grow. Where is the possibility for growth here? Resignation is an old place for you—no—don't accept it. Dig for the new change; the new choice. Go! Sounds like a parent/child thing. Look for links with how you have felt in the past.*

Who is The Laird for you? Powerless, weak, out of control—use the event; don't fight it. It is for you. Look to younger days. Good luck. I am standing by. But please respect The Laird's requests. Let's stick to our agreements—only with his blessing, even texting. Can we be strong? Let's stick to it. Work hard. Enjoy what's being revealed. If you are feeling flat and down look into what the mind-talk is saying—be the ferret; root it out. It is your turn—go.

Lots of love and blessings all around you. Call on your Angels; Christ. So much help. Just don't get stuck and hopeless. Artemis and Apollo, twins; draw on mythology—strengthening images. You and The Laird have been drawn together in some way that complements your old, learnt patterns of behaviour. All of us are co-dependant until we explore our relationships. You have acted out, and The Laird too. Now you have a chance to look at your patterns. Who is The Laird for you? And who are you for The Laird? Your feelings will guide you to your mind-talk. Go! Go to the core through your flat, resigned feeling; through your stubborn, 'don't want to' feeling. New, fresh thoughts await you.

Mouse: *Expect you are right. Thanks for the coaching—I'll try.*

A heavy heart with an awful, dragging feeling sits like a lead weight inside my usually happy person. Is this depression? I hope not. *"Look for the mind-talk. Ask the questions."* Haven't I been doing that with my writing over the past months? I suppose it is complicated and needs to be unearthed. But couldn't it just be a straightforward case of The Laird and I having completed our Earthly journey and the choice to let go and embrace something new needing bravery and harmony? Oh, I don't know. Adrian's encouraging coaching—his forte—doesn't fill me with positive vibes or get up and go. It annoys me a little, although I know he means well. I don't get a buzz from self-analysis. I know it's useful but I find it can err on the side of selfish introspection. I am a sun-filled Angel. I am meant to dance in the light and lead others there too. The dark places are not for me; I honestly don't need them.

There is a strange smell in the kitchen. It has been there for a couple of days. Could it be a gas leak? Is that why I am feeling so peculiar? Perhaps. I must call the gas company; our stovetop runs on gas and we have a bottle attached to the cabin wall outside the kitchen window.

The Laird is happy again today; thank goodness. We were close and loving this morning, which always puts him in a better mood. It doesn't change me though. How can I dismiss the glory of playing in Heaven's Garden with my Angel? I sometimes wonder if it was a mistake to walk through The Garden Gate—once visited a return to the Earthly Realm loses its appeal. Is that what happens if you meet your Angel on Earth? And have Adrian and I chosen our encounter as a near impossible challenge or is it a mistake that we ever met?

Mouse {Unsent}: Hmm; yes; I know a lot of that stuff-it's what I have relied on all these years. I have always looked beyond to find the 'true essence.'

To find the 'true essence' in the here and now; well, that is a new treasure; an amazing realization. Is it fantasy? Is it unsustainable in real life? I really don't feel the need for the constant life coaching. All I need is to be loved and celebrated for who I am; perhaps only recognized and given a voice. I suppose I can live without a physical completeness within the treasure. If my true person is acknowledged in companionship and love I can go forwards to grow the other relationships in my life. But I will NOT deny the truth that I have found. I will NOT live without it—even if only in an etheric form; unless you tell me it is not a truth we share, My Friend.

Are you perhaps on your martyrdom mission, Lord Swallow? Why such urgency in pushing The Laird and I back together? Are you guarding yourself against guilt? Or are you preparing to face a grief if I turn my back on us? Perhaps you want me to move away from your arms—back into my husband's care? Is this your way of saying; 'Let's stop altogether?' I can see how the virtue would strengthen you. But for me, I am depleted by the thought; the action. I have no need for a buffer of that kind. I feel so strong and sure about our connection. In fact, I can get on better when we are joined as one.

However, I do hear earthed reasoning in your tools of self-analysis. Perhaps my fault is that I dismiss an Earthly attitude towards my emotions. Perhaps you have been sent to make me pay attention. Okay—I'll spend time Earthing myself. I know this would make you happier. Hmm—I am stubborn. I feel my reluctance to face the Earthly reality of my person. I dislike being questioned. All I want to do is play in The Garden.

Tuesday 3rd January 2007

A.m. Adrian: Distant roar of surf and the first stirrings of the family—an eventful day leave me a bit bleary-eyed and croaky. Heading home today. Good times; deepening connections with everyone. Sharing of intentions for the year. Heaps of singing, hence the croaks.

Many thoughts of you—wondering—thinking—worrying. Does she struggle? Does she despair? Does she feel rejected by me? Have I done the right thing? Did I sound too harsh? But I am here, standing by; somehow trusting. Intuition says there is learning now for The Castle Folk. The hunter lies out in the Forest and waits patiently until his Lady walks freely through the Castle Gates with harmony behind her and gentleness in her heart— strong—centred—and he is patient. There is plenty to do while he sits at his camp. There are bows to craft, arrows to shaft, fires to tend, thoughts to think, words to write and songs to sing. He can wait. Very well.

I like the image Adrian paints—of a nobleman waiting in the Forest for his Lady. He is patient; busy with his woodwork projects, his sword lying quietly beside him. I turn to the poem he gave me for Christmas; one he wrote for a boy in his class. I Like the Celtic border around the words. He has laminated the paper.

THE WARRIOR

Strong he stands at Castle wall,
Sword, sharp in its sheath,
Doubtful dreams of dread and doom,
Banished bold by scene beneath.

The Morning sun magnificent
Spreading light o'er tree and stone,
The land and lakes he hath laboured and loved
With his hand, his heart—his home.

Yes! He would to battle go,
Yes! His armour he'd don.
With sword held high, and kinsman nigh,
Charge out with heart in song.

Mouse: *Dappled sunlight filters through the Native Bush as she strolls, matching her mood of impending hope. Her Woodsman; her Swallow Man; courageous and true—waiting for her. Yes. One day she will walk free and in harmony, singing with sure steps that guide her to him. She knows he is there. She knows because together they claim The Key and The Gate—The Bird and The Maiden—The Prince and his Lady—The King and his Queen. And a pair of the finest crowns imaginable. Yes, one day she will walk free.*

Yesterday was a bleak day for her. So heavy—a clouded heart with heavy eyes and sluggish movements. That his absence can affect her physically as well as mentally—that scares her. She needs his daily contact;

then she can manage a joy-filled heart and give her all to the Castle Inmates. With her treasure beside her she can give her best. That is a reality she cannot deny. Only if Lord Swallow tells her it is not a truth he shares could she bear to let it go.

Early P.m. Mouse: *Oh trusty chariot, faithful Toolbox, carry My Love safely home to me, even if only geographically. Travel with a gentle, happy heart. I am thinking of thee. Come home to craft, to find a workshop, to sing and to write. Yes, to write, My Friend—for this will be our chance to change the course of life's pattern. You and I—My Woodsman true—X*

I really don't know what is going to happen when Adrian returns. The Laird is not happy; his often generous nature has departed; perhaps with the close of his holiday excitement.

* * * * * * *

Later on, Mouse: *A Houseboat moored in Waikite Bay—with a workshop on the shore? Just a thought. What are the rules about houseboats? Hope you are home safely? I am home alone this evening—thinking of you—X*
P.s I bought some green paint for your workbench; you might want it to go to your new abode but it's looking a bit tatty; needing a re-paint.

Adrian: *Thanks. Ha, funny idea about the houseboat. Back home nicely around 4p.m. Just visited more family staying at Pillans Beach Caravan Park. Heading home now.*

Thursday 4th January 2007
Am. Adrian: *Home to a delighted pussycat. Home to a big, warm, safe bed. Home to a hundred exciting projects. Home to new things—new promising. How does it all work now? How does my Special Friend weave in? Buoyed up by the acceptance of Big J, Lottie and family he feels so positive. Talking, talking—so much talking. And his niece Cathy is very interested in the same teaching philosophy; and his stepsister is keen to do the 'More to Life' course. His family appreciates him. A high. Definitely a high. High success. And so much to come. Freedom.*
He feels guilty—too good, unbalanced. Not considering others. Hmm; to bask in that glow without indulgence; to trust in the guides for when change needs to take place. Life-shock guidance. So, forgive me, My Lady. My thoughts are far-flung and busy. Now let me integrate—an air lock. Life has been so rich and full in different ways, but looking forward to the tranquil waters that surround you.

Mouse: *Good morning, My Friend. How lovely to hear of your right-placed welcome home. This is an important lesson—to carry with you at all* times. *You are ever-loved and appreciated by others. It is only your self-perception that removes the belief. Lovely to have you home. Wish I were in The Leafy Glade with you. I am still abed. Laird is in town—children slumber on. The pig is rooting in the kitchen. Better get up!*

I am reading a very interesting book: 'The Power of Now' by Eckhart Tolle. I think the philosophy is one we share. I have only just begun reading—I'll keep you posted. So, My Darling Friend—here we are. And what next? We have lots to discuss—plans and beautiful love to work on in ways that keep integrity and Kingship. Mmm. Are we permitted a phone call?

Midday, Adrian: *Phone call is good. How is The Laird with you being in contact with me? Have you two found your level ground? It is very important to me. I want him to know what you are up to and to be in agreement. Possible? If not I will wait in the woods—patient and calm.*

Mouse: *The early summer sun beckons me outside, newly bathed with wet hair—clad only in a bath towel. Definitely time to restrict the consumption of festivity morsels. No breakfast—just greens to drink. I lie face up on the back door step, naked as a teenage maiden, aware of her supple sensuality for the first time, her alluring qualities and childbearing potential. Perhaps I bear him even now? This child I see so clearly in my dreams.*

My lovely piggy joins me; lying as close as possible. Little grunty noises, happy in my presence. I offer myself up to my Angels' direction, such a glorious feeling to bond with the natural world without a stitch of clothing. The strong rays of the sun, the gentle breeze, the chickens mumbling in the nearby grass—mmm; lovely. And wonderful chats to family over the Internet—so soon will they be here. 18 months is a long time to be parted from loved ones.

He leaves her a message—'out in the sun from now on'. But The Laird; extending his stay in town to swim, he would probably not accept their contact. Such a leap of faith for him to let go and open himself to unconditional love. I think Cordelia may be our helper here. I feel secure about being in touch, My Love, but the decision is yours. The pig has just decided to get even closer; is now lying across my back! Oh-so prickly; and my bottom is beginning to burn. The gasman is due any minute. Oops; better get dressed! X

We have a lazy day. The Children play quietly and Cedric lies in all morning. It is very hot. The piggy continues to be adorable; she is so friendly and loves the attention we dish out. The Laird stays in town for a long time. When he returns he cajoles the boys into building a dog kennel behind the second cabin. The Bog-Brush will need containing when we head off on our planned 'Tiki Tour,' {road trip), with my parents later this month. Kind neighbours have agreed to feed and walk her every day. The wobbly wire and metal stakes turn our Mountain stronghold into even more of a 'shantytown'. Oh well, as long as it restricts the hairy monster.

I think we are beginning to realize just how much cash it would take to turn this lifestyle block into something decent. A couple of hundred thousand dollars might level some garden, fence a paddock or two, tarmac the drive, join the two cabins, add a large deck and plant some wind-breaks. I don't think we will ever achieve our dreams.

MY PIG

Golden slumber in the morning,
Bulky addition to the kitchen doormat,
You bask in over-stuffed recline,
Long eye lashes flicker in happy welcome.

My friend,
Snoozing on legs and laps when time allows,
Constant food, snuffle and barge.
You stand on my bare feet,
Pushing your heavy self against my vegetable-chopping stance.
Why do you always fart when I say hello?

Saturdays, you seem to find a way inside,
Twice when we have been away,
Pasta and muesli bin emptied in piggy disarray,
Sad, indigestion countenance and guiltless grunt.

And now you begin the garden rampage,
Snout as turf-digging apparatus,
Stripping away the victim grass.
Our lawn attempt is rolled and ready for stacking.
You should work for a turfing company.
Each day you grow larger, my piggy friend;
A gift to keep me from straying,
You are meant to tie me down;
What secrets we might share.

Bernard and Felicia invite us to an evening barbecue at six and the kennel builders are more than happy to head away for some refreshment. It is The Laird's birthday on Saturday, so this provides a little celebration for him. Bernard has been out in his boat today. He often takes The Laird diving for scallops just out of the harbour. I recently learnt that one in four households owns a boat in this part of New Zealand. The fresh haul is being laid out neatly on the barbecue as we arrive. Hau and Abbey have also been invited and the younger children muck about happily. The children are younger than Cedric and the Go-Getter; our two soon ask when we are going home, so we let them watch a video. Bernard throws the empty scallop shells across the terrace into the garden for Sally the dog and we chat into the evening as the sun begins its bedtime slide across the bay.

P.m. Mouse: —Shining—X

Very late, Adrian: *Just home, and dropping off fast—NEWS! Found a workshop—lovely flow—and guess where? At Vonny's house; right next to school. Perfect! Heaps of space—feeling unclear about Vonny; something hiding; shy? But I can live there as well. She has a spare room. I'm pretty sure I can live with her—*

Friday 5th January 2007

Early A.m. Adrian: *Where are you, My Lover? I'm mid process after full-on day yesterday. Need to read your words and imagine your voice. So much change. Touching base would be good—but not secretively. I will no longer be hidden in my actions. Today I'll tell Big J. that I'm moving out, to Vonny's, in two weeks time. It may be what Big J. is wanting too. I had the thought this morning—making way for something new in her life? I have done my time in the Queen's kitchen; answering the calls, polishing the silver, ordering things just as Her Majesty requests. Now it is time to be in the garden—working in the sun once more. Coming up a level, yes. Vonny's feels easier—spacious—looser. Out-breath with challenges of a different kind. Thomasina for one—young girl needing a father figure. She talked about him as we cleaned out the workshop. She thinks we are cleaning it for him to come and move in! He once joked that he would and she's held on to the idea. And Vonny herself; I don't quite get her. I might be walking into a storm, even though I feel positive vibes. She says she has imagined me being in that room. Have you seen it? The little room behind the garage?*

Here come my rose-tinted glasses and the rescuing knight; but I'm up for it. I think it will be the out-breath I am wanting; the proximity to school; combined work and living. And a definite need—a worthy cause; using my strength and intuition to strengthen Vonny's parenting and help her manage the home and garden. I am leaping in faith. I feel sure. Okay. Stop! What are my options? Stay at Big J's in the relative comfort of The Leafy Glade? This may or may not be a possibility. Perhaps Big J. wants me to leave. I would continue the lessons in standing up to her; learn to speak my mind. Perhaps I am running from her too early? I think our friendship—

Anyway—how are your days filled? And your evenings? Depth of connection, honesty or surface living? Activity focus; status quo? Intuition says you need to maintain your blazing fires. A low flicker in the household at all times—always striving for more expression; more of you—more of The Laird. No more false harmony where you suck in all the family garbage and pour out your sweet essence to cover the plop. Enough sacrifice; it shouldn't be this way. All should be heard. Gruff! No laughing until you are all happy; 100%. This is not to be inflammatory or to incite a riot—but come on—voices have been given to us to use; holding them back only damages us.

Find your voice fair Artemis—gentle-firm—strong-probing—reasonable-undeterred-steady—understanding; love-bringing; the nurturing hunter—with all people.

Mouse: *My Friend—how I long to fall into The King's enfolding arms—to talk through all these very exciting changes and developments! Well—news indeed! Yes, I certainly know Vonny's home and the spare room behind the garage. I first met Vonny when I was house-hunting early on—high up in the hills behind Waikite Bay. She was living up there at the time and I stopped to ask directions. A few days later I bumped into her in town and said hi. I was most surprised to find her at school the next week; small world really. We have a few connections—she is English; she comes from the Midlands. I understand she's been a Kiwi resident for some years, living a bohemian life in the remote Northland, she told me. She and her partner split up and she came further south for Thomasina's education—something like that anyway.*

The house she used to rent was in the property pages last month; I remember pointing it out to you; the one next to the deer farm. She must love living so close to school now; I notice she is becoming involved on various levels. I imagine it gives her a real boost. Is she shy? Does she have other issues in which you would find yourself involved? Perhaps that's just what's needed. Had you considered just having the workshop there? Would it be a good idea to ask Big J. for her opinion?

As for us—Vonny is a close friend of Felicia; they often spend Christmas and holidays together. Felicia talks to The Laird and I know he talks about us, although she wouldn't gossip. She is a counsellor herself and understands discretion. So—I suppose we wouldn't be able to meet there very easily. Perhaps that's a good thing. Hmm.

I really need to speak to you, or see you, My Friend. I am trying to find the right words to say to The Laird, to open things up as we have suggested. I'd like to find a new level of relationship with him. However, he seems quite happy returning to familiar patterns and behaviours. He would rather just forget his wife's mid-life crisis! Last night a few of us gathered at Bernard and Felicia's for The Laird's imminent Birthday. The trouble with being completely open is that I'd have to admit I haven't been properly in love with my husband for many years. I don't think he could bear that—I don't think I could be that cruel, for we do care deeply for one another. I can only explain things as I have before—that a different part of me needs recognition; recognition by another. I think I can ask again.

But you, My Friend—do you in fact need a clean break from our relationship? Do you need a fresh start without complications? Do you need your freedom? How much do you want me in your life? I need an honest answer if I am to continue treading this tricky path. Is our love as true for you as it is for me; as I sense it is? Tell me—X

Adrian: *Thanks for filling in the picture so well. The Laird is in denial—*

his old pattern. And you don't speak up because you have learnt to bottle up feelings and retreat into a private world. Perfect match. Just as well you are having a mid-life crisis or what a sad old couple you would be in later years. But how to proceed? Hit him right between the eyes—parade your nakedness before him; don't allow any surface living. Am I just a stirrer? Rock the boat-look at—

But I hear you too; the difficult position you are in. Unfortunately you're stuck because I won't be secretive. If you want to see me you have to get his blessing. This is the Quest. You have to use all your craftiness. Go Artemis—use your huntress skills—acknowledge your cunning—seduction too. Straight up honesty could be necessary as well. Can you speak on the phone?

Honesty? The Laird and I can achieve that on one level—but not when it involves our personal emotion. And why hasn't Adrian answered my direct question. I need to know what I mean to him. I need to know now.

Later, Adrian: *Hi, my Friend; a business question first. I need some turkey, goose or maybe pheasant feathers. Any around? Will answer your other question when we have a chance to speak—not sure about that yet. Need to be lying down for that one.*

Mouse: *Dear Friend, I have various large feathers—when do you need them? I can be yours tomorrow afternoon for about an hour if you would like my company. I could try and get permission. Thank-you for your message. Need to lie down too—preferably beside you—X*

We have a lazy day. I continue to enjoy the book; 'The Power of Now.' The content rings many bells with me. The most striking element speaks of being 'present to the moment'. If we let go of past and future we let go of fear and unhappiness. This is the gift that Adrian and I share—the ability to be totally present to the moment. Eckhart Tolle also speaks of the need for change if one's situation becomes negative. He offers the opinion that as humans we operate on two different vibrations, or levels. The language of the more intuitive means little to those of a more earthed level. This all makes sense to me—but I was surprised this morning by The Laird's inability to understand the book's message. Here lies our fundamental difficulty. Of course, if he did resonate with the content I would not have needed to find another's close companionship.

I spend my lazy day wondering about Adrian's reluctance to answer the questions I pose. Perhaps I am just imagining his attachment. Am I building it into something more than it is? The friendship we share is priceless—that is a foregone conclusion, if nothing else.

Midday, Mouse: *Are you home? Do you want me to phone? I am alone for a short while.*

Adrian: *Sure; phone call now is good.*

I call. We chat. Adrian sounds distant and flat. He even calls me by my real name, which leaves me feeling unsure. I have to cut the phone call short when the family arrives home earlier than expected.

Early P.m. Mouse: *Sorry, My Friend—hate to cut you off like that. I should be able to talk openly to my best friend; all out in the open from now on. I'll continue to work on it. Lovely to hear your voice. X*

Later on, Mouse: *Hi there. I still can't find the right thing to say to The Laird. Don't want to spoil his birthday tomorrow. I might have Cedric in tow needing 'Mummy Time' this afternoon while the others head to the cinema. However—a few clear hours tomorrow in the early morning may give us an opportunity to meet. The Laird is off fishing at 5.30 a.m. I will try to get permission for you to come up for breakfast. Maybe a window—X*

Saturday 6th January 2007 The Laird's Birthday

Early A.m. Mouse: *We have permission, Lord Swallow—for you to collect tools and have a cup of tea only—as long as it doesn't make me all 'swoony' and lead to texting for the next two weeks!! A trip up here may not work for you, My Love, but the offer is there should you feel so inclined. The Laird is driving out right now—X*

Laird: *Might he not come to collect tools when we are out?*

Mistress: *Perhaps; but I need to see my friend as much as you need to see your friends and go fishing. We have placed a new balance inside our creative friendship, so you needn't worry. I love you. Happy Birthday, My Darling Laird—X*

Adrian: *Okay—I'll get the trailer attached and barrel on up. Be with you in 40 mins.*

He comes to me; walking in through the back door and holding me for a long time. We don't say anything. This is where we belong. I relax into my man, knowing the feel of him; the smell of him. He is my Lord Swallow and I am his Lady. I am both surprised and not surprised by his powerful claim. The children slumber and The Mountain wakes gradually to the summer morning as I nestle into his clean, linen shirt. I love him. I love my Adrian. Despite his permanent quandary I know he loves me.

The King is centred and strong. He does not kiss me, even though I wouldn't resist if he did. He is so handsome; brown and windswept. There is a new determination about him, making his Queen so proud. I am impressed by his patience and tireless endeavour. His excitement over the move is infectious. "I still haven't decided one hundred percent about moving in with Vonny," he tells me. "We had a long, honest discussion yesterday. I laid my cards on the table. We spoke about spirituality and Christ; my need to unearth deep-seated issues and tackle chaos." I am pleased to see him deliberating.

He takes my hands gently in his, asking; "How are you, My Love?" I am afraid the tears come again—I feel so at home with him, even though I cannot have him. "I still don't know where I am with the questions over us," he admits. "I can connect with you when you are centred and deep, but not so easily when you are off on some trip before we have earthed each other; especially if you are all 'twittery'. I think I need to experience more of the world before I can see around 'us' clearly. These are huge life decisions and I am not ready for them right now."

Fair enough. I can't really expect anything other from him in my married state. "Artemis and Apollo—twins?" He reminds me. "Hmm—yes, but no," I answer. "I sense our magnetic attraction all too readily. I'm not sure we would avoid incest." "You have to continue to dig deep," my counselor advises; "everything should be shared with others; yes, even The Garden Gate."

I listen and hear the sage advice. My heart tells me that all I have ever wanted is to share deep communion with another. I know our connection isn't about lust or fantasy. I don't think I would be feeling such grief and desolation if this were some imaginary trip. Perhaps I have wrapped my need in a fairy tale cloak. And although Lord Swallow states he prefers the *real, earthed* me, I know the *real* me he claims lies both inside and outside the fairy tale. The 'twittery' tendency he refers to is the ever-positive overlay I tend to dish out; that all too British habit for small talk and polite banter that smoothes the waters and covers over *'the plop'*. This is what Adrian dislikes, not the storyline that we weave together. That intrigues him; he cannot deny himself the pleasure of our magical world.

Together, we climb the steep hill to find his plants. They are piled beside the top cabin. They have been there for weeks; waiting for something; rather like our relationship. "I wonder if I'll ever come up to The Mountain again." He voices the question in both our minds. The polystyrene seed trays join the seedling pots and bags of compost in the back of the trailer. "I'll plant up the garden at Vonny's," he states. "I'm feeling strong now; ready for a new challenge and less battered by life. Look after the Ribbon Wood sapling won't you? Perhaps plant it somewhere special." He drives away to begin a fresh chapter—a new family awaits his touch; both his soothing presence and his relentless 'digging'.

Midday, Adrian: *So; she cries as she gazes at him. His penetrating look that she has missed and longed for turns towards her—and he demands more from her; asks that she reveal more. So used to sitting in that place he doesn't realize how lucky he is; how hard it is to achieve when a stream of constant life-shocks and unpleasant behaviour from children keeps knocking* *her, not 'out', but 'in'—the only place that is clear. He softens—seeing how it is—understands the relief that she feels. Hmm.*

__P.m. Mouse:__ She thanks him for his kind message; for coming to see her on the Mountain—for holding her so close. It has been a busy day with birthday celebrations; starting with an après fishing rendezvous at Pillans beach; The Laird inviting himself to Martha's house for a birthday breakfast. We joined him there. After that beach delight, {good to see Martha enjoying her holiday so much}, I took Cedric shopping at the second-hand warehouse; his favourite outing. {I found you a jumper} Then we left the kinder at home in The Scowler's care while The Laird and I headed off for his birthday treat; a ride along the beach just out of town. What bliss—2 hours of glorious sunshine and soft beach just waiting for a comfortable canter. The horses were great—not too speedy but certainly not plodders! We shared a cup of tea afterwards at the café adjoining the stables where lots of questions were asked and answers given. I even admitted to having been out of love with my husband for a long time. Oops—not so good for his birthday.

Poor Laird. He systematically lectured me on the objective truth; his perception of our relationship, you and me—partly true I am sure, but understandably misreading our position. I tried to explain that we are not a single unit. He said we are kidding ourselves—texting and seeing each other being the evidence. I told him you are beginning a new chapter; you have new things in your life and that we are standing apart to open up our connection. At times he was understanding and considerate. There is more to say; more thoughts from The King's neighbouring Queen, but right now I am stressed and tired. I need my bed. Hopefully The Laird and Mistress can build something strong from this base-line when sleep has woven its magic. I'm not sure where it will lead. Just keeping my Apollo informed. Sleep well.

__Adrian:__ Thanks for the update. Well done—to both of you—and it is true, we have kept to our agreement. There has been a big change in our relationship. May your sleep be blessed with peace, clarity and penetrating insight. Big J. and I just watched an involving N.Z movie called; 'In My Father's Den'. We then had a terrific chat until midnight about life and her own husband's betrayal. Great. I decided to hold off speaking about my plans to move out; just until it's all a bit clearer. Sleep sweet.

I turn out the light and let my thoughts dwell on the day. What a busy time. The Laird is engrossed in the usual television. I would rather think over the day's events and invite the beautiful pictures into my dreams. Pictures of sun-speckled orchards beside quiet roads float across my mind; roads so broad compared with those back home. Rows of high Casaurina windbreaks too—we cantered beside the kiwi fruit planting, the enticing vine tendrils encouraging us to go faster. They dangled in front of us, dancing in the breeze as we dashed by. The fruit hangs heavy under low canopies that make for easy picking. I often see the ground-crawling orchard vehicles that are designed to fit under the fruit ceilings; they make me think of mechanical caterpillars or military, amphibian trucks as they move between the various fruit farms in the area. The harvest will begin in four months or so.

The Laird's delight is central in the next picture—a young spirit—excited by the action and his wife's participation. "I told the stables I was an experienced rider," he called over his shoulder. "I've only been on a horse once before!" I had to grin as he thundered past. The horses were perfect; a chestnut and a bay. **7** others were riding with us, among them a fourteen-year-old American girl who chatted away in a strong, southern accent. She was on holiday and this was her treat; "I ride every day back home," she informed us with an air of confidence.

How blue the sky was today, and how glorious the beach views. The panoramic seascape was ever-present; the volcanic Mount majestic in the distant harbour. We passed several large houses with ample gardens and ornate gateways. The region is highly desirable, and expensive. I spied new homes under construction between the orchards and above the curvaceous coastline—grand residences that climb down to the bays with terraced gardens and impressive decks. The beaches looked so inviting from our elevated position. I watched a child playing with a dog on the warm sands while the horses walked sedately along a grassy bank. When we reached the sand the horses took off at speed along the familiar stretch of coast. What fun—the wind whipped any loose locks off our faces and the waves ran beside us, enjoying the chase. This is one of the reasons we have come to New Zealand—to taste exhilarating, wild adventure in the 'great outdoors' of the Southern Hemisphere. We certainly enjoyed ourselves, especially The Laird. I smile wryly to myself; haven't I already found the exhilarating adventure for which I abandoned an established, secure life?

And afterwards we shared tea and the picture of our unwelcome conversation returns to me, the conversation that had to come at some stage, where I admitted to my husband that I have been living a half-truth for many years. I was clear and levelheaded, knowing the truth needed to be aired. The Laird adopted his unemotional, psychologist attitude. His view of my extra marital relationship was harsh and sometimes accurate. Of course he tore Adrian to shreds, insisting that we have never had to share anything other than an idyll, so how could we possibly know we are meant for each other. Any mention of our relationship's new level was dismissed. I listened—I let him give me all—and yes, there was some kindness and understanding too. I tried to make a point about the danger of a judgmental attitude. Did he hear me? Hmm—he rarely lets others get a word in. Tricky times.

As my eyes close I think of my Ribbon Wood sapling—still waiting to be planted. It must be pot-bound by now; passing time in a plastic tub until its new home materializes. Adrian gave it to me just before his European departure last July. We were searching out plants for the new school border on another of our exciting excursions. Adrian had taken on the project of laying a school path between the library and the playground; the border alongside needed planting. We wandered happily together in the winter afternoon, choosing plants in a local garden centre. *"And a Ribbon Wood for My Lady,"* he decided, passing the rows of delicate, twisty stems in their pots. It was so cold that day.

I remember the English proprietor directing us to the plants in question. A thin blanket of low-lying fog lay between the rows of interesting ferns, shrubs and fruit trees. Situated in the hills behind Waikite Bay the place is a professional gardener's treasure trove. Interesting posters on the office walls displayed the native plants and nursery specialties; many of the plants were reasonably priced and the English woman was enthusiastic and knowledgeable. What a happy time that was. I wonder where I should plant the little sapling. It should grow into a good-sized tree.

Chapter 2 Passing

Sunday 7th January 2007

A.m. Mouse: Dear Friend—I have some thoughts for The King that need consideration before our side-by-side adventure continues. What would you say if I questioned your tendency to 'dig deeply'? For all the rich reward and well-meant unearthing I sense a hard-edged insistence behind the intention— a relentless 'dog with a bone' undertone. Might I be so bold as to suggest this, in some obscure way, could be an unconscious reflection of your need to acknowledge and feel self-love? This is just a suggestion, for I sense a barrier within you against your right to claim love. I am not looking for declarations of undying passion—no—but I am surprised, even slightly hurt, that you cannot openly acknowledge and delight in receiving love on a private, personal level. You appear to possess a driven desire to ignore the comfort of a resting place within its truth, on whatever level it is for you.

Of course, I know we should never stand still, but surely some stilling, some kindness to self in allowing this quiet, would enrich you no end. I would like to see a softness surround you—there is great wisdom in letting go and acquiring a soft edge. I know it would help with your tendency to 'think afterwards'; to help you feel compassion before, rather than after, you have acted. Because you don't allow yourself this kindness you cannot bestow it upon others when it is needed. Might I also suggest that you give yourself a big 'pause' before you leap in as the rescuing knight and 'dig deeply'? This isn't to say I don't recognize the benefits; just that perhaps these life lessons need to find a lasting and sustainable home in you first before you can administer to others. I don't suggest abandoning your gift; just adopt a measured, kinder approach with empathy and lower gear unearthing. A soft edge to The King would bring great wisdom to all his actions.

As for the neighbouring Queen—well, she has always been treated with kindness, despite her suggestions, and perhaps he hasn't claimed the love completely because it isn't as true for him or that he is respecting her married state. It is The King's relationship with others that she addresses; not so much his relationship with his Lady. All she has ever striven for is profound communion with him in acknowledged divinity; a recognition of Spirit within which they dance and delight—even for a short while—for she knows it gains them entry into Heaven through a beautiful Gate. It offers a chance to return home—a key to The Gate—a knife-edged keel—a set of billowing, white sails and the recognition of a fellow sailor.

P.s. having said all that, you know I appreciate the soul-searching you have led me to face. I have never felt unkindly treated by you. You have been lovely throughout the journey. It is kindness to yourself that I refer to in our relationship. I will ever be your Lady—some truths cannot be undone, whatever the future holds—M—X

We attend church as a family. The Laird is softer today; perhaps some clarity may appear. A game of squash is next on his busy agenda. I sit in the park while the children play. I like to write at times like these, using the small screen of the phone of course.

Midday, Mouse {Unsent}: Here, at the very spot you made me the beautiful, green, seaweed heart, wondering how you are, My Love. Finding myself no further away from you than on our dusky, nighttime stroll at Whatipu Beach in West Auckland. I hope my hard-hitting, Sunday lesson wasn't too much? I hope you could find my undeterred love for you between the lines and sentiment. I keep asking myself the question; 'why so sure? Why so certain I should walk beside you still'? And now it is really open; the truth of it within my marriage. Yes, I sense a new start without hidden agendas; an exposed base line from which to work.

Today we celebrated The Epiphany in church; the arrival of the 3 kings, although yesterday was the actual day as today is the 7th. Hmm—the 7th-a special number for us I think, in this year 2007.

I imagine the green heart you made me. I am standing beside it as I watch the children swim in the shallow water and play on the sand. I encourage them to be creative with the seaweed. A figure appears in the slippery, green sculpture we make together; jaunty, shiny legs, arms akimbo; he is itching for a dancing partner. Sadly she doesn't appear. Alone in his imaginings on the ever-moving shoreline, he sighs. Alone, yet not alone, she hopes he knows.

So, The Kings have arrived—or should I say The King and Queen? They have achieved another rung of their daring ladder; standing apart, yet on the same level nonetheless. And today's Sunday revelation? A church service full of renewed hope, a humbled, hurting husband and a wife who feels no guilt—unchanged in her realization. She imagines Lord Swallow in church with them, standing more in the background than before; hat clasped quietly before him, perhaps even hopefully. And out of the blue comes the picture of a dear, elderly man that I befriended in his latter years. There was a strong bond between us. We were part of a group pilgrimage in Southern France many years ago. We spent a moving evening together in the hospital ward where we were staying. He was in his wheelchair and didn't feel like socializing in the town bars with the others. It was dark and I sat beside him, holding his hand. He was tearful, always so tearful—full of regret for past misdemeanors. I could feel his grief; it was overwhelming for him. How sad to see a man laid so low. He had been in the army—I don't remember exactly, although I recall some reference to violence. The details don't matter now. All I remember is how my heart met his and the sure knowledge that the Good Lord would hold him close; that in the hour of total humility and despair he would come to him. When he died a year later I made a special trip to his funeral. How strange that I should think of him now; why today? And then I realize—his name was Adrian—Adrian Calver.

I look out across the bay, wondering at the significance of the names of the two men—the strange coincidence that not only the Christian name but also the first letters of the surname should be the same. My attention is suddenly diverted by The Laird whose squash game is over. He strides towards the beach-"What? Are you texting again? I don't believe it!" I try to explain about using the small screen to write up my diary—my thoughts. "I don't send the writing to anyone—honestly, I don't." The Laird is unconvinced; of course he is. Perhaps I *am* kidding myself. The barriers of mistrust shoot up again. The black cloud descends. "I wonder if your relationship would ever have taken off without the mobile phone," he asks. "My patience isn't limitless; the next time I see you using it I'll stamp on it; smash it and throw it far out to sea!"

We have an unpleasant drive home, The Laird's cruel words accompanying us as unwelcome yet inevitable fellow travellers. We stop at the local Dairy for extra provisions. "And the menus are getting repetitive and boring," he adds as a final stab. We have guests coming to supper. I am tired—it's that time of the month again and all I want is my bed. I manage a small, restless kip on the sofa before snapping to in the kitchen.

P.m. Mouse: —X—

Our extra guest is interesting—Conrad, an Englishman from Cornwall, {goodness me, another southerner at last}! He is great company and we have a fun evening. If you can call it fun; my husband is upset and cannot bring himself to even meet my gaze.

Monday 8th January 2007
A.m. Mouse: {Unsent} *A grey dawn in my heart. A husband who no longer trusts—who cannot hold his wife at the moment—who is understandably harsh with his words: "I'll smash your mobile phone if I find you using it." I try to explain that it's my diary but he doesn't believe me. A busy day yesterday with church and The Laird's game of squash. We delivered the Go-Getter to his friend's house and then came home. A hasty scramble to produce a meal for guests—13 arrived for the evening. Should have made The Laird happier. Then every family member started complaining about the repetitive menu I provide. I got cross—"I have been out all day, looking after you lot while you have fun! When did I have time to cook?!" Sammy and family arrived, plus a few others. Conrad's family is abroad at the moment; his son is a new friend of Cedric's at school. The evening was a success. We started off in the garden but headed inside when the sun went down. Everyone met the pig and lent a hand with the big puzzle.*

I am so tired. Cedric kindly gave me a foot massage; he is being lovely after his shopping trip. Gifts are definitely his love language. And so to bed— at last. I am heavy of heart; there is a lot of cleaning and bed-making to organize before my parents fly in. They should be in the air now. The pains are bad in my middle; no Small One this month then; not exactly any lovemaking going on anyway. I wonder what the strong feelings of bearing another child are all about. The night sky is slow to welcome the dawn and I keep my head upon the soft pillow. No word from you yesterday, My Love? For obvious reasons you are silent. My eyes close again on this Earthly realm. I am accepting; but sad. No Husband; no Lover. Where might it all lead?

Later, A.m. Mouse: *Are you there, My Friend? I need to know your thoughts. Are you offended by my strong message yesterday? Do you want a clean break? Do you want to hear my daily ramblings? Please let me know where you stand—otherwise I cannot feel clear. I am home alone with the children who slumber still. I could phone if you would prefer. I am in a lonely place right now—no Lover—no Husband.*

The day is filled with endless chores. The Laird is absent all morning, off on his usual round of sporting fixtures and social engagements. My ears are bad. I am stressed.

Early P.m. Adrian: *My Dear Friend—I'm sorry to cast you into uncertainty. I took your suggestion yesterday and had a quiet day; felt like communing with nature in the evening, so I went out to the bus where I used to live. Thought I'd have a fire-bath but talked late with the neighbours up there. It was cold in the bus—I didn't sleep well. I had an early start to meet an old man who had some perfect wood for bow staves. I'm just busy— thinking about your words—on the go right now. I'll text once home and see if a phone call is possible. Lots to talk about I think. I'm still unclear about where I stand, but not concerned. I know it will unfold as it should. Thanks for your bold honesty—well done. I'm probably 2 or so hours away—X*

Mouse: *My Darling Friend—thanks for letting me know how you are— relief—that's all I need for now. Funny; I can get on so much better if we keep in touch. I shall continue with the housework with more vigour. My parents arrive on Wednesday! Help! Not sure if I am mentally, or physically ready. You must be preparing for the Bow and Arrow Workshop. Wish I were helping you run it. Don't worry to text later—unless you feel like it of course. Just a little update is fine—X*

Midday, Adrian: *Hi—heading on a spontaneous mission to Rotorua in search of goose feathers for the arrow flights—be so nice to have you with me. I'm resting in a Rotorua Park. I'm feeling tired and a little stressed. I need a swim but the good lakes are across town. I'll head back via Points Road. What are you up to?*

Mouse: My Love; what a nice message. Wish I was with you; we would make an excellent goose-feather-hunting-team—The Woodsman and The Country Lass guise I imagine. Mmm. I am busy tackling lots of jobs at once—drives the single focus of The Laird mad. I am in even more trouble, which makes life pretty grim.

Poor Laird—he does have a reason to be cross. I feel no regret but I am stressed. My ears are rough today and it's that time of the month again. 28 days comes around quickly. We are beginning to make headway in the general household chaos. The Laird will be out all tomorrow on a sea-fishing trip. The Go-Getter will be away for the night and I will find somewhere for Rinky to spend the day. What are you up to tomorrow? T'would be good to catch up. Hope you get the feathers—and a swim. Love—M—X

Late P.m. Mouse: Would you like me to send on my recent diary thoughts?

Adrian: Did you phone me? Just missed it. Shall I speak to you on my workshop phone briefly?

Mouse: Sorry Friend—no, t'was not me that phoned. {In fact, it was The Laird.} I'd love to chat but no chance at the moment. Laird is cleaning the floor like a maniac and I am cleaning the mouse-infested larder. So—you have a workshop phone now; great. What is your number there? I'll phone if a chance appears; otherwise meet at our usual etheric rendezvous at 11p.m-X. Sleep well.

The Laird suddenly lays into me after his floor cleaning session; a verbal assault that shocks me. His good friend and squash partner, Simon, spoke to him earlier about my relationship with Adrian. Simon is the chairman of the School's Board of Trustees and Big. J. had just informed him of our situation in accordance with school ethics and management regulation.
My husband is furious; his pride is understandably injured. "I am about to telephone Adrian and give him both barrels, so watch out." My poor Laird-this is a terrible situation to have thrust upon him. I have treated him badly, without intention, and he is hurting. Does the management team have to rake up the issue again? Despite the disaster I remain upright in my choice, quickly reaching for my phone to warn my unsuspecting Friend.

P.m. Mouse: Dear Friend; Laird is on the warpath—I'm afraid he's going to get shirty and phone you. Big J. has spoken to Simon in her official capacity regarding our liaison and he has informed The Laird. Just to warn you. So sorry, My Love. Need to speak really soon. X

And then I hear him—out in the garden beneath our bedroom window. He is shouting at Adrian on the telephone, refusing him any say. "No, I don't wish to hear your side—you are not to set foot on my property again, do you understand? Don't even try to give me your view of things; I won't listen. And you may *not* see my wife unless in the company of others. I shall inform The School Principal that I have spoken with you."

Wow, he certainly lets both barrels fly. My poor Swallow Man. I feel awful. I imagined the reality of two men fighting over the hand of a Lady to be the stuff of romantic legend or wildlife performance. I wouldn't wish the experience on anyone. A cold shroud renders me numb with disbelief. I manage to stay calm, despite the shock. The Laird storms off to the top cabin and I hastily telephone Adrian. "Are you alright?" I ask. "Hmm; better get off the phone, My Love" he says. "We will have to decide whether to go underground."

I replace the receiver and consider his words. He was loving and intimate; hushed shock and anxiety in his voice. Although we are insisting on a changed emphasis our connection laughs in the face of maintained, physical restraint. This is true love, without a doubt. So, what do we do with it now?

Late P.m. Mouse: *I am here my Love—by your side. So; others throw us up, onto the next level. The Laird is particularly cross because I haven't been totally honest with him. There are things I have kept secret—to keep him from harsh assault. He asked the big question—"Have you slept with him?" I didn't answer directly. He says you and I need time apart to test our love. So; he is aware that it is more than a 'flash in the pan.' I continue to say we have changed our emphasis, because on a physical level we have. Unfortunately he cannot believe that. What next? Let's speak tomorrow—X*

I sleep fitfully and alone. The pressure in my ears moves to the back of my head. I hope it doesn't make me ill. The Laird comes to me in the night and we talk. He cannot get over the upset of my night in Auckland with Adrian. There are tears from us both as we look back over the past years. This is hard-"My beautiful Angel has enfolded me in his mature spirit and I cannot leave him now," I admit. "You haven't changed the emphasis of your relationship, whatever you believe," my husband lectures me yet again. I suppose he is right. We are kidding ourselves while wrapping a cloak of discipline and integrity about our relationship. We all know it is more than friendship. We talk openly for a long time. The Laird continues to call for a six-month separation between Adrian and me. I speak of unconditional love—of peace and fulfillment—of joy. My husband speaks of years where children always came first, of having to play second fiddle and of watching me fill my life with other stimulants apart from him. He admits to being wary of emotional outbursts—of passion. Childhood years of parental discord have taken their toll. I cry, he cries. We face a lot of work if our marriage is to survive. I'm not even sure that's what I want.

Tuesday 9ᵗʰ January 2007

   A.m. Mouse: *Help—My Darling, we need to get down to the Boat-Yard quickly. Some high-ranking Marine Officials are making a report on the movement of our precious Boat. They are in the process of condemning The Celestial Sea. They are manhandling her. I even saw the Harbour Master throw a large stone against the hull. What should we do? Until we make headway with our Book we are stuck. We have no alternative but to stick with the present dry-dock situation. Our presence at The Marina fuels the Officials into disquiet and action. They do not trust either of us.*

   I have a very busy day ahead of me; less free time than I hoped. There are major developments after the stone hurling; a definite pressure release. We need to talk soon. The temptation to leap aboard and sail away is very real, but we both have heavy anchors and positive work is afoot. You can text, My Friend. Loving you. Hope the stone didn't catch you a glancing blow—M—X

P.s I'm heading into town on my own. Can you let me know if you are okay, My Brave Friend? X

   Adrian: *Dear Laird—sorry. I can see from your perspective. With a contrite heart I send this, hoping you will read it. I promise—for what my word is worth now—not to have any further contact with your wife. I am prepared to stand up before The Principal and the Board and admit my error. I will accept whatever consequences they deem fit, even resignation and leaving the district. I would prefer to work it out privately with you. If there is any way I could restore your trust and good faith in my word I would go there—a flogging or a beating come to mind. I would talk with you more. I am sorry for the effects of my actions on you and your children. I have learnt. Adrian.*

   I hear nothing more from Adrian this morning. I am worried. Is that it? Has he cut our contact entirely? I imagine he will keep to his word. Did he send me his message to The Laird to tell me he is washing his hands of us? Cold reality shudders through me from top to toe. Have we really come all this way for a negative finish?

   Mouse: *Are you not going to speak to me, My Friend? Have we come all this way to face silence? I need to tell you what has happened, unless you don't want to hear. I will take my lead from you, Sir. My feelings are unchanged. Is this really our only choice? I need to know if you feel cornered or if it is your sincere wish to halt contact. Please, please let me know—I can't bear to leave things like this. I need to tell you about a conversation I had this morning and I really do need to know how you feel about US. Am I meant to show your previous text to The Laird or have you already sent it to him? If I don't hear back from you by tonight I will show him the text and try* *to guess your—*

Adrian: *Please wait. I need to hear from The Laird. He has the text—unless he has deleted it. Please wait-*

Mouse: *Will do, My Love. Sorry for the urgency. I am in the supermarket—just been for the final dentist appointment. Feeling wobbly; am by your side. My Parents arrive tomorrow.*

The day is busy. Preparations for the grand arrival are slow but thorough. The work is tinged with sadness and excitement both. I am resentful that The Laird has taken my friend from me. I feel robbed. I cannot turn to him in bed as a wife. He tries to make conversation throughout the day but my heart and soul are shattered.

Wednesday 10th January 2007
A.m. Mouse: *Mist hangs like an expectant shroud over their Mountain—a place forbidden him. She feels dead inside. Without her Angel beside her she is but a shroud herself. But not expectant like their Mountain—for him the sun will definitely return. She sends her love, knowing he cannot reply. She will think of him today as he crafts with the children. Wood and feathers, knives and linseed. Bows and arrows, mastery and manhood-X*

My parents arrive at last. They are tired and travel worn; both have aged over the past eighteen months. A delay at Auckland airport for the local flight sees them arriving three hours late. It is wonderful to have them here. "How pioneering," was their comment upon reaching The Mountain. The house has never been so clean and tidy. Everything sparkles in the afternoon sun. Even my desk is in order; the shelved paperwork receiving attention after months of life-changing adventure. Cedric the Scowler has moved into the top cabin so we can have his room. My parents have ours, which is of average size with extraordinary views.

So—we are set—ready—but for what? *"Wait—please wait,"* he asks of her. So, she will wait.

The coldness in my heart increases. The Laird has torn and burnt my Angel's wings. He has set an icy stone inside of me. How can I love if my true person is denied? I need to go to Adrian. I need to lie in his arms and ask how he fares. We need to discuss all that has happened. Why doesn't he reply? He is a man of his word—he cannot reply. Does he want me to keep writing to him? I have not sworn an oath of 'no contact'. I know we belong together in some way; yes. My Darling Friend, I will try and wait.

I wonder why Adrian corners himself behind such impenetrable, noble fences. Time and again I watch him make punishing promises. These promises affect me too; they are harsh. Perhaps it is the only way he can make himself tow the morally acceptable line, or perhaps he likes the drama; the attention of being shown up. Is he testing himself? Is this part of his martyrdom tactic? I imagine there is a little truth in all these suppositions.

My parents have retired to bed for the night, The Laird is watching T.V and I have completed some more deskwork. My head is cold and dead. I must go upstairs.

Mouse: —X

Thursday 11th January 2007

I hear nothing—no evening message or morning greeting. Oh my Love, what are you thinking? I fear a return to normality. I dread the steady pattern of unquestioning dependability. I have walked the dull path for twenty-five years; do I have to continue in the same vein? I yearn for you to unearth of my essential essence. I resent the exacerbation of our relationship into unnecessary drama, just when we had the situation under control. I am empty and hurting inside. I feel no guilt or concern over others' judgment.

We have a gentle morning looking after Ma and Pa. We let them rest while we potter quietly at home.

P.m. Mouse: My dearest Friend—I am hurting. I miss our contact. I know you have promised to keep away but I have made no such promise. Do you want to receive my daily missive? Or would you prefer not to hear from me? I understand that you cannot reply. My parents have arrived—so lovely to have them close, and a good distraction too. I am finding it hard to forgive The Laird for so brutally tearing your wings. I am empty inside—nothing to give him at the moment—not sure if that will change.

How are you, My Love? I hope the bow and arrow workshop went really well. I'd so like you to meet my Ma and Pa. I feel robbed of my one, special joy—an illicit joy, I know. Can you let me know if you want my messages to continue? You could phone me from your landline with a blank message, or send a blank text; then I would know you are happy to hear my news. If I don't hear I shall stop texting and continue guessing your thoughts. X

I hear nothing. As the days pass the wound deepens; the hurled stone was jagged and lethal. Something truly beautiful has been cast into the tray marked 'ugly', 'dangerous', 'unworthy'. Others' opinions have filed it so. Perhaps I am deluded; caught in a spell that I cannot break. I have no other choice but to soldier on, pretending that all is well; that I feel quite normal when this is far from the truth.

The bond shared by The Laird and I is ever-present but no longer enough. We do not meet each other personally. We have been found out. The Laird is too scared of being hurt; of being abandoned. He will not stand upright and face the truth of the situation. He is one hundred percent earthed; he cannot see the full learning potential. Oh—why can't Adrian let me know how he is; what mind-talk takes centre stage during these silent days? I just need one more conversation to clarify our standing. Has The Laird's aggression highlighted the domestic reality of our connection? I wish he would let me know. I must return to a place of silence and imagination. I am used to that. I shall return underground. I cannot share my essence with someone who doesn't see me; much as The Laird is loyal and caring; a special person in my life.

I am a 'Frodo' character and he is my 'Sam'. The analogy fits. Frodo is a ring-bearer. He needs to leave with the Elves. Sam cannot hang onto him forever. He must let his friend go to other places; to others who need him. Frodo can let go and maintain his friendship with Sam. He is prepared to be the back-up for his loyal friend. He will hold him still; comfort him when needed.

But my personal comfort? The Laird denies me it. He is a prisoner of fear and misunderstanding. His cell has no windows. His lack of light spirit; his tendency to heaviness and depression, keep him anchored to misery. I ask him to accept unconditional love; yes; to allow me a lover of celestial influence; yes—a literary partner, an intimate friend—just occasionally—just enough to keep enlivened and free. "Please."

Friday 12th January 2007

The Laird is away all day—fishing. I would rather he was out than heavy and brooding in the cabin. The sea kayak is a great success and he usually returns with tales of challenging swell or calm water. Last month he hooked a dolphin and had a hair-raising ride back to the beach, thinking it was a shark! Red snapper and Kawhai are often brought triumphantly into the kitchen. The Kawhai is excellent smoked in the tin smoker. This is The Laird's domain; he enjoys providing for his family and claims the door-less 'shid' outside the kitchen to prepare the fish.

Mizzle, mist and endless rain overtake The Mountain and keep the rest of us inside all morning. The overpopulated rooster troop is waking our guests unsociably early. We move some of them to the Twealm Realm; might they stay down there?

At midday I receive a blank text message. Lord Swallow wishes to receive his Lady's thoughts and observations; he still holds her in his heart.

A.m. Mouse: *My Darling Friend; thank-you for your indication. I hope all is well? I am so sorry about the stone hurling; something The Laird needed to get off his chest. He had to release the strong emotion he keeps under wraps as a result of early childhood experience. He admitted recently to a fear of domestic disharmony—his parents' violent arguments made him feel unsafe as a child. The outburst—only noise I think—meant we could talk honestly. However, he is pretty devastated by my revelation of a lack of* *passion and chemistry between us. We have a long way to go towards a healed marriage. I know I should back down and get on with it. That's hard when in your heart of hearts there is something other that you want, even though you try to choose with your head.*

I suppose the entire situation is such a massive shock. He never thought I would go behind his back. I should be feeling dreadful but I am only a little rattled. There were tears from us both. I explained what we are to each other; you and I. Any sexual reference I left out. I tried to lighten the scenario. Perhaps I have credited him with more stability and independence than he possesses. Anyway, I hate not being able to talk to you. I don't know how to proceed without knowing your thoughts. I will place my trust in our Guardian Angels—and in time. Have you moved yet? What are you up to? I am at home with my parents and the children. The Laird is out fishing all day.

Our new English friend, Conrad, invites us to supper this evening, although we leave my overtired Ma to baby-sit and recover from jet lag. I had forgotten to tell Conrad my father doesn't eat fish; oops; he hastily finds some chicken and puts it in the oven without turning a hair; the perfect gentleman and host; so British. His wife and children are away. A large fish pie is waiting for the rest of us. It is delicious. "We're just renting this easy house until we sell land on Waiheke Island off Auckland," Conrad tells us. "A relation picked up a section for three hundred pounds many years ago and left it to us in his will. We have bought a section here, on the other side of town. Would you like to see the architect's drawings? We're building a house as soon as the land sells."

What a gentle, interesting man; even my Pa has connections with our host through a common military background. Conrad works as a counselor and his wife is a Special Needs expert. They moved from Cornwall a year after our departure from the U.K. We are fascinated by his past career—"I was in the army for many years; as part of the peace-keeping force in the Congo around the diamond running. I was so appalled by the effect of this unnatural commerce in the villagers' lives—you can imagine the devastation to their otherwise civilized, tribal lifestyle—that I left the army. My wife and I became involved in establishing the Fair Trade element of a well-known, global company. After that I took up counseling work. My present career was easy to bring into New Zealand; so here we are."

The Laird and I chat late into the night; we are slow to unwind after a sociable evening. "Adrian sees the whole of me," I explain. "Yes, but what exactly *is* the whole of you?" My long-suffering husband tries to understand. Of course I can't explain. The language I use to suggest the essence is beyond his comprehension. "Can't I have *some* pleasure?" I ask again. "You pleasure yourself at *every* opportunity."

Our conversation goes round and round; The Laird understandably questioning the type of pleasure I have granted myself. I cannot admit I am in the wrong, although of course I say I'm sorry to have hurt him. I will not denounce the joy and delight in my relationship with Adrian. I will no longer blur the edges. "We are speaking from different places," I continue. "I wish you had been open and honest from the start," he comments. "Then perhaps we wouldn't be facing this problem. You know I would give up my fishing; my other busy hobbies; I would give them all up to have you properly beside me." I consider his words, knowing the reality of a bored, moody Laird at home would be far worse than an occupied, busy husband. "I need to move with ease; with a lightness of spirit; with joy. I don't sense any joy when we are together. In fact I'm not sure you 'like' me very much," I tell him. "I know you love me, but I also need to be liked."

Saturday 13th January 2007

A.m. Mouse: Your Lady lies in her Angel's arms—hoping he is happy to hold her; wondering about his thoughts. More in-depth discussions last night. I still won't move from the reality of our bond. The Laird struggles with the realization that he is not at the centre of my life. Difficult trying to keep a normal face in front of my parents. I'm not sure they could cope with the situation.

But my Ma has been asking about you and Rinky nearly said the wrong thing yesterday. The truth will probably emerge before the month is out. Not sure how that would be. The Laird would feel supported; I might feel hounded, even in the face of claiming a close friend. The quandary lies between you and me and The Laird—nobody else. The Laird finds this very hard. He relies on others at all times, speaking his mind and sharing with a large audience inviting discussion. Hmm—a challenge for him; a challenge to find greater self-reliance. He continues to give me the cold shoulder and cutting, short-tempered remarks. I suppose I am used to that. One day at a time. Sorry to load you.

Do you like to be kept in the picture? Wish we could keep in touch. I'd like to share these life-changing revelations—so central to the relationship we share. But I can feel you close, in whatever way fits with you, My Love. I don't have lots of time now, so will send you my beach time reverie from Sunday 7th. I always save my diary writing. Loving you—M-X

P.s we have a problem with the Bog-Brush being left with neighbours—they are going away unexpectedly. We leave on Monday for 6 days. We thought we might take her with us but the camper van company doesn't allow dogs. Help! Are you able to take her for us? You are allowed to text me back—Laird's permission. Gulp—nothing like a Bog-Brush to bridge the gap! Big love—M—X

Adrian: Sure, My Friend. Had thought to go on a 'Tiki Tour' myself, but lots to do here anyway. Told Big J. that I'm moving and started the big sort out today. Now ready to line, plaster and paint the new room at Vonny's. Sure I can work the Bog-Brush into my plans. Let me know when you're going-X

106

Sunday 14th January 2007

A.m. Mouse: Dear Friend—good morning from a very wet and bedraggled Mountain. My parents seem to have brought the bad weather with them. Thank-you so much for your offer to have the hound. Will let you know what The Laird says. He is being kinder at last. I want to tell him that when he smashed My Angel he smashed any love left in me. Perhaps I will. We are off to church. Wonder what this week's revelation might be? I'll let you know. M—X

At last the sun comes out and we enjoy a pleasant morning on the deck. My parents are amazed by the incredible views. "We were really excited when we flew over the beach before landing," they tell the children. "We wondered if you were down there, waiting for us to arrive." After church The Laird heads off with a colleague while Ma and I spend a pleasant half hour in the local café. The College Principal is there, sharing coffee with some staff and a local Judge. Ma enjoys meeting them in the friendly atmosphere of the modern cafe. Some of the tables spill out onto the broad street curb where a huge Camellia tree shelters other church goers from the sun.

*P.m. Mouse: Part of this week's sermon was about 'celebration'—especially in sharing the blessed wine at communion. "The Mass should always be likened to attending a wedding party." The priest went on to discuss the miracle of the six stone jars of water; an imperfect number. "Bring in another; there, now there are **7**—the number of **perfection.** They were turned into the finest wine."*

I sense holiness around us today, My Love. And you, My Friend, how are you feeling? Being out of contact means I am unsure what you would be happy receiving from me or what we can be to each other. Might we speak soon? Just to clarify where we stand? The question mark makes me so sad—and frustrated. Please send something to tell me your position—your thoughts. You asked me to wait, but for how long? And tell me straight up; do you want me in your life or not? I would delete your return message immediately. Please—X

P.m. Mouse: Dear Friend, The Laird has found another neighbour to care for the Bog-Brush and animals. I couldn't face asking him to overcome his anxieties yet again. Thanks so much for the offer. I passed you on the road earlier—trailer—Thomasina with you? Hope all is going really well; a poignant reminder that I am part of you now. It feels strange not to be helping you move. I am with you in spirit; a dampened one, but still a spirit—X

Chapter 3 Poignant

Monday 15th January 2007

The big holiday trip to the Northland begins. The skies are aglow with summer promise and we are excited, discovering anew with our guests the beautiful scenery. The packing up and animal arrangements have left us tired and frazzled but the need to collect the camper van by midday meant a nine o'clock departure. Despite the sense of adventure I am low in spirit. The Laird is kind and tells me how much he loves me. I am unable to respond, knowing the truth of the gift I have received; the gift I am denied.

The Camper van is spacious and rattly. It isn't very comfortable but the children are thrilled and quickly grab the top bunks and cosy cushions. Cedric takes up residence in the very back; his earphones constantly plugged in and an air of resigned boredom on his face. No wonder I wish to change our family dynamic. Ma and Pa are generosity itself—they are treating us to this holiday and the first night sees us way up North, staying in the Hokianga; the family homeland of our Maori friend Hau. My parents book into a comfortable hotel while we park up at a local campsite.

The hotel is wonderful, with beach frontage straight onto the Hokianga Harbour. This unspoilt location on the west coast of the Northland is beautiful and especially calm. Also known as Te Kohange O Te Tai Tokerare, {The Rest of The Northern People}, it is relatively under populated. The mangrove-lined estuary extends for 70 kilometers inland, punctuated by small inlets and family owned farms. The climate is mild throughout the year and the region is home to one of the oldest Maori Iwi in the country; the Nga Puhi. Oral tradition speaks of Kupe, the great Polynesian explorer, stepping onto Aotearoa's soil for the first time here, in the Hokianga. He is said to have settled in the area which he named; 'Spring of the World of Light.' The name stayed until Kupe's old age when he returned to his original homeland of Hawaiki. "Hei kone ra i te puna i te ao marama ka Hoki nei ahau, e kore ano e hokianga nui mai," he said before he left; "this is The Spring of the World of Light. I shall not come back here again." So the name Hokianga-nui-a-Kupe was given, becoming 'The Hokianga' over time.

My parents are delighted by the setting and we enjoy a seafood supper on the copious deck as the sun sets. Other hotel guests soak in the swimming pool next to the dining area and the children play on the large expanse of grass that meets the sands. Hau's brother joins us for a drink; he works as a builder at the resort; an eye-opener for my father who usually socializes with those from a similar background and culture, and certainly not with labourers in shorts and steel-toed boots! I grin to myself as the British Colonel makes small talk with the Maori local. "You should go sand-surfing while you are here," Jim advises. "Just walk to the pier and a boat will take you across the harbour to the sand dunes. The boat goes regularly; reception will give you the times." We don't manage to finish the generous meal and head to our various beds before the dark sets in completely.

Tuesday 16th January 2007

Waking to the summer sunshine we join my parents for a stroll on the beach before breakfast in the hotel. There are a fair few staying at the resort; it is high season of course. The atmosphere is one of holiday relaxation and we duly set off with others for a morning of sand surfing. What fun that is—even I have a go! The enormous sand dunes reach to a height of one 170 metres, falling to the harbour waters where we are told we might see dolphins, orcas and seals. In the afternoon we find Hau's mother in the tourist shop she manages and after directions we locate his step-father's puzzle workshop and retail outlet buried in a rural hideaway. What a delight—the pentagon building with colourful wind chimes of intriguing design houses an artist's Mecca. Shelf upon shelf of hand-crafted puzzles finds us asking questions and hearing about a major puzzle award recently achieved by the Maestro himself. Leonard looks just like Father Christmas; a large Dutchman with a long, white beard and a merry twinkle. We come away with various treasures. I treat my Ma to a Kauri wood kaleidoscope while my parents buy the children a 3-D globe puzzle. We would like to stay longer but everyone needs tea. Perhaps we might return one day.

As we drive away from the area I notice a derelict building for sale; an iconic, Kiwi shack from a by-gone era sitting above the quiet lane with a pretty paddock alongside. I wonder who owns the land. Will the shack be done up? We haven't seen any 'posh' homes yet. The region isn't affluent. There is something rather appealing about The Kiwi Shack—I have seen several over the past eighteen months. The corrugated iron is usually painted a rusty red colour. My favourite one lies close to the road we take to Auckland. The door is broken and weeds climb in through the single window. I'm not sure if it is still in use—knowing the Kiwis, it is probably a regular shearing shed.

Wednesday 17th January 2007

A.m. Mouse: He is ordered out of the Dry-Dock enclosure. She is left behind, tear-stained and desolate. The Harbour Master understandably refuses to countenance sharing her with another, despite his constant irritation with her female presence and his life choices indicating a bachelor existence. He tells her she can't have her cake and eat it—but isn't that just what **he** does? And where is Lord Swallow? He keeps agreeing to conditions that separate them. Perhaps that is what he wants or is he on his martyrdom trip? She wonders—he cannot tell her. She is left to guess; left to rely on the intuitive truth that haunts her every thought.

The beauty of the Northland is startling and majestic all around them; a welcome distraction as their marriage boundaries are shaken and redefined. She told The Laird yesterday she has little left to give—with her Angel wounded she has nothing to share. He listened. She told him of her need for honesty from now on. "I want you to have time apart from Adrian—distance; before you can judge correctly," he continued. "And then we shall see; make changes if we have to." She knows his tendency to depression. Would he ever handle the truth? Could he ever let her go in peace?

And how is The King? The neighbouring Queen has been taking him with her on their exciting travels—his hand in hers as she walked through the impressive Kauri museum at Matakohe on their way north; famous for the world's largest collection of ancient Kauri Gum and extensive Pioneer Memorabilia. I couldn't believe the width and length of the Kauri panels on display; one was 22.5 metres long! The largest single pieces ever. Have you seen them? Staggering.

I enjoyed the life-sized room sets from the 20th century—the reproduction of the 1900's in the Southern Hemisphere was intriguing. Room after room took us from kitchen to bedroom, as well as a host of tree-felling and logging equipment to view—and a large collection of photographs from pioneering days that was so interesting—the men and women—such hard workers who endlessly forged paths and cut down thousands of the magnificent Kauri trees. The timber industry in the Northland was extensive. I see the face of my beloved in those early woodsmen and Kauri Gum collectors, knowing I am privileged to walk beside a man such as them. He is strong and able, wise and industrious; a fine man from this beautiful land. Yes, you were with me in the museum, My Love. Together we shared information, finding similar interests and inspiration. We enjoyed every detail—eyes meeting—fingers knowing—ideas taking flight like your handcrafted arrows. A real pleasure.

And then to sand-surf in the Hokianga Harbour with the children; an outing especially for them yesterday after breakfast. How the boys enjoyed themselves. Cedric smiled all morning and managed to stand upright as he rode the sandy wave, greeting the ocean on his board to the applause of onlookers. Even the Castle Mistress went hurtling down, bouncing into the sun-sparkled sea. The massive dunes outline the Northern side of the harbour. They are so silent. I stood at the top and imagined the phantom canoe that Hau told us is regularly seen crossing the water.

"Come on—let's give ourselves a rite of passage," I challenged The Laird. "Let's begin a new chapter." He followed my lead reluctantly, not rising to the excitement, although we hurtled to the water at the same time. We played and splashed. I was in full flow. He was slow and unsure.

I want to teach The Laird to let go—to experience joy. I long for him to feel safe; to take the freedom without inviting negativity as convention demands. Our foundation will not crumble. We are held by loving arms. Does he really not feel that assurance? We retired to the hotel for lunch after the sand-surfing, followed by an outing into the rural hills. Now, that is somewhere you would have found interesting. Hau's stepfather and his workshop would have intrigued you. When we returned to the resort Rinky and I enjoyed a 'dolphin' splash in the pool, and to close the momentous day we joined a night walk through the Waipoua Kauri Forest following Maori guides; meeting the two giant trees in the dark; the oldest trees of them all. The Maori sung greeting was awe-inspiring and awakening in the presence of such natural majesty. The boys were open-mouthed in wonder. And the King and his Queen? How were they as they stood before Tane Mahuta'? Well— she would have to be lying beside you to dare tell—X

P.s—Keep waiting—X

Thursday 18th January 2007

P.m. Mouse: Yesterday; Wednesday; a day of traveling and sleeping in the bus, all of us tired after the busy day before. A vanload of children and family enjoying each other's company, despite the scratchy youngsters. We stopped several times for snacks and lunch, introducing my parents to the regular availability of the Kiwi, heated pie; "There are pies in every shop!" My mother remarked.

The scenery continued to keep us spell-bound, although we thought we'd never reach the end of some bush-covered inclines with their wiggly roads. We travelled through steep, rugged terrain and then over soft, rolling farmland with voluptuous curves, reminiscent of home. We have generously been lent the holiday house of an Auckland wine merchant. His family company owns a liquor importing business—the people who entertained us in their Ponsonby wine bar when I took the boys to Auckland before Christmas. We found their family history of Hungarian origin very interesting. The Laird is going to represent them at a Whisky fest in a few months' time. You can imagine how pleased he is about that.

We eventually located their remote farmhouse and stretch of river in the hills behind Kaitaia. Once we had claimed bedrooms in the comfortable home we headed off for an evening stroll through an established walnut grove. A lonely horse greeted us from behind a hedge; {I don't imagine he has many visitors}, and a beautiful backdrop of steep, bush-covered hills in the near distance, regal in the evening sky, put me in mind of a carefully constructed oil painting. I noted the way the light fell to catch the onlooker's eye; a group of ferns at the summit was defined even from where we stood.

As the evening light undressed the landscape, withdrawing its colour, we headed to bed ourselves. I fell asleep to the sound of the shy river running at the end of the garden. I felt your smile waiting to greet me there—

My dreams are full of the night excursion to meet the 'Lords of the Kauri Forest' -in particular the enormous tree, Tane Mahuta. The reverent footfall and quiet explanation of our Maori guides who pointed out the insects and creatures of the night fill my imagination like rich ingredients in a regional soup. "Listen—hear that haunting call? That's our native owl; the Ruru, commonly known as the More Pork. It's called that because of the sound it makes—*more-pork*". Our party of ten walked the forest boardwalks in single file. We noticed every wing flap and insect call in the gathering dusk; the ghostly brush of ruffled foliage surprising us in the quiet. The native Weta bug was found under a bank of tree roots and we stopped at the sound of any undergrowth rustle. "Sometimes we are very lucky and find the nocturnal Kiwi bird, although they are rare," our guides informed us. "There are five kinds of Kiwi bird in fact; three very similar; the Brown Kiwi, the Little Spotted Kiwi and the Great Spotted Kiwi. They are New Zealand's only indigenous, flightless bird apart from the giant Moa, which was hunted into extinction between the 1500's/1700's. Kiwi feathers played an important part in Maori culture in days gone by. They were woven into Kahukiwi, {Ceremonial cloaks}, and worn by high-ranking Iwi members. Of course, nowadays the Kiwi bird is a protected species and every effort is made to protect them and their habitat."

"The Kiwi birds belong to the Apterygiformes-Ratitae family and are only found in New Zealand," the Maori guides continued. "Their feathers are almost hair-like and they have slender bills with nostrils at the end. They feed on insects, worms and grubs, supplementing their diet with bees. They mostly live in dense forest, although some make their homes in scrub and native grassland. Surprisingly, the Kiwi can outrun humans and have survived because of their alert nature and sharp, three-toed feet with which they slash and kick their enemies. A female Kiwi can lay up to two eggs in a season, although not at the same time. The egg will often weigh as much as a third of her body weight. The males incubate the eggs. Very few New Zealanders have seen Kiwis in the wild."

Walking deep into The Bush a wide platform eventually brought us to a standstill. The Maori guides began their reverent greeting. The ancient song echoed through the forest and I sensed other's eyes watching—perhaps stewards of these Earthly treasures.

Ko tenei ki a koutou,
Te hae kainga, nga Tane Mahuta— {Greetings to you, Tane Mahuta}.

And then the guides switched on powerful torches. We stood quietly, waiting, looking ahead but seeing a continuation of the boardwalk and dense Bush. "Turn around," we were instructed. The strong light beam bounced us forwards, straight into the face of Tane Mahuta himself! He was behind us— waiting to shock his nighttime guests. We were speechless. The tree we had come to see was so close—and immense. I cannot describe the sensation of standing before this giant.

Tane Mahuta—Lord of the Forest—over two thousand years old and standing fifty-one meters tall. Although not the oldest or widest tree, this giant is considered the biggest because of its massive volume of wood. The enormous tree towered above us. We were but vermin beneath the serenity and huge quiet. Kauri trees are protected these days, only being felled to provide wood for a ceremonial, Maori canoe. In days gone by the younger trees were felled by the hundreds. Known as 'Rickers' they made perfect ship masts.

PIONEERING STEEL

Pioneering Steel—The men who forged these paths through native Bush and ancient hill. Did they know what they did? Did they know what they took with their years of backbreaking toil? Did they realize where they stood; what ground they claimed as theirs? The sacred, virgin landscape; She feels it, knowing its significance. He feels it too. Their breath hardly dares meet that of these Giants-these Lords of the Forest.

Friday 19th January 2007

A.m. Mouse: *Good morning, Lord Swallow. Your Lady Thumbelina sends special love and greetings. I am sitting inside our camper van, a beautiful view of the falls at Hururu in front of me. The sun is shining and I wonder how you are? Where you are? Have you moved yet? I imagine you enjoying a creative time; making yourself a new Leafy Glade. I wonder if I'll ever be allowed to visit you there.*

Yesterday The Laird and The Go-Getter braved the freezing cold river for a playful splash while the rest of us watched and got badly bitten by sand flies. We all have horrid bites today. Would you believe it, we found one of my sister's newly published books under a mattress in the attic bedroom! You can imagine how surprised we were. She must have made it as a writer to achieve the remote N.Z. Northland! She will be amazed. We had an interesting walk yesterday through the grounds at Waitangi; {the site of the famous agreement between the Maori and Pakeha settlers on February 6th 1840; the Treaty of Waitangi. To this day controversy remains over The Treaty. The Pakeha wording didn't echo Maori understanding and agreement. Land entitlement was left unclear and in many opinions, unfair.} We wandered over beautifully manicured lawns; a surprising contrast after the untamed nature of the landscape through which we have recently driven. My Father was definitely more at home in the historic British history of the first Governor's home. Now, that is a pretty house; I particularly liked the red roses in the garden and the old-fashioned courtyard at the back. I would enjoy living in a house like that.

The sense of dominant, European structure was obvious; the National Park attendant, {a Maori woman}, was noncommittal when The Laird tried to draw her into political debate. Her raised eyebrows were enough. The Whare, {pronounced 'fare'; a Maori meetinghouse}, is located centrally, although in a shady corner of the extensive lawns. We removed shoes and entered quietly. The silence spoke of powerful tribal holding and a more real spirituality than a Pakeha's less-connected religion.

I missed your hand in mine as we walked back to the car-park along wooded paths. The cicadas were loud as they played their ode to the sun. We return home tomorrow evening. The Laird then leaves for Christchurch for a week of leadership seminars. My Friend—can you let me know if you are still happy to receive messages? I would like to see you next week—introduce you to my parents. I will see if I can get permission. After all, you are what my life has been about these past 18 months. If you are still with me can you send another blank message? It will be totally anonymous if sent from your landline; if that still exists? Lots of love. M—X

The final afternoon of our holiday sees us visiting pretty Russell across the water from Paihia in the Bay of Islands; an attractive town with a colonial feel. "I like it here," my father announces. We take the ferry across the still water and step ashore on to golden sand that is the gritty sort. The little town of Russell has an interesting history since Captain Cook stepped ashore here in 1769. It was the first, permanent European settlement in New Zealand. Originally known as Kororareka, south sea whalers from the early 1800's found the small port a useful provisioning stop. I like the story of the town's first name; legend tells of a wounded Maori chief asking for nourishing penguin to eat. On tasting the broth he exclaimed: "Ka reka to korora;" {how sweet is the penguin}.

The port continued to expand until the country's first capital, Okiato, moved to Auckland. Kororareka and the Bay of Islands began to decline and loose its trading prowess as a result. Two powerful Maori chiefs, Hone Heke and Kawiti, ransacked the town and exacerbated the decline. After that the port was renamed Russell and since the early 1900's has been considered a quiet, historic town.

The leafy, village atmosphere of Russell is delightful. Cafes and historic houses sit quietly above the beach, exuding an air of gentle permanence. We stroll happily under the Pohutukawas and eat ice cream in the shade of a giant fig tree. An older gentleman chats to us; he is staying at The Duke of Marlborough Hotel beside the water. The tree is very old and we admire the huge canopy that keeps off the sun. The Laird and the children disappear to find the historic homestead of the country's first Catholic Mission, established by Bishop Pompallier in 1842. As we watch the ferry returning to the pier I find myself thinking about our beautiful Boat and wondering if a return home will find The Celestial Sea a thing of the past.

Chapter 4 Past?

Saturday 20ᵗʰ January 2007

We are home at last; a tired family after the long drive. Unfortunately we discovered a flat battery when we collected our vehicle from an Auckland suburb. We were held up for a couple of hours while we located a replacement after Saturday trading hours. My parents treated us to a lunchtime morsel from an Italian shop in Ponsonby—and then we motored the three-hour trip home. Ma and Pa have been so generous. The children have enjoyed various extra activities this week. Rinky had an hour's ride near Dargaville while the boys tried their hand at cross-country go-carting, as well as a host of delicious meals and excursions enjoyed by us all. We have certainly been treated. We reached Matamata by teatime and found a good pie shop that hadn't sold out; "try the ones with steak and cheese," the children encouraged their grandparents. "What, more pies?" They exclaimed. "The Kiwi's seem very keen on them; pies, pies, pies—at every stop along the way!"

The menagerie is delighted to have us home. "The Bog-Brush escaped from the kennel every day," our neighbour informed us. "We just kept her at home. She enjoyed the other dogs and was no trouble. She didn't like being alone on The Mountain." Monty hadn't been seen all week but appeared at dusk.

The Laird turns his mind to Christchurch. He is unhappy about leaving us for a whole week on another College excursion. C'est la vie; it was ever thus.

Sunday 21ˢᵗ January 2007

"How would you feel if *I* went off with someone else?" My perplexed husband asks as we drive to College this morning. The Christchurch trip is made up of twenty students and three staff members. They are travelling to Rotorua airport by coach and then flying to the South Island at midday. "I'll try to imagine that one," I answer. Of course the idea is unpalatable. "Do you want an open marriage, and if so what would that mean for me?" He asks again. Questions, questions.

I sometimes wish my beautiful adventure had taken place in my mind and on the screen; not in reality. The complications are increasing rather than decreasing. I hate upsetting my husband to this extent, yet in the same breath I can't ignore the reality of the bond I share with Adrian. Will I ever be allowed my pleasure and joy? No, not at the expense of others; only if everyone is in agreement. I suppose I will have to shelve it—can't bear it—well, I suppose I can but I am left sad and empty instead of fully able to dance in the light.

Midday, Mouse: She has said goodbye to her husband for a whole week. He realizes that changes are afoot, but in what way? Still unclear—and alone; she heads for the Everglades to ponder awhile.

I hope Adrian might be brave and join me at our special place beside the Raupo Reeds, especially as The Laird is away. But he doesn't respond. He probably isn't even at home. I find it so hard to have lost contact. Others have rendered our beautiful union dangerous and sad. Drat them all.

Monday 22ⁿᵈ January 2007

It is a day of errands; the supermarket, the recycling and the library. Our library fines are exorbitantly high. My thrifty parents are very shocked. The Mistress' head can't have been straight these past few weeks. Cedric undertakes an afternoon's work for a local animal centre and the rest of us pass the day in a domestic manner. The summer weather is glorious and our town trip is made special by the flowering Jacqeranda trees lining the main drag in town. Their delicate, dark green leaves and striking, purple flowers always make me blink and wonder if I am seeing straight.

P.m. Mouse: Dearest Friend, I am free if you would like me to call. Just send a blank text. Perhaps you think we shouldn't chat? If I don't hear I shall stop bothering you—X

I hear nothing. It is unlike Lord Swallow to be so distant.

P.m. Mouse {Unsent}: Dear Friend—how strange to have flicked the 'off button' in our woven togetherness. I feel dead inside; normal, flat. What is the meaning behind recent events? Why this beautiful journey and then? And what do you make of it all? I imagine you have sworn to keep your promise; you are a man of your word—an honourable person. No contact or togetherness unless we can be open, as we have agreed time and time again. No more hiding.

Perhaps you think I am playing games with you. I am trying; in all honesty I am trying to find a way. I know you don't respond because I have yet to establish my standing with The Laird. You don't tell me how you feel because you don't wish to be party to any marriage breakup. "Wait; please wait," you tell me. That final message makes me hopeful. Perhaps you are serious about our relationship. Perhaps it does mean as much to you as it does to me. But there again, maybe you have been humouring me, and yourself, all along. Are you afraid of The Laird and his threats? Maybe you

118

want to end 'Us'; to walk away.

My obvious need to know your thinking seems to fall on closed ears. Is this because you cannot risk contact? Job—Male Honour—Morals—Danger. Or is it because you like the unanswered question; the knowledge that I am left hanging in mid-air? Do you see this as a test? Can I be true, even in the face of uncertainty? But, there again, I suppose you are very busy with your move. Your single-minded focus is occupied elsewhere. The question of 'Us' is on the back burner.

Hmm—I really don't know. The strongest part of me says; "continue trusting; he is beside you still." Another, smaller part of me asks; "If he were beside you still, surely he would send some signal; some courage snippet?"

P.m. Mouse {Unsent}: *Goodnight, My Love. I am here, resting my head upon your chest, knowing we are one despite the quandary, the judgment and others' condemnation. We know this connection goes way beyond the earthly boundaries of convention. Perhaps we ARE meant to resist each other. Perhaps this is our 'Test'—so strong is the pull to be one. Who knows? I am almost past trying to figure it out. Anyway, you are certainly stronger than I in self-denial. What will be, will be. Over to you, guiding Angels—X*

Tuesday 23rd January 2007

A.m. Mouse {Unsent}: *Tuesday—normality takes the upper hand. Say goodbye to intense presence. Shopping bags and car trips; the window overlooking personal joy and excitement closed—locked once again. Resign to never-ending workload. Find the sun in mundane toil. Shelve the truth.*

Today we picnic at Pillans beach. It is a perfect afternoon. We paddle in the waves and make sandcastles. For some reason our children are never too keen on the beach; disgruntled youngsters once again although they get stuck in after fifteen minutes. Experienced surfers tackle the waves and we watch a family of ten arrive and establish themselves with professional organization. Beach trips are integral to Kiwi, summer life. We couldn't even persuade The Scowler to get in the car. I think he's had enough family outings for a while.

Wednesday 24th January 2007

A.m. Mouse {Unsent}: *Should I text Lord Swallow or should I leave him be? I know he'll be hoping for my message—well, I think he'll be hoping. I could be wrong. He hasn't sent a blank text so I suppose I should stick to my word and not keep in touch. He asks that I give my marriage a second chance; to honour The Laird's request for 'no contact'. I have my pride to consider too. I shouldn't push for his attention. If he really wants me he'll let me know. His eagerness to assume harsh sentence and respect my married* *state makes his choice clear—I think. I could be wrong.*

The day begins. Established order and calm, flat spirit, although a rooster dispatch this morning should be amusing.

The rooster troop have NOT stayed put in the Twealm Realm. There is nothing for it but to either chop off their heads or take them to Kopiro Falls. We decide on the latter. With The Laird absent I am certainly not happy to be the murdering henchman, although none of us is squeamish and would happily prepare the culled birds. The Laird has dealt with a couple before—there wasn't much meat on them really, although they *were* tasty in the slow-cook-pot. I think a dawn trip to Kopiro Falls will suit us better this time. There are **7** of the noisy fellows to catch and I envisage an interesting escapade with my parents as our roosters join others at the national park—a taste of modern, Kiwi pioneering life; the soft kind. There is plenty of the hard sort out there.

The only way to catch your surplus roosters on a ten-acre, mountain hideaway covered in gorse is to creep up on them in the dark. Yes, you are tired and bash your head on the cabin's foundations as you clamber over bikes and dusty tools; the only option. "Watch out for the nest of eggs; Boadicea is broody—and the Go-Getter's recent spray paint job. No, Bog-Brush, you can't join in the hunt, much as you would love the opportunity. Ah; there they are." The sensible head-torch picked out the flock last night, perched at the back of the under-house space.

I bless my supple frame at times like this. "Got you" the first rooster was clutched under my arm while I backed out carefully. Drat, I banged my head. Adrian's stack of wood was suspended directly above my path. My mother was waiting with the large dog cage inside The Laird's car last night. Once they were all contained I drove the old Ute halfway down the drive, out of earshot. The dawn chorus must have been impressive inside the vehicle but we certainly didn't want to know about it. And what peace this morning! We weren't woken at four a.m—a pleasant change. I slept right through until **7** a.m, which is late for me. A farming life calls for harsh decision-making and action; even hobby farming.

We set off early, my dusk rooster raid contained down the drive and waiting for dispatch. We get the giggles as we enter the park, looking over shoulders in case rooster dumping is illegal. There aren't any notices to the contrary. Hmm-"quick, before anyone comes, can you take this side of the cage?" I ask my father. Nobody appears and the surprised fellows strut out of their overnight prison to a life of sexless foraging and male company. Feeling like a bunch of gangsters we head home for a cooked breakfast. My law-abiding father assumes a perplexed expression all the way home-"so unlike the life of our own dear Queen!"

Thursday 25th January 2007

It is The Go-Getter's eleventh birthday; a hot, humid day—siesta weather. The celebrating fellow decides on a quiet, family day. "Let's do something exciting with Daddy when he comes home." A trip to the toyshop for Lego is high on the list of priorities. We start the day with a swim in my favourite outdoor pool at Monument Park. The temperature is perfect; how I adore that welcome cool where you slide under the liquid envelope and linger under water, watching the reflection of the sun through the ripples.

My parents sit comfortably in the sunshine while I get some exercise and the children splash about together. Cedric refuses to join in and stays in the car. I suppose we should be grateful he got out of bed early to join the family outing.

"Shall we stop at the German deli before we visit the toyshop?" I suggest. The delicious aroma of German sausages and garlic pate lures us inside the delicatessen. This is the only place in town to sell a decent sausage and the modern shop located in the same shopping complex as the toy emporium is a 'must'. All the employees are German. They look charming in their red gingham aprons. The walls are decorated with enticing pictures of the Rhine valley. As well as the wide selection of meats the wooden dressers display German chocolates and spiced biscuits. I come here every fortnight and often notice German shoppers amongst those waiting to be served.

"And now for fish and chips on the wharf—who's up for that?" Cedric looks brighter; he enjoyed helping his little brother choose the latest Lego Star Wars Fighter. Any mention of food always helps. We drive to the centre of town and park outside the fresh fish market. We like eating here; they serve the best fish and chips in town. Tables spill out, onto the wharf from a covered deck. There are no frills—straight up, Kiwi fisherman and their families running a thriving fast food outlet and fish shop. Their fishing boats bob alongside. I notice the covered deck has a fabric partition that unhooks to allow the fishermen direct access into the shop. The sunshine is glorious and we watch a group of local boys in togs, {swimwear}, daring each other to leap off the wharf into the water below. My father takes a wander with his camera. Several boats are moored alongside and the circling seagulls wait for any leftovers.

"Number 97", a loud voice calls from inside. "That's us," I say, jumping up to collect our lunch. The friendly Maori lady passes me a tray fit for a king. "Blue Gill today, freshly caught this morning," she says. I smile and give my appreciative thanks as I head back to our outside table. All the fish market workers are Maori; they wear purple cotton overalls with caps to match. They have white gumboots on their feet. I like the way the walls are hung with framed pictures of fishing vessels braving the high seas. A stack of Green Lipped Mussels in the near corner of the shop is mechanically watered from above. I watch the water trickling over their jewel-coloured edges, highlighting the surprising marine emeralds.

The Book is important,
It keeps our love alive, lending rightful standing
And permanence when we are denied communion.
My fingers on the keyboard go part way to ease the ache for my fingers touching yours.
The use of word; the replaying of our story brings back the vitality and imaginary worlds we enjoy.
The Alchemy we spoke of recently; I know The Book is its vessel, steadily continuing to surprise and delight.
Come join me in this journey; together we give solid form to its conception.
The living presence of sacred joy is to be shared.

P.m. Mouse {Unsent}: *Thursday and where is he? My beautiful Lord Swallow. I sense he is away; away on a trip somewhere. What is he seeing? What does he hear? What are his thoughts? Does he still write them down? I dare not go near The Marina. I heard talk of padlocked gates being installed. I will not leave our Boat. I shall keep watch from afar. The Celestial Sea is whole but so sad. She is resigned to her shrouded state. Will she ever sail again? Why was she ever launched? For what purpose her fine lines and impressive Angel sails? Her proud hull and knife-edge keel are wasted in the dry-dock. Her sailing ability is a joy to behold, let alone experience.*

I am trying to view the situation from a distance. Can I see the full extent of the damage? The Harbour Master has insisted we keep apart; the stone hurling his final say. Did he wound you badly, Lord Swallow? You have been so courageous but your livelihood has been threatened, and more importantly, your standing as an honourable man. Of course you are keeping clear. Your Lady comes with a danger warning; a large sign about her neck.

And so, I view our lovely vessel from afar; bound but alive. I wait. Little Arthur and I will wait together. Patiently wait; for what? For decisions on my standing with The Laird? "Wait, please wait," you told me.

P.m. Mouse: —X—

Friday 26th January 2007

A.m. Mouse {Unsent}: *Grey uncertainty covers The Mountain this Friday morning. Hints of blue sky and impending heat tease us across the valley basin. Normal routine emerges. Deskwork continues—floors cleaned— piggy barging about the place; Monty recovering from his undignified operation, {we need to stop him roaming if possible. Sometimes he is gone for several days}. We mend the dog kennel. The car is fixed and registered and my wonderful mother tackles the mending pile. The Go-Getter's birthday cake is enjoyed; his birthday over for another year. Have a good day, My Friend-X*

My parents encourage me to tidy up the loose, domestic ends. Inspiration has moved on, vanished over the hill with the man I know in my heart of hearts I am profoundly, one hundred percent in love with—no question. And he with me? I am ninety-five percent sure he feels the same. For obvious reasons he will not tell me, so I cannot be certain. My marriage is based upon immature love with a strong element of familiar care and support. We have adopted a mother/son relationship, true in its own way of course; upheld by family and cultural framework. The routine of school timetable, childcare and social events have cemented our relationship. We have never been that comfortable on our own, without the crowd. I can honestly say we have never achieved real harmony together; there has always been a lack of vitality. Of course we love each other; years of dogged sticking together and hard graft have forged a strong bond. And the children—the most important factor—we adore our darling trio, although they test us sorely and must pick up on the unspoken dull tone between their parents. When we are alone as a couple or immediate family I cannot sense any joy in my husband. His depressed person is oppressive. He is only happy when he bounces off others. But we don't live with others all the time, and 'others' do not sustain a marriage.

The sad truth is that we dance to a different tune. We are out of step with each other, physically and spiritually. I cannot even move in time with The Laird on the dance floor. Add the components of my health issues after Cedric was born, constant, financial struggle, hefty working timetables and The Laird's depression and subconscious dislike of women, and bang—a disaster waiting to happen. My husband has always turned to heavy commitments and interaction with lots of different people. I have always filled my life with learning and initiative that goes some way to fill the gap felt in my marriage. Have we both been avoiding the deep-seated issues? Have we filled our lives to replace a lack of depth between us? Is this why unease and dissatisfaction have set in?

And then we make the rash decision to abandon our support structures for a 'better life'—as far away as possible from everything that might keep us safe; the Southern Hemisphere for goodness sake! Little do we realize it is our marriage from which we run. Well, *I* know something has to change. My idealistic tendency hoped for an easier answer and I certainly never imagined it would come under the guise of a magnificent Boat with Lord Swallow at the helm. Would we make the same decision again, knowing the true state of our marriage? Probably not, although I wouldn't turn the clock back for all the tea in China.

Of course, our move has only compounded the issues rather than rectifying them. Our acquisition of land and crippling mortgage does nothing to ease the situation. We are stuck without an income to improve The Mountain ten acres. The Laird's short temper increases. For the first time in our married life we are property owners with every bill to pay. There is no boarding school picking up the telephone or heating tab. We are tired and overworked, filling our lives with uncontrollable livestock and over-sociable diaries. We try to replace our known support structures but find our roots are too shallow here, on the other side of the world. We have been found out—caught in the spotlight. Maybe if we sell our U.K property that might ease the looming problems. "You have to go out to work," The Laird tells me. "You have had long enough sitting around doing nothing."

I can't see any clarity over our situation. Maybe we have to travel the long road and learn our lessons the hard way. I cannot sense any joy looming on any horizon. The Laird drowns his problems in whisky. And then Adrian appears, offering the joy I have dreamt about for so many years. The unattainable is suddenly handed to me on a simple platter. I honestly thought I would have to wait for paradise to experience this delight and happiness. What to do? There is no way I am turning this golden gift away. But how do I rejoice in it and keep the established order?

The Laird is coming home today. I take the family to meet him at Rotorua airport. He is in good form; buoyed up by a successful trip. He introduces us to an older Maori lady whose grandson has been with the school party. "Marama is an influential Maori elder; we are privileged to have her input at College," he explains. Her twinkly dark eyes meet mine as we shake hands. I introduce her to my parents, telling her we are off for a family visit to the geothermal, Maori Heritage site and traditional carving school in the town.

We have visited the centre several times before. The bubbling mud pools and impressive geysers are so exciting. The centre is beautifully laid out with enticing tracks and board-walks between the sulphur-stained rocks and steaming outcrops. Inside a specially constructed cave Kiwi birds forage behind glass in the dark. I hope the lights are turned on for their daytime sleep every night. A Maori Marae, {meeting house in a fenced, grassed courtyard}, in the middle of the centre hosts an impressive cultural show with singing, poi swirling and of course the Haka dance with tribal tira, {sticks}.

There is so much to see and learn—the presence of traditional carving with its rich story telling is always fascinating. A walkway around the workroom allows the visitor close inspection of the beautiful pieces. Flax weaving is also demonstrated; the rolled flax makes the ceremonial, piupiu skirt and is a complex art to master. And the smell—my goodness—flatulence hasn't anything on the powerful pong of sulphur throughout the whole of Rotorua! After a while you stop noticing the aroma and the children get bored of blaming each other for over indulging at lunch, but it certainly knocks you out at first!

As we take in every detail and share information I realize what a privileged position we are in. As a family we experience the living presence of Maori culture every day in our normal lives; not just at this cultural, living workshop, intriguing as it is. I come away with a brochure from the site:

124

New Zealand Maori Arts and Crafts Institute—Created in 1963 by an Act of Parliament to protect and teach authentic Maori arts and crafts.

Rising from the geothermal valley above mud pools and steam vents and originally a pallisaded fortress, this area protected the people and its culture from warring tribes. Today our centre stands majestic as a symbol of protection for our arts, crafts and culture; upholding the values of Maori—past, present and future.

Imagine standing on the Earth's thinnest crust. It is raw and powerful. See boiling mud leaping and playing, hear steam hissing as it escapes the ground around you, feel warm water raining down as the geyser explodes up to thirty metres high, right in front of you. Smell the sulphur, the boiling mud and steaming rocks. To really experience the valley, take off your shoes and feel the warm ground. You may even feel the Earth's vibration beneath your feet.

For centuries, Maori learned to weave baskets, clothing and mats. Our history was carved into meetinghouses, canoes, weapons and jewelry. Carving and weaving were like breathing for us; part of our everyday lives, but not in this modern world. The loss of these skills would be a tragedy and we are making sure that won't happen. Students of the institute will share with you the stories of their carvings, their weaving and their ancestors. You'll see fine examples of their work, and the work of other carvers, which you can buy and take home with you.

Our culture is about 'manaakitanga'—welcoming and caring for the visitor. When you visit us you will experience true hospitality. You'll arrive as a stranger and leave as our friend. Tours depart regularly throughout the day. Hear the legends and stories that have shaped our rich and colourful history. See for yourself how the vegetation has adapted to survive in this mysterious landscape. Marvel at how Maori lived in this environment—cooking and bathing in natural, boiling water, growing food, making medicines and carving and weaving from the abundant, natural resources. Visit our living 'Pa' village and be amazed by our intricately carved designs in our fully carved meetinghouse.

"Carving and weaving our history before your very eyes. Experience our centre with all of your senses—sight, sound, smell and touch."

When we reach home The Laird and I walk the dog and sit on the far bank, away from the house. We need to discuss our situation. The Bog-Brush hares about with her enormous speed. No wonder we all find her exhausting. What should we do with the property? Should we sell up and move on? Every conversation returns to the same question. "But will you still be my wife? I need a decision." The Laird is insistent. "I can't say," I reply. "Without being in touch with Adrian I have no idea about anything." My lack of resolve makes him irritable and cross. I do try to be caring and clear but all I feel is empty. I am incomplete. Any remaining love for my husband is lifeless.

P.m. Mouse: —X-

Sunday 28th January 2007

A.m. Mouse {Unsent}: My Friend—are you there? Can I speak to you by text? I need you. X

Midday, Mouse {Unsent}: This week's Sunday message-'be true unto yourself. Faith hope and love are the most important virtues, and of these, love is the greatest'. The theme of today's mass is: 'Recognize each other's talents.'

My Friend, you drove past us this morning and you waved. How lovely to see you; if only fleetingly. I sent you a quick X by text as you drove on your way. We are still in a state of waiting, and yes, I sensed you beside me in church, a little behind but still there. I love you. X

Monday 29th January 2007

A.m. Mouse {Unsent}: Monday morning and I have allowed The Laird to hold me as a wife should. I have let myself fall back into the normal routines and patterns of life. The child in the Laird demands it so. His negative energy, especially after the whisky drinking, is too damaging for us all. I cannot let it fester. I am plastering over the cracks, I know. We need to reach an even keel. I have to diffuse some of his fear. I will let things rest a while, although I will maintain my stand of no decision-making without speaking to Lord Swallow. I held The Laird close—he released his male tension—and afterwards he turned to me and said; "I think I'll have some toast now. Please send one of the children upstairs with it. Thank-you. And now I need a snooze."

A happy Laird—normality reclaimed. He doesn't ask me how I am or how I really feel. He is probably afraid of the answer he would receive. There are more questions regarding our future but he is matter of fact about the issue. I sigh, there is no other way. If I want to see Adrian it will have to be underground—hidden, and we have rejected that scenario. Hmm, My Friend, I really need to speak with you. Why are you not there for me?

Tuesday 30th January 2007

My mother and I visit our favourite charity shops this morning—always a popular pastime. Ma is an expert patchwork quilter. She and a team of friends run a sewing group in Hampshire. "Look what I've found," she calls me over to the bulging pile of knitting patterns filling a bottom shelf. "An old patchwork quilt pattern book, published in 1968." We buy the booklet, and some clothes. We chat and laugh together, enjoying the abundant presence of old-fashioned sewing and knitting craft. I have noticed that many Kiwis possess practical skills, even the younger generation.

After choosing a 'seconds cheesecake' in another shop, {the base is slightly squashed}, we chat to an Israeli kitchen builder whose workroom lies behind the industrial kitchen. "There are a lot of wealthy people in the town," he tells us. "I'm always busy—yes, you'd easily find interior decorating work. Can I give you my card?" I have wondered about returning to the decorating world. I can't say that I am overly keen on the notion. Been there, done that. And most of the people I know are certainly not wealthy; we find many struggle to keep their heads above water, let alone spend on such luxuries as interior design. All I really want is to curl up with Adrian and write—and ponder—and smile.

It is good to spend time with my Ma. We chat about marriage; how easy it is to get stuck in a rut. "Pa is quite happy to sit about without instigating any change, expecting everything to be laid on," she admits. I don't say; "but he isn't consistently short-tempered; he doesn't swing from ego-boosting exuberance to lifeless depression affecting the entire household." I do mention the difficult atmosphere at home with The Laird; the negative vibe. She is understanding and expresses concern over Cedric's constant black moods. "Is he depressed?" Pa asked last night. "You must be careful—the younger two will begin to copy his behaviour."

I speak honestly with Ma, admitting that the atmosphere is improved when The Laird is away. And then I speak about my friendship with Adrian. I keep the content light. She doesn't offer any judgment, apart from questioning the children's interpretation of my friendship with another man, adding—"the preservation of marriage is the most important factor." I think she understands the situation. I really need her support and friendship right now. Thank-you Angels for organizing my parents' arrival to coincide with Lord Swallow's banishment. As always, your timing is impeccable. How I wish I could introduce them to Adrian; it is really important they meet him. I will continue to look for opportunities before they leave.

Wednesday 31st January 2007

This morning I lie in bed for an hour, feeling my Lover spiritually close. I know he is with me. My eyes focus on the macracapa beams in the sloping ceiling.

MACRAPAPA BEAMS

My eyes are fixed upon them; strong and solid above my head,
Light reflecting off their honey warmth.
I am with him; my hand resting upon his Greenstone,

127

Connected in time and space by a moment shot through with
Fragments; fragments of whisper truth; of love, of us;
Like splinters in the beams, they form a living presence.

A.m. Mouse: *Dearest Friend—are you around? I am taking the family to Tui Park after 1p.m; mud flats and crab watching. 4 children, including a couple of friends. I have various items of yours from under the house. I could deliver them, or leave them somewhere for you to collect if you would rather not meet; just let me know. M-X*

I receive no reply; nothing whatsoever. Oh my Love; what are you thinking?

The children take boogie boards right out into the bay at Tui Park. The water is shallow and safe. I wade out to join the fun; the Bog-Brush on a long rope. My father paces up and down the beach, muttering to himself and happier when we return to the shore. As he ages I notice his anxieties about our safety increase. My mother produces a picnic under the shade of the trees. "What is Pa muttering?" I ask. "I never know," she replies; "poetry or something. His muttering has always been a mystery."

P.m. Mouse {Unsent}: *I watched for you, My Friend—I waited and I watched in case you came my way. I miss you. The atmosphere between The Laird and his Lady is stilted this evening. He steers the conversation towards the meaning behind faithfulness. "What do you understand by that? What is it that you really want? Not a conventional family life it appears." "I am a reluctant Angel," I reply. He takes himself off to sleep in the top cottage, saying; "you won't talk to me."*

I sigh. I *have* been talking to him—for months. I know it is my language and intuitive sense that he doesn't understand. How can I make something indefinable fall into any sort of clarity? Am I meant to make a black and white choice and stick by it? Probably, although that would go against the grain of whom I am.

Thursday 1st February 2007

A.m. Mistress to the Laird: *My Darling—I know we need to talk. Yes, we are different from other families because of our vocational gifts; especially yours. We face an interesting crossroads where discussion needs to take place. I intuitively sense the future picture and my friendship with Adrian is part of the make-up; in what way I am unsure. I am sorry to put you through sadness and heartache. I know that what we have to learn lies beyond initial, natural emotion. I know that all our future plans depend upon the decisions we make now.*

However, I cannot be clear myself without speaking to Adrian. I know he will not respond unless he hears from you first; to receive your permission. He has given his word of 'no contact' and will stick by that. My relationship with Adrian has come about for a purpose. I cannot fathom the reality without being in touch with him. Please know that our marriage will always be with me, but perhaps it needs to change form to allow us to grow as individuals. X

The Laird lectures me for a long time today. I am the errant pupil and unemotional handling is the only way forwards; in his book. My dear Laird; he responds in the best way he can. And I bless him for his efforts. He asks me about my choices; my idea of marriage. "I could let you go off with another, to be coupled elsewhere," I admit. He is shocked by my statement. He continues to call for an extended separation between Adrian and myself; "to test if being *in love* leads to *loving*," he says. "Then you may go with my blessing."

I speak of the need for deep levels of intimacy to sustain love. He listens without interrupting. "I'm not sure our recipe has the right ingredients for that," I suggest. "So you would *really* be okay if I went off with someone else?" He asks. "Yes," I say, taking a big gulp. Of course the idea is peculiar but it doesn't fill me with horror. "If it brought you deep joy I would be okay."

"Well," he replies; "that's a surprise!"

P.m. Mouse {Unsent}: *Thursday evening and we have been together, My Love—moving as one in the Ocean swell; our Dance in time with the ever-moving waters. We are an integral part of its essence. When I hold your Greenstone you are with me. I can feel your breath upon my brow. I know your eyes demanding my connected attention; here and now—present—no excuses. Yes, we are approaching The Garden Gate, but slowly; seriously; no rushing ahead before we are grounded together—you have taught me so well.*

"I can see you better when you are serious," you tell me. "Your face is really a long face, not a round one." I think I know what you mean by that. My constant smile betrays my intense, serious nature; my face rounded instead of long; thoughtful. And you have found it—exposed it in me as of course you would. That is the truth of our love, just as I expose the waiting King. We challenge each other deeply on every level. We excite each other profoundly on every level. We delight in each other's presence with real joy on every level. We are one hundred percent synchronized in our physical longing and spiritual connection. The only place we are less united is in my past; my English life—and in your Kiwi roots. Sleep well, My Prince.

I have noticed a slight unease in Adrian when I chat about my past. He often stops me, telling me straight up that he isn't interested in connections or trivial information about people and places he doesn't know. This is the Kiwi way—no polite niceties. He can be intolerant and short with me if I waffle on. Would that become an issue over time? I remember his discomfort when I instigated a classical carol singing performance at a Mid-Winter feast last year. He didn't know I could sing in that way—a way that we don't share. I remember feeling surprised at his partial dismissal of the event. It wasn't his initiation and he was less interested in being involved. He likes to be in charge; to be the one introducing new ideas. I recognize myself in the trait. Are we too alike? What might Adrian make of my English family and friends? Would it have to be a Kiwi existence for us? Would our relationship flounder in the everyday world?

I wonder how we would tackle these questions. The thought excites rather than worries me. I love Adrian's humility; his desire to self-question and remedy issues. I think we would rise to the opportunity. An interesting time lies ahead if things progress in the way I instinctively sense they might.

I cut out an article in a magazine today that took me back fourteen years; highlighting the vitality and sensual spark I knew was missing in our marriage, even then. One spring evening The Laird and I happened to watch the film 'Dirty Dancing'. I was transfixed by the magic; the sensual grace and chemistry of the young lovers; by their rhythmic dance and sheer attention to the moments they found themselves enjoying. I remember jumping off the sofa in great excitement, dragging The Laird to his feet and trying to rouse him to dance with me like that—to move together as one. My attempts fell on disinterest and unsynchronized feet. I remember feeling rather stupid and heading to bed in the usual fashion. "I'll just stay put and watch the rugby; be up in half an hour," he said.

The film article interests me-"**Dirty Dancing taught me how to do a love scene,"** {Patrick Swayze writes.} **"It was about connecting on a soul level. We lived it and it shows; one of those times where the camera accidentally caught something magical."** The article tells how nobody thought the film would be a hit, until they realized just how much they had, in fact, lived into the beautiful sensuality and spiritual physicality. I fold the article away carefully. I always wondered why the film made me jump out of my seat. Now I know. Fourteen years later, a massive adventure under my belt, and I know the secret. I have moved like that with a partner—oh yes—across oceans and magical worlds—I have moved like that.

Friday 2nd February 2007

"No, I won't speak with Adrian. I won't give you permission to communicate." The Laird will not discuss the matter further. "You will be seeing him at school anyway. I won't be able to stop you then." I try to reason with my husband, explaining how things are:

"You don't understand—Adrian won't speak with me, even if I see him at school. It's really important to him that you give your blessing to any meeting. He has his career to consider, and moral integrity, quite apart from honouring his agreement with you. No, he won't speak with me."

I will have to get used to no communication. "Just forget it," I state. "It's too complicated."

130

Cedric the Scowler is in very bad form today. Why is he always so bad-tempered? My parents are concerned he has psychological problems. He has been this way for a long time. Have the difficulties increased over the holidays? Possibly. The Laird and I try to draw him into conversation. He admits to missing home, although he was bad tempered there too. He doesn't like his brother and sister and he can't communicate easily with us, he complains. A normal teenager? We hope so.

P.m. Mouse {Unsent}: Where are you, My Friend? Everything's pretty grim here. Wish you were beside me. I'm fed up with constant negativity. I am empty without our creativity and happiness. M-X

Saturday 3rd February 2007

The Laird continues to be on edge. As a family we drive to the Historic Village, located in a little-frequented suburb. I can't think why the council chose a location without a surrounding community—the lovely collection of colonial buildings are dead and empty. A handful of craft shops are in residence and a market is here today, but nobody is about. What a shame.

We take a wander over the attractive gardens, stopping inside the tiny church. I like the traditional church buildings here—they are similar to those in America with their white, clapboard facing and neat bell towers. The windows and doors are often painted a rusty red; like the corrugated, Kiwi Sheds and traditional Whares. I have noticed several on our travels around the country. They are often positioned beside Maori Maraes. I stop beside the old school house, my active imagination taking me back to those pioneering days. The sunshine is lovely today.

After an hour of sight-seeing we visit Bernard and Felicia's house, taking their two children home for the afternoon to play in the sunshine. We make dolls food and laugh uproariously as we wash the pig; she has a common skin infection and needs to be lathered and showered. Goodness, it's not an easy job bathing a pig!

Bernard and Felicia join us for tea and the afternoon passes in a pleasant stream of sociability and domestic chores. In the evening The Laird admits to the return of his depression—bother—blast—and other rude expressions. I am going to have to abandon myself; brush my needs back into the tunnel. Can't he sort himself out without my single focus attention? I am missing Adrian.

P.m. Mouse: —X—X—X

Mouse {Unsent}: Sleep well, My Lovely Companion. Are you still there with me? How are you this night? I am listening to music and wondering if you are too. What are your thoughts? Do you miss me? I wish I knew. Sleep well. I am here for you. I am unchanged in our unity. Sleep well with The Angels—X. My hand is on your Greenstone—X

Sunday 4th February 2007

A.m. Mouse {Unsent}: It feels like a fresh start as we walk into church today. The new organ looks magnificent. A whole week of installation and now the full choir and organist are voicing their classical polish. The choirmaster is blind; he has the most beautiful singing voice. What are today's revelations? There is a sense of family harmony; so good to have my Ma with us. My father never attends our church. His own, Anglican Church in the Hampshire village is his niche. For several years he has been a Sidesman and likes to ring the church bell on Sunday morning, strolling across the meadow to reach the 15th Century building before the handful of parishioners arrives. He has stayed behind at home with the animals today.

My Darling, I sense you beside me again on the pew this morning and Little Arthur is sitting on my lap. You are holding his hand. Our Copper Bands, {we both wear one}, link our belonging. A quiet contentment spills from our togetherness. There is a mature peace surrounding us all. The Laird and the children are present. I imagine The Laird as happy—he has something new in his life as well—a light shines upon him. The warm sensation fills me right up and overflows from my thinking to the tips of my fingers.

I take your hand, pressing it against mine. Little Arthur plays with your waistcoat buttons. A few days ago Rinky said: "You should have another baby Mummy; a little girl for me to play with." And then in the next breath she added; "he would be very sweet." Recently I have wondered if Little Arthur might be female. Rinky's contradictory remark confirms the ambiguity. Today is the 4th of February. This time last year you left a message on my answer-phone, calling me 'beautiful.' Do you remember? I kept it for ages. Recently I found it had gone. Did The Laird remove it? Or did the telephone company cancel it? I passed you on the road driving to school earlier. I delivered some curtains to Class 1 and hoped I might catch you. It's important that my parents meet you—

A verse from a church hymn:

Ponder nothing earthly minded,
For with blessing in his hand,
Christ our God to Earth descendeth,
Our full homage to demand.

Are we entrusted with a mission? I keep wondering where these events and images are heading. Are they linked with school? Or with The Laird's school ideas? Is the church involved—and who is Little Arthur? The questions stay with me as we leave the building. The Priest shakes our hands at the door, saying: "May 2007 bring your family great fulfillment."

* * * * * * *

132

"Why is The Laird so low?" My mother asks the delicate question as we walk on the drizzly Mountain this afternoon. "Because of my friendship with Adrian," I admit. I am not going to lie. I talk about the lack of harmony within the family; The Laird's increasing mood swings and short temper disturb us all. I speak of the delight in my new friendship with another man. Of course I am advised to keep my distance; that I must preserve my marriage at all costs. "Busy yourself elsewhere; complete your kindergarten qualification; something to take your mind away from Adrian." I listen, hearing the sage advice but knowing I am not ready to move away just yet. Will I feel different in six months' time? Would The Laird be depressed anyway? The summer fun is nearly over. Are my choices the cause of his mood swings, as he would say, or would they happen whether or not I was a faithful wife?

"Is Adrian some sort of Guru for you?" The Laird asked yesterday as I chopped vegetables for supper. "Do you consider him a prophet or something?" I was genuinely surprised by my husband's question. For a while I was stumped for words. "Oh no, nothing like that," I replied. "I suppose you could say he is my Guide; My Golden Guide. Together we access a certain divinity. It isn't each other that we worship." I am thoughtful after that, asking myself; "but if he had asked the same question about Little Arthur I would have replied; 'I don't know, I really don't know. All I can say is that he/she is someone special.'

MY GOLDEN GUIDE

He offers my spirit his care,
He leads me by the heart,
He directs me with his eyes;
"Come into yourself.
Come into me.
Where is your centre?
Not up high but in your earthed presence.
I can join you there."
He brings my Garden Gate inward,
He makes me welcome it, truly.
And he loves me there.

Mouse P.m. {Unsent}: *Goodnight, My Darling. How was your day? I expect it was full of meetings and classroom organization. Children need The School's structure and rhythm now the holidays are ending—mothers and fathers too; all thirsty for the impulse. Term-time discipline is vital after a long summer holiday. My ever-optimistic mind continues to play out unlikely scenarios. I even see The Laird smiling and shaking hands with you in agreement; bringing you home for supper no less! I laid an extra place at our table but it remained empty; I think? Perhaps Little Arthur sat there.*

Sleep well. The Laird is feeling so low and unhappy. For some reason I am stable within his turmoil. I love him in the way I have always loved him. I feel no guilt having given myself to you. I know this is meant to be—that we can't even begin to fight it. May the Good Lord bless and keep us all within him. Amen—X

LITTLE ARTHUR

We have seen him.
We have felt a constant presence in our deeper selves.
First on a beach; in the shape of a shell discarded
Until our loving eye beheld.
And then in a pastel picture, displayed on the bedroom wall;
The embryonic potential waiting in hopeful curves.

We have seen him as a babe in arms, or is he a she?
The quiet, patient eyes will not say;
 Memories of a loved grandfather bring a name.

We have seen him sitting on a church pew,
Little legs swinging joyfully.
Leather boots and green shorts,
Curly hair just like his father,
Eyes to match her own.

He has travelled to meet the family in Auckland,
And been swaddled on his father's chest;
Up steep beach steps and on a fiery steed.

And the red hat beside him, ready for his step outside;
Outside into a needy world.
Yes—we have seen Little Arthur.

Tuesday 6th February 2007, Waitangi Day, a National Holiday
A.m. Mouse {Unsent}: Bright light greeted me this morning. The Laird was away at dawn to welcome in the famous Treaty day with Maori reverence at the top of The Mount in the harbour. His college students were amongst those who crewed the ceremonial waka {canoe} that beached at the foot of the ancient hill. The tribal ritual must have been quite a spectacle; next year we shall all go. Apparently a local politician made a crass speech, which angered many. Supposedly he ended with the statement; "when I die I'd like to be buried on this spot." Someone responded: "If you make any more speeches like that we'll make sure that you are!"

Good morning, My Friend. I wonder what you are up to today. Go well—
X

134

I rise early and walk the dog, marveling at the different trees with their branches reaching for the sky. Each is unique; a single, yet unified world of its own in the morning quiet. A crooked tree at the end of its life catches my attention. The few remaining branches are entirely covered in parasitic creeper. I admire the tree's dignified resignation. The Bog-Brush is all ears and nose, responding like her mistress to the clarity of the day. There are possum trails around every corner. We listen to the Tui birds calling and flitting between the trees. Their white, tufty bibs stand out starkly against their black feathers. This two acre piece of Bush is packed with native trees and plants. I especially like the Punga and Mamacou ferns, integral to the intriguing landscape. They are prominent along our driveway. The tall Mamacou stand alone; beyond the Bush they break the skyline over the gorse-covered Mountain. I stop to pull some weeds from the drive; dandelions; yes, they have them in New Zealand.

My thoughts today? I sense Adrian must think ill of me; of my ability to deceive my husband, even though I am trying to keep things in the light. He is probably right. My skin is itchy all over; not something I am usually bothered by. What does that mean? That I am in denial? That I no longer fit inside my own skin? This is my parents' final day in New Zealand. I persuade Cedric to join us for a family outing to Mallory Falls. We take a picnic and sit on the bank of the reservoir above the Falls. It is a peaceful location; part cultivated, part wild. We watch the paradise ducks feeding in the fields across the park and we walk right around the pretty stretch of water. The ornamental planting is lovely and Ma and Pa are amazed to see so many black swan—they are rare at home. In fact, every swan in Britain belongs to the Queen. Last year The Laird took part in a black swan cull in the harbour. Hundreds of the birds were shot; that was something different for the British sportsman.

The children enjoy paddling about in the kayak today and Cedric zooms down the steep hills on his mountain-board, happy for a change. The Laird joins us from College after lunch. Like Adrian he is busy getting ready for the start of the new term.

I am overtaken by a crashing tiredness and have to retire to bed when we get home. I snooze while the family completes the complex globe puzzle we bought in the Hookianga. A sudden thunderstorm shakes the cabin and I reach for my copious diaries that hold all our recorded text messages. I re-live our lives from the previous months—my goodness—page after page of spiraling passion and mystery captured; throw in the emotional wrangles and various adventures across Aotearoa and the story reads fluently. Our romance is becoming an epic tale. I love Adrian; our connection is so exciting— magical—dramatic; certainly not boring. I have been longing for a change from boring. I suppose my wish has been granted. Love of this quality is a rare and powerful surprise. I cannot deny its truth. As I turn out the bedside light I wonder what tomorrow will bring. Might I see Adrian? Will he say hello? I am sad that I haven't managed to introduce him to my parents; he is what my life has been about for the past year. He is an integral part of me now; my best friend in New Zealand.

Wednesday 7th February 2007 Beginning of the New School Year

The sun shines. The house is full of busy adults, children, lunchboxes, school bags and cars reversing in the drive. The dog shows concern at the sudden activity. My parents' cases are packed. The Laird leaves for College with Cedric after fond goodbyes from grandparents on the deck. I shall take Ma and Pa to the airport at two o'clock this afternoon for their own departure. By eight thirty we are away to school ourselves, driving down the hill in the sparkling sunshine. The visibility is perfect this morning and the views are ever-present. Wild honeysuckle fills the hedgerows and the scent greets us through the open van windows. We are all excited—nervous too for various reasons.

School is sociable and friendly. Compared with the start of our English school year the atmosphere is gentle. With summer at its peak a relaxed attitude puts everyone at ease. Teachers say hello from the open door of the staff room; spilling onto the deck with cups of coffee and easy, Kiwi welcome. The abundant gardens and attractive paths are ordered and ready for the new term. Smiling children and parents greet each other, delighted to be back within the happy embrace of this rural school community. We settle the children in their various rooms—they are pleased to be back amongst friends and proudly show their grandparents around the classrooms. They open desks and greet their personal belongings that have been waiting patiently for the start of term. Although their teachers haven't changed, their rooms are different.

I spy Adrian heading across the playground beside the fence. He looks up and sees us. For a split second we hesitate—and then I make a move towards him. He turns to meet me and I introduce him to my parents; at last.

136

Part Three Outrigger

The new working year begins. The long haul looms ahead without any sign of change. Holidaymakers depart, despite the beautiful summer weather. The air is heavy with sultry haze and endless sun. Faces turn to shield themselves from the strong rays, rather as they might step back from the heat of a winter fireplace. Sailing boats are fewer upon the ocean and the dry-dock makes way for new residents.

The Celestial Sea can no longer view the water. The Harbour Master makes sure she is moved; placed in the back of the yard where her only outlook is of machinery waiting repair and a dozen, rusting oil drums. Some days she even wonders if The Craftsman has lost interest in her welfare. One or two of the dockworkers treat her kindly; they intuitively know something else is going on beneath the now-ripped, plastic cover. One of the men always says hello when he walks past, winking at her in a friendly manner. One day she overhears him say to a workmate; "I don't know why, but I think that pommy boat's lonely. You'll think me crazy but I'm going to ask The Boss if we can put the fishing vessel next to her; the one that's just come in. What d'ya reckon?"

Her new neighbour certainly raises the interest levels. For several days The Celestial Sea is captivated by the vessel's stories of recent travels; a trip along the Northland coast is full of intrigue. She listens avidly, sensing the adventure and living every detail. She finds her imagination razor sharp. She can bring anything to life when she applies her mind. But now the storytelling is over and the daily routines resume their lifeless mantle.

The summer days go by slowly. The predictable heat is both heartening and arid. Without the watery embrace The Boat becomes malnourished and unkempt. Her woodwork feels scabby and scaly; like a snake she is ready to shed her skin and glow anew. One day a group of officials peel back the plastic cover and climb on board. What are they doing now? She sighs— more paperwork—another report. She watches one of the men take a black pen from his top pocket before he begins a thorough inspection of her deck, even leafing through the pages of her log. Why can't they leave her alone? She isn't doing anyone any harm.

"You're causing quite a stir, Hon," the friendly dockworker says one day. She recognizes his kind voice and the orange worker's bib he wears; it is stained with green paint. He runs a hand gently along her hull. "The Marine Officials are busy measuring up for a set of gates; to be installed before the month's out. We've never needed Marina gates before now. I heard them mention your name. What is it you've done? Who, or what, are they trying to keep out?"

Chapter 1 Outlook

Wednesday 7ᵗʰ February 2007

P.m. Mouse {Unsent}: Smart new shirt my Love—you look very well. Thank-you for greeting my parents so graciously. I felt proud to call you Friend, let alone Lover of my deepest longing. I hope I didn't life-shock you too much by appearing there, in the playground, just as you were about to enter class. It was very important that my parents met you. Thank-you Angels. Did you notice the date?

Well, I am horribly overtired tonight. I feel unwell with the exhaustion; that unpleasant sensation where drowsiness is replaced by nausea and insomnia. Yuk—I can always sense it coming on. I suppose the past few days have been busy and full of anxiety on different levels. I said goodbye to my parents this afternoon. I thought I would be tearful but I wasn't. Their visit has been lovely but the new term is beginning and it is time for everyone to knuckle down. They have been so generous. My Pa has offered to pay for our return tickets home every year; he even bought a fire extinguisher to keep us safe in the wooden cabin—bless him. The Laird appeared at the airport before they flew. I had to collect the children from school so I left him to wave them off. I hope he didn't fill their heads with worrying details. I don't want them returning home with tales of doom and gloom.

Towards the end of their stay my parents mentioned concern over our financial position and choice of lifestyle, as well as disapproval over Rinky's late reading development, {usual for children in the alternative school system}. I bless them for their care and questions at this difficult time in our lives; certainly a challenging position for my father who likes everything secure and taped. I fear they will reach home and tell everyone we are 'all over the place'—'a walking disaster'. Knowing their family is in strife on the other side of the world is difficult for my parents to handle; a life lesson in letting go perhaps? They desperately want us to come home of course, so they can offer help and keep an eye on us. Tricky times.

*I didn't spy you at the end of the day, My Friend. To see you and say hello this morning filled my heart with joy. My Spirit leapt in recognition and delight when you turned to face me with your beautiful smile. I know I love thee still. And how do you feel, Sir? Hmm—what **are** we going to do?*

I return home to more student lectures from The Laird; "You are acting like a fifteen-year-old; your mother is terribly upset. She thinks you won't talk about the situation because you are ashamed. Your infatuation is based on an immature idea of love." "Oh no," I correct him. "This connection is of the very highest nature; it is profoundly mature. Do you really think I would be interested in anything other?" I want to say that our own married love is immature and based upon juvenile intimacy, but I save my husband the wounding. "It would be better if you went off and lived with him—you'd be back pretty fast, I can tell you." He states. "What you share doesn't include children, illness, financial struggle etc. It is unreal. Your parents are beside themselves with worry. I find myself living a lie everyday when you refuse to move from your position."

My poor husband. I know I am being unfair. I have been unable to turn to him properly as a wife since he banished Adrian. I can't bring myself to tell him we have slept together. I really need to speak with Lord Swallow. It had been so good to see him earlier. I was nervous and delighted both when he turned to face me. He was looking beautiful—organized and Kingly with clean clothes and tidy hair. He was wearing a yellow and orange checked shirt, which set his summer glow off so handsomely. I was pleased to see him standing straight and tall, his nobility shining and undaunted by recent events.

As part of The School's holistic philosophy the teachers wear certain colours on different days. Monday is a purple day; Tuesday is red. Wednesday they wear yellow and Thursday is orange. Friday is a green day. "If we had school on Saturday the staff would wear blue," Big J. informed me recently. "And of course Sunday is all white." I smile to myself—Adrian's new shirt will see him through both Wednesday and Thursday. I keep meaning to read up on the significance of the different days and colours. I know the practice will have some important, spiritual indication.

I sigh, wishing I could speak to Adrian. I really need to know what he is thinking.

Late P.m. Mouse: *My dearest Friend, I don't know if you want to hear from me or not but I need to inform you of certain events. The Harbour Master has invited several others to inspect our Boat. They are in the process of climbing aboard The Celestial Sea and making yet another report. The visitors are conducting a thorough search. Unfortunately they are making quite a fuss over our private property—rather odd really, seeing as we signed and sealed our dry-dock papers some time ago.*

The Harbour Master is only ever happy when supported by a crowd so although full of disquiet, in a strange way he is pleased with the attention. On the other hand, your Lady, {if you still consider her so}, feels calm—calm in the centre of the storm whipped up by others. It is a strange place to be. My parents know a little of our situation. They will take the news back to England. I have been unable to act as a normal wife to The Laird. I have told him many home truths. I have said that I cannot move forward without his permission to speak with you. This in itself makes him realize how important your friendship is to me. I suppose it makes him more anxious. He can't understand my lack of any need to talk through my 'problems'. I have tried to explain that the last thing I feel is the presence of any personal 'problems.'

My Friend, I really do need to know your thoughts. Perhaps it is all over for you, so what is the fuss about anyway? The Laird tells me you have been to see Simon today—to discuss our situation. The Laird will see Simon tomorrow to hear what you have to say. What exactly is going on? I seem to be none the wiser on every front. Are we ever going to be allowed to talk? The Laird seemed surprised when I told him you wouldn't speak with me. He expects us to be back in contact now that term has begun.

Events seem to be out of my hands. I am watching as an interested onlooker; calm—wondering. Thank-you for meeting my parents this morning. I am sorry if it life-shocked you just as your first day back at school began. It was important to me. You were very Kingly. I felt proud to call you Friend. And yes; the new shirt is very smart.

Thinking of you—needing to be in touch soon, before they tow away our Boat and leave her to perish on the rocks—M-X

Thursday 8th February 2007

How still The Mountain feels today. He is relaxing. I sense The Mountain is a 'he'. The sun is glorious and my thoughts turn to Ma and Pa winging their way back home across the world. Sheets flap companionably on the washing line while I busy myself with domestic work. I drive into town with the recycling and face the supermarket for another big shop. We find the cost of food high; I can easily spend three hundred dollars a week. I meet my friend Hannah in Countdown, {supermarket}. She is a lovely person with an interesting family. Her husband is Israeli whereas she is a Kiwi. For many years they lived on a Kibbutz in Israel. We chat away, blocking the spice isle. Her middle son is a new student at The Laird's College.

Reaching home I find that Wonky, {the rooster with the crooked beak}, and one of his girlfriends have been inside the house. What a mess! Molly helps me clear up the cereal and butter party—it's quite a while before the shopping is stacked in the larder and *all* the livestock dispersed. I love the cuddles I share with my piggy; she is really friendly. Together we enjoy the smell of The Go-Getter's cake rising in the oven; he has requested a late birthday treat for his classroom celebration. I write up my diary and get more of The Book down while the cake cooks. Waves of passion and chocolate aroma propel my tapping fingers as I record our precious messages. I am both subject and object; a bizarre reality. The story unfolds each day without any need to invent the next chapter. I sometimes wonder if something other is writing this tale; perhaps I am just a willing recorder. Would Adrian like me to send him more of the completed story? I would like to ask. After all, The Book belongs to him as much as it does to me. If I cannot have the man I love The Book will endeavor to fill the gap. There is a wealth of potential in the storyline. I find it exciting and life-giving. Thank-you Lord. Please send reassurance to Ma and Pa as they head home. There is no need to worry or to be afraid. I know you are holding us all. Amen—X

Friday 9th February 2007

Rinky the Minx is at home today with a wobbly tummy. She isn't too bad but I decide to keep her with me. The Laird continues to be angry, hoping I will admit my error. I tell him that I am sorry; that I am wrong to have hurt him. However, I cannot deny the perfection of the relationship shared by Adrian and myself. "What has happened has been so very 'right' for me." "Well," replies my exasperated husband, "you had better move out then, hadn't you?" He leaves the room, slamming the door behind him.

Oops, I write him a long text, which makes my thinking more coherent. My phone battery is low; bother. I'll send it later. Apparently Simon saw Adrian in his official capacity as Chairman of the School Board of Trustees. Adrian admitted he was wrong to have taken another man's wife. "You will have to hear the rest from Simon, or from Adrian and Simon together," The Laird told me earlier. "What?" I replied; "Oh no; no way. I am not going to stand up in front of others and speak of my relationship with Adrian—never."

Whose idea was that to have a facilitated meeting? Was it Adrian's? I can understand his need for the honourable approach. I could possibly speak to Simon on my own but certainly not with him as a facilitator between us both; I couldn't stand that. I head to my lonely bed, sad and confused. I need Lord Swallow's Angel wings right now.

P.m. Mistress to Laird: My Darling, I am sorry to cause you grief and pain. In this I admit that I have done wrong. I kept the reality of my relationship with Adrian from you because I didn't want to hurt you like this. I hoped to keep my two lives separate which was again wrong of me. I naively thought I could make it work in line with your increasing bachelor lifestyle and time away from the family and me. For many years now I have needed my deeper, spiritual essence to find love and nurture. I know this to be my true person and to share and learn with another is a gift I have not denied myself.

For many years my imagination, coupled with my desire to be in control, meant that in a way that side of me was alive; I made sure that it was. Through having children and being unwell I lost a large amount of control and began to realize that what I thought was something we shared only came from me. Any spiritual, mystical rhythm was mine alone. It was one-sided. I sometimes wonder at my self-sufficiency; did I never question why I didn't receive anything back? Have my years of boarding school cemented a sad acceptance of a solo playing field? I think we are emotional strangers without ever having acknowledged the fact. This problem creates our immoveable block to deep communion; one we cannot override because our 'love language' is different. To meet someone who not only gives me as much as I can give, but challenges me there, emotionally, is an extraordinary

142

experience. In a way it is the greatest humbling. I know it is the only way anyone would ever knock down my bombproof defenses. When I stand in front of Adrian I am naked; totally.

My Darling, our marriage has always been about going out to others. We both know this. We build community and we make things happen. Of course we share a solid love in this. It is our life, our family, our friends and our vocation together. My relationship with Adrian is teaching me that I don't need to be in control any more. He guides me, encouraging me to bring that private side out, into the open. In this way my Spirit bows to his superiority. Far from being an adolescent love it is, in fact, the most profound of human connections. I cannot deny the truth of this. To do so would be the ultimate abandonment of self. "Be true unto yourself"—Sunday's lesson in church.

In my mind none of this concerns our marriage, although in conventional terms of course it does. It all depends on how we view life—and of how free, or afraid we are. I know this connection would enable you and me to go deeper as a couple. Once I am earthed I can meet you there more easily. But in asking this of you I am stepping right out of line. I would be asking the impossible. So, until I know how Adrian is truly feeling about our situation; until I can gauge his standing, I don't know whether there is any reason to pursue this path. Once I know I will either act on it, or put it to bed. I can wait for Paradise if I have to. I have been hanging out for an invitation to go home for many years. I'm sure I can wait some more. Never in my wildest dreams did I imagine Paradise would find me first; and this gift could bring such wondrous, inclusive Light all around. "It could be very important in a larger sense," Adrian's words some months ago.

I keep asking myself; "why us? Why now? Why such finite beauty and for what purpose? There must be one." The recent, powerful events are a fact. They are solid and earthed, despite their esoteric nature. Adrian, for all the negativity you like to pin on him, is strong in his Christ-centred integrity. And he is most certainly earthed himself. Yes, we have been tempted but I can assure you that at no time has our integrity ever been sidelined, unlikely as you will consider my statement.

My Darling—thank-you for your kindness and long-suffering patience. There is nothing to fear. In my mind our marriage is not altered. I will always love and care for you. The situation between Adrian and me is something different—unique if you like. It has come about for a reason. Could you bear to stand by? I love to see you strong and inspired, feeling safe and balanced in your vocational work. I ask that you embrace those vocational gifts, knowing I am here for you and stronger for you with my own support structures in place. I love you. Thank-you for listening.

Will any of my message ring true with The Laird? In many ways he *is* able to grasp new ideas. Will he ever see the potential? Will he ever believe it could work in our lives? Hmm—sometimes I am certain this is the right path to be treading. And then at other, more earthed times, I think; no, of course he will never entertain such a notion; of course we couldn't make it work. I sleep eventually but wake again before midnight. After an hour of swirling thoughts I decide to send Adrian a message. Something has to give.

Late P.m. Mouse: My Friend—so you want me to talk to a third party; to discuss our hallowed secrets with someone else present? I understand your noble desire for the sun at all times. I applaud your bravery and clarity. However, I am more of a moonchild. I need an equal amount of sunshine and moonlight. To discuss the intimacy of our precious Boat; our private Ocean—to invite the Chief Marine Official on board and reveal the pages of our log—do you really want me to do that? Could you honestly go through that? Our story is so personal. Your Lady might be destroyed by such strong sunlight. This territory is my last bastion of private strength; the very core of my essence. You ask that I bare my all; open myself to the ravages and possible destruction of the regular world? Yes, I know you do.

In a way I could stand proud. I am not ashamed of something so beautiful. But I really couldn't discuss the complexity of our personal standing with someone else present; especially when all I long to do is lie in your tender embrace and hear from your own lips how you are; what you see as our ending; or our way forward. It is either one or the other.

The Laird wants me to contact Simon, to organize a time to meet with him. I suppose he is asking me to pluck up the courage to speak with someone other, rather as he shouldered the difficult task of speaking with you before Christmas. Can I not telephone you instead? You can tell me 'goodbye' quickly if that is what you want. The Laird is away in town tonight; not home until tomorrow evening. I would tell him that I phoned you. Nothing hidden any longer; everything laid out on the table. My marriage is on the line and I really, really need to speak with you. Whatever you have to say to me, I will take. I will try to be clear and brave—not swoony—I promise. If it is okay for me to phone, send a blank message with your new number. If I don't hear from you? Hmm—

I sleep at last, sad and wondering if Adrian will be in touch. I am unsure.

Saturday 10th February 2007

A.m. Mouse {Unsent}: My Darling Friend—good morning. I don't know if you will respond to my request. I wonder how you are. How were the first days of term? The King reigns often in my mind. I wonder how he rules his Kingdom; how he finds his new Palace? Has he moved in properly? I can see his woodworker's hands, skillful and inspired at the new workbench. What is he working on right now?

I imagine you gardening with Vonny and being such a joy for the little one there. And how does our own Small One fair? I hope he is really well; busy with his father, planting up the garden and building shelves. I imagine him following you wherever you go. I know you will have given him his own little hammer and chisel. Please tell him I am missing him so much. Kiss the

144

top of his curly head for me. Tell him to look you in the eye and there you will see my love for you still.

I am awake by **7** a.m. I sense Adrian holding me. Animals, sunshine, demanding dog—the usual rounds of domestic routine. The Laird seems to leave the dog duties to me these days. He is strict with the animals; never tender. I take The Bog-Brush on our morning amble down the drive. The Tui birds serenade our footsteps. The ducks follow us with their hungry eyes from the pond below the drive and the hazy sky promises another hot, hot day. Instinctively I reach for my apron pocket; my phone accompanies me everywhere. I pull it out to check the screen; in case there is a message. I didn't hear any text in the night.

There *is* a message; just a number; nothing more. It is from Adrian, indicating that I may telephone him. Back inside I make up my bottle of warm Supergreens, take a deep breath and walk over to the desk. Better get this over with. I dial the new number and a sleepy sounding Adrian answers. It is still early. After the past silent weeks we are awkward with each other; neither of us knows quite where to tread or how to be with each other. Hesitatingly we talk about his new life; yes, he has moved into Vonny's house. He is relieved to be free of Big J's ruling presence. The 'out-breath' of Vonny's home suits him well. "I had some problems moving out," he tells me. "I had to clean the carpet and tidy up the garden; extra things like that."

"And guess what? I've bought two milking cows from a lovely old couple in the Kuwharu Hills. School has accepted my proposal to rent the top paddocks and have them on site. The cows will graze the school land and fertilize it at the same time. I'm milking them every day, driving up into the Kuwharu Hills until I can move them over." He sounds really excited. He thinks he may be able to bring some other animals on site too. "Oh, do you still need the rabbit cage?" He asks. "If not could you bring it down to Vonny's house? I've persuaded her that Thomasina needs a pet of her own."

"I'm not doing the morning circle in class anymore," he continues. "I don't have to turn up until ten o'clock! How's that for civilized? And I'm about to start teaching woodwork." I am pleased to hear him happy and fulfilled. Adrian isn't the kind of person to hang around in the doldrums; he always finds the positive in every situation. I smile to myself; how alike we are, although I have certainly been in the doldrums in my emotional turmoil. That must be the feminine compared with the masculine. He had a trip to Wellington with Big J, he tells me. "We chatted as we drove. I told her how it is between us. She was very understanding and really hopes I will stay at school. That buoyed me up no end. I want you to know that I spent time with Jules. We had fun together; I still have warm thoughts for her. And Delphine is helping me milk the cows."

So, he has moved on, filling his life with other maidens and not lingering over 'us'. I couldn't really expect anything other, but a gaping sadness wells up inside me. After all we have been to each other, am I not more important to him? Is he such a 'Peter Pan' figure? A wandering Minstrel who never settles? "There is still love in my heart for you, My Lady." He consoles me, "but I am not holding out for you." I try to draw him on how he genuinely feels about us; deep down. Has our love really moved away? I cannot *believe* the nature of our bond leaves him as ambiguous as he claims. He is silent. He will not respond.

"Ask me in a different way," he eventually replies. I pose the question again and he is thoughtful before answering. "I am in the Forest still and you are in the Castle with your husband and children, where you belong. I am not waiting. I may well stroll with other maidens. But; if you walk out to meet me I will come to greet you. If you walk with harmony and happy agreement between yourself and The Laird I shall be there for you."

"So—am I still your Lady?" I tentatively ask. "Yes," he replies—although other things he says confirms the ambiguity and the conclusion that 'no', I can't really consider myself as such. Despite the crashing sadness there is a part of me that refuses to deny the truth. Although he won't speak of it I know he acknowledges it too. Adrian has chosen to return to the light; to drop our connection as any man of integrity would. The world of the Leafy Glade has passed; he has moved on. "I am concerned for you, My Friend," he says. "I have filled my life with cows, woodwork, other ladies and new projects. I am concerned for you. I want you to let go of your secret world and stand in the sun. Please don't grieve any more." "But I need to maintain my private, sacred world," I tell him. "It is central to who I am. It is my spirituality. Without my secret sanctuary I am undone." "Are you?" He continues to push me. "Are you really undone? Oh—don't listen to me; I'm not offering any remedy."

"Perhaps I have to *make* myself disengage from us," I reply. "This is hard when eighty percent of my mind shouts 'NO', and the other sensible, twenty percent says 'yes, do what is correct." "You don't have to disengage; it is your own choice," he says. I am thoughtful for a while before replying; "but if *you* have then there is no point in *me* holding on. Thank-you for your honesty."

We continue talking for a long time. Adrian tells me of the fear he felt after The Laird shouted at him on the telephone; "I was filled with anxiety over being reprimanded again in front of the management team—of having to leave my community and the district. Feelings of shame overwhelmed me when I realized I had broken my Christmas promise to The Laird—our night on Whatipu Beach was a grave mistake, despite our maintained restraint."

I hear the plea in his voice; I know he is really saying: "I don't want any of that again—not even for 'us'—I cannot take further negativity. Can you understand?" I ask if he would like me to send on The Book so far—perhaps he would consider being involved in the compilation. "Not yet," he replies. "Perhaps in a year's time. The spark between us would reignite all too easily.

146

It is too soon. I would be going against the pledge I have made with myself. Ask me again in a year's time." I want to tell him what I wrote to The Laird, but he is unsure and to be honest, so am I.

Filling him in briefly I give an account of events to date. I don't mention my parents' sadness and concern although I thank him for greeting them so graciously. "We can still see each other sometimes, eh?" He suggests in a lighthearted manner. "Perhaps," I reply with despondency. "I suppose we can say hello in the car park." We both know the conversation is nearing an end. Neither of us wants it to finish.

"Maybe we might be together again one day, even though I'm not holding out for that," Adrian adds hopefully—waving a limp flag of possibility. "The Laird has called for a six month halt—to test our love; to discover if it's more than infatuation," I tell him. "That sounds like a good idea," Adrian replies. "Then he would let me go with his blessing—although would he really?" I add.

Adrian mentions his talk with Simon. "I really trust Simon; he was so good to talk with. He is a friend—I am his son's teacher—he is Chairman of our School Board of Trustees; he was very understanding. I think it would be beneficial for you to talk with him. He knew what I was speaking about. He certainly resonated with the mythology and mystical essence of our connection; he could see that in us. 'There could only be a beautiful connection between you two,' he said. As a close friend of The Laird he understands his difficulty with expressing emotion." I have promised Simon that our relationship is over. In his official capacity as Chairman he has to be sure of that. You and The Laird need to drop your British inhibitions. Come on—you have joined the Kiwi Experience, so go for it." Adrian is greatly heartened by Simon's attitude. "I really want you to speak with Simon. He is a good listener. You mustn't carry everything on your shoulders, alone. I worry about you, My Love." Adrian tells me he would like to meet The Laird with Simon acting as mediator. "I am scared of your husband's anger. I really can't be afraid of bumping into him around every corner. I know there is work now for the Castle Inmates. I sense you have a long, hard path to walk. I am praying for you, My Friend. You know, I was so scared and shocked after The Laird yelled at me that I fled to Auckland, to spend time with my parents. I told them our night at Whatipu had been a terrible mistake, even though we were restrained. We prayed together—we prayed for us all."

"I sense The Angels telling me to disengage. My parents agreed that a total cut off was the only course of action. They advised me to be tough, in order to allow a deeper level of understanding to develop between you and The Laird. I am sorry that I hurt you. It was the right thing to do, although sending the blank text was stepping over the line. Thank-you for keeping me informed; it was good to hear how you were and to accompany you on your Tiki Tour."

And so we bid each other farewell—that unwanted ending yet again. "Goodbye Mouse"—"Goodbye Adrian."

I replace the receiver. I am sad, relieved, disbelieving, held—yet alone. This cut off is more final than before although as always the ambiguity gilds the quandary. If truth be told I am devastated. As I remove my hand from the telephone a little bird flies into the French windows, stunning itself and collapsing lifeless on the deck. Rinky is walking down the stairs as I run outside to ward off the dog and find the injured victim. Together we administer Rescue Remedy. I hold the delicate creature tenderly, realizing with surprise what kind of bird lies helpless and struggling for life in my hands.

Final Message, Mouse: *A bird—a delicate little bird just dashed itself against the French windows. She ran to it and held the gasping creature in her hands—exquisite markings; iridescent against her skin. Soft, dappled under-feathers and bright, bewildered eyes met her own, beseeching her to comfort him; to make him well and let him go. Carrying him into the sun she waited with tears in her eyes while the Rescue Remedy took affect. "Goodbye Little Swallow," she whispered as he spread his wings. Goodbye—X*

As I press 'send' my own phone signals an incoming message. It is from Adrian. We are synchronized yet again.

Adrian: *She is not back with The Mole, however, for during her absence The Mole pondered and began to realize his confining attitude and with these thoughts his burrow began to crumble and the first rays of light shone into his home. The face and body of The Mole began to change with the light— slow but gaining momentum. She realized that she could love this transforming being—but only now, because the winds of change; fanned into being by her departure with Swallow, had begun to blow, fresh and cleansing through the burrow. She set to work and began alterations—long conversations with The Mole, uncovering their shared history—the shy, woodland creatures they both had been.*

Yes, My Lord Swallow, that would make a fitting end to our story. I am crying inside, for my loyal Mole may or may not change but I will have to say goodbye to shared, mystical rhythm and artistic creativity. I will have to turn my back on synchronized chemistry, and most importantly, the woman in me would have to deny the man who holds me in his ownership; as guide, as protector, as master—welcoming my vulnerability and desire to be consumed. Words alone cannot convey what these gifts mean to me, or how much I desire the passion. I know this gift is ours and ours alone.

For many reasons, especially the moral quandary, you do not allow yourself the recognition. Your hesitancy over my questions says a lot about how you view our bond. "I don't know," meaning; "I am not allowing myself the gift that we are." Oh, I should stop trying to guess your thinking. I have said it all before. Perhaps my female intuition is at fault and you don't really feel as I do.

148

Hmm, how come you knew how to continue the story from my last message? Your words complimented mine as if you had already received my text.

P.m. Mouse {Unsent}: I am grieving again, My Love. Such sadness—why, oh why? Things you have said in the past give me clues as to how you really feel about us. "I don't think she will ever be mine," you told your stepmother a while ago. "Oh, don't be so sure about that," had been her reply. You have held me in your arms and said; "but what if you are 'the one'; my life's partner?" You said in a text that you were experiencing the most even-paced event of your life through our relationship. You have counted the years before the children are grown up; the years before we can be together. You have told me that you love me, but you have not been able to look me in the eye and say: "I am totally and irrevocably in love with you, for now and all time. This is the most exquisite, unique relationship my life has been blessed to claim as gift. Never, never will I allow our essence to be taken from us, even if you are unable to stand beside me."

Part of me wonders if this is all in my imagination, and yet the woman in me knows it to be just as true for you as it is for me, My Friend. If it were not so we would be denied access through The Garden Gate.

Sunday 11th February 2007

A.m. Mouse {Unsent}: Good morning, my disengaged Friend. Another Sunday greets me and I feel the need to keep by your side. The disengaged state is too harsh for me. An early morning amble with the hound takes me into crisp, clear air, reminiscent of early autumn at home. The Kuwharu Hills are tinged in soft lilac, their message one of hope for the future; whatever that might be—and something about choices too. I can choose to hang on to 'us' or I can choose to take up my old life, hopefully with new learning.

Oh, My Love, I can't bear the thought of never sailing The Celestial Sea again. After all, she was built specifically for us. Are we to let her disintegrate and perish?

I am feeling so sad today. The tears come easily. Rinky and I go to church. I am unable to engage properly with The Laird. **"True happiness comes from trusting God and letting his love fill our lives,"** the Priest preaches from the lectern. "Hmm—chance would be a fine thing," I mumble to myself. Returning home I apply myself to Ma and Pa's e-mail, which simply reads: "We are very upset, Darling." I had better reply in a way that calms everyone down:

"Dear Ma and Pa—please don't worry about my friendship with Adrian. Our liaison has obviously caused upset, but it has been blown out of proportion over the holidays as Adrian was away and I have only just been able to speak with him, to clarify our standing and keep to agreed levels of friendship. We don't want to upset

anybody. He is my best friend here, in New Zealand. We get on famously, which can obviously lead to problems for others. Anyway-to cut a long story short we will no longer be in touch. Adrian is involved elsewhere and I need to get a job before long. So, sadly for me, but happily for everyone else, I will no longer have my friend. So be it—husband and family before personal joy. Sorry if it worried you; the timing was tricky. All is fine and dandy now. I shall endeavour to become an expert housekeeper instead."

P.m. Mouse {Unsent}: Goodnight, Fine Sir. I wonder what you are thinking this evening. Am I foolish in my hopes for our future? Could I really make my Laird that sad? It would only work if it became a life-giving choice for him as well. Dear Lord and Father, please guide us on these questions. Please bring clarity to the situation we face, for the insistent spark refuses to extinguish, despite Lord Swallow's claimed absence. Something, or someone, is keeping the flame alive. Could it be Little Arthur who calls us with such urgency?

Church today was quiet and lovely. You were not there beside me, My Friend—not even present at the back of the congregation. We met the new Priest today; a young man returned home from America, full of enthusiasm and sparkle—a breath of fresh air for the church. He has clear, alive eyes and an arresting manner. The Laird is going to enjoy him, especially as he will be involved at College. Sitting quietly on the bench I could see both the men in my life as fine priests themselves.

The message from the lectern today was about love—and happiness. As we drove away from church I sensed you walking ahead of us on the other side of the road, perhaps casting a wistful glance in our direction. You were definitely focused in other ways, a solitary, noble figure heading towards town. Is this our new level then? A hard place to stand; together yet apart. A set of large padlocked gates has been erected between our Boat and her crew. The family and Marine Officials have made sure it is so. We are cornered with no other choice. I never imagined a place as sad as this for our love—

Monday 12th February 2007

The sun is ever present as I garden for the elderly Dutchman renting Sarah's house. Bill is an interesting character and has been in New Zealand for nine years. Sadly his marriage ended recently and he lives on his own. His wife has retained the family home, which is close by. He is not too keen on gardening-"or housework," commented Sarah when she asked me to help out. "I wouldn't use the bathroom if I were you."

I deadhead the white roses growing in the front garden, enjoying the immense views and single focus of the task. Bill is a musician and the house if full of beautiful instruments of every shape and size. Before retirement in Holland he was a musical conductor; I enjoy hearing about his working life.

150

He has an artist daughter living in Auckland whose work is currently on exhibition. He shows me a brochure of her paintings. I notice that he is reading 'The Power of now' by Eckhart Tolle—what a coincidence. We end up engrossed in an exciting conversation about spirituality. "Here, you can borrow the tape that accompanies the book," he offers, joining me as I weed the lower flowerbeds. I enjoy his positive attitude and enthusiastic conversation. As I pull clover from the succulent ground covering plants he sweeps up the hedge cuttings that have landed in his driveway from the neighbour's property.

Working companionably together I hear all about his new girlfriend and her legal custody case over a truanting son. Bill is a dear man. I am pleased to hear he has a new lady in his life. He shows me a picture; she is a lot younger than him. I wonder how old he is—mid to late seventies perhaps. I empty my bag of weeds in the chicken run and head off to school, arriving five minutes late for school pick-up. As I turn into the school entrance I see Adrian's ex-girlfriend, Delphine, pulling out of his new lodgings in her little yellow car, also running late for school pick-up—just as I always was last term. Ouch.

Chapter 2 Ouch

Early P.m. Mouse: Well well, you replace me so soon Lord Swallow? Same routine—same late mother for school pick-up, leaving your driveway in a rush. For weeks you keep me wondering, holding me in agonizing suspense so I am unable to move forwards, unable to prevent the worry for my family. I reach a point where The Laird is almost ready to let me go—and then you tell me you cannot be there for me—that you have moved on—that you cannot say what we mean to each other. You leave me as a prisoner on our Mountain while you comfort yourself with immediate distraction. I, on the other hand, have months to grieve our thwarted love.

Perhaps there is no reason to feel as I do. Yes, I know the circumstances are impossible. I know you have been afraid. I know the questions of integrity sit uncomfortably upon your fine shoulders. However—surely, if we truly love in the way I believe we do, then surely, My Liege, My noble King and jointly crowned Lord Swallow, you would allow yourself to be loved— would acknowledge the gift we have received and give yourself time. For it is not impossible—X

Mouse: P.s Sorry, My Friend. Just feeling really hurt and sad—and angry that I cannot visit you—grieving that other maidens stroll with you in our Forest—needing to know if Delphine and Vonny know about 'us'—not sure how to face everyone. I know you don't mean to hurt me. I know you need to move on. I know there is no other way. I am just sad to have so little acknowledgement of our gift. Needing to get these thoughts off my chest— no one else to talk to like this. Sorry. I won't text again-X

As the day closes my mind goes round and round; should I have sent those messages? I needed to speak to someone and I always let Adrian know how I am feeling; personal honesty is what our relationship is about. Seeing Delphine leave his home this afternoon stabbed me through the heart. Hmm—I probably shouldn't have made contact.

Tuesday 13th February 2007

I am not hungry these days. Food has lost its appeal since Adrian and I spoke on the telephone. I decide to make the most of the easy diet and eat only at lunchtimes. At least I might tone up and get fit. It is cold this morning. I start the day in warm trousers and a woolly jumper. I expect those further down the mountain are donning shorts and T-shirts while coastal residents are taking a morning plunge. The dramatic temperature differentiation around the district is surprising. A mountain life certainly calls for warmer clothing. A spare hour sees me completing more of The Book—how I wish Adrian and I could work on it together; it is our story after all.

Once the children are delivered to school I take The Bog-Brush for a walk on the sands at Memorial Park. Then I find a parking place under a row of leafy trees. The fresh start to the day gives way to the ever-present sunshine and I decide to swim in the outdoor pool. My hairy companion seems happy enough in the car—she has a lovely view of the park all around. The pool is so quiet today; a pleasant change after the busy holidays. There are only a couple of other people here. How lovely; there is nothing quite like slipping into a still swimming pool in the summer heat, the rest of the town humming through its Tuesday morning routine outside the sanctuary. This is just what I need.

An elderly man swims in the lane across the pool from me. He must be quite an age; he has pallid skin and a hunched back. He uses a snorkel and goggles, stopping to catch his breath every few minutes. I notice he wears a wedding ring—is his wife still alive? Is she preparing his lunch? Somehow I think this unlikely; knowing the Kiwis; if she were still in this world she would surely be swimming alongside him. I am constantly impressed by the national attitude towards fitness, whatever your age. Many parents at school participate in a sport; a wide sporting knowledge is considered 'the norm'. Several mothers at school readily don shorts and whistle, stepping in to either coach hockey or referee a netball game.

I swim for half an hour, stopping to pass the time of day with my swimming companion. I can't help wondering if I will reach old age with the ability to maintain the same levels of fitness. Will I still be married? I can't imagine myself and The Laird as an elderly couple, whereas the idea of a companionable old age shared with Adrian is very real. Perhaps that's just the way my mind is working at present. I swim for half an hour; the clock by the lifeguard's office window keeps me informed. Bordering the road on the steep bank above the pool the trees greet the skyline as friendly onlookers. The sun highlights the sinuous, many-branched Eucalyptus. Beside it the greyer, stronger rooted Pohutukawa tree appears almost somber. The native Australian tree beside the native New Zealand tree—the Antipodes united—friends and rivals both; one flamboyant, the other more reserved. It is interesting to see them together like that.

The children have hair appointments after school pick-up today. Shawn looks after them this time—what a great name for a hairdresser! This is the first time Rinky the Minx has had a haircut. Through the Kindergarten philosophy in the U.K I learnt that many consider a child's physical strength to be enhanced by not cutting the hair until the age of **7**—in line with loosing milk teeth and beginning a practical way of learning in Class 1. I remember being surprised when Cedric first began the alternative Kindergarten in Sussex; "why are the children all girls?" I remember asking a teacher, only to be informed that half of them were boys with long hair! Well—I didn't travel that path with my boys but I definitely have with Rinky. She was **7** last April so she is ready for the ceremonial cut. This is quite an occasion, I have to say. As we finish at the hairdresser my phone bleeps. I have a message. It is from Adrian.

P.m. Adrian: *Dear Mouse, thank-you for letting me know how you are. I can imagine how you felt, seeing Delphine, but—she isn't my new lover! She was making compost with me. What a pang your words gave me. Why could I not simply have told you it was over for me, instead of leaving you hanging? I don't know the answer. I'm sorry to put you through that. I bless you everyday—at least think of you with care. I don't know how to proceed here—feeling for you, but cautious.*

Mouse: *Dearest Friend, thank-you for being in touch. Sorry to accuse you wrongly. It was unfair of me to say those things when you have been dragged over the coals for us. I just needed to unload; yes, I can sometimes be human; not very often though; too Heaven-bound most of the time. Wish I was making compost and milking the cows with you. The Laird is being kind and caring. He just wants me to be happy—to be the person I am called to be, even if that means losing me in the long run. He makes these statements when I have no place to turn, yet he sings a very different tune when my path ahead lies clear. He says things should be sorted by May, one way or the other. We might decide to go back home earlier than planned. I can't help feeling an outcast at the moment. I am still unable to be a proper wife. Yes, a new light is certainly with us; The Laird is trying really hard. Perhaps things will change. However, my dear Mole may learn many things but he will never learn 'The Dance'—for that is ours alone—X*

Wednesday 14th February 2007 Valentine's Day:
Will Adrian send me a discreet Valentine message today? My vivid imagination plays out several scenarios—a red velvet ribbon in a tree perhaps? Or something written on the side of the road that only the two of us would understand? Hmm—nothing—of course not. He has moved on. He has made a pledge with himself. The Laird is right; I am acting like a fanciful fifteen-year-old. I wait all day in case something happens. I would really like to place a flower on Adrian's pillow; his reply to my reactionary message rests quietly in my heart. My kind husband brings me a present of some dancing dolphins; a candleholder for the centre of the table. I don't deserve his attention. He is at home more often these days.

I spent another hour gardening for Bill this afternoon, the sound of the cicadas so loud in the overhanging trees. There were dandelions galore through the driveway and tough Karaehi rea roots, {a type of couch grass}, that I plucked from their stolen hideaways; among them some exquisite violets. The purple flowers with a splash of gold raised their heads to catch the sun. Such exquisite detail—are they really a weed? I placed two aside, not wishing to discard their tiny dignity. Below me the valleys and orderly orchards lay spread like a banquet. The high windbreaks that protect the kiwi fruit and avocados divide the dips and hollows of the volcanic landscape. The sky is *so* clear today. Beyond the farmland the town spreads wide, reaching its fingers into the many bays along the coast.

I swim again after school drop off this morning, the water welcoming my tired body and offering kind comfort. My shorts are beginning to fall off me; I still don't feel like eating. I like the discipline of measured diet and exercise. I hope I can keep it up—at least something positive may emerge from these sad days. Our financial situation is definitely *not* positive. To maintain our current lifestyle I must bring in at least five hundred dollars a week. How on earth can I work the hours to reach that goal? I continue to take on small, part-time jobs like the gardening for Bill, as well as various painting jobs. The work is sporadic and badly paid. I really can't get enthused about anything other than my writing—that is really all I want to do, as well as lying in Lord Swallow's embrace that is—for hours of peaceful meditation with him; My Prince; My Soul-Mate.

GIVE IN

I feel a need to withdraw,
Ponder in reflection, prayer and lyric.
I have spent many years giving out; now I need to give in—
To myself for a while with him, My Prince; My Soul Mate.

I feel a need for his artistic hands covering mine,
Gently exploring my secret places;
Lips and eyes and tears that dissolve in our exquisite union.
Yes, I need to give in—
To myself for a while with him, My Prince; My Soul Mate.

Thursday 15th February 2007
A chocolate brown moth greets me on my walk this morning. It has cream tints on each wing. I wonder what it's called. It says hello a second time as the dog and I return from our pre-breakfast amble. Monty the cat has taken off again. His operation doesn't seem to have helped the wandering tendency. Molly and Wonky are as enthusiastic as ever when the mistress' face appears at the kitchen window. Molly has taken to lying right across the back door; we are finding it difficult to budge her increasing bulk every time we need to go out to the 'shid'.

The tape that Bill lent me—The Eckhart Tolle lectures—confirms the gift Adrian and I share. I have had some exciting thoughts on the topic, which I'll send on to him. This is important and I'll *try* to make it my last message.

A.m. Mouse: *Dear Adrian, I have discovered something really important for us; perhaps something that explains our connection. I have been studying 'The Power of Now', {you told me you had seen the film.} I urge you to read the book; its relevance is uncanny. There are references to 'processing techniques', 'portals'; ie: Garden Gates, and even 'distant shores.' This is all part of the Alchemy—especially the chapter on relationships. This is why I cannot deny the truth of our bond; what I intuitively know but find difficult to put into clear language. It is all in the book—in coherent phrasing. Acknowledgement is all that is needed. Although I long for your physical presence with the chemistry, artistry and shared laughter, I can just about forgo their actual presence if we acknowledge our gift. Does this make sense? Then, although it would be intolerably hard, it wouldn't matter where we were; together or apart. So, My Darling Apollo, I am firing an arrow to you from afar—X*

It is the Go-Getter's turn for a 'Mummy Day.' The wee chap is a little under the weather, although I know that won't stop him from being great company. We spent half an hour in the library earlier, which he always enjoys. He came out clutching 'The Guinness Book of World Records' and duly entertains me in the car all the way home. "There's a man in here that eats metal, Ma—really he does. So far he has consumed eighteen bicycles, **7** television sets, five beds, fifteen supermarket trolleys, a pair of skies and a Cessna plane. He's in his sixties and still going strong. He gets an upset stomach if he eats ordinary food. He sprinkles his salad with metal bolts!" I don't swerve off the road but I *do* laugh all the way up the hill. My wee fellow is wonderfully uplifting; his enthusiasm as welcome as a shaft of sunlight. I expect he has arrived in our family to counteract the negative male vibes in the home. "I feel like making a robot," he announces as we walk in through the cabin door.

Friday 16th February 2007

Mid-February means mid-summer in the Southern Hemisphere. But the mornings and evenings are dark compared with Europe and a mountain life calls for warm jumpers first and last thing. It is strange to have really hot days with dark nights and mornings. Ma says the days are beginning to lengthen in England; the snowdrops and crocuses are out in the cottage garden, announcing spring as they always do. The back lawn is covered with the prettiest, lilac crocuses in February. I miss their shy appearance.

The Laird retuned home last night, admitting that people are asking him questions. Yes, he can definitely feel the return of his depression; it has been hovering in the background for a while now. I know he blames me for the way he's feeling, but this isn't a new state of affairs. As he gets older the negativity appears more often. When he isn't bouncing off others his ego is depleted and a dull spirit takes over. I realize it is the underlying reason that I've allowed myself the illicit joy of falling in love with another man; a man for whom positivity is as natural as breathing.

I drive to Vonny's house after morning drop-off, depositing Adrian's workshop items inside his car. How strange to see it in a new place with a new family; my Lord Swallow finding nurture and community within another home. He needs the companionship, friendship and provision that others provide. Another replacement mother figure is central in the scenario.

The 'Toolbox' looks industrious and messy as ever; I pile Adrian's bits and pieces on the front seat; including the giant Teapot. As I wrestle the old rabbit hutch off my van's roof, Vonny returns from school and lends a hand. "Oh, thanks for bringing that for us. Adrian reckons Thomasina needs a pet of her own; we're getting a bunny at the weekend. How are you doing?" We chat for a while, catching up on holiday news as we carry the cage to the back garden. I can't help wondering if Adrian has told her about our relationship. I leave a discreet love-heart on the inside lid of the hutch—a small token with the initials A & M; hardly noticeable. Adrian probably won't spy the message but it makes me feel better.

Poor Rinky has a nasty leg infection from an insect bite. "I reckon that needs a trip to the doctor," says her teacher, Little J. "She's been complaining all day and I think it's getting worse." I take her to the surgery as soon as school ends. I like the system in New Zealand where emergency surgeries are open all hours for anyone needing attention. This one is on the corner of a wide avenue in the centre of town; our own surgery didn't have any free appointments this afternoon.

Unfortunately Rinky needs antibiotics and has to keep her leg up as much as possible; the infection is angry. One of her school friends is staying for three days while her parents, Freya and Justin, sail their new boat down from Auckland. Having collected Cedric from College I drive the gang home. Lucia is one of Adrian's pupils and I enjoy hearing about the day from his enthusiastic class member. How nice to have her with us—a friend for Rinky and a small link between Adrian and myself. I care for our guest morning and evening while my Lord Swallow takes over during the day.

Lucia and I take the Bog-Brush down to feed the ducks before bedtime. Our crazy, over-bouncy hound manages to pull me right into the muddy pond! I fall in headfirst, which amuses the little lady no end. I am mud-caked from top to toe. We laugh all the way home. She must think we are the maddest household. The Scowler asks for an evening foot massage and our regular, quality time together takes up part of the evening. The Laird has a College function but I can't accompany him when Rinky is unwell. He is cross with me for putting the children first, yet again. As he drives away I realize that he often complains. His cup is half empty rather than half full. He draws on my unconditional love and positivity while moaning that I am not there for him. He can't see the repeating pattern. He relies on me one hundred percent, while admitting he is often happiest when away from home. I am beginning to realize that what annoys him is my inability to provide a bouncing board, as well as the growing dominance of our immoveable, emotional block. I cannot supply him with sustenance at every turn. Yes—I am certainly a replacement mother figure for The Laird, however much he tells me that Adrian sees *me* in just such a way. Hmm. A mother is unable to provide her son with a certain intimacy, but she loves him and would never turn him away.

Saturday 17th February 2007

The Laird and I are up and about early this morning. A day's fishing is on the agenda and I busy myself making his sandwiches; the least a failing wife can do for her husband. We continue our tricky conversation wrangles while I slice and spread. Plucking up courage I admit; "You don't nourish me. I know you care for me—and provide for me—but you don't nourish me. I really need to see Adrian every now and then; we have stopped any physical contact. Can't I see him once a week? Please?"

"No—certainly not. I know you consider your friendship to be a blessing, but if it damages others it is definitely not positive." I hug him before he goes on his way. For the sake of others I must shelve my spiritual comfort—or transform it. He knows I love him as I have ever done. I will try to be a good wife. As he drives off I realize that I am bored in my husband's company. Our union is safe and solid—but I am bored by it. What a terrible thing for a wife to admit.

A.m. Mouse {Unsent}: *And what will today bring? An early morning discussion with The Laird reveals more home truths—our agreed bottom line is that what makes us tick, fundamentally, is different. It will never be the same.*

I managed to track down my author sister, Mizzie, at last. We have been trying to talk over the telephone all week. The different timings between the hemispheres makes for tricky communication. I know she will want to unearth the truth of the situation. "Our family is notoriously good at smoothing over any difficulties, Darling Sis—you can tell me anything. You know I'm not exactly Mrs. Chaste myself!" My lovely sister, offering me comfort and confidence; reassuring me that nothing would shock her. It's good to chat freely. "I have quite a story to tell," I begin-"In fact, a large part is already written down. Would you like to edit my Book? Could you give me your professional opinion?" Yes—She would certainly like to understand more. She could take a look at the writing. We will speak again soon, probably by e-mail. What a relief to speak to family at last—to share all.

"Mizzie-I'm having the adventure of a lifetime," I admit. "Imagine finding yourself caught up in a live, mystical romance, where passion, sensuality and thwarted love are wrapped in real magic—well—that gives you some idea."

As I write this message, a message I won't send, I am sitting under some beautiful old walnut trees bathed in warm sunlight. Speaking to my understanding sister has made me a little tearful. So—My Lord Swallow—it is really out there now and we might even have ourselves an editor into the bargain. Dear Angels, please show us the way. Save my Laird from too much pain. May truth and learning come upon us all through this unusual adventure. Thank-you.

Early P.m. Mouse: *Dear Friend, I know I shouldn't be in touch, but I need to know if you plan on attending the school picnic tomorrow. Life is difficult at the moment. I still can't move from my position. The Laird is very hurt. He might not be in a good frame of mind to meet over a sandwich. Just let me know; we can stay away. If you need to be brief send a 'yes' or a 'no.' Things should improve soon; looks like I might have to be untrue to myself though. Thanks. M—X*

Bernard's business partner, Reg, has invited us to a birthday party this evening. He has a Lifestyle Block up in the hills; close to our Mountain. The Wood Exporting Industry keeps the partners well-heeled and amongst the affluent of the town's population, so they have the income to develop their property. Reg's wife is Korean. They have four adorable little girls and a houseful of Korean relatives who tend the gardens and pigs, clean the house and help with the children. Reg runs quite an empire; it's an unusual set-up. Lucia knows the children from violin lessons, so she and Rinky quickly find their feet. The boys refused to come with us.

Various relatives are scattered about the sitting room when we walk in— grannies, uncles, nieces and even a great grandmother! I get the impression that some have recently arrived in the country. Reg must be taking on the role of giant benefactor. He is a large man with a jolly disposition and a hedgehog haircut that his wife sometimes douses with the henna bottle. A huge television screen dominates the main room. A cookery programme followed by rugby seems to be entertaining them all.

The majority of the party sits out on the deck by the barbecue where some twinkly blue Christmas lights frame the wonderful view. A Korean relation stands over the sizzling beef and chicken. I understand he's responsible for the massive vegetable garden—it's a field, really. "What do you do with all your vegetables?" I ask Reg. "You must have an abundant harvest. Does your broter-in-law have a market stall or anything?" "Oh no, nothing like that," he replies. "Eric has everything he needs right here— anything we don't eat we give away to neighbours, don't we, mate!" he turns to a friend at his elbow and together they raise their whisky glasses with loud guffaws.

Of course, Reg is totally hooked on the whisky. The Single Malt Society that Bernard and The Laird instigated enjoys his avid support. He's even roped in the immediate neighbours. Judging by the noisy gang around the birthday table they thoroughly enjoy the new society. I am not altogether sure it is a healthy passion. The man sitting next to The Laird is interesting—

160

an expert kiwi fruit grower he surprises us with his biodynamic, organic farming knowledge; informing us at the end of the evening that he was involved in the land purchase for our now, twenty-year-old school.

Well, surprises all around. You never know what might emerge during a Kiwi barbecue. I even overhear The Laird engrossed in a conversation with the Korean brother in law; they are discussing Buddhism and Karma while they dish up the meat. Mountains of salad, followed by a lavish Pavlova, keep everyone satisfied. The Laird's tartan trews and Scottish anecdotes go down a treat. The whisky drinkers pass him a glass of mystery malt; one he hasn't met before. Those gathered eagerly await his opinion. While they are engrossed in the merits of the golden liquor I venture into the kitchen to lend a hand. Everything seems to be in order—'many hands on deck' is an understatement. I wander over to the sofa and sit next to the Korean great-grandmother. She turns towards me with a toothless grin. I take her hand, introducing myself. As I point out my family using sign language she laughs with her hand covering her mouth; I think she is embarrassed by her lack of teeth and slightly overcome by the attention. Her watery eyes tell a thousand tales. We sit together companionably for a while.

Sunday 18th February 2007

A.m. Mouse {Unsent}: I lay beside you this morning, My Love, close and quiet, warm and tender—my hand upon your Greenstone and your lips upon my brow. We lay together for a long time. I know you were there with me, our limbs entwined and our fingers walking along favourite paths. A time of stolen joy and waiting; our precious Boat secure in the Marina, resigned to everlasting dry-dock. The freedom and joy of our private Ocean is but a wistful memory.

I walk the dog as usual. The sunshine is brilliant this morning. I stop beneath a Punga fern at the corner of the drive, its hairy trunk highlighted by the golden light. Like giant fans the exotic branches reach for the sky. The ferns behind the Punga belong to the Mamacou. They are taller and don't have the hairy trunks. Their frondy leaves appear out of the top of the plant like umbrellas trying to shield the plants below. I often spy their trunks without any fronds at all; they always surprise me as they rear up, out of the Bush like menacing serpents. Are they emerging or dying off? I must ask someone.

I gaze into the Wheki Punga fern for a long time; a world of its own in the variety of colour, texture and form. Dark green to fresh lime, black to muddy brown the knobbly protrusions and flapping strands of the dead branches give way to the graceful fan. And in their very heart the extraordinary, coiled youngsters raise snake-like heads from a hallowed nest. They unfurl themselves in prehistoric ritual. I have described them before. The Punga fern is synonymous with New Zealand. I have seen the trunks used as garden fencing and the distinctive fronds adorn much Kiwi memorabilia. The 'Koru' shape of the young fern is arresting. I can see why the spiral design is used as a national symbol, along with the 'Silver Fern' of course. We have plenty of that in our strip of Native Bush along the drive, the underside is most definitely silver; also a Punga, it is a different variety to the Wheki. I wondered who had spray painted the plants when we first arrived on The Mountain.

Strolling home I consider my Sunday lesson. Perhaps I *am* being asked to relinquish my need for a private Gate into Heaven; my secret world. Perhaps The Angel in me needs to join the human race. Should I leave my private home? We are heading down to the harbour later this afternoon. Freya and Justin will sail their new boat into Parrot Bay around two o'clock.

"Come on Rinky and Lucia, let's swim out to the buoy; it's not far. See who gets there first." The Laird is away, challenging his willing daughter and friend to take the plunge. The sunshine sparkles pretty and perfect across the ripples today. The intrepid sailors have arrived and wave from the deck. They have had rough weather, extreme heat and a dose of sunstroke, but apart from that they seem exhilarated by their adventure. I volunteer to get everyone an ice cream and saunter off towards the pier. This side of the harbour is quiet. The beach is gritty and not so good for swimming. Several boats anchor here instead of berthing at the expensive Marina.

P.m. Mouse {Unsent}: *Ice cream and seagulls—gritty sand between my toes—The Mount towering above me in all its rugged wildness. I like to see the sheep grazing its slopes, watching their unlikely neighbours in campervans below. The tower blocks of the holiday apartments make an incongruous frame as they munch away. I wish you were here with me—X*

This evening The Laird takes me to bed, peeling off my clothes and remarking on my weight loss. I certainly feel light; hardly present on the Earth if truth be told. He is caring and gentle but I have nothing to give him. I am empty. I am missing my Angel too much. How can I explain that I need Adrian to feel whole?

Adrian didn't reply to my message about the school picnic. We went along briefly but he wasn't there. I helped Cordelia hang the new curtains in his classroom. It was a treat to step inside my Lover's sanctuary and walk over to view the latest chalkboard drawing. He has drawn a small picture of every child in the class; I wonder what the Main Lesson this week is about? I know a beautiful story will accompany the artwork. I took a piece of chalk and left a small message in the bottom corner, {-X—}, nothing he'll notice, unless one of the children points it out, of course, but perhaps he may feel some love as he steps into the room on Monday.

Monday 19th February 2007
Today Rinky has her first riding lesson after school. The young couple running the stables rent a steep-sided valley at the bottom of our road. My

goodness; I thought the hills were steep around *us*; these are even steeper! It feels strange to descend into such a depth from the road above. I hope my brakes hold out. Phil is American and his young wife, Carol, is friendly. She wears heaps of make-up and tells us she was a beautician before she met Phil; "I didn't know anything about horses before I married. I'm totally hooked now." She takes Rinky over to a pony called Boris. "He's twenty three years old and very gentle. Come on, you can help me groom him." She encourages The Minx who is slightly anxious. A small 'yappy-type-dog' barks around my feet as I walk back to the car.

I spotted Adrian twice today—just fleetingly. He was carrying cardboard boxes out of his classroom as I drove past. Our eyes met for a second. Later he was driving Vonny's car, parking at school just as I was. I hesitated, and then walked quickly past as Vonny was sitting beside him. I couldn't meet him with others present; polite conversation would be unbearable. I won't see him unless we are alone. I really need to be held by my man—in silence—nothing less, nothing more. I hate it when he uses my proper name when he says hello. I just need him to acknowledge the truth of what we share; that's all. I am sad and hurting. Maybe it will always be like this. We aren't meant to remember Heaven after all. If we did we certainly wouldn't be happy to hang around on Earth for longer than is absolutely necessary.

Chapter 3 Others

Tuesday 20th February 2007

There is a random Toitoi grass growing along our drive today. I haven't seen it before; a seed blown onto The Mountain perhaps? Or a bird, dropping a fertile morsel as he passed? The Bog-Brush is all ears and nose in the morning air. I love to see her Pointing instincts—paw uplifted, tail and nose indicating the bird or possum in the bushes. "No, my Friend—not today; one dunking in the pond was enough for this tired mother. We aren't going down there."

The Woodsman's Den hasn't had any visitors for a long time. I stop a while and study the Pukatea tree base that marks the right-hand entrance. Our Bush has a number of Pukatea trees; their wide spreading, skirt-like trunks are beautiful. They thrive in swampy ground. The flanged skirts are known as Plank-Buttresses. The one in the Woodsman's Den has a long limb coming out of a fold before entering the Earth. I decide it is rather phallic, like a male entering a voluptuous female. Perhaps the magic I sense about the place is steeped in fertility. The sky is different today; darker than usual with a golden glow behind the cloud cover. My senses are alert and my mind turns to the Pa Site and the living presence of The Mountain Ancestors. Are we to move away? Is the magic linked with the story I am writing? Perhaps I should claim the top cabin for my work. As the dog and I reach the end of the long driveway I half expect Adrian to walk towards me, silhouetted in the magical glow.

We visit the library after school for our weekly dose of new reading material. The children love this regular outing. I bump into Delphine as we leave the building. We say hello and pass the time of day. We don't mention Adrian. "You can talk to me anytime," she adds, before getting into her little, yellow car.

Oh——

P.m. Mouse {Unsent}: *And so, you ask your ex-girlfriend to say I can talk to her any time, My Friend, knowing I need a friendly ear but not understanding that I couldn't speak openly with her—lovely as she is. You haven't listened to my plea for some indication as to who knows what; for instance, what does Delphine know of our relationship? You spend every day with her while I am an outsider. She is there by your side, part of your life. No, thank-you for your care but I couldn't talk to her—not before I know* *what you have told her; what you keep telling her?*

How are you? Our eyes met briefly as I drove past today and we waved tentatively, our tiny caged boxes suddenly large and enclosing of our very selves-sad and strange. I imagine you have moved on in a surface kind of way. My Smiling Minstrel; your melody as pollen settling in many places but left to drift in the breeze. Were do you shed it now? But I know, deep down, you are still there with me; could not be anywhere else for 'we are', and you know that 'we are'.

Goodnight, Fine Sir. I shall meet you at 11p.m tonight, even if only fleetingly in your mind.

MONUMENT POOL

The town pool is my sanctuary of welcome ripples,
It draws me under a liquid buffer,
As friendly as a cup of Earl Grey tea, if you know what I mean.
Each time I take a breath I greet the ancient tree line above the Park.
I hear the seagulls and occasional children's voices
From the playground next door.
The Cicadas sing so loudly in all the trees,
Their clicking calls synonymous with the summer heat.
I am at peace.
I will miss this pool when we leave,
It will remain a strong memory for me of my life here,
In this town in North Island, New Zealand.

Wednesday 21st February 2007 Ash Wednesday

A.m. Mouse {Unsent}: We lay together again this morning, Lord Swallow-for over an hour. I meant to get up early but found my hand upon your Greenstone and couldn't pull myself away. Your eyes held mine for long, long minutes. You stroked my brow as we chatted, telling each other all the things we have been unable to say. We didn't make love for a while. We were not consumed by our usual fiery passion—a genuine sense of care and unconditional love swept over us both; an oasis in this barren time.

When we did make love a surprising urgency overtook us, as if we knew it would be short lived and was to be taken quickly before morning routines kicked in and our copper boxes locked once again. Goodbye, Lord Swallow. If I see you at School I shall wave. May your day—our day-bring steady, held blessing. I am yours—X

Ash Wednesday and I have already given up a major part of life; my meager food intake a Lenten abstinence unachieved in previous years. The scourge of mind, body and Spirit is well under way. Red and blue flags surrounding the pool catch my eye as I swim; a swimming gala will take place later this week. I am feeling slim and toned. Management officials

166

wander around my sanctuary while I breaststroke up and down the pool. I overhear a conversation; a face-lift is being planned for the old-fashioned site. A workman is busy with hammer and chisel in the water this morning. He removes a panel from the tiling. I swim in steady rhythm, the sun warming and glorious as ever. A small Asian man walks out of the changing rooms and stands at the pool's edge. He is well toned and obviously 'works out.' Is he trying to catch the ladies' eyes as he stands there? 'Sorry Sir—you are *definitely* not my type, in fact you couldn't be further away from the two men in my life. No, I shall not catch your eye.'

The watery bliss holds my sublime reverie and I face a peaceful surrender. I will go with the flow. Our precious Boat is a reality. Although she may remain dry-docked for an eternity her living presence is a fact. Part of the Quest is complete—The Boat exists in the regular world. Perhaps she is safer behind locked gates and our red-hot sparks contained in their copper boxes. If our love had to face everyday life with all its domestic chaos and stress I suppose it could lose the alchemist's heat. At least this way it survives intact. Yes—a comforting thought as Lent begins in this year **2007**. Our year, I feel.

Thursday 22ⁿᵈ February 2007

The Laird continues to be tolerant. He is kind and present but my feelings remain unchanged. I cannot turn to him as a wife. Poor man. I hate to hurt him. I cannot live a lie. I know I should move above all this; show unconditional love even when I am hurting. "Come on, let go; move on," I tell myself. I cannot let go. I cannot be untrue to myself. In my deepest person I am sad and longing. According to Eckhart Tolle I am just feeding my ego, but it refuses to retreat. The magnetic force is ever-present; my connection with Lord Swallow too powerful for me to deny.

"You can teach me how to reach these spiritual heights," The Laird suggests. "How do you get there? I'm ready to learn." I meet his gaze; my dear, willing Laird. "I don't know," I reply sadly. "My lessons have been axed. I am unable to continue learning. I'm sorry, I can't teach you."

After school drop-off I drive to town where the organic butcher sets me up with some mince and chicken for the Japanese students who arrive tomorrow. My younger brother, Wilf, and his family are also 'en route' to New Zealand; he and a couple of brothers-in-law are competing in the Taupo 'Iron Man' competition next month. Life promises to be busy over the coming weeks. I slip into the waiting water at Monument Pool after my shop. The temperature is perfect. Aquarobics for retired folk is well under way and my quiet sanctuary is not so peaceful today. I shan't take part in the jolly jumping, splashing, and noodle whacking display. Everyone seems to be enjoying themselves. Loud music adds to the hullabaloo. I complete my lengths without any prayerful reverie. One overweight lady is laughing so much her canvas sunhat falls off. I notice it has a floral neck flap to prevent sunburn.

Early P.m. Mouse {Unsent}: *I am missing you, My Friend. If you asked how I was, I would look you in the eye and reply honestly: "Well—I am all the S's: steady, settled, soulful, silent, separate, seriously smitten, spent, surrendering, sad, simple, sorrowful, sacred, sanctified, a solo sailor, a spiritual spiral, sometimes, slim, simpering, secluded, sliding, snatched, soldiering, shouldering, shackled, seeing signs, sealed, stolen.*

The Laird wants me to take on a part time job at College organizing the details of a community service project for his department. I can't say I am overly keen on the idea but I have agreed and tossed him the completed employment forms before he left for work this morning. I feel trapped with no alternative. My suggestion of having the top cabin for my writing is met with disapproval. "It would be better to put Cedric up there," I am told. I must bow my head and surrender to being a good wife; give my husband the love he deserves. I need to keep him steady. I realize he is a depressive character and not as strong as I imagined. His energy feeds off mine and mine is all dried up. I have been replenishing it with our friendship this year, My Fine Sir.

Before nightfall I climb to the top of the Pa Site with my hairy friend. The views are astounding. I really can't quite describe the panoramic glory. The sun is gentle and the breeze ruffles my hair; unruly after my swim today. The cows swish their tails lazily on the opposite bank and the neighbour's bougainvillea is vibrant with colour. The neighbours used to own all this land; their cabin bungalow is just visible across the wetland and positioned high up, above the road. They painted it a grassy green last month. We have met Moira and George a couple of times, weeding the shared part of the drive. "We planted all the ornamental shrubs and trees at this end of the land," they informed us. Their steep driveway is pretty; lined with Golden Elm and the blue and white Agapanthus that grow so well in the climate. I sit and meditate for a while, watching the sun begin its nighttime ritual; "over to you, Angels and Ancestors—over to you." I close my eyes and let the evening breeze take my prayer.

Friday 23rd February 2007

Early p.m. Mouse {Unsent}: *Here I am, parked outside your classroom, knowing you are a stone's throw away. I am missing you so much, My Love. I am looking at your class garden, some orange Canna Lilies directly ahead of me. Their exotic, broad leaves are tinged with veins of red and gold.*

I imagined you accompanied me on my morning walk today with Little Arthur—nice. As I thought of our mystical trio, three dandelion seeds floated high above my head. They were joined together so lightly. I watched as they climbed higher and higher, enticed by the blue sky and quiet, watching clouds. My eyes followed them for a while—and then they drifted out of sight. As I sit here, waiting for school to end, I decide I am in a truly

168

extraordinary position. What a rare gift to be recording our very own, romantic epic. I relish each moment I steal to write; to record events as they unfurl and to write retrospectively at the same time. The pages of the first Book are growing. Like a child in the womb, an individual emerges with the potential to breathe unaided. This is our gift to the world, My Friend. The present diary writing is for the second Book. I wonder how many books are waiting to be written. Will we ever have a 'Setting Sail'?' I hope our tale exudes the drama, mysticism and comedy we have recorded. If life is an illusion that we create as we progress, then we are doing pretty well. I saw Sienna outside the staff room today; she asked me twice if I was okay. Have you told her about us? I wish I knew what was going on—I really do.

The Bog-Brush made us hoot with laughter this afternoon. We arrived back on the Mountain after school and disembarked in the usual fashion. Well—a dog has to do what a dog has to do; there she was in mid defecation when she let out a series of painful howls. We all winced, wondering if she had eaten some gorse-"or maybe it's my school pencil she was chewing this morning," piped up The Go-Getter. The Japanese students must have wondered what on earth was happening; their surprised expressions made us laugh all the more. What a hilarious introduction to The Castle on The Mountain. Poor dog, she really is a handful at the moment.

"Are you sure your relationship with Adrian is God-given?" The Laird asked me before breakfast this morning. "Most certainly," I answered; "the most profound gift ever." "You can use all the pretty words you like," he replied, "but you are still not addressing the destructive element of this liaison." "For you, perhaps, but it couldn't be further from that for me." I tried to explain that I don't feel any worry or sadness because I exist on another dimension; I am less affected by earth-bound regulation. I must have appeared cold-hearted. "My depression is back again—all my plans are up in the air," my poor husband replied.

"Why does everything have to be founded on me?" I asked plaintively. "Can't you be more independent?" "Yes, I could. I could just bugger off. You are blackmailing me. You will only give yourself to me if *he* is back in your life. Do you really think you can have him as *well* as me? Sorry—no go. Do you still want to be married? Who will pay the mortgage? Who will look after the children?"

"It would have been better if you had never known," I concluded. "We *were* in love—I know we were," the Laird continued wistfully. "Yes, we were," I replied, not adding that we have always had an immature understanding of true love. Emotional blocks in a relationship prevent it from deepening. I didn't mention the profound levels I am capable of reaching; the levels I know we cannot reach together, although I did admit to being depleted by the lack of joy and regular depression that accompanies us so much of the time. Our emotional blocks are a shared issue; neither of us is well versed in negotiating that potential minefield. Our British private schooling and similar, services background bequeaths us the same difficulties. What should I do? Blow apart our foundation for something I can't even have? Why, oh why am I being so bull-headed? Why can't I return to the earth-bound love of before? I don't know. I really don't. Adrian probably won't ever speak to me again; he has been badly rattled.

My brother, Wilf, and his family have arrived in the country. They telephone and we chat. How wonderful to have them here, on this side of the world! Half-way through the flight their three-year-old announced: "I think I'll go outside and play now!" They have rented a house in Taupo and their Iron Man training is well underway.

Swimming at the pool this morning felt clear and steady after the honest talk and big 'out breath' The Laird and I shared earlier. I chose a double lane and swam between the black lines of the pool's floor; feelings of freedom filling me like the wind inside billowing pillowcases on the line. I like watching the flapping linen as it dries in the Mountain breeze. What path do I tread? The path of a double life? In many ways that works well, but probably not for long. I swam through the watery eddies of neighbouring swimmers, strong and undaunted. My Love, are you there? Might you wait for me at the end of the swimming lane one day?

I walked the dog and tidied the top cabin for the Japanese students when I got home. And then I wrote more of the story—sixty-seven pages of Microsoft already written and only halfway through the second notebook. Oh my, this is a huge story. Is it of interest to me alone or could others find it exciting? I must run it past Lord Swallow.

P.m. Mouse: *Hi Friend. How are you? Only texting to ask if I can talk about a business idea. The Laird is away in Christchurch for the weekend. Can I phone you? Just tell me when. Don't reply if you would rather not—M—X*

Mouse {Unsent}: *Our Asian guests—2 boys aged 15—are settled. Lasagna and dog walks in beautiful sunshine—greeting the pig—trampoline and card games. All domestic and peaceful. Laird away in Christchurch giving whisky talks; unsettled and gloomy. Do I have to sacrifice my happiness for his sanity? 'In sickness and in health', I promised—don't feel like it though.*

I don't hear back from Adrian. I need various things from him for our story; e-mails from Europe, the Pa Site photo with its angelic light, diary writings—and has he seen the missing 'Stamen Gazer' poem I might have left with him? And then I wonder; how will he feel about having his inner thoughts recorded? Now that he feels others' accusation might he shrink from our highlighted infidelity? Would he rather not open up the wound? He mightn't be able to rise above his constant feelings of shame and guilt. And he did tell me to leave it be for a year.

Do I offer our caged sparks their freedom? The Book could open our copper boxes, re-igniting the fire. Where does Lord Swallow keep his copper box? Has he lost it? Reading our script, let alone partaking in the compilation, would fall into the forbidden realm and go against his promise to Simon and The Laird. But—we have a powerful story to tell, a couple of proofreaders in the U.K lined up, {with an editor into the bargain}, and a business opening. This holds golden possibility. The story reads well so far. It would be unfair not to offer Adrian the opportunity and I know the time is right. It's tricky, for we need our passion to drive the story. I also need his permission to send his personal writing to proofreaders.

This is a lot to digest. Our writing is a joint project and I know we could make something of it. Is it important? Is it the underlying reason for our connection? I need Adrian to cast his eye over The Book so far. We could work by e-mail; not spend any time together. We could keep our love alive— but allowed. Oh, I don't know. I'm not sure Adrian's integrity would allow him to go there. He lives in fear of losing his job if he oversteps any mark.

Saturday 24th February2007

The Japanese boys are pleasant and understand very little. They work their way around the complications of knives, forks and table etiquette with serious expressions. Last night's lasagna proved interesting. I hope they liked it. They enjoy the card game 'Happy Families' and the livestock outside the kitchen door is a big hit. I found them gazing at the immense views after supper last night, standing on the deck of the top cabin. They had changed out of school uniform into traditional Japanese shirts and shorts. Later on I spied them chatting to the pig and chasing chickens before disappearing over the hill to explore The Mountain. My boys aren't too keen on interaction so it's left to me to be sociable, although Rinky is happy to play cards. The students belong to a school group and have lessons at The Laird's College in the mornings and excursions in the afternoons. They are here for two weeks. We give them bed and board for twenty-five dollars a night each, which isn't bad. We had a couple staying last year. I have to prepare their lunchboxes everyday and entertain them at the weekend. I am *not* looking forward to coping with the whole household alone, today and tomorrow.

The Laird calls from Christchurch—"It's cold and wet here," he tells me; "just like the last time I visited." I send him a text saying that I am missing him-*"My happiness is not worth the cost of your depression returning."* And it isn't. Only if all parties are happy can my liaison with Adrian be acceptable. What a mess we are in—all good learning, I'm sure. I can't explain how I feel; that nothing has changed. He knows I am hurting inside because my spirit is wounded. On a purely domestic level how can a husband accept that? He can't, certainly not when I keep the flame alive through the keyboard. Our copious text messages are extraordinary in their quality and quantity. What are they meant for, if not for a story? I need to record the unusual events. Have Adrian and I really written so much to each other?

Halting our literary connection means I might get to catch up.

There is no reply from Lord Swallow. Is he cross that I've tempted him to regain contact? Perhaps he blames me for cheating on my husband. Or does he make me wait, increasing my desire for our union and propelling me to leave The Laird? I don't know *what* he is thinking. My mind tells me many things about Adrian's mind-set. This is the most likely scenario:

'Our union is unique and beautiful. You are my perfect woman; my Soul Mate. But I will not destroy a family for the sake of your hand. Only if you step away yourself, without any encouragement from me and with harmony behind you, will I come for you. I cannot tell you how deeply I care; I won't even acknowledge the profundity. I will not give you any clues. I will not work on The Book. I live in the present; I never turn towards past or future; you know that. What will be will be. The Angels are in charge.'

A.m. Adrian: *Hi Friend, a call would be great. Call anytime. Now is good.*

Adrian's message arrives an hour after it was sent. How lovely to see my screen light up. Did he have to pluck up courage to contact me? Or has he genuinely lost interest and texts me out of curiosity only. I wonder. And why was the message so delayed?

Mouse: *Dear Friend—am busy at my desk. Now would be fine except that Rinky and the Japanese students we have staying are busy with the puzzle beside me. Not that I plan to whisper sweet nothings in your ear. I will text if a clear moment appears. Hope you are well—*

No clear moment appears and the phone line is crackly and dies suddenly; strange? The day begins in its whirlwind of guests and children, constant food and animal tending. The Go-Getter stays in bed later than usual. We drive into town when he wakes, leaving Cedric at home with the mad hound. "Keep her inside," I remind him. "She's learnt how to jump over the deck." Drat!

Negotiating the skiddy gravel The Go-Getter asks: "Do you think 'super-grip' tarmac will ever be invented?" We chat about the possibilities; how the road industry must have various recipes up their sleeve. "And just think of all those other items we use everyday; imagine how *they* were invented." I continue. "Imagine the toothpaste lid, for instance. Think how complicated that must have been to make." "It probably took more than one person," answers my ever-chatty chappie. "And cocktail sticks," he pipes up, "whose idea was *that*?" "Cocktail sticks?" I ask. "What on earth made you think of those?" I chuckle to myself over his imaginative capacity. I wonder where he gets it?! I deliver him at a classmate's house for the day before heading to Monument Pool with Rinky and the Japanese duo.

The Japanese boys enjoy the hour we spend in the swimming pool, although I notice they get rather chilled. Afterwards I take everyone to the fish market for a warming lunch of fish and chips beside the wharf.

Midday, Adrian: *Are you free?*
{This message took over an hour to reach me—again.}

Mouse: *Hi Friend, I'm at the fish market on the wharf; Japanese in tow. Might go to Tui Park after lunch. Am free after that—will take them home at some stage. What are you up to on this fine day?*

I am both excited and surprised that Adrian is responding to my message. A warm glow fills me like a shaft of sunshine syrup. We spend a short time at the park before driving to the other side of town to collect Caleb—a school friend of Rinky's who is spending the afternoon with us on The Mountain. Rinky wants to show him the big swings in the Twealm Realm.

Early P.m. Adrian: *Going to school to cut weeds for the haymaking— about fifteen minutes.*

Mouse: *Hi Friend—am back on The Mountain. Just collected Caleb. Will be free when I take him home later this evening. Happy weeding.*

The afternoon and early evening is busy with cooking, animals, hair washing, writing and general domestic chores. Rinky is overtired and Cedric is grotty. I imagine they need a good meal and some sleep. Bread dough on, omelettes made and eaten and lots of trampolining use up several hours. Weekends are hard work, especially with Japanese guests.
All set—down to town again, leaving Rinky with Cedric and the students.

Mouse: *Dear Friend, am just heading back down the hill with Caleb. Am free for a short while before picking up The Go-Getter at about 9p.m. Are you around?*

I hear nothing. Has Adrian lost his nerve? Unlikely. I expect he is busy elsewhere, perhaps expecting me to turn up at school and help with the weeding. I pull in to Tui Park and watch the sky turn from lilac to grey. The tide is right out. I listen to gentle music and wait. I'll give him another ten minutes. I don't have long before my next child collection and the park gates will be closed soon. If I don't hear I shall head home. Perhaps we aren't supposed to meet today. Our connections are being stalled at every turn. I'll wait until 8.30 but not longer—time to write up my diary.
I enjoy being the observer with time on my own, enclosed in a private capsule with the world going by; music and reverie filling my soul. I am warmed by the thought that Adrian is happy to meet me, that he knows I would like to see him. My phone rings. Why is my Father telephoning from

the U.K? He never uses my mobile number. "We couldn't raise you at home—just wondering how you are." We chat for a while. More precious time lost.

8.15-p.m. Adrian: *Hmm—wondering if I should invite you round here. Business, eh?*

Mouse: *Hmm—wondering too. I do have things I need to discuss. Am running out of time now—*

Adrian: *Impulsively he says—come around. Quick visit. Cup of tea; careful tea.*

I look at my watch. I consider Adrian's hesitancy, realizing it is the Prince's impulsive, less honourable brother that speaks. I had better not visit. I don't want to tempt him. I think we might fall into each other after such a long parting.

Mouse: *Dear Friend—would really love to—have run out of time now. Maybe just as well.*

I collect The Go-Getter and we drive up the hill together, passing a road sign that says: 'Slippery when wet'. "I don't think they've used the 'super-grip tarmac' here!" I laugh. "Mmm-It's probably too expensive," he replies. We telephone The Laird when we get home. He sounds well, although lonely. I don't like to think of him lonely. The whisky talks were a success. "I could have a new career if I wanted," he tells us. Once the smaller two are in bed and the Japanese installed in the top cabin Cedric and I spend quality time together. We like our peaceful moments; he is a quiet boy who prefers one-to-one companionship. We watch a crazy film about a museum caretaker where all the displays come to life at night. Later on I cook some buns, write up more of The Book and wonder about our day—mulling over the thwarted connections between Adrian and myself. How many obstacles did we meet? I count them:

Unusually long delays over receiving text messages; our dodgy phone line that suddenly went dead; children and guests beside me when we could have chatted; missing our potential park connection; my father phoning when I might have had time to see Adrian, occupying the line and making his last message so late. I hope Adrian wasn't upset by my refusal to meet at the last minute. There were other reasons I declined. If we had had more time I would have said; "I am unsure; I don't know if Vonny knows about us—I don't know where to park—I don't know which door to use—I don't know how to be together—what we can be to each other. Too many 'don't knows' for a quick cup of tea. Sorry my Love; can't do it. 'Quick' is fine when we are clear and knowing, but not otherwise. We need to catch up quietly—in the way that suits us both. Ten weeks is a long time to have been parted. If I am honest I also have my pride to consider. I don't want to appear over anxious to see you, especially if you have lost interest."

I curl up in my duvet and switch off our busy day, saying a little prayer: "Dear Angels, please give us clarity. We are submitting but frustrated. I sense a maturity edging its way towards The Laird and I, but not a 'together maturity'. Is he moving towards letting me go a little? I don't know. My Lord Swallow wishes to see me; that is clear, I think? His contact warms me. Please guide us."

Sunday 25th February 2007

A.m. Mouse: "Come to me"—she whispers into the dawn. "Come to me as pollen on the breeze. Come settle on my brow, my limbs, my lips. Come to me," she sighs across the valley—knowing that he cannot—X

There is no reply from Adrian. I check my phone several times but he doesn't make contact. I suppose I am testing the honourable King, testing him sorely. I wish I knew his thoughts. Does he welcome my messages? Wonky the rooster brings his girlfriend inside for a shared porridge breakfast this morning. They are rather sweet together. I shouldn't think it's easy for him to woe the girls; he looks peculiar with his crooked beak. The Japanese are managing admirably, even learning to barge the pig off the back door step and negotiating chickens as they pour themselves cereal.

At midday I bundle the whole family into the van with a picnic and drive to Rotorua. We are collecting The Laird from the airport at one-thirty. My brother and his family are driving up from Taupo and meeting us there. The Rotorua airport is larger than our local one. It offers the closest flights to and from the South Island. Trying to explain away the flatulent, sulphur pong of the thermal geysers to the Japanese as we approach the area is hilarious. Turning around I make a series of raspberry noises while holding my nose, indicating that the children are *not* the culprits. Our guests look even more confused than usual and I get a fit of the giggles. Cedric scowls at me although I notice the corner of his mouth twitching.

What a joy to be reunited with my brother and his family; the little boys are adorable. Rinky The Minx is thrilled to be the big cousin today. We picnic by the lake and walk around the attractive park, ending the day in a thermal hot pool together. The Tudor style Bath House in the centre of town is interesting. Opened in 1908 as a South Seas Spa it boasts an incongruous, Bavarian image. I find the European structure rather odd alongside the native culture and geothermal activity, but I suppose it gives a good indication of the multi-national, multi-layered make-up of the nation. The building is huge with luxurious interiors and marble sculptures behind the imposing façade. The established gardens around the building make a restful stop; the little boys play peek-a-boo behind the rich planting. Apparently the building was the government's first project in the then, newly launched tourism industry.

My brother has a chest infection after the flight so we take things easy and relax in the sunshine. The spa pool minerals should do him good. I enjoy hearing about his present career as a solicitor in the City. He works long hours in London, including involvement in a new leisure website, hopefully launching later in the year. He has undertaken a massive exercise program for the coming Iron Man competition. He is super-fit and two brothers-in-law join the family party in Taupo tomorrow. Serious training resumes in the morning. The competition is only six days away.

A crock-pot lamb supper welcomes home The Laird. After the meal the children disperse and we hold each other close. "I'm sorry I said I don't value our marriage," I tell him. "Of course I do, really." "I know you need to grow," he replies. "I'm sorry to have chosen an unconventional path;" I try to console him.

Chapter 4 Only

Monday 26th February 2007
   A.m. Mouse: From her turret vantage point the Lady of the Castle looks out over the valley. She imagines him resting in the heart of the Forest; she knows her Lord Swallow is there. Sunshine filters through the trees, tracing patterns across his linen shirt—she knows the way it moves. She sees him look up, smiling a warm welcome at the dancing light. He is collecting herbs for a woodsman's brew. The early morning breeze has woken her—Lord Swallow's watching, waiting heart is her's today. She can sense his gaze. He has walked to the Forest edge, his Woodsman's axe over his shoulder in readiness for any woodland treasure—and as protection—for The Laird's henchmen may lie in wait. He worries they may track his movements.

His Lady is waving a white scarf from the turret. It flutters in the gentle breeze—flutters in his mind too—a message that she is his for a while. He stands, gazing up at the Castle. He is feeling bold today; the risk-taking Prince to the fore. He lights a small fire away from the tree-line. Might she see his smoke signal? Will she know what it means? For he has given his word and the honourable course of action is a challenge he needs to achieve. His livelihood, and most importantly, his Kingly bearing are at stake.

And yet—his Lady calls—he has not seen her for weeks. He hasn't been able to smile into her eyes to let her know everything is all right; that he is here. All he has been able to do is tell her their love is over; over for him, knowing how his statement will make her heart bleed. The red stain is visible, even from the valley floor. Lord Swallow makes a decision and hurries to the Marina, remembering the way with ease. It is a long time since he ran this way. The route comes back to him instantly—the twists and turns, the quiet passages and short cuts that take him swiftly through the town's back streets to the Marina and beckoning Ocean; their Ocean.

Knowing the Harbour Master is out of town he dares steal a look through the fence at their beautiful Boat. Why is she parked around the back? And why have they installed such high gates?

Oh—she looks so forlorn. His heart sinks. At least she is sound and whole—remarkable really; the recent weather has been inclement and her crew unable to attend to her needs. With a practiced, seaman's eye Lord Swallow scans their precious vessel carefully. He notices areas that need attention; peeling paintwork and rusting cleats—cosmetic details he knows. All the same, he wishes he could spend time repairing the damage. He longs with a fierce passion to run his hands along her fine keel; to remove the ugly

*'No Entry' sign that hangs crookedly from the middle mast. But he cannot fit through the narrow gap between the gate and the fence. A sudden determination fills his heart; she belongs to him. He **will** find a way to gain access, despite the locked gates. But not as a thief in the night. He is a nobleman after all. His Lady knows he waits in the Forest—that he hasn't forgotten her.*

He looks more closely at the rigging; has his Lady been solo sailing? Would she know how? The Boat appears weather-beaten, salty, slimmer even than he recalls. He must warn her about sailing alone. He knows The Laird doesn't take the helm. But where is she now? He was sure they would meet here today. Has she lost courage? Like sand through his fingers she has slipped from his grasp. There—yet not there. The Angels have denied them permission. He turns away sadly, glancing over his shoulder a couple of times. He could not find a way in and perhaps neither could she. Anyway, he has his life to get on with.

She watches from behind The Boat as he walks away. Did he not realize she was there?

I only manage a short swim today—half the town's primary school children arrive for a gala and I splash through my lengths before the pool is closed to the public. A sea of children clutching rucksacks pile into the changing rooms as I hurriedly dress. They laugh and chatter, grabbing pegs closest to the showers. I notice a microphone being installed beside the office and friendly staff walks about with armfuls of clipboards and swimming caps. One blousy lady in an orange bid is holding a starting pistol.

My father phones me again on my mobile. Our main line is still on the blink. Is he checking up on me? He is anxious to hear about my brother's arrival and our day out in Rotorua. He loves to hear about the grandchildren; what did we think of the little boys—aren't they adorable? An expensive supermarket shop sees the van groaning up the hill by midday. Over three hundred and fifty dollars worth of food takes me a good half hour to unload and install in the larder and fridges. We have another student friend arriving on Tuesday. I receive two phone calls from The Laird. Is he checking up on me too? Perhaps he senses my happier mood and wonders if I have been in touch with Adrian. I suppose my voice is brighter and my touch lighter. He is pensive—maybe a little sad; "I miss my friends at home," he says. "I miss England. I haven't heard from anyone since Christmas." I know he hasn't spoken to friends because of his depression. He would have to admit to a breakdown in our marriage—the humiliating fact of his wife's betrayal and his inability to make her happy. How can a man admit such a truth to his male comrades? That his wife has replaced him with another? I suppose he faces the ultimate humiliation. A hard place to stand for an often-arrogant man. For I have not, cannot and will not deny my love for Adrian. I cannot promise never to see him again.

The Laird must realize this and suffer daily as a result. Nevertheless we were loving and close this morning. I do sense a shift somehow. Perhaps I feel some freedom in the air. Do I need my own space? My own life where Adrian can feature? These thoughts are still uppermost in my mind. The Telecom engineer from Suffolk appreciates the cup of English tea I provide. He has only been in the country a couple of months. Poor fellow—he is here for ages, starting with the faulty line investigation at the drive entrance, scrambling over the gorse-covered Mountain and eventually locating a mouse-chewed wire in the corner of 'the shid'! A stark contrast to Colchester—better make him another brew.

I spend more time on The Book while the engineer is working. I am pleased to see my writing improving; it's not as waffly as it was in the beginning. I have edited a lot this week. I am so excited about this creative process. I intuitively know we could keep our love alive, and allowed, through the writing. I hope The Angels haven't forgotten us. Perhaps I need to establish my path with The Laird before Adrian and I can come together. Or maybe there is an all-together different outcome for us.

These thoughts swirl through my mind like wind-tossed leaves. The predominant image taking centre stage shows a man and a woman unable to resist the magnetic force of their birthright; *'deep in embrace, softly— gently—quietly.'*

I see Adrian at school pick-up today, just in passing. He walks through the car park as I pull up. He looks well, wearing jeans and colourful waistcoat over a white T-shirt. Angels interfere again by way of arguing children who dash to the car and try to claim the front seat. I cannot meet my Lover's gaze. I reverse away quickly, not wanting to say hello in public. The Bog-Brush tries to squeeze onto the front car seat too; the noise inside the van is quite something. She escaped The Mountain stronghold *again* this morning, depositing the bedraggled body of a baby Pukeko on the sofa when she returned dripping and muddy from the pond. Oh, the joys of arguing off-spring, mad hounds and unsound dog-kennels.

Tuesday 27th February 2007
A.m. Mouse {Unsent}: Good morning, Fine Sir—was that you waking me at 1.30 this morning? We were off on another road trip in a vivid dream. You were kissing me with such urgency that I woke up and took two hours to get back to sleep. Eventually you made love to me and then I slept comfortably. The ache at the back of my head continues—X

I have reached the height of our passion in the story, reliving those weeks is a powerful drug and the strange ache moves higher up, above my ear on the right-hand side. The script increases. My touch-typing speeds up.

I wait with other mothers beside the school seesaw this afternoon. The children come out at three o'clock. I chat to Karen and don't notice Adrian joining the group. I am nervous and agitated; oh-no-I can't meet him like this, please no. I won't speak pleasant banalities with others present, pretending everything is fine. We can't skip the past year. I am not ready to burst this bubble. I turn away quickly as my conversation ends, knowing he will notice. Ours was the next hello and conversation. I feel bad walking off like this. I know his eyes follow me. Does he notice my marked weight loss? Does he want to speak to me? Our thwarted weekend rendezvous was both unsettling and frustrating. I hope he realizes why I cannot say hello in public.

P.m. Mouse: Sorry, My Dearest Friend—I cannot greet you after ten weeks as if we are casual acquaintances, using our formal names and chatting about the weather. I need to spend personal time with you first, and then I could play those games in public. I'm sorry if it hurt you when I walked away. I want to be with you so very much. I would come and visit but I don't know if Vonny knows about us-I don't know which door to knock on first—I don't know if you want to hear from me. Too many 'don't knows'. Easier to stay in my solitary, Mountain bubble. Sorry—

Wednesday 28th February 2007

I was cold last night and wrapped myself up in one of Adrian's shirts. The Laird came to bed and tenderly stroked my head. "My little one," he said gently. Yes, we are closer again, although he senses I need to be elsewhere. I need my strength back. I am hardly present on the Earth. Three weeks into my meager diet of one meal a day. There is nothing like thwarted love to subdue the appetite. "We are both determined people, aren't we?" The Laird states. "Yes," I agree.

Perhaps it's time for us to use our strengths elsewhere. My husband is getting on with life, despite the return of his depression. I turn to him and give him a hug—half feeling like it, half not. He doesn't understand the strength and intensity of my connection with Lord Swallow.

I miss my swimming this week—the pool has been closed for various galas and other club functions. My soul is less content without the enveloping relief.

P.m. Mouse: {Unsent}: My Darling, I am missing you so much today. Yes, we are all steadier. Yes, The Laird and I are close again. Yes, he thinks I am over you. But no, my Lover, I will never be 'over you'. How could I be? The house is tidy and the larder well-stocked with various ingredients that meet with the Castle Inmates' approval. The Laird took me in his arms during our picnic at Tui Park this afternoon; "I love you", he said. "I admire your knowledge. I'll take an axe to anyone who meddles with my wife." I said nothing, smiling weakly. I poured the thermos tea and quietly packed away the picnic supper.

Yesterday I sent my author/editor sister, Mizzie, a synopsis for the story. I am pleased with the way it flows. I think The Book is well-represented. I am excited by her response; high praise indeed from a professional writer. If we could make something of the story and become financially stable—well—lots of doors would open. Impossibilities would melt away and the world might welcome our eager feet. I do need to speak to Lord Swallow; to pass the ideas by him.

E-mail from Mizzie: **I am honestly intrigued by this, Sis—well done! You've grasped the essentials of a synopsis pretty well. There are several things you can do to improve it further, though. Remember that a publisher is coming to this cold and will need more direct pointers, eg character names, some more details regarding plot (explain what the Castle on the Mountain is, for example) and, I would suggest around 3 chapters to help put the synopsis in context. I'd be delighted to offer my assistance as ruthless editor. What do you think?**
Supper's boiling over - work is shouting at me - la la la...

P.m. Mouse: {Unsent}: My Friend, I find it so hard when you are out of touch. I really need to speak with you. Are you testing me? Or yourself? I wish I knew. I felt more alive at the festival meeting this afternoon. I spent time with Sammy after the meeting; she and I got excited about a new 'After School Club' that she and Bruce are opening. Would I like to be involved? I said I would be interested. They are naming the enterprise 'Camellia House' and will operate out of a building they own in town. And so, My Love—goodnight. I am lying beside you in your new chamber, holding you close as you read and I snooze. Lover—oh yes—most certainly that. Sleep well. X—X

Thursday 1st March 2007

The weather is cold and damp today. I don't sleep well. I sense my Lover calling me at four a.m. I am beside him instantly, close and intimate before I fully wake. My diet is making my monthly cycle slow and half-hearted. The mornings are noticeably dark and some of the trees in Monument Park are losing their leaves. The seasonal changes assume less drama than at home. Apparently they are more marked in the South Island.

After delivering our student friend to the bus depot I walk the Bog-Brush in the bay at Monument Park. The tide is right out and we have a wonderful dash along the sands. We walk beyond Dragonfly Cove and I let her run on a long rope. My goodness, how she loves the exhilaration of allowed speed! She nearly pulls me over several times but I manage to brace myself against the wet sand. I encourage her to run in huge circles around me, splashing into the water as she chases seagulls. She is too disobedient to be allowed off the lead. We pass some impressive houses on the water's edge that I haven't seen before—large homes; they must be expensive. One is particularly pretty; a classic design with a bay window and white roses growing up the coffee-coloured walls. The house resembles a giant wedding cake with a couple of elegant pillars completing the effect. A bouncy Golden Retriever barks wildly as we pass. The water is as still as a glass mirror today—lovely. We must come here again. We are both having a grand time.

Mizzie has sent me another encouraging e-mail; she likes the title of the first Book. Eagerly I tackle the writing; this is going to take months. But the creative project will keep me focused and alive; a good thing. I *must* speak to Adrian soon. I am feeling bold. I decide to take the bull by the horns and send him another message.

Midday, Mouse: *Dearest Friend of the beautiful smile and tiresome Lady Friend—are you home today? Sorry to bother you. I would like to be in touch. I do need to talk to you. Shall I phone? I am home alone until 4.30 p.m. M-X*

Adrian: *I have a meeting starting in 10 minutes. What do you need to talk about? I sense a life-shock coming. Will I keep my word to The Laird if I speak to his wife about anything other than business? Is she coming out of The Gate or is she firing notes over the Castle wall? What could it be about?*

Mouse: *Don't worry—no life-shocks. Does it shock you when I send a message? I would hate to think I was a negative presence in your life. I need to talk to you about our writing; nothing scary. We have an opening with a professional, U.K editor and contacts in the publishing world. The editor is keen to start proof reading. So yes—in a way I am firing notes over the Castle wall—100 Microsoft pages in fact. If they take off and sprout their own wings then I would indeed have my ticket to walk out of the Castle Gates. But, and this is the tricky part—our writing is a joint project. This is our story; our creativity. I sense it is important for us to complete The Books together—perhaps by e-mail if we cannot meet. The difficulty is that it needs to be soon, otherwise we will forget. I know this goes against your decision of not being involved for a year. So—think on it. The synopsis is looking promising. It may come to nothing but it would be unfair not to offer you the opportunity. I also need your permission to put your beautiful words into print, anonymously of course. I am not expecting you to desire me back in your arms, My Friend. Just let me know your thoughts; that's all. You don't need to pack your bags or saddle the stable's swiftest gelding just yet. M—X*

Adrian's tone upsets me. It is hard-edged; concerned more with self than anything else. Is he annoyed that I am trying to contact him? Does he want me off his back? His claim that he would walk to meet me if I were a free woman suddenly appears unrealistic. The King would stand up to meet me but possibly not The Minstrel; too many life-shocks for him. He has been badly rattled. Bother and blast. If The Laird hadn't slammed him I would still have my friend. I cannot feel close to The Laird; he has hurt me, for the right reasons of course, but he has hurt me nonetheless. I suspect Adrian will refuse to be involved in the writing. I don't think his risk-taking side will rise to the challenge, not if I remain at arm's length and out of his life. He doesn't do 'partial involvement.'

Friday 2nd March 2007

Midday, Mouse {Unsent}: Dear Angels, if only these two men of mine could scale the impossible mountain, could shake hands and make an agreement–if only that was possible. As peculiar as it seems I know it could work in our life situation. I walked the dog through the glistening water at Tui Park this morning. We followed one of your sparkle paths where prayers and hope danced before our tentative feet. We walked a long way, following the golden trail, letting the sand and estuary mud slide between our toes. The hound swam while I waded in thigh-deep water. I like the way she is so silent when she swims. My bare shoulders started to burn so we stood beneath an old Pohutukawa tree to watch the dancing sprites a while longer. The tree beards hang like stately whiskers from the oldest branches. I have never touched the hanging parts before. They are surprisingly stiff and solid, like substantial, stable brooms. The tips of the beards are pink. As we stood there another dog dashed past, jumping gleefully through the water. I didn't let the Bog-Brush off her lead; she tends to pick fights with other dogs and would disappear for hours. Dear Angels, if you are listening please hold us in these challenging times.

"Hello Hon;" my friend Carla calls across the playground as I wait for children to finish School this afternoon. She has been relief-teaching in Class 2 this week. "How are you doing?" She asks. "How are your Japanese boys getting along? Mine is awful; he eats with his mouth open and leaves the table before everyone else has finished. He stays in his room all the time. I'm looking forward to him leaving!" I laugh, telling Carla that ours are well mannered although they like their own company too. "Hey, Damian," she beckons a twelve-year-old boy sauntering through the playground with a bag of sports kit. "There's something of yours on the deck that is embarrassing the girls—you had better go and collect it." Turning to me she whispers; "It's a pair of his underpants, Hon." We laugh together. I do like Carla. I know Adrian has spoken to her about our relationship, although I haven't done so myself. Before leaving School I catch Cordelia to ask her advice over the strange pain at the back of my head. "It could be that you are ducking out of facing something," she says. Hmm—ducking away from meeting Adrian? I wonder. Ducking away from standing up to The Laird? Or maybe ducking away from the truth that Adrian will never be mine?

The Laird comes home clutching a new book that interests him—"It's about life choices; the importance of our 'Choice Worlds.' We each have an individual world that needs to be happy. The people around us should compliment and support that world." I am pleased to see him brighter this evening, although I suppose the book subject is another lesson in disguise. He walks the dog this evening for a change, returning with another announcement for his undisciplined wife; "You know, you and the dog have many similarities—you are both impossible to train, you are both unruly and you definitely require space and high boundaries. Oh—and I've invited the English student from school to supper; you remember Tim? The eighteen-year-old whose parents have moved to Hong Kong, leaving him here, alone. He's in a bad way—a stepfather in the picture and abandonment issues running riot. He'll be here at eight, okay?"

P.m. Mouse (unsent}: Good evening, Oh Noble Friend of the apparent cold heart and indifferent attitude. I think I understand your tactics but I wish you would be kind to your Lady and give her a little opening. I suppose you cannot trust her to keep it in proportion; that even one tiny, friendly tone might send her hopes soaring? Probably. I hope you are okay? The Book is reading well. I so wish you could be a joint adventurer in our writing, My Lord Swallow. Goodnight then. We are off to Bernard and Felicia's later on. A film and night-cap evening. Should be fun.

Part Four Navigation

Oh, for the interminable unknown to reach conclusion. The ambiguity is a place of stolen succour for The Celestial Sea, yet uncomfortable under its blanket of dull acceptance. She has her private world that exists in all reality, albeit denied in the physical, but it is a heavy load as well as a joy. A happy outcome is unlikely, whichever way the die is cast. She has risked everything for the chance to sail again. Her faith has never once deserted her. The golden light around her intention does not fade.

Sweet memory and hours of word-play keep her occupied. The storyline weaves naturally as if another guides her hand. The waiting game is perfect for reverie and fairy tale creation as she revisits the travel log entries. She is surprised by the quantity of script—an entire bookshelf in the galley is stacked with notebooks of every size and colour. She picks one with a floral pink cover and glances through the pages—why, even alighting upon the notes takes her sailing for a spell. The atmospheric detail is captured intact. She spends every available minute reliving the adventures of last year. She hopes nobody notices her constant absorption. She concentrates when few are about, although she suspects her friend in the orange worker's bib has spotted her distraction. She can't risk losing her creativity to The Marine Officials; that would be her undoing.

"Hey, Hon—something on your mind? You seem far away. Where do you go? Her friend whispers as he passes; "do you sail again in your dreams?"

The friendly dockworker is increasingly drawn to the abandoned vessel. Last week he stayed late to scrape down the peeling paint on his charge's hull. Areas of the claret paintwork are flaky and weather bleached. He likes to spend time caring for her. He needs to re-stow her sails too; has someone been on board? After half an hour he turns back towards the office, deciding to 'borrow' some of the flowers from the vase in the Boss' room. He will place them on her deck in the last of the evening light.

As he leaves the office a woman walking up and down outside The Marina's locked gates takes his attention. Does he recognize her? He hides in the office doorway with the flowers, watching. What is she doing? Maybe he should ask. Just as he decides to make a move she slides her slim frame between the gate and the Marina wall, running quickly to The Celestial Sea and ducking down behind her stern. A pile of metal sheets shields her easily.

The dockworker is surprised; unsure what to do. The woman is trespassing; he should haul her out and ask what she thinks she is up to. As he steps towards The Boat he notices someone else—a man—also approaching the Marina gates. He too is looking to gain entry. He tries the narrow opening beside the wall but can't fit through the gap.

The woman doesn't show herself. For many minutes the man gazes at The Boat with a softened eye. The dockworker knows he scans the vessel for any damage. Does The Boat belong to him? To her? Are they the distressed couple who crewed The Celestial Sea when she was first brought into dry-dock; the couple that was ordered to keep away?

The office doorway keeps the dockworker hidden. He intuitively knows not to interfere. Whoever the couple, they are integral to the mystery that surrounds The Boat; of that he is quite certain. Once they have left The Marina he places the flowers on The Celestial Sea's deck, as he had planned. Somehow, his gesture seems important.

Chapter 1 Notes

Saturday 3rd March 2007

The day of the Taupo Iron Man Competition has arrived. The weather is clear and fresh. My brother, Wilf, and his two brothers-in-law are ready; carbohydrate stuffed, adrenaline pumped and in the lake by **7** a.m. We follow the competitors' progress on the television before packing the car for a day of spectating. To the haunting sound of the ceremonial, Maori Waka, {canoe}, arriving on the lake and a full Powhiri on the shore, {welcome ritual with Haka dance}, they are off; fifteen hundred athletes braving the water for a 3.8 km swim like a shoal of slippery, shiny sardines. They vie for places in the water; a mass of white hats slither across the television screen— "Apparently it's the most dangerous part of the race," my brother told us last night when we telephoned to wish him luck. "Competitors are ruthless in their quest for speed and thrashing limbs can be vicious." I walk the hound in the crisp morning air before we set off, texting Adrian the message I deliberated all night about sending.

***A.m. Mouse:** It is colder this dawn morning as she looks out of her turret window. She feels distant from the world below The Mountain. She cannot sense Lord Swallow's gaze any longer—or his intention. With a sinking heart she feels his impatience; he does not linger at the Forest edge. Yet—she will send one more note over the Castle wall; the last one, for she has found a way for them to record their story without undermining his honourable promise. Is he willing to listen? Might he grasp the potential? She knows he doesn't linger in the past—but—perhaps he might consider solo sailing for a while. It would mean a rekindling of their spark, but in his imagination only. He need not share it with her. He wouldn't break his agreement. She would place her 'flashdrive' in an envelope, along with an explanation of the story to date. There are suggestions from the editor as well. He could download all the files and return the 'flashdrive' to the office for her to collect. His Lady need not even see what he is writing—not until the time feels right anyway.*

As summer dwindles and the autumn chill sets in, now could be a good time to dig out the caged spark and place it on his desk—still contained—but alive and present for a while. She hopes he hasn't tossed it into the estuary? Perhaps he has. If he is happy about this idea he needn't reply. If he would rather not be involved, he should just text a short 'No thanks.' She would understand. Her phone remains private.

She is unable to be a proper wife to The Laird. She cannot pretend to feel things that don't exist. In pulling her harshly back inside his tunnel her Spirit has been wounded. She doesn't know if it will recover. She doesn't know what The Angels intend. And how is he? Her Fine Sir—she wishes she knew. The Castle Inmates are off to support her younger brother in the Taupo Iron Man Competition today—X

We leave The Mountain by eight o'clock, delivering Cedric and the Japanese to friends for the day. The beautiful drive through Rotorua and on to Taupo takes a couple of hours. Approaching the town we join a traffic queue as others with the same intention crawl into the heart of the sporting venue. The famous lake accompanies us on our right—the town is strung along its shore in a lengthy ribbon of guesthouses and fishing shops. We locate the comfortable house my brother is renting and duly take our place to watch the bicyclists go past. The raised house sits right on the sporting route and in between catching glimpses of the athletes we retire to the spacious abode, which enjoys grand views across the water. The morning sun shines down on the competitors; an endless stream of peddle pushers intent on this next leg of the endurance test; one of the toughest races on earth. What excitement when those of our party dash by, managing a quick wave as they sail past. The children are thrilled and shout out encouragement from the driveway. One competitor has a metal leg and several elderly athletes leave us admiring and questioning our own fitness. A mere 179.2 km ride is underway before participants run a full marathon!

The Laird inspires The Go-Getter to complete his own mini Iron Man Competition. Together they swim out to a buoy in the lake, bike a couple of times around the town and then complete a short run. The Laird is keen to bike with the competitors for a while and enjoys feeling part of the great day. He keeps the women and children informed of the men's progress. How he would love to be competing himself. I walk the hound—as always. I can't believe the heat of the lake's water. We happen to stumble across a volcanic upsurge and I encourage the Bog-Brush to swim, giving her some exercise. I have to hop from one foot to the other on the black sand to prevent my feet from burning.

We tuck into spaghetti bolognaise for lunch. The sun-filled upstairs room with wooden floors and huge windows is lovely. A copper jug with crimson silk flowers catches my eye; the furniture and furnishings are definitely 'up-market.' We haven't seen much of the wealthier side of Kiwi life. I expect we would come across more of it in Auckland and Wellington. We leave Taupo as the competitors begin the final stretch of the 42.2 km marathon run, passing Wilf as we drive away from the town. Holding hands out of the car window for a second makes us feel part of the exhilarating event.

We drive home in silence, appreciating the immense views and sunset skies. The hills in the distance appear veiled and massive. They are almost mountains. We pass acres of farmland with sun-kissed windbreaks glittering in the light winds. Rows of hay bales and fields of satisfied cattle complete the scenery and butterflies scatter as the car disturbs their sanctuary. The road is almost deserted. The atmosphere is stilted between me and The Laird. He made love to me last night but I couldn't respond with any enthusiasm. "Thank-you for trying," he said. There was a sarcastic edge to his voice. Fair enough.

"I am living a lie everyday," he continued. "You have to get a job; it's not fair otherwise. You have to stop grieving." "Do you think this is something I can just walk away from?" I asked. "We were in love—I know we were," replied my patient husband. "Perhaps you can rediscover the boy that you fell for all those years ago." I was silent. I didn't say; "but we were so young. My idea of true love was mostly in my imagination. Single sex schooling did me no favours in respect of male/female chemistry. Yes, of course there was a love; a good love, and there still is, but you never responded to my true love language; you have never been able to meet and challenge me there emotionally. I cannot sense your authority over me.

So, you see, I have been living a half-truth for many, many years. The love we share is kind and caring, solid and dependable—and there. But it has only been 'adequate' for me for a long, long time. And then, as our last child reaches her **7**th year I meet a man who is my match-mate in every *single* way and I find myself gifted the most beautiful, true love. I hardly dare believe it to be real, but it is—and I have to walk away from that gift. I have to deny myself the deepest pleasure imaginable. Yes, you are right, I am grieving. I will grieve forever but I cannot tell you this. I cannot hurt you even more than I already have, for the love I *do* feel for you is ever-present. Dear Angels in Heaven, please help us."

We arrive home to find the pig has ransacked the kitchen and eaten a vast quantity of dried dog food. Oops—she isn't meant to consume meat products. I presume she drank water with it. I head to bed, hoping the morning won't find her collapsed on the back door step with listless ears and drooping eyelids. I would miss her.

At ten p.m my sister-in-law phones to say Wilf completed the Iron Man competition in thirteen hours. A great result; we are very proud of him. Apparently a grand party with noisy fanfare greeted the last runners in the Taupo Reserve. Several competitors have yet to come in; the gates stay open until midnight.

Sunday 4th March 2007

Midday, Mouse {Unsent}: Hello Friend. How are you? I wonder what you thought of my suggestions about The Book compilation. Does your lack of response mean you are happy for me to proceed? I shall presume that it does. We had an exciting day yesterday in Taupo. My brother completed the impressive race in good time—what an achievement!

The Bishop opened the new College Sports Hall this morning during a church service. The Maori students gave a Pohiri welcome to initiate proceedings. The Laird was away early to complete the organization. The new building was packed with College families although it didn't feel particularly holy, despite the effort to make it more than a utilitarian space. The Bishop spoke about 'The Transfiguration'-"Have you noticed how **Mountains** *play an important part in many holy events?" He asked. "Transfiguration; finding Heaven in the here and now." Well—*

The vision today, My Friend? The same one—that of The Laird handing me to you with peace in his heart—and Simon involved in some way— stepping through a high gate all together—and The Small One; Little Arthur of huge importance. Yes—definitely Little Arthur. I was proud of The Laird this morning. He looked so smart in his white shirt and Indian waistcoat that he was given by a London waiter a few years ago. He was shining and pleased to be able to introduce us to the Bishop after the service. I love to see him shining. Have a good day. Thinking of you. X

The Laird stayed in town after the service for a lunch party with the Bishop. I brought the children home. They were happy to potter quietly and I documented more of our story. There is a lot to it. I wonder if it will be too long and boring for others. I am missing Adrian today; seriously aching for our Love. Does he feel waves of longing as I do? Perhaps that's just a female thing. I'll send him a little message to let him know I'm with him. I probably shouldn't but I'm going to go with the strong sense of feeling him close. Perhaps his Spirit calls mine—anything's possible in this epic tale.

P.m. mouse: —X—

Monday 5th March 2007
"Oh, lovely husband of mine—today is not a good day to demand my van; yours is not adequate for my domestic duties, although I know you have college students to transport."

Trying to explain to our Japanese students the need to pack their bags for a night away with friends, {my brother and family are coming to stay the night in the top cabin}, adds to our Monday morning chaos. Cedric The Scowler is furious at having to wrestle rubbish and dog out of my van into the inadequate space of the old Ute in the college car park; especially as the rubbish bags have been 'pigged' in the night and are not properly contained. He leaves us hurriedly, hoping none of the college students notice the family antics as we swap vehicles.

I am late; rubbish even less contained, children complaining and the Japanese polite as they wave goodbye. We leave the college campus in a dash with children squabbling and the Principal's wife looking on in surprise; the Go-Getter seems to have his legs sticking out of the window. My backside is soaked from a wet car seat—The Laird left the window open all night. "Argh-husbands," I mutter under my breath. Arriving late at school to deliver the two youngest inmates I sigh with relief. The Bog-Brush and I are left alone. Peace at last. As I reverse away Adrian waves from the classroom deck. He is wearing his patchwork hat, which completes the Pied Piper image. I love him. I know we belong.

Today is my English friend, J.J's birthday. I send her a message when I reach home. I mention our thwarted, lover's connection—she already knows about Adrian. "We are writing a Book instead of being together;" I type, "although Adrian isn't communicating at the moment." My brother's family arrives at four thirty and we spend a fun evening together, showing them around our Mountain Eyrie and introducing everyone to the livestock. Monty the cat is spectacularly sick after supper, which impresses the little boys no end. We chat late into the night.

Tuesday 6ᵗʰ March 2007

Wilf and family accompany us to school this morning. The sun shines as ever and I introduce staff members as we stroll around the grounds. I am so proud of our delightful and different School. The side door of Adrian's classroom is open and I tentatively look inside. Adrian is busy at the chalkboard and steps outside to meet my brother. He is friendly and quickly realizes what we are about. I hang back a little, pleased that Wilf shakes his hand and hears about the teaching philosophy from a professional. He is clutching a pile of yellow Main Lesson books and flicks through some students' work depicting the biblical lesson they are currently studying. He is as enthused as ever and speaks beautifully about the artistic way of delivering the curriculum, inviting my brother to step into the room and view the latest drawings. Our eyes linger in each other for a short while—

"Adrian is my best friend in New Zealand," I tell my brother as we leave The School. "I'm so pleased you met him." "So, have you fallen in love with New Zealand, Sis?" Wilf asks, climbing back into his hired car. "Hmm," I reply; "maybe" —
Wilf and family are off to the Northland for a two-week holiday before flying home. We won't see them again.

P.m. Mouse {Unsent}: *Goodnight, My Friend. So—we met more normally today, my brother surprising you through the side door—watching the master at work. You bounced out to say hello, realizing who he was. Thank-you for that. I felt proud to know you, yet sad that it felt a little flat; a slight anti-climax. I hate the spark dying on us. I don't think it shall, but meeting you felt so ordinary today. I don't want it to be 'ordinary' between us. I want the magic; the excitement—yes, I do. My life is dull without your vibrance. You thrill me, Sir. Sleep well.*

Wednesday 7th March 2007

The days go by in their usual drip, slide fashion. The clock ticks and the toast pops. Washing-up and trips to the local diesel pump recur with surprising frequency. The workload lessens not—the apron always waiting on the kitchen hook. No matter the hemisphere or her state of emotion, a mother's life is mapped. Perhaps I fly a flag against the tedium; a flag for all kitchen-sink-slaves who dream into the soapy bubbles. My story gives the answer—what if? Perhaps my adventure is designed to offer light relief to all those women folk with soggy cuffs.

__A.m. Mouse {Unsent}:__ Good morning, Lord Swallow. I feel like a chat. How are you? How did you receive my recent messages? I wish I knew. I wish the giant bubble containing our love would burst. This waiting game is endless—beautiful but endless. Last night the Japanese party at College entertained us before they leave tomorrow. We laughed a lot; they were very funny. A crisp eating game in pairs made us giggle—the partner eating the crisps was fed by their blindfolded companion standing behind; hilarious! It reminded me of those crazy Japanese T.V shows resembling our British, 'It's a Knockout' competition. Did you ever see that show over here? Oh—when I say 'crisps' I mean the N.Z equivalent, 'chips'.

The Laird and I continued our 'chats' last night. They seem endless and caught in a giant bubble like our love. Round and round we go with no way out, although The Laird's honesty was more light-filled than usual. "I question the depth of our married love. I am questioning myself," he admitted last night. "I am not going to play the depressed card. We all have choice—we choose these things. If you left me I would marry again. You would go to Adrian if he called, wouldn't you?" "Yes—I would," I answered truthfully. I was surprised by his declarations—and relieved. Will those sentiments stick? Will he really be able to shake off the depression?

The Bog-Brush and I had a lovely walk up to the Pa Site yesterday evening. We followed the antics of a large dragonfly, turning this way and that, not sure of its direction but determined and busy—like me I suppose. We watched until it disappeared behind the pine trees. I slept badly. The back of my head is sore. My heart is filled with the ever-present care for The Laird and the all-consuming passion for you, My Lord Swallow, which refuses to abate. A frustrating quandary. I think I am missing my swimming. I must go tomorrow. Autumn is definitely waving a flag. Take care, My Friend-X

Thursday 8th March 2007

Mizzie's e-mail is waiting for me when I come downstairs this morning. She has read my synopsis and—I'll talk about that later. Best get moving before the children wake up.

The hound and I enjoy our regular soaking in a seagull-chasing dash through the bay at Monument Park after school drop-off. I forgot the dog lead so make do with the roof-wrack bungies instead. Another crazy mother idea—we must look bonkers out in the water; the dog propels me along like a puppet on elastic. She drags me over sharp shells and oozy mud, pulling me with her huge strength in uncontrollable directions. We eventually stride back to the shore with wet shorts and knickers; both.

On to swim, at last. Bother, the aquarobics is in progress again. Never mind. Sliding under the water my head begins to clear; The Laird's honest comments inviting the freedom that laps at the corners of my life. Strolling back to the van after my swim I pass an elderly man and his dog. They are enjoying the quiet park. I smile; old friends. My shorts are practically falling off me! Four weeks into my meager diet and I am feeling fit and lithe. Blessings in other ways these days. I miss Lord Swallow. Once home I complete the letter to Adrian accompanying The Book compilation so far. I shall deliver the flashdrive to his house before school pick-up today. Mizzie's reponse to my synopsis is encouraging. I am rather chuffed to have a word of praise from my published sister. Adrian hasn't sent a 'No Thank-You' message, so I shall take his silence as an agreement of sorts.

My Darling Adrian,

So, our longed-for Alchemy begins in all its truth. Thank-you for agreeing to yet another part of our amazing adventure. I have a feeling this could be very important for us; I'm not sure quite how, but I continue to trust in my intuition. Enclosed is the precious 'flashdrive', {I don't have duplicates}, with the beginnings of 'The Celestial Sea'. To make things clear I am not handwriting this! {Even *I* struggle with my scribbled notes at times.} I shall work in bullet points to separate the different questions. Are you set? I hope so.

i. **I have sent our editor, {my sister}, a beginning synopsis. She has responded favourably, with some pointers. She suggests we include 3 chapters with the synopsis for professional presentation. I am waiting to hear if they need to be the first 3, or could they be from another part of the book? I shall send you copies of all her e-mails from now on, as long as you don't mind family natter. Her real name is Larch, although we call her Mizzie. She knows you are on board now, {I presume your silence means you are considering being involved?}. She would be happy to hear from you. This is her profession, so we couldn't be in better hands. She is also unshockable, or so she claims! Although I am unsure how she will handle family loyalty and politics. Let's hope she can see the bigger picture. I don't think she's particularly interested in this kind of spirituality, which could be a problem—we'll see. She has direct access to several Publishing Houses for whom she works as an editor on many projects. She is based at home in Surrey, where she works very hard in her** tiny office. She has two small boys, Alfred and Gil. Her husband Edward is a solicitor in a local market town; in fact, the town we used to live in before we moved to N.Z.

ii. I have started the Book at Part Four, from the beginning of our texting life-i.e.: August; your return from Europe. I have yet to allocate Parts or Chapters.

iii. I hope you can treat this as a joint project. Please feel free to change wording, grammar, detail etc. Add things which you feel would work better or delete where needed. We have sooo much recorded text writing that I am wondering if it might be too long and boring. Our friendly Editor will advise, I'm sure. I have been filling in between the texts with an account of our adventures. The texts end up being a little flat without input in between. You need to decide if you want to add to my writing, or take some of my accounts out to replace with your own. By the way—the pink floral notebook you gave me is just the right size; where did you get it? I need several more.

iv. I would love to see you tackle the weaving of the nautical element into every Part. This is our main story line and needs to run from the beginning of the book. I have imagined a passage at the start of each Part, {it could be in a different font}; either a poem or a piece of your stunning prose to reflect the chapter's content. In other words, the everyday routines and happenings of our life, transformed into mystical, nautical language. {Something like that anyway.} You may well come up with a better idea.

v. The fonts I have been using so far are 'Verdana' size 12 for the writing, and 'Segoe Print' 12 for the poetry. I did wonder if we should have a different font for the text prose. Also, you may decide the layout should be different. It would be good to have a fresh eye cast over the work, as it has been my close companion for many weeks now.

vi. At some stage the script turned red? I must have pressed something odd. My computer skills are still limited so can you sort that out please? Also, I tried to number the pages but they did something strange. The passage where we are stacking wood at Cordelia's narrowed into bullet point. That needs mending too. Sorry, Doctor!

vii. I haven't started writing Parts One, Two, Three and five although I have lots of notes. Also, you can see from the early writing that

194

the story is weaker without paragraphs between the texts—although I did wonder if going from domestic dialogue to intense, text passion runs smoothly. I will probably go over the early texts and add more domestic prose, and please do so as well.

viii. Now, this is going to be tricky for you, My Friend, I think. We need to keep the intimate detail as real and explicit as we can. This is what makes The Book something special, but in a beautiful, poetic way—nothing base. I know there are aspects of yourself you have expressed upset at having down on paper. Your constant companions of shame and guilt hate any reminder. I don't know why, because you are lovely and there is nothing to be ashamed of. But I know you; I know you might cringe at having to revisit yourself. I am throwing you a challenge. This is the ultimate way to learn to love yourself—could be a good therapy session too. Please don't cut out too much about yourself. Of course, do correct anything I have got wrong and please write about your interpretation of my character as well. We will remain anonymous so it shouldn't be too much of a problem.

ix. I have tried to disguise place names, people's names etc. There is probably more to do. Any comments? We don't want the paparazzi chasing after us if The Book takes off!

x. This is the order of the folders; it would be best to read them in the right flow. Can you get the 'flashdrive' back to me for the weekend? Thank-you my Friend.

xi. The Celestial Sea. How Blessed are we. The Synopsis. Index. Part Four.

xii. Are you set? Light a candle, dig out the caged spark; {make sure you have a mat handy—it's likely to burn your desk.} Play some of our music, My Love, and enjoy.

xiii. The wind is up; a spell of fair weather forecast, so imagine pulling up the anchor. Make sure The Small One wears his life jacket and head out to sea. I shall be in the Crow's Nest; just call if you want me. {We can communicate via e-mail if we need to. Mine is totally private.}

xiv. I love you. Sail safe and happy. Your Mouse, always—X

The envelope is addressed and precious flashdrive wrapped in bubble paper. For obvious reasons I don't have any writing stored on the home computer. I hope Adrian will read my message and return the flashdrive soon. I can't work without it. Will he even look at the files? I am unsure. I place a dab of my scent on the seal to remind Lord Swallow his Lady still exists. I hope to catch Vonny at school to ask if she'll deliver the package for me. Unfortunately I miss Adrian's landlady and decide to drop the package in her post box myself. I discovered the house number by checking the school address list earlier.

I leave my vanload of children at the bottom of the school drive and dash over to the row of post boxes. I am about to post the package when Vonny's blue car leaves her driveway. Adrian is driving—and alone. Oh—I am unprepared to meet him like this. I take a deep breath and apply my jolly smile. "Hello there," he says, looking surprised as he leans across the passenger seat to unwind the window. "Here, My Friend—the package I said I would deliver. I was just about to drop it in your post box." He takes the envelope and places it carefully on the seat beside him. He is looking boyish; dressed in a green T-shirt that doesn't really suit him. How strange to meet like this, as if there is nothing between us. "How are you?" I ask. "I'm very well—how about you?" He replies. "I'm fine—busy. I'd better dash—car load of children waiting for me—bye." I turn away quickly but not before I notice his softening eyes inviting me to blow a little kiss through the car window.

Chapter 2 Natter

Friday 9th March 2007

A.m. Mouse {Unsent}: All night she tosses and turns, wondering if he has opened the files; if he dares read any of their precious story. And if he does, what thoughts go through his mind? Does the idea excite him? Or is he wary of being dragged back into their shared longing and passion just when he had it nicely under control? Perhaps he is too busy to even bother opening the package–quite likely, she knows, although she feels his arms about her as she lies awake early this morning. She hopes he will have the courage to set sail alone. She loves him-X

The Go-Getter is unwell again; another chesty cough brings the worrying asthma we have to watch carefully. He stays with me today, resting in the car under the shady trees while I walk the dog in Monument Park. The Angels' dancing path stretches right across the bay this morning, beginning at our feet on the shore. What an invitation–one we don't refuse. The Bog-brush and I stride through the shimmering path, correct lead and swimming shorts donned today. Perhaps this path might take me to Adrian as King. I know it is The King who takes my breath away, more so than The Minstrel and The Prince. The King has the authority I admire. A small grey heron flaps into the air from the Pohutukawa trees as we pass. It lands further out on a sandbar in the bay. It passes close above us; the distinctive white head and yellow legs of the bird stand out sharply against the blue sky. The Bog-Brush hares after the exciting target, leaping and splashing in the water that thankfully slows her progress. The heron lifts off the sand and lands beside a large pile of pinecones back on the shore. I wish I was an artist. The picture is beautiful. A tumbling plant with exotic pink flowers and broad green leaves frames the composition. A Monarch butterfly in brilliant orange flutters about my head when I step back on the sand, its slow-motion dance so lovely in the bright light. I stop in front of the fountain; the water droplets catch the sun and create a perfect, mini Rainbow that arches away into the edges of the spray. I decide it is surely a symbol of the truth in magic; the living presence of mystery and wonder in our everyday lives.

My young patient seems to be responding to the various inhalers and homoeopathic treatments. I take him home for some rest and clear out the back of the car. Yesterday's clobber is still littering the boot. How come my young lad managed to explode his banana inside his lunchbox? Yuk—

exploded is an understatement! When I say exploded I mean unrecognizable, to the extent that his entire Thursday's lunch was rendered uneatable! "It wasn't me, Ma—honest." Hmm—"I've heard that before," I answer. "I've seen you swinging your school bag over your head, bashing your school mates as you muck about together. Please consider your lunchbox more carefully. It was the yogurt last week."

I let the Laird take me this evening. I endeavour to show willing. "Thank-you for trying," he repeats before turning out the light.

Saturday 10ᵗʰ March 2007

A.m. Mouse {Unsent}: I am lying in your arms, Lord Swallow. I imagine you reading our messages and my writing; all the work I have completed these past months, delivered to you for safekeeping and continuation. I wonder if you have read any of it. What do you think? Does the storyline delight you, or do you cringe at recognition of self? I am watching you in your new Leafy Glade—is it a Leafy Glade? Maybe not. Something different—a King's Chamber perhaps? I see you snuggling into your cosy duvet, wrapping yourself up in our beautiful memories and ongoing adventure. Hold me a while and I will settle against your chest and kiss your neck. I like to feel your long limbs covering mine. Let's enjoy our story together, My Love. It is our precious gift to each other—and to the world if we are destined to share the joy.

A.m. Mouse: Darling Friend—are you able to return the 'flashdrive' to school by 2p.m? Perhaps put it under the lid of the barbeque outside the office? We will be out and about on weekend errands so I could dive in to school and collect. If that's not possible I shall wait for Monday morning and collect it from the office. Thank-you. I hope you are well? Thinking of you—X

Wilf phones from pretty Russell this afternoon; the attractive place we visited with my parents in January. He and the family are having a wonderful holiday up there. Half way through our conversation Rinky lets the dog inside. "She's a bit smelly Ma," is all the warning I get. My goodness—SMELLY? That's an understatement!!! Whatever she has been rolling in is quite honestly the most disgusting pong ever—YUK! I am rendered speechless and helpless with giggles. All I can do is scream with asphyxiated laughter and try to explain to Wilf what all the fuss is about, especially as the culprit tries to sit as close as possible to her mistress and with the phone in hand I can't escape. The Laird hears the commotion and strips off to hose down the ashamed monster in the garden. Honestly—whatever next!? No wonder Lord Swallow would rather keep his distance from this mad family. "She's definitely *your* dog," The Laird says, dragging her outside.

After a trip to town I try to collect the flashdrive. No sign—as I suspected. Adrian doesn't play by other's rules. He rarely does what I suggest. Perhaps he is away in Auckland. Sammy mentioned he was diving in to see them on Friday after school and they live a good thirty minutes away, en route to Auckland. I wonder why he was visiting them. His participation in our Book compilation seems unlikely. Teenage idealism should surely have deserted me in my mature adulthood. Obviously not—once an optimist, always an optimist. I am just so excited about the magic that keeps happening; weaving a story I don't have to invent. I would like to share it with others. Before switching off the bedroom light The Laird closes his book and turns to me; "What are we gong to do?" He asks. "Let's not worry," I reassure him. "The Angels are holding this one, that's for sure." I kiss him goodnight and roll over onto the deck of The Celestial Sea for a thrilling, nighttime voyage.

Sunday 11th March 2007

The Laird is away early. A triathlon on the far side of town calls for his participation this fresh, summer morning. No church for us today—shame. I enjoy day-dreaming on the weekly pew. The children play contentedly while I wash up and send various e-mails. I also send Adrian a message with a few things I need to say.

A.m. Mouse: Sunday—their day and his Lady can fly a white kerchief from the turret for a few hours. She has been in her Lover's arms all night—sailing the high seas—wondering if he was on board with her. Wondering if he ever feels like sailing. Is he away for the weekend? She thinks of him with their creative script in his hands—has he even looked at it? And if he has, what is he thinking? She is worried he might want to smash the precious flashdrive. Is he unhappy to see their lives in print? She trusts him—trusts her intuition. Will she find an envelope in the school office at 8.50 on Monday morning? She is with him. If he is unhappy he only has to say. She just wants to speak to him in this—their intimate, well-loved way. M—X

An image of The Book's front cover comes to me today. I see a background of striking blue in dappled tones—sky and sea merging as one—a chalkboard drawing of The Boat in the centre. Perhaps the Boat should be slightly undefined? I imagine the rich New Zealand ferns and Native Bush covering the inside of the jacket. I wonder about pictures at the chapter beginnings—or photos? Photos would be okay if they were mystical/ abstract shots reflecting the storyline. In fact—I know just the person to ask. Would Cedric ever rise to the potential? His mother writes a book that could undermine his entire family and she asks him to be party to that. Hmm—this second Book strikes me as more sombre; a pale lilac cover with The Boat in dry-dock as inset. The pictures or photos could continue from the first. Well, that's enough dreaming for now. On with the domestic duties. What is that horrible smell? The dog again?

"You mother must have dropped you in a vat of magic at birth," states The Laird as we drive to Castle Rock this afternoon. Cedric is joining others with their mountain-boards; the park has some good bike tracks incorporating the necessary jumps and he is keen to join the handful of pioneers in this new sport. We travel for an hour-and-a-half to reach our destination. "Oh, yes—I have lots of magic surprises in store for you, My Darling." I reply. "Maybe in a few months' time." "I know. That's why I married you," my good-natured husband remarks. "You and the dog—and the pig—you are all out of control on The Mountain; must be something in the water."

Very few Kiwis know about mountain-boarding and we are pleased that Cedric finds himself included in the group representing New Zealand's participation. A couple of months ago they visited Cedric on our Mountain. The neighbour's field offers the perfect, downhill venue with its steep basin and gentle bumps. Our guests were amusing. They arrived in a beaten up old Datsun; twenty-two-year-old Biff, {New Zealand's current champ}, sponsored by a fizzy drinks company; thirty-five-year-old Sam, the enthusiastic mountain-board promoter with his chubby, twelve-year-old son and their seriously overweight dachshund that puffed its way up our deck steps, promptly peeing on the carpet once inside! "Here," offered Biff— "anyone for a box of fizzy drink? I've stacks to give away."

Biff and Co have already arrived at Castle Rock and as soon as the car door opens Cedric kits himself out in helmet, gloves and pads and heads off to find everyone. The Laird follows with his camera and I am left with the perpetual dog walking. Lucky I am happy in my own company—and that of my hairy mutt of course.

I enjoy the different scenery on our walk today. Huge rocks with lichen-stained faces rise out of the gently rolling hills and cattle snoozing under the trees surprise the Bog-Brush with their swishing tails. We walk past banks of pink and white columbine flowers that tumble to our feet and butterflies accompany us much of the way. As always, my thoughts turn to Adrian. I wonder what he is up to right now—how he finds this new rung of our ladder. Does he feel the alchemy? Although we didn't go to church earlier my mind takes me there. Adrian isn't sitting on the pew beside us but I imagine the children dashing out to the foyer after the service where he is waiting. They take Little Arthur by the hand and run outside together to play under the cherry trees.

Arriving home we find Molly the pig inside, AGAIN! "Who left the back door open?" Roars the Laird. We work to clear the mess, The Laird helping himself to the cheese-cracker jar as we sweep and straighten the ransacked larder. "These crackers are stale, Wench," he accuses. "I know—I'll replace them soon," I say. "Probably all I deserve anyway," he sighs. "Oh no—you deserve much better," I tell him. And rightly so—he does. He deserves a better wife too. "Who would have thought it possible?" He continues. "After all the hard work I have done building you up, that this should happen." "But I need breaking down, Sir," I reply; "breaking down, not building up."

Monday 12ᵗʰ March 2007

Pink clouds float in a threatening sky as we walk this morning. The ground is damp after last night's rainfall. The Bog-Brush's Pointer instinct is razor sharp; I notice an increase every week. She looks at me from under shaggy eyebrows as we listen to the sounds in The Bush, the drizzle threatening to divert our attention. The Tui birds warble and croak; their white chest bibs occasionally visible amongst the foliage. Their call is varied and evocative; a haunting sound through the stillness of the morning. The first time I came across the iconic creature was in the blossom trees at school. The distinctive birds were feeding on the deep pink flowers of the Taiwanese Cherry soon after our arrival on Aotearoa's fair shores.

I work in Class **7** this morning. The class is preparing the seasonal story at assembly and I am helping with the detail. Once they know their way around the week's theme I head to the office to use the photocopying machine. I ask if an envelope has been delivered for me— No? Hmm—drat. Still no sound from Lord Swallow. I have some free time today and want to press on with The Book. Heavy hearted I drive to Monument Pool.

Mouse: *Do you want me to come and collect it?*

As I plough through the water I wonder—is he playing games with me? Is he keeping the flashdrive hostage, enticing me to him; making me take the first step so he isn't responsible for breaking any promise? Or has he just forgotten? I often find his attention diverted but never forgetful. Hmm—I don't know. Lord Swallow's silence both worries and excites his Lady. How should I proceed? Well, two can play at this game. I won't send another message until tomorrow.

Today's grey sky is shot with occasional sun. The dog and I stride out into the bay at Tui Park. We run and run together. I wish I had a surfboard to skim through the shallow water behind her; she makes me run so fast. Maybe I'll bring one tomorrow. The water is scudding; the ripples eager with the incoming tide. The high wind tears the bark off the Eucalyptus trees while the solid Pohutukawa watch patiently. There is no Angel path to guide us today. The bay is different and exciting. We wade right out; the warm water teases my waist while the dog swims. That's better—less pulling. My shorts are falling off me. I've lost a stone through my love-struck trauma. It is time for my swim.

I share a swimming lane with another woman today. There are more people than usual in the pool. The water is cool and I let it slip over me like a silk sheet covering the possibility of 'maybe'. I wonder if my swimming partner delves into daydream as she swims a professional free style. Cedric is having a home day. He is exhausted after the sport at Castle Rock. A quiet time is needed and together we share a slap-up brunch of Mountain eggs and cold meat from the German Deli. He claims to be suffering from a painful tum. I expect his overworked stomache muscles cry out for some respite.

Early P.m. Adrian: Need to speak with you. Tomorrow—by phone or after school in the car park? School question—and another one too. Thanks. A.

Mouse: Phone might be best—or text if you would rather. When is a good time?

Uh, oh—that sounds ominous. Sometimes I prefer silence to any contact. It threatens to burst the bubble. I like my bubble. I expect Adrian is going to refuse any part in The Book compilation. I imagine he is unhappy about his words being printed. SH—T. Excuse me. I saw Adrian this morning as we drove in to school. He was casually dressed in a linen shirt and woolly blue jumper. He walked with his Kingly bearing. He smiled and waved, filling me with certain joy.

Early P.m. Mouse: Am free now until 5p.m—could meet you—or could phone once I'm home. Just let me know. M—X

Adrian: Tomorrow—midday? Cows coming to school today. Very busy time of life.

Mouse: I'm excited for you, My Friend. A School Farm at last! We will have to donate our livestock if and when we move back to the U.K. Wish I was there to help. Midday tomorrow would be fine. I am free. Where? Sorry to give you more things to think about when you are so busy. It's all happening. M—X

So, I don't imagine Adrian will be interested in The Book. He has a new focus that will exclude other pursuits. I must remember that he doesn't look back. Perhaps this is how it's meant to be. I just hope he'll let me write the words for him. I'll have to wait until tomorrow to find out.

P.m. Mouse: The Lady on the Mountain bids Lord Swallow good night. She hopes the cattle are safely bedded for the night. A gentleman farmer now—how fitting. She realizes she assumes too much, asking him to contribute to their story documentation. Of course he is too busy. He has moved on. He does not need to be reminded; too complicated. She understands. She will complete the writing alone.
Please give me permission to print your words, Good Sir. I promise to make it anonymous and of course recognize you if it takes off. You need not

*tell me. Am I right? I know you to be a man for the present moment. So, as the rain lashes The Mountain my thoughts turn to home—the weather comfortingly familiar. I miss England—my family and my friends. I miss the roaring fires and the chestnut trees—and the smell of apples being stored in the garden shed. I miss our ancient churches and village walls covered in ivy—and the sound of the telephone ringing with close friends sharing news and laughter. I miss the full diary of sociable events and family gatherings highlighted in marker pen. Perhaps it **is** time to go home, our lessons learnt. Sleep well, My Friend. Warm thoughts for the Farmer—X*

I don't hold him as I drift off. I can let him go. Adrian's lack of response in ten weeks has taken its toll. The thoughts at the forefront of my thinking make me question his lack of kindness to either himself or to me—hardly an ounce of recognition or acknowledgment of our shared gift has willingly passed his lips or his pen. He can harden himself with ease. I know his reasoning is noble but aren't I as important as his personal honour? Obviously not. He can be hard—and life is full of ups and downs where kindness to self and loved ones needs to come before personal concern. Perhaps I am being unfair. Am I making too much of our fairy-tale romance? Why can't I let it go? These thoughts are born of a lack of communication, I know. I don't like the guessing game. I sleep alone tonight, my husband sad and unsure; my Lover absent.

Tuesday 13th March 2007

A sore throat signals the start of a cold as I wake early this morning. I sense Adrian's arms around me and I roll away, trying to disengage. I don't succeed. The magnetic pull is too strong. The house and home feel organized; The Mistress has the situation in-hand—she hopes. Today heralds the end of our Boat's interminable dry-dock sentence. Today should tell if Lord Swallow and his Lady are definitely 'over' or truly 'on'. Dear Angels, please guide us. Dispel the ambiguity, much as I like that state. Give us right-placed wisdom and clarity at midday. Amen.

Midday, Mouse: *Are you at home? If so, how long for? I could come to you in 20 minutes if that still suits.*

Adrian: *Still up at school; bricklaying but heading home in about 20. Yep—come around. Think it's okay?*

Mouse: *Should be. I'm fighting a cold, so I'm not in top form. I should be safe to handle. Will park in Kindy and stroll over. Text when you are in. Does Vonny know about us? I need to know.*

Adrian: *No, she doesn't. I'm rocking back home now. Come have salad and fresh cheese.*

I arrive, nervous and unsure. I am on edge, although I am outwardly confident. What will this meeting highlight? Adrian is sweeping the kitchen floor as I enter the house. I say hello to Vonny and we chat about this and that. "You smell nice," she comments, noticing the scent I sometimes wear. Bother—I hope he doesn't think I smell nice just for him. Of course I do but I don't need attention drawn to the fact. He is looking well, thinner than ever and handsome in his jeans and white T-shirt with ethnic waistcoat. He gives me a friendly hug hello before we take cups of tea into the sitting room. The normality of the situation is an anti-climax; as always. Vonny continues her gardening work while we chat.

Adrian makes sure I don't sit next to him. He sinks into a brown velvet sofa, indicating I should take an old armchair opposite. He tells me about his new school timetable; woodwork classes, guitar lessons and the cows. He milks them at dusk every evening. "I love being out in the fields as the dark sets in; it's much easier having the cows on site," he says. "Do you know—someone did a survey recently on the ideal milking time. Guess what hour the cows chose? Midnight. How strange is that! I'm sure that's why it feels good to milk them at night. Oh yes; and I'm making Pecorino cheese; some Italians showed me how. Come and try it."

My Minstrel Friend is away, as enthusiastic as ever and totally engrossed in the current projects. Vonny's back lobby has been claimed as 'The Dairy' and her shed as a 'The Woodwork Room'—and her under-house storage is full to bursting with the wood collection. Hmm, I hope he doesn't overstay his welcome. He is good at taking over. I wonder what Vonny makes of it all? 'The Dairy' sink is overflowing with various milk bottles and cheese sieves. The strong smell of milk and all things 'moocow' is apparent. However, the Pecorino is very good, especially the one incorporating sun-dried tomato. We share a delicious cheese and lettuce salad at the kitchen table.

"And how are you, My Friend?" Adrian asks at last. Our initial nerves take flight and I notice a softening of tone. We achieve some level ground. "Oh, I'm okay—same old life—you know, this and that." What is there to say? "I'm really enjoying my writing and I'm swimming every other day." I don't need to give lots of detail. My messages have kept Adrian in the picture over the past few weeks. He has the inside track on my life. A sudden downpour brings Vonny running inside. "Where did that come from?" She exclaims, dripping onto the cork floor of the spacious kitchen. "I'm heading into town now; can you bring Thomasina home from school?" She asks Adrian.

Once she has driven off Lord Swallow takes me to his room—the space behind the garage that was painted a dark blue the last time I visited. The room is smaller and darker than I remember. It's strange to see all the familiar objects in a new setting. Adrian has painted the walls in milky terracotta and some old carpet in the same tone lends a cosy atmosphere. "I don't have to pay any rent," he tells me. "I work in the garden and around the house, helping out with Thomasina instead. It works well." He sits in his desk chair while I perch on the bed. He asks about the children and I tell him about Cedric's film-making on The Mountain. "He's made a couple of clever videos of the mountain-boarding. They are good; the music and special effects are great. You can see them on 'You-Tube'. He press-gangs The Go-Getter into cameraman duty." Adrian laughs. He is always pleased to hear news of the children.

"About your recent text, My Friend. You are wrong in thinking I wouldn't like to be involved in The Book. That's not how I feel. I'm just so busy at the moment; I haven't even opened the flashdrive. I'd like to save it for the winter when I can go to a deeper level and give it the time it deserves. I'm still feeling tender-hearted and wounded. The Laird's onslaught has really upset me. I'm not ready to step back into anything. The time isn't right. Perhaps by the end of June—mid-winter solstice. Yes—that feels good. I should be clearer by then. I still feel for you, although I am not dwelling on 'us'. I have shelved that side of my life for a while. I can't stand in the shadow any longer." Adrian admits to feelings of fear around 'us'. "I need to look at that," he concludes. "I am waiting for you to clear the way."

I speak about choices, mentioning The Laird's disquiet and my inability to give myself, as a wife should. "The Laird knows I need something more," I state. I speak about the choice of being untrue to myself in order to maintain others' happiness. "Perhaps I should fill my life with other riches to compensate, as I have always done in the past. Sometimes I feel brave," I admit, "and then, at other times I cannot face the upset. The Laird's entire world seems to hinge on me. Is that healthy? He's found a book on Life Choices that is taking his attention. I'm pleased to see him tackling the situation positively; although I worry his depression will undo any good work."

"Have you spoken to Simon yet?" Adrian asks. "No," I reply. "Perhaps I will soon. You know, a little swallow really *did* crash into the windows when we said goodbye over the telephone last month." "Did it kill itself?" He asks, surprised. "No," I say; "it was only shocked and dazed for a while. I'd really like you to read my synopsis for The Book—soon. I think it would make you smile. I'm really enjoying the storyline. I *do* think we could make something of it. Please say you'll look at it?"

"Oh—it's good to catch up like this," beams Lord Swallow, ignited by my excitement. "I can tell you are going to get me all fired up again. Here, I'll download the files now and return your flashdrive. I've got some music for you too." The sun is shining again and we head out to the front deck. The sparks between us are alive and well; I know we both feel them testing the lids of the copper boxes. "I don't know how to meet your eyes," I admit. He smiles at me and we sit together on the swing seat. My Lover places an old straw hat strategically between us. Some deterrent! *Better not squash that, Sir,* I think to myself. Why are we kidding ourselves like this? We are playing one big game—a frustrating, tantalizing game. We both know we are still in love. "I don't like the thought of you leaving the Southern Hemisphere," Adrian continues. "Will you definitely be going home?" I tell him the likelihood is real. I also mention The Laird's recent conversation; where he told me he would marry again if I left him. "The Laird knows I would come to you if you called, although he doesn't understand the part about positivity—only if we are *all* one hundred percent happy would I make as radical a move as that. I suppose that's the bottom line isn't it? It always has been, and how realistic is that scenario?"

"I'd like to find a new footing with The Laird," Adrian states. "I'll be playing hockey with him later this year. Martini asked how that would be. He suggested it might offer some healing opportunity." "I think I'm about to be expelled from The Mountain," I laugh; "along with the pig and the dog!" "It really *is* good to see you," Adrian says again. I ask him an important question; "Do you like receiving my text messages?" "Yes," he says, "but no; I find it frustrating that I can't answer your thoughts and questions. So," he pauses—"you need a Book out of this, do you? How will that be for The Laird?" "He knows I am writing," I respond. "I'm sure he has read some of the story. I know it must be hard but he hasn't forcibly objected. Far better that his wife dallies away from him on the screen than in real life. Yes, I need The Book. It isn't just a story. I suppose it's my way of making our relationship permanent; birthing something positive from our beautiful months together. Does that make sense? I have the time right now."

"Poor Laird—poor you." Adrian is thoughtful. "Oh, I'm okay really, although it's difficult for The Laird," I admit. "I'm not the same person I was twenty-five years ago. Are we meant to stay married if the joy has departed? If we feel called to something other?" I ask my pondering friend the difficult question. My phone rings, surprising us both. It is The Laird, asking me to join him for lunch. Why is he asking today? He hasn't phoned at lunchtime for weeks. Adrian is right. We must be psychically linked. I decline, claiming errands and school business as priority. Today I am *definitely* Adrian's. This meeting is long overdue. I don't feel guilty.

Adrian leads the way back to his room to collect my flashdrive and guitar for his afternoon lessons. "What happened to your lovely big bed?" I ask. "No Leafy Glade?" The narrow single bed is meager in comparison. "It fell off the back of my trailer when I moved across the road," Adrian says with a nonchalant air. "I went back later but it had disappeared. How's that for a telling sign?" "Well—I shan't be so tempted to sneak down The Mountain and climb in beside you without your large, cosy bed to welcome us, you'll be pleased to hear," I laugh. Adrian smiles, adding; "Hey, I think I should take back that music C.D I just gave you. Sorry—just a sudden feeling. I don't want to ignite you all over again." "Okay," I say, surprised. "Take it back. I don't mind. And you needn't worry about igniting me—I'm permanently ignited. My imagination provides plenty of tinder."

"I'll look at the files as soon as winter arrives," Adrian promises. "I'll look forward to that; I can see myself getting stuck in. Mid-winter it is then. And I hear we might be involved together at Camellia House? I saw Sammy recently and she spoke about the After School Club. I might offer them some Workshops. Angels trying to push us together again, eh?"

"Eh, indeed. See you then, Fine Sir. Can I kiss you goodbye?" I ask hopefully. "No—you may not." He backs away but I sneak a quick peck on his cheek anyway. "I have an appropriate Celtic prayer to send you. I stumbled across it yesterday," I say as I turn to leave. "Goodbye, My Lady." He waves from the sunny deck. I walk away with a warm tingle. Ambiguity dispelled, eh? Eh, indeed.

P.m. Mouse: *A Celtic Prayer:* ***"Spirit of integrity, you drive us into the desert to search out our truth. Give us clarity to know what is right and courage to reject what is strategic; that we may abandon the false innocence of failing to choose at all, but may follow the purposes of Christ. Amen"***

I found this yesterday as I cleared my desk. Nice to see you today, Sir. Strange too—where were your arms—where was our spark? Odd to have the lids locked tight. And where was the Leafy Glade? Please don't feel bad that you can't reply. Although it saddens me to be denied your daily balm I suppose I am used to the silence after 10 weeks. I know I have no right to any claim over you. Perhaps you can do what I often do—write a message in a notebook—a message you never send. Perhaps you could reply like that; your words would become a diary like mine with recorded dates and times. I know the intention would reach me. Tell me about your day; the cows, the children, the woodwork and the cheese. Tell me about your ups and downs, the chalkboard masterpieces and all your adventures. Maybe we might use your writing one day. Whatever, I shall hear you. Extraordinary things keep happening to us. Sleep well, My Friend. I'm pleased I can picture you in your new room at last. Shame about the bed. M—X

My sleep is patchy. Desire for Lord Swallow overtakes me again and again. All night I sense his hands stroking me so tenderly. I move with him in our Rhythmic Dance for hours. The pleasure is excruciating yet frustrating. Perhaps it's just as well he took the music back. I'm not sure I can take any more forbidden love. I know Adrian would worry The Laird might ask where the C.D had come from. My mind goes over our meeting today. Does Adrian trust himself so little that he had to place a hat between us on the swing-seat? I suppose I should feel honoured he desires me to that extent. My desire for *him* is certainly overwhelming. His voice rings in my ears; "In your last message you said you imagined I had moved on, My Friend. Well—you are wrong. I haven't moved on; it's just that I'm not dwelling on 'us' at the moment."

Thank-you for that, Lord Swallow. Your words are sweet balm to your Lady who loves you with a fiery passion that refuses to abate.

YOUR BED

You lost it off the trailer when you moved, My Friend?
Your bed—large and soft; a waiting nest.
You made it yourself; raised it on high wooden blocks
As a perfect Leafy Glade for our Love.
You only moved one street away—how could it have disappeared?
Your bed—holding us perfectly as we sailed across uncharted seas;

Duvet waves and pillow clouds our Celestial escape.
It had disappeared when you went back for it? Who could have taken it?
I miss your bed. The narrow replacement is less inviting;
A pledge to celibacy, a 'sign' you say.
Perhaps our Leafy Glade has sprouted wings and gone to Heaven.
We certainly showed it the way.

Wednesday 14th March 2007

It is cold today. The Laird leaves early for a men's prayer group he is not really enjoying. He is hostile and unloving at the moment. Does he realize I was with Adrian yesterday? Would he be unhappy about our restrained, platonic meeting? I expect he would be. I wish he could let go of fear. I will need to make a decision soon. Rain accompanies the cold day. I drive to Sultan's Point in the harbour. The Laird needs me to collect a salmon for tonight's Celtic Fundraising evening at College. He is hosting the event wearing his Whisky Society hat. It should be good. The Laird will don The Kilt and give an educational talk about The Single Malt. His natural showman skills will be much appreciated.

It's fun to explore a different region of the harbour this morning. I locate the commercial fish packers; the business and smart premises are surprisingly posh. I am directed to the shop on the waterfront and wander around, looking out of large glass windows into the harbour alongside. I see several fishing boats—one is named 'Huraki', a Maori name perhaps? I can't find any meaning in the Maori dictionary. A man in a white coat packs up the college order while I look at the different fish displayed. Green-Lipped Mussels, Kahawai, Blue Gill, Kingfish and Red Snapper lie in submissive rows in glass-fronted cabinets. Water sprinklers douse the aquatic line-up. I say hello to six inquisitive cray fish that claw the sides of a glass tank; someone's next meal. The salmon and three kilograms of fresh shrimp are expertly wrapped and handed across the counter. A friendly Maori fellow called Kini carries the heavy box to the car.

The swimming pool is closed again this morning, so I drive home and continue my writing. I am constantly amazed at the time consuming nature of documenting our story. I lose track of time. It takes hours to produce something worth reading and I relish every minute. The Laird and I continue chatting when he comes home—he is definitely in a better mood this evening, telling me he has moved away from shock and recognizes the lack of emotional passion in our marriage. He is accepting and warm, still clutching the book on choices. I tell him I spoke to my sister Mizzie—how she had been so helpful. "I want to be here for you," she told me. "You have to make a decision soon; this limbo state is bad for everyone concerned. Whatever you choose you'll have to be prepared to face the fallout. It's important to remember selfish desire—and neglect of responsibilities. Remember how we used to talk about that? How the 'free love' element of the Hippy World didn't sit comfortably? I always consider my future memories—what elements of my life will have been positive? What actions might I regret?"

The Laird and I feel much closer as the day ends. We have peeled away the layers to reveal the truth. And it isn't as frightening as he thought. Will he maintain these sentiments? I hope so. I cannot let go of my bond with Adrian. I am eighty percent certain I belong beside him. "It is three months now since you stopped seeing Adrian, isn't it?" He asks. "Yes, it is over three months since we signed our agreement." "You are right, we are not in love any more; you and I," admits The Laird. "Something has to change, and soon. I know it's why we moved to the Southern Hemisphere. I just wasn't expecting this kind of change."

P.m. Mouse: *Huge—real life-changing discussions this evening. Yikes! Just touching base. Sleep well—M—X*

Thursday 15th March 2007

A.m. {Unsent}: Waves of passionate potential overtake The Castle Mistress as she leaves The Mountain on her trusty steed. Could they really make it work? She has some thoughts—various ideas keep popping into her mind like the last pieces of corn in the bottom of the popcorn pan; there is always one more pop. Could I have a trial time away? A time where I see both my men folk? I suppose it would be a choosing time. Hmm—It would be good for me—and The Book—but probably not for the men. We shall see. Goodness, it's chilly this morning! I am wearing a woolly hat and leggings. The sky is crystal blue.

The Laird and his Lady were in a frivolous mood this morning. "I could write a poem about jam sandwiches," she laughed while buttering the eternal lunchbox demands. "Ode to a crust." They enjoyed the rare moment of silliness. "It's good to see you laughing," he said. "The book I'm reading talks about a woman who had a four day love affair. She admitted she couldn't ever return to her previous life. She said she felt like a frog in a swamp. Perhaps that's what you are—a frog!" "Oh no Sir," I replied. "I am more of a dragonfly—or a Thumbelina wee girl who needs to fly away with her Swallow every now and then." "Hmm, Perhaps I am the frog in the swamp then," he said. Last night he was tender and kind, stroking my face; "what are we going to do with you, Little One?" He is generous hearted—most definitely. How can I explain my deep ache for Adrian? What else can I do? Haven't I explored every gentle avenue? This situation is not about unkind choices and selfish desire. I will never rest easy until I am safely returned to Adrian's ownership; Adrian as King.

Lord Swallow walks over to my car at school pick-up today. The Bog-Brush is with me and goes completely mad with joy at seeing her friend again after three months. I smile; she is my little alter-ego, displaying the emotion I keep demurely under wraps. Another parent joins our conversation. Adrian is looking pale and tired today.

P.m. Mouse: *My Darling Friend—you look tired. I have not been able to care for you recently. I haven't asked how you really are. Tell me about 'tender-hearted' and 'wounded'. I am sorry to put you through these difficult times. Am I being selfish? I have no right to intrude upon your life. My Love, as the autumn appears know that you are held in my deepest care. My prayers are with The Angels; perhaps they know what the future holds for our friendship. Thank-you for being there. I do sense a steady shift each day; a shift towards some decision. I think it will come before mid-winter. Is it all right to keep you posted? M—X*

Chapter 3 Nonchalant

Friday 16th March 2007

I slept better last night. I get up early to complete more of The Book, although early risers disturb my morning routine. I notice The Laird's Spirit is much lighter today. He is trying hard to regain my adoration. Noticing the change I realize how debilitating I find his usual, heavy mood. I suspect the prospect of an ego-boosting whisky evening is the reason. I work around the kitchen, watching him down his cereal and tea, catching a glimpse of the boy in the man—the boy I fell in love with twenty-five years ago. Are we meant to return to that place? I am a mature woman now; my intuitive knowledge about male/female bonding has tasted the truth and I don't want anything less. My morning is taken up with domestic errands and dog walking; the normal routine, although an impromptu hair-cut makes for a change.

At midday the College Principal telephones to talk over my part-time job in The Laird's department. I am to co-ordinate the community service placements for the senior students. The job entails visiting various nursing homes and meeting with the student groups as they complete their obligatory twenty hours. I can't say I am over-enthused but it will bring in some cash and keep me occupied. I would rather concentrate on The Book. Ho hum- "Will we see you at the Celtic Party this evening?" He asks.

I bump into Adrian at the end of the school day. He has been busy on the farm applying biodynamic treatments to the land; burying a cow horn filled with particular herbs and applying a solution that needed an hour's stirring in both directions. Class 5 were roped in to help. He appears the satisfied farmer, munching an apple as he hangs over his classroom deck. He waves and I stop for a brief chat. It feels so normal to pass the time of day like this. We must be perfecting the art of 'Spark Containment'. "So—you've been having life-changing conversations, eh?" He asks in a nonchalant manner, waving another flag with the apple. I am in a rush and don't wish to speak of serious matters without our considered tone. I need to be lying close to him, snuggled in our usual intimacy, or writing him a message to disclose such truths. "I'm in a dash," I say. "I'll tell you later."

Before collecting Cedric from College I pick up a liquor license for The Laird's Celtic Soiree. I deliver it to his office. "I like the new haircut—and the skirt," he remarks. I can fit into my skimpy clothes these days. I kiss him hello. I suppose there are some benefits to this hopeless love business. Rinky The Minx is staying with a school friend tonight and Cedric is in charge of The Go-Getter for the evening. Once they are fed and watered I head down the hill for the 'College Do'. The Laird is in top form. He looks splendid in the new Kilt and wows everyone with his whisky spiel and amusing banter. Bernard and other whisky friends mingle with college parents. I sit at a table with Felicia and her Dutch guest, Stuart. We enjoy the salmon and other delicious food. I don't taste the various whiskies being passed around the tables, although I always enjoy the smell of the different malts.

Halfway through the evening I escape to the 'ladies' and send Adrian the long message I prepared earlier. Is it the right thing to do? I don't want to worry him or give him false hope. But I need to tell him the truth; the truth of our present situation. It is a long message and takes five texts to send. When I eventually return to the festivities Scottish Reeling is on the agenda. I enjoy a twirling reel with Stuart who is a tall, artistic man. As he spins me around the dance floor I can't help imagining how it would be to dance with Adrian like this.

P.m. Mouse: *"It has to be an exit through the main Castle Gates," she has been told by both The Laird and Lord Swallow. "You have to make a decision and come out into the light, through the main entrance. Yes, we know the gates are rusted and the key mislaid in the many-storied building, but the time is fast approaching when you must decide. It is not fair on anyone to keep up the 'limbo' state. I think you might be surprised at how helpful everyone would be. Even your Sister gave you the same advice last night. And haven't you noticed a big shift this week anyway? You managed to meet Lord Swallow, distant as it was, and now you can bump into him in The Forest, and on the farm, without feeling anxious. You have noticed an increased presence of those special Guardian Angels too—all this week they have been closing in around you, giving you extra attention."*

Strange how all of them were outside Big J's office today—Hau, Felicia, Simon, Cordelia, even Freya, Big J. and Martha. She realizes there are about 40 people who know of their union, {this fine man, Lord Swallow, with The Laird's wife}. That is quite a number; school colleagues and friends, family and loved ones on both sides of the world! My my, novices or masters? Can they really sail this sea without causing alarming waves? The tide will tell.

She has been quietly busy these past few days, attending her thoughts to the impending decision ahead. She is not eating or sleeping. Swimming and writing are keeping her steady. She has discovered the key at long last— inside one of The Laird's discarded trunks in the dungeon of all places! He finally admitted he had mislaid it; that in his heart of hearts he didn't know whether he truly desired it any more. Of course, he would like to polish it and make it function again but was there any point if it wasn't a joint decision? "Perhaps our time is up; our learning done together? Perhaps we are needed elsewhere now?"

They smiled at each other and hugging as the closest of friends she took the key away, on her own, to oil it and try out the lock. To her very great surprise, the key fits! She can even get it to turn, but is she brave enough to push open the old gates? The offending noise may upset many neighbours. And what of Lord Swallow in the Forest? Will the noise be too much for him? Does he really want her to walk out to meet him? She thinks she knows, but cannot be 100% sure. And could she actually face the biting cold wind as it whistled in through the Castle Gates? The autumn chill is upon their Mountain and she knows their time is nearing. She is missing him so badly—a deep ache; a steady longing that keeps her awake all night. But when they meet she cannot tell if their spark is alive. The copper boxes remain tightly locked. How can she possibly make any choices when they are unable to touch; unable to be close and honest with each other?

She knows what she must do. She will ask for a trial walk out of the Gates; a slow, tentative footstep. This feels right. She wonders if her Fine Sir has been back to the boat-yard—to check the sea-worthiness of their vessel. She will need a re-paint, that's for certain; three months' neglect is a long time. And a change of tone; perhaps a richer claret red over her keel to match his Lady's velvet gown—and a pale blue trim; the colour she likes to see him wear. Yes, that would be fitting. As her thoughts turn to him she wonders what his heart is saying—

Saturday 17th March 2007

All night I lie awake, wondering what Adrian thinks of my recent texts. The quandary I face involves the tipping of my personal scales. My Heavenly home or my Earthly abode? I need them both. The step I take is a tentative one—nothing definite—as close to a decision as I can make. I hope Adrian doesn't think I am about to turn up on his doorstep with my suitcase. He runs in the opposite direction if decisions are made for him. I feel sick. After weeks of abstinence last night's rich food takes its toll. I definitely shouldn't have had that pudding.

VALLEY GAZING

And so I stand,
Between here and there,
An impartial, safe haven;
A valley basin—
Water, stone and tree.
At what cost if I move this way, or that?
I feel no guilt. Why not?
Here stands a rock;
Solid, strong foundation, loyal and true.
How can I shatter and displace?
There moves a whisper breeze,
Deep echo in my soul.

How can I refuse Celestial embrace?
I have ached so long for this.
I am valley gazing,
Impartial in my soul/heart quandary.

The dog and I step out into the morning silence. A pink hush behind grey clouds greets us with mizzle that curls our hair. The stillness whispers sweet nothings in my ear and the gravel skids beneath my feet. The Bog-Brush disturbs a covey of quail above the duck pond. They look strange with their protruding feather that appears to grow from the top of their beaks. They put me in mind of a regimental platoon; they run so fast on brisk little legs, tumbling out of the undergrowth in matching uniform. They alert the ducks and geese to the Bog-Brush's presence.

Dewdrops balance on every fern and spider sacks stand out, silky and obvious on the gorse. I have to keep the hound on a long lead to stop her running wild. The Bellbirds in the pine trees welcome the day and we walk to the end of the drive, passing the old log and stepping onto the neighbour's tarmac strip. No post for us today, just a continuing quiet that matches my expectancy. The only sound is the Bog-Brush farting surprisingly in The Bush—her digestion must be in sympathy with mine this morning!

The Laird is pleased with the eggs on toast I deliver to the bedroom on my return. As he tackles the yummy platter I joke with him; "please, please let me out of the Castle Gates, Sir." "No—I shall pull up the drawbridge; you cannot escape. I won't share my wife with another." "Oh please," I continue. "Just imagine how exciting she'll become." "I'll have to give you three more children instead. That'll tie you down for a good few years," he threatens.

Oh dear—less freedom today; the recent, honest conversations are forgotten. The high of the whisky exhibition is over. *There might well be a child waiting in the wings,* I think quietly to myself—not that I can reveal such a scandalous thought.

The computer frustrates me this morning. Somehow I manage to delete a big chunk of work. B—GG—R, {rude word}. I am unskilled in this technological world and have no idea how to retrieve deleted script. I wish Adrian could help. I fiddle with a few keys and The Go-Getter lends a hand. We don't win. I take a deep breath and begin again. I think I remember the content. Adrian would probably tell me it is a 'sign' that I shouldn't be writing such an intimate account of our lives. However, I shall press on with my intuition—or my stubborn mind-set.

Mouse: *Good morning to you, My Friend in the valley. Can you help a Maiden in technological distress? I touched something at the base of the computer and have lost pages of script. S—H—T. Excuse my French. Is there an easy way to retrieve the work? Only reply if you have any answers. The* *household is recovering after a lively Celtic evening at College. Don't worry if you can't help—M-X*

We spend a couple of hours at Tui Park with Sonya, {the potter}, and her family this afternoon. One of her children has a birthday party and Rinky is invited. The children enjoy a game where a cloth full of different coloured lollies, {sweets}, is laid out before the eager children. Participants take it in turn to step away from the ring for a minute while the rest of the party choose a single lollie from the display to be 'it'—the one to avoid. Once the child is invited back to the ring he/she chooses lollies one by one, hoping to avoid the chosen 'it'. The child gets to keep all the lollies until they pick the unlucky one. At this point everyone shouts 'Tick!' and a new child is chosen to step out of the ring. What a great game.

I enjoy meeting Sonya's close friends from Coromandel. One couple talk about their twenty-three-year old twin daughters—professional acrobats performing as a double act in the circus! Well, that's certainly different. "Can we play 'Tick' at my birthday party, Mummy?" Rinky asks as we head home. I check my phone before we drive up the hill. Adrian hasn't replied to my plea for technological assistance.

P.m. Mouse: *Hello, Fine Sir. How goes the milking? I hope your day was good. Mine was full of bad luck. I was awake most of the night feeling sick after the rich dinner at College. Not a good idea after 5 weeks minimal eating. Then I lost 15 pages of vital writing and just now the wind blew shut the French window so hard that the bottom glass pane shattered. B—GG—R. Sorry. I am dog-tired-alone with Rinky while the others are watching the stock-car racing. Not back til 10.30. Wish you were here. Just saying goodnight. M-X*

Sunday 20th March 2007
I re-write **7** of the fifteen deleted pages of 'The Celestial Sea' this morning. Lucky my memory is good. I also work on the last pages of this current Book, putting the text messages onto the computer in an effort to make sense of the unfurling events. The Laird knows I am writing. I decide to show him The Book's synopsis as well as the long message about walking through the Castle Gates. We are being honest with each other and I *do* need him to know what's happening. I hand over the printed scripts with a bacon sandwich. "No more secrets," I tell him. "I need you to give Adrian permission to see me. I cannot move forward without his friendship. You told me to give it six months. I have been without Adrian for three months. Now I need three months with Adrian in my life." "You would have to move out completely—think of the consequences," he says. "You want me to give another man permission to make love to my wife, so my marriage might end? Is that right?" "Well—sort of—If that's how you understand it. We need to move forward and this is the only way I can envisage. Once I know our true needs and desires we can make choices," I state. "Perhaps you should

go and live in a motel for a while; then you'd see what life would be like," The Laird retorts. "But I want to continue looking after everyone," I respond. "We can decide how it is to be. We can make it positive or negative. The choice is ours." The time has come for honest talk. Recent conversations have revealed truths that cannot be sweep under the carpet.

P.m. Mouse: It is in The Laird's hands now. She opened it right up; showed him the front cover of The Book; the synopsis and Friday's long text about walking through the Castle Gates. No more secrets as he would want. She asked him to give Lord Swallow permission to see her as more than just a friend—a trial time to see where they all stand—if their love is over or just beginning. He raised his eyes in disbelief at the cheek of her request. Then he gave her a kind hug and took the dog for a walk. Lots more was said, with understanding and kindness. The atmosphere was much improved on his return. "Thank-you for showing me The Book," he said. We shall see. Goodnight, Dear Friend. May the Angels hold us as we slumber; their intention in our dreams—M—X

Monday 19th March A.m

A.m. Mouse {Unsent}: My Darling Adrian, the dawn breaks on the feast day of St.Joseph the Carpenter—your feast day too, I imagine. What will today bring? My busy routine kicks in with work for College and cooking for our School Raft Race. I'm still getting used to the clock change—we are well into autumn now, on the Mountain, although the middle of the day is still hot. Chill winds and thick jumpers in the morning though. I wonder what thoughts drift across your mind, Sir? I love thee. M—X

Tentative new beginnings; The Laird and I feel our way round them as we breakfast together this morning. "What's this?" I pick up a stray piece of plastic. "We found it under the fridge, along with a playing card," The Laird tells me. "Oh, and you retrieved my long-lost cookery book too; thank-you." "Hmm—now it's the marriage we need to retrieve," sighs my patient husband. He has a wistful look this morning. I hate to hurt him, but I won't be untrue to myself any longer. "Hello, Monty;" the cat jumps on my knee, home for a change. "Are you hungry?" "How can you switch from a conversation about the predicament of our marriage to one as trivial as feeding the cat?" My husband throws me his perplexed question. I have an answer but I save him further wounding. My answer would have been: *'Ah-that's my lively, entirely versatile mind that needs stimulation, Sir. I am bored without intense passion and mind-play. I can spring from here to there in a single leap.'*

I see Adrian twice at school today; the second time he is walking up the drive at school pick-up time. I wonder—does he come to see me? We wave and my heart turns over at the sight of the man I love.

216

P.m. Mouse: "Come to me," she cries into the dusk. "Come to me as silent dew upon the hill. Come bathe me with your tender balm. Come move in me tonight and I will greet thee with our love-drenched nectar in all its sticky sweetness. Come to me; come inside me," she calls into the night, hoping that one day soon—he might-X

Tuesday 20th March 2007

I complete the deleted pages of The Book this morning; relief. Perhaps I was meant to re-write them. Perhaps I have included vital, extra passages. I certainly added some kind words about The Laird. He was distant and cold again last night. His school board meeting had been long and his supper unappetising on his return. Cross Laird. I know he finds my messages mixed. I am trying to find a way. Do I have to be unkind? I can't bear to hurt him. I can be close and cuddly with him still—he thinks this means all is fine; he cannot understand the mature, emotional passion that I share with Adrian. As far as he is concerned, 'passion' means physical lovemaking; and he is a strong lover in that respect. How can I explain the difference? Of course, if he did understand I would never have needed to step outside our marriage.

I see Adrian in the distance at school today. I wave. He's wearing a shirt that doesn't suit him; a dark caramel colour; one I shall encourage him to discard if we see each other again. The sunshine is glorious. The heat burns my bare shoulders as I leave Monument Pool. I jump up and down on the hot tarmac to unblock my waterlogged ears. The cicadas are noisy today and I look up into the native tree line for a while, knowing there are hundreds of insects there. The outdoor pool is closing for the winter in ten days' time—winter? Surely not; this heat is beautiful. The dog and I sit together in the car under the Plane trees. We listen to classical music and I write my diary. Life is really exciting at the moment, with delicious pockets like this to gild the hovering potential. I pray for The Laird—that he may grasp the future and let go of fear. We don't need to lose the things we value; community, family, friends, caring and sharing. We can make the future whatever we like. His vocation and bachelor lifestyle can run free. Will he ever grasp the possibility?

I have noticed an odd change since yesterday; since the seriousness of our situation reached a more realistic level. Rinky has started acknowledging Adrian whenever we see him. She waves enthusiastically. "Adrian says hello to me everyday," she informed me last night. How strange. I often ask if she has seen him at school. She would never be drawn until yesterday—the feast day of St. Joseph. Does she know something we don't? As I wait for children Adrian dashes past the car with his guitar on his back. He takes the path on the other side of the flowerbeds. Is he avoiding me? Is he late for guitar lessons? He looks boyish, free, playful—and mine. I love him.

P.m. Mouse: Goodnight, My Silent Friend. Nice to see you dash past me *earlier—guitar on your back, shorts flapping—the boy in the man. Laird understandably angry with me today. If I don't appear at school tomorrow you may have to drag the Castle Moat. He is hoping to see Simon soon. Thinking of you—M-X*

Wednesday 21st March 2007

"Please wake me at five-thirty a.m and then again at five-thirty-five;" my instructions last night. Does my husband realize how much he relies on me for all his domestic needs? "I'll bugger off with the children, then," has been one of his recent statements. "What are we going to do?" He asks. "I would never abandon my children for selfish desire," I reassure him. "I will not make any move unless there is harmony for all concerned. Trust that the way will be made clear. Please let go of fear." Sleep was slow to take me last night. The Laird finds my messages mixed and I have to say, I am finding his confusing.

The Go-Getter's class is studying 'Indian Religions'—their current Main Lesson. Our wee lad is filled with enthusiasm for the dress-ups day, {Kiwi term for dressing-up}. He raids my wardrobe for an embroidered waistcoat and string of beads. He fashions a turban out of an old T-shirt. He helps make the Dahl we are contributing to the shared lunch party. I join a handful of other parents for the meal and chat with Andy—Kieran's father—the same Andy whose workroom Adrian occasionally uses. "I've been doing some carpentry work for your neighbours on The Mountain," he tells me. "Did you know their marriage was over?" I look up surprised. "Really?" I wonder if The Mountain Spirits have something against happy couples. "And you remember the guy you called 'Yellow-Tooth-Dave? The decorator who never paid you? Well, he went belly-up; never paid me either. All I got out of the deal was his old caravan. I gave it to Adrian."

P.m. Mouse: *Goodnight, My Lovely Friend. Want an update? I find this so tricky, not really knowing if you are okay hearing the detail of my present life. Anyway, I shall dish it out and you can either ignore—or not. I have just had another session in the psychiatrist's chair. The ever-reasonable, patient Laird reduced something he will never understand into a series of numbered points, in dull, earthed logic. No, he will not give his permission—far too demeaning to his manhood. And no, he would never share his wife with another man, {understandable}. "If Adrian really felt for you he would be in touch; he would not choose safety over your love. He does not need my permission to see you. He will not lose his job. Why don't you just go and knock on his door in the early hours? It would be out in the open if you did. Even if he doesn't want you anymore, I won't play second best." {Fair enough}. "I want a companion who shares my life; you never want to do anything with me. I'd like us to spend three days away, WITHOUT children."*
Hmm—she listens to his reasonable calm, dropping like damp earth

upon the fire in her heart. "Where is he"? She calls. She needs him.

Thursday 22nd March 2007

A.m. Mouse: Dear Friend. Can we borrow your gas ring for Class 5 today? If so, can you deliver it to the classroom by midday? They are cooking again this afternoon. I am coming in to help. Don't worry if it's not possible. The Laird is doing the school run later—just warning you. P.s— there is a sign up at Tui Park claiming the water is currently unfit for swimming, {or raft races}. Pollution problem. What time do you want me to serve up the soup lunch tomorrow?

Adrian: Hi Mouse. Thanks for making soup for the Raft Race day tomorrow. Probably say grace around 12/12.15—Okay?

My day is filled with vegetable chopping and cake baking. Busy, busy. I don't know how many will eat at my café table tomorrow. The children bring home a message saying that the Raft Race venue is changed. The event will take place at an alternative Park on the other side of town.

Friday 23rd March 2007

The dog and I start the day early. We are both restless. Will Adrian speak to me today; the day of our school Raft Race? He will have to say hello; I am bringing the cafe lunches he has requested. Something is in the air. The dark morning greets us with a veil over the future. The Bog-Brush and I tread carefully.

Early A.m. Adrian: Icy fingers of fear have played a dirge on his heartstrings all night—her courage stuns him—she is opening The Gates. Suddenly it is his decision. Now he must decide. His first instinctive cry is "NO!" He thinks of his cows chewing their cud contentedly in the field, a picture of his own comfort and security in the unfolding developments and settling at school—into school. Her exit brings with it a mighty storm, strong enough to blow it all away—strong enough to blow him and the cows right off the land—right out of the district. "NO!" he cries again, fear gripping him. But a breath brings back his courage. Where are his feelings for her? They have been hardened for three months.

He looks for his heart—the storm of outrage and accusation brews while he searches. He feels that she sits upon the top of a powerful Tidal Wave and that when The Gates open all its power will descend upon him. She will want him to be a rock in the overwhelming scratching and cutting tides—mourning children and husband—angry friends and family—disappointed colleagues— mocking children—scornful community. And his love for her? Is it strong enough for this? He searches on.

A wind from a new quarter is blowing through the rigging today; the south, south/east—cold and strong. He walks the fields, his dog banned from free running at school, now on a long rope. He watches that she doesn't crap anywhere. He checks the water-top up and a shot of vinegar. The cows keep pulling the hose out. They drink a good 60 litres a day. They are awake—grazing. The pasture is tufty with bare patches. New seedlings are springing up in the bare parts. It will be ready in a month. He and Delphine will be spreading preparation 500 this week. She would have him back like a shot, he knows. Two mothers; a childhood reflection for him of torn loyalties. What an intricate web is being woven. He will speak with his Lady today—that is a term he has not used for a while. He wonders how it would be, could be?

Mouse: She cannot sleep. The dog whines for a dawn amble down the familiar route. Newly cut gorse surprises tender paws—a graceful side step and they continue in their dusky welcome to the day, wondering what it might bring. The wind is up; a call to action ruffles the ready and aching sails above her head. Once inside she checks her phone, ever hopeful that he might be there. The optimist in her doesn't fade. The screen is blank.

She makes a cup of tea and wrestles with the computer which is slow to activate today. And then she decides—she will tell him. She will let him know that she has indeed opened The Gates, that all restrictions are lifted. But, she does not want him to think it is just on his account, although she would love to see her friend, of course. There are other questions that need answering; the main one being; 'Can she live the rest of her life with a man with whom she shares a strong commitment but with whom she cannot reach the depths of creative passion she needs?' And she needs deep—oh, yes, she really needs deep, because she **can** go there. She reaches for her phone—"What is this"? She cannot believe her eyes—they are synchronized again! His words send her already scared heart into a fast tremble. Yes, she is riding the crest of this massive and frightening wave. Something prevents her from gaining the easier waters. Will she only back down at the point of crashing spume?

My day begins. I drive the children to the alternative Park for the Raft-Race outing. Tui Park remains banned to swimmers due to the temporary pollution warning. Vonny helps me unload the trestle tables and raft building supplies that we have brought—a paddle, some rope and the body-boards. I drive home quickly to start the café lunches, the journey taking a good half hour through this unknown area of town. An open region, the green suburb is lined with kiwi and avocado orchards along straight roads. I glimpse neat homes and tidy lawns through the established hedges. I enjoy the different route today.

My Lord Swallow was not at the park when I dropped the children. I expect he is involved in collecting some last minute component for the raft building. I look out for his car and trailer as I drive home but he doesn't pass by. I am very organized this morning with a speedy completion of the soups and cakes; a chocolate topping to be applied on arrival, more seasoning in the saucepans and lids taped down to withstand our steep drive. The soup is more watery than I would like—never mind. The show is on the road at last. The Castle Hound is meant to be with The Laird but he forgot her in the bad-tempered, morning dash. I manage to squeeze her in alongside the café paraphernalia. I don't blame him for the bad mood. I am leading him on a most unfair, and certainly not merry, dance. He awaits my declarations of undying love and request for forgiveness, both of which are slow in coming. I am walking out of The Castle Gates with his knowledge but without his happy blessing. There is another man I love as a profound 'completeness'; something I have never experienced before. I am aching for Adrian. I need him. Forbidden as it is, I cannot stop the reality of these feelings.

Re-joining the children at twelve noon I am amazed by the carnival spectacle in the bay. The entire school, divided into teams of children and adults, are either busy in the water or reclining on the grassy bank. Picnics, sun-hats, paddles and chatter—the park resembles a shot taken from one of those elaborate, action-filled puzzles with lots of people engaged in a hundred different tasks. Happy bods in togs, {swimming things,} and wet tea-shirts fill the bay with makeshift craft of differing size and design. Small boys and girls, alongside various intrepid adults, are busy with barrels and rope, tyre-rings and polystyrene blocks. I smile and quickly enrol helpers in Louise and Lisa. We choose a spot to place the tables and start serving soup and bread to hungry takers. We hastily erect a discarded umbrella to keep off the scorching heat; a lucky find.

A Sausage Sizzle, {sausage barbecue}, is already underway and I am slightly anxious there will be no hungry mouths left for all the food in the back of my car. I needn't worry. Familiar faces soon appear at the popular café spread; chocolaty fingers and soupy grins make it worthwhile. Some passers-by stop at the tables and ask: "What school is *this*?"

My Lord Swallow is in the thick of proceedings, as you might imagine. Sporting swimming togs and white hat he manages a quick word as he passes the café; "Yes, he might come back for soup if he has a minute—maybe later". He smiles broadly. After the festivities have died down I walk the Bog-Brush along the sands for her long-awaited exercise. The sun is still blazing and I bless the dense tree shade under which I managed to park all afternoon. My keen raft-builders were on the same team they announce. "We came third out of ten teams!" One of them departs with a friend for the weekend while the other hunts for trophies on the beach with a buddy from his class.

A handful of staff and parents remain to clear the lost property; forgotten lengths of rope, sun hats and brightly coloured swimming towels. I watch them from my amble/dash through the shallow waters of the bay. The sharp shells crunch under my feet. The dog and I enjoy the different venue. I spy Adrian in the distance, busy loading up the trailer. He disappears along a path at one point—was I meant to follow him? There is no opportunity to talk today; he didn't even get time for his soup. I stay until the end but so do several teachers who know of our connection. He drives away with a wave and a loud "goodbye" in my direction. I hear nothing for the rest of the day.

P.m. Mouse: *Wonderful atmosphere—a joy-filled day. Well-done, Sir. A spectacular event, without any Tidal Wave threat either. I am proud to call myself chef to the Maestro and his team—X*

P.s I am sending you an e-mail with an Easter song for Monday. Sleep well.

Saturday 24th March 2007

A.m. Mouse: *A frightening hush lies in her heart and soul, the caged spark so alive in her abundant mind-play, but in the cold reality of worldly presence has it been extinguished? The hard-heartedness of his months towards her—oh, she knows there was really no alternative—but her constant stream of tears that went unheeded may have killed the fire forever. She is part-scared, part-relieved if it is so. His truthful text of yesterday in all its clear and negative realism is matched by The Laird's sadness and picture-painted family split across hemispheres. These Angels have picked themselves the most impossible of scenarios; on purpose I am sure. So, why can she not climb down and turn her back on the impossibility? But—she will not be an equation in his split loyalties; there is another who shares his life now. Perhaps it is better left that way.*

My morning passes in growing agitation, agitation that I haven't heard from Adrian when he said we would speak, and anxiety that my message this morning was too harsh; that he must be growing tired of this unwanted complication. The Laird's heavy Spirit continues to sap the joy out of life. Dear Angels—*please* give us some answers. I shall send one more message to Lord Swallow. Then I'll leave him be.

Midday, Mouse: *Waves of stress overtake her this morning. Why now? She has been in tight control for months. Her breathing fast—her ears and back of head aching. Vigorously, she cleans the cooker hob. She was too harsh this morning in her message to him. Deep down, she knows the spark is alive and ignited in their own, private passion. It may take some unearthing but the flame can never fade. They both know that. She was unfair to say she would not be part of his split loyalties—doesn't she ask that of him everyday? And isn't it better he has those around him, caring for him when she cannot? She is alone this evening if he does want to see her, but she will be okay if he would rather stay away. She loves him. They have an epic tale of romance to write and she has cleared some sort of path to whatever the future holds—M-X*

Adrian: *He is driving, having just been to a real Country Fair in the Kuwharu Hills. Ideas—he waits to read her message, still a little stung by her slap. His instinct was right—not to send his reply straight away, or at all—*

222

just live with it. He is relieved that he does not have to harden to her. He thanks her for her understanding. Maybe a phone call tonight. She wounds him with her words. The disappointment pointed and hard. She understandably misunderstands—assuming his fickleness has been right from the break. She's wrong. The warmth has only just come into the time spent with Delphine. She is not my Lady—a dear friend and companion—needed to explore what was there; betrayal?

P.m. Mouse: Thank-you. Sorry. Take care. A phone call later maybe. I will text if a free slot appears and the boys are away from my desk. M-X

Later, Mouse: I am free until dark—cannot get boys away from desk, so phone call is off. Am able to text, or meet somewhere, but that may not be appropriate, My Friend. What do you feel? M—X

I receive no response from Lord Swallow. I walk the dog in quiet contemplation, thinking, thinking and waiting for inspiration.

Late P.m. Mouse: A sudden impulse ripples through her evening stroll. 'They should be bold—take what is theirs and strike out, much as they did into the waves on Maketu beach in December. This pussyfooting around each other will only continue for weeks if they do not go there again, even if only for a trial period.' She is feeling bold tonight—and frustrated by the lack of knowing and the fear on both their sides. She has decisions to make; for herself and her family. The wait is taxing them all. To return home or to stay here? To move out for a trial period, as suggested by The Laird, or not? To move closer to town or to purchase 2 properties? To go back home in September on the college trip or to go at Christmas as the family has offered to finance? To place The Book writing as top priority to pave smooth paths if it takes off?

The life-changing questions are many. And the most important one, upon which the others hang—their bond, and where, if anywhere, they are meant to take it? They need to lie close and still for a long time. The formal meetings are past. Neither of them will be satisfied until they are in that sacred place. This will not go away—it is too strong—whatever they decide 'it' is; whatever alchemy they become. What say you, my fellow Sailor?

Adrian: Going to sleep on that one. Just back from a 'More to life' meeting in Hamilton. There's a lot going on for you—my God. Need sleep. I'll let you know tomorrow.

Mouse: Sleep well—X

Sunday 25th March 2007

A.m. Mouse {Unsent}: She sleeps fitfully, if at all. Her over-indulgence of the day before claiming her gut; making her feel sick and bloated. She *cannot rest. The wave is about to crash and will she stay riding it to the very last or will she chicken out and leap to safety before it hits the shore?*

I hear nothing. I do not contact Adrian today. The Laird sits with another family at church this morning. A new parishioner and parent at College enjoy his community welcome. The Go-Getter and I sit together; Cedric is at home and Rinky is still away for the weekend. I imagine Adrian beside me on the pew. I feel his arm around my waist, his fingers locked with mine. Little Arthur sits between us. He watches the Go-Getter drawing all over the service sheet.

The gospel before the homily tells of the adulterous woman stoned and set free; even God granted her forgiveness. "Imagine yourselves as that woman," the Priest suggests. I did and felt I could easily stand up and tell the crowd about the God-given nature of my illicit love affair. He talked of forgiveness and compassion—of letting others be who God has called them to be. I listen, intrigued, although The Go-Getter is distracted throughout by two little girls in the pew behind who copy every move he makes.

"Did you notice how the reading and homily were so relevant?" The Laird asked after the service. "I imagine you were rather pleased and would tell everyone you would do it all over again. Funny how our situation is highlighted all the time, even the film we saw this week; 'Miss Potter'—did you notice the relevance there?" Yes—I had noticed. The lovers' forced banishment for three months; the true love and shared, creative spirit that was only allowed a short time to live. Hmm—yes, I had noticed. "Just don't watch *Shakespeare in Love,*" I tell him. "Leave that one on the shelf."

Monday 26th March 2007
The dog and I turn left instead of right in Monument bay this morning. Another hot day scorches and entices us further than we have walked before. I let The Bog-Brush swim as I wade, waist deep in the tidal water. Despite the heat I am aware that autumn is around the corner. I can't say I'm looking forward to another winter battering The Mountain; a winter without Lord Swallow and a depressed, rugby-watching husband for company. I realize I need the support of family. I couldn't be further away from them. "You really enjoy writing your Book, don't you?" The Laird asked me yesterday in a brighter moment. "Yes, I do," I admitted. "Well," he said, "you had better get on with it and make us a fortune."

I am feeling empty today. I have taken my truth as far as I can. Whatever happens happens. I am almost past minding. I can let Adrian go if we are 'over'. As The Laird said, if he truly loved me he would come for me, no matter what. He has others in his life these days. As the evening draws in I find myself unwell—a kidney infection? A flu/cold? Or is it stress?

Tuesday 27th March 2007
I feel worse this morning, even my chest is aching. I manage the vital

chores but the dog swimming isn't possible. The bay at Tui Park is warm and inviting—shame. We stroll around the grass instead. I stock up on the basics at 'Pak N Save', {the cheaper supermarket where you 'save' by 'packing' the groceries yourself}. I chat to a dear old lady who pulls up beside me in a battered, Nissan Civic. She has a panting dog sitting in the passenger seat with the window wound down. "I'm seeking dog shade, like you," she says. "There isn't much in these car parks is there? He's waiting for his walk, aren't you, old boy? I'm off to shop first."

A tap on my window surprises me when I arrive at school this afternoon. It is Adrian. I climb out of the car and say hello. "Have you got the story for assembly?" He asks. "Yes, here it is. I was going to give it to Big J." "I'm reading this week," he informs me. I hand over the script with a grin; a farming story with a couple of passages he will enjoy. Cordelia and I take turns writing the assembly stories and this one is rather apt. A repeat of last year's tale our story tells of the farmer tending his livestock and tidying his barn; the villagers prepare for something important, reflecting the end of Lent. I have added a couple of sentences highlighting the cattle.

Lord Swallow looks gorgeous today. He is glowing and sun-kissed. I like the blue shirt he's wearing. Our eyes hold each other for a while. We are happy to be together and stroll towards the staff room. "How was the Celtic evening?" He asks. I tell him about the success; the whisky and extra guests who arrived at the last minute, boosting the ticket sales. "I danced with a tall, dashing Dutchman who whisked me across the dance floor in great style." "Did you have live music?" Adrian asks. "No, sadly we didn't." "Shame I didn't know about it. The Irish band I play with was free on Friday. Perhaps we should have some reeling here at school one day; that would be fun."

We say goodbye. I'm pleased Adrian will read my story at assembly. "You have ink on your lips," I tell him before I leave. I don't add that I'd like to kiss it away for him.

P.m. Mouse: She bids him goodnight. She is alone tonight and fighting a flu bug. The Laird is away, camping with students. She does not want Lord Swallow to think she is waiting. She knows it is impossible. Just saying; "sleep well"—M—X

Wednesday 28th March 2007

A.m. Mouse {Unsent}: It rains. She wakes, alone and in pain. The mystery ache around her lower back and kidneys is draining and odd. It is painful to sit up but she drags herself downstairs for the usual rounds of dog walk, herbal brew and writing. She is pleased with The Book's progress— every day the words leap out of the diaries, spilling from her memory. Her life is vibrant in this domain where Lord Swallow takes her hand and dances across the pages with her.

225

I am exhausted by the domestic duties. The Laird is still away so I have to cope unaided with grumpy children, a messy house and lunchbox organization. Eventually we arrive at school and I can relax; a little. The Bog-Brush stares at me, ever hopeful for a ten-mile hike. "Sorry, my friend. Another grassy stroll for you today." My phone screen remains blank, except for my faithful Laird who sends a morning greeting.

Laird: Gd. Mrng. How R U feelin?

Mistress: Shitty—on my way to visit another rest home for the College project. Hope you are having fun.

Laird: Ask them for a bed! I'm ok, feeling old and fat, surrounded by fit young things.

Mouse: Surely not The Laird? He's in his prime—a mature, handsome man. Those whippersnappers cannot hold a candle. 'Tis all in the mind-X

How kind of The Laird to send me messages. I don't deserve his ongoing care. I miss the content and poetry of Adrian's texts. The Laird's are so different. I view the over-packed, sad state of the elderly in their home by the sea. The front door has a childproof lock to prevent escapees. Like babes in high chairs they sit in rows around the edges of the main room. The smell of old age and spilled gravy precedes the inevitable. The lady manager has an interesting history. Of Swiss origin she trained in Cornwall before working in South Africa. Her partner is Kiwi but they find life difficult here. "It's too cold in the winter," she says, "and the pay is bad."

"Adrian made up his own version of the story at assembly," Little J. tells me at our Festival meeting this afternoon. Of course he did. I can imagine. Rinky informed me that someone borrowed his computer to watch a film; I hope they didn't open 'The Celestial Sea' file. I am well in to Part Five now; the pages keep coming. Might it be too long? Oh well, seeing as something other directs this storyline I shall continue to record, word for word, and see what the completed script reveals.

*P.m. Mouse {Unsent}: Oh my Love—where are you? I cannot hang on much longer; please contact me. I need **something** from you. I am tired and ill and unsure. Last night I overheard The Laird speaking to my mother. I caught the words, "her decision," and "passion." I also heard him mention the children's schooling. I can't believe you don't acknowledge our bond. I am through The Castle Gates. Restrictions are lifted, {although without The Laird's blessing}, and I was free last night. Can you really not call me—if only as a friend? No, you cannot. Doesn't that tell me something? Either you have truly forgotten you said you would speak with me or you think our car park meeting was 'the chat.' Or perhaps you want shot of our relationship* *but can't bring yourself to say so; maybe you hope it will just fade away. Can't you make up your mind? Is this why you wait, keeping me in constant, ambiguous suspense? Deep down I think you know what we are to each other but you are afraid of the consequences. Do you want me to make a move towards you, relieving you of any blame? Or do you need to honour the six months suggested by The Laird? Perhaps you don't believe I have walked through The Castle Gates. Will you only be happy if The Laird gives you his permission personally? The decision has been mine with The Laird's knowledge but without his happy agreement. Hmm—I don't know. I think I favour the scenario that finds you acknowledging our bond yet afraid of the consequences. I should just accept the indecision—after all, if you are indeed serious about our love you need time. If you decided to make a stand for me it would be the biggest decision of your life—and of mine. A decision like this could take months—even years. So, My Distant, Silent Friend, I bid you goodnight. I will limit my messages. I am spent. The ball lies in your court. My part is complete. I shall wait without expectation. Sleep well. M.X*

Friday 30th March 2007

The rain is pouring down on the land—torrential; like the worst downpour we would get at home. 'Home'. Yes, home beckons. I am feeling sad; so sad this morning. My screen lies blank. He cannot even reach out to me when I have cleared a way; cannot even send me a goodnight text or a small acknowledgement. What is he afraid of? That even the smallest show of contact will open everything up? That the force is so great he dare not give himself an inch? That he doesn't trust himself, or doesn't trust me, more likely? He even placed a hat between us on the swing-seat when last we met and then took back the music he had just given me. He shied away from an ordinary kiss when I said goodbye.

Thanks, Lord Swallow. Where is your nobility now? Can we not rise above this fear? Your apparent inability to do so, alongside the prioritising of your self-protection, means there is no point in my heart-felt sadness. It was never deep enough for you all along. Hmm—but your Lady knows that it is, in fact, deep and you know that she knows. You understandably cannot get past the practicalities and yes, the fear—the fear of The Tidal Wave—the fear of The Laird. You were badly frightened by his outburst in January.

The Laird bumps his way down our drive with all on board. "Can you do the school run today"? I asked earlier. "There is no point in me going down the hill if I don't need to." My female belly is in pain and my back still bad. Is my meagre diet playing havoc with my monthly cycle? Is this why I have been feeling ill? I overindulge in a greedy cooked breakfast; there will be no lunch for me today. I am left alone in peace on The Mountain, the complications and impending decision-making as impenetrable waste before me. The comfort of my Lord Swallow's embrace is a thing of the past and I grieve.

Saturday 31st March 2007

I wake at six a.m. It is hot and muggy. We had to close the windows to keep out the rain last night. The restless dog entices me out of bed and my love for Lord Swallow hurries me downstairs to check my phone. The screen remains blank. It has been that way for days. Grey mizzle shrouds The Mountain in eerie awakening. The birds are silent this morning. The dripping trees claim the stage while the stream on the neighbouring property bubbles and crashes with the sound of water playing over boulders. We head that way to watch the rain-induced frolic. As we stroll home the sky changes behind the mizzle to a misty shade of lilac. I spy lacy thin clouds high up; one cloud is chubby; like the face of a young bride it smiles shyly behind a veil.

A.m. Mouse {Unsent}: I am with you, My Love. Are you with me? I sense you strongly this morning. I curl up close beside you and place my hand upon your Greenstone. I look sadly into your eyes. Yes, I am here, but are you really with me or is your attachment only present in my imagination? Perhaps you already lie in another's arms with little thought of me. I like to imagine your mind-talk. This is my optimistic take on today's version:

'She is waiting for him—even though she says she isn't he knows she waits for the phone to light up. He has been hard, cruel even with his silence and ambiguity. At times he doesn't care, yet at other times, like now, he knows their love eats into him; his fear destroying the potential for this most important love of his life. He has tried to ignore it. Unacknowledgement and lack of response have tried in vain to dispel the truth. Her courage and steadfastness amaze him. Yes, she has completed her side of the journey. And what is he doing? Hiding in the shadows like a coward to protect his personal position. Is he unable to accept the challenge? Does she risk losing more than him? Her family, her friends and even her global belonging are on the line. His career, community and honour are at stake. Even his cows are threatened by the Tidal Wave—URG—he wrestles with himself. She is right; it will not go away. The truth of their bond is too strong and it will not disappear. Denial is a false companion. He watches his cows grazing in the drizzle. A surge of anger explodes from his usual composure. He kicks the ground and yells unprintable words at himself. He kicks the tufts of grass and kicks himself in the shins with self-fury. Spreading wide his arms he shouts—"YES, I LOVE HER—I WILL NO LONGER DENY THE TRUTH. I AM INCOMLPLETE WITHOUT MY LADY BY MY SIDE. I CANNOT LIVE WITHOUT HER— YES, NO—NO-YES."

Wow-that makes him feel much better. Honesty at last, the monsters of guilt and shame have run away, over the hill. Yes, he will contact his Lady now. He will tell her it isn't impossible; they will

find a way. Whatever it takes he will have her beside him again. A cold draught springs up from the southeast, troubling his thoughts. Will she still want him? Her silence over the past few days worries him. Has she jumped off the tidal wave to avoid the crashing spume? His dream last night returns; her face looking out of an aircraft window as it taxied down the runway—the sensation of running after the moving aeroplane-"TOO LATE, TOO LATE," others shouted above the roar of the engines. "YOU LEFT HER STRANDED TOO LONG. YOU ARE TOO LATE." He is filled with desolation and dread. How could he have been so hard? He woke in a cold sweat, his heart thumping and a roaring sound in his ears. He prays he is not too late. Is she still there for him? He cannot be 100% sure. She knows he needs time to make a stand. She has plans, he knows. He is not used to being led. Remember what he said when she read him The Celestial Sea poem? "I'm sorry—I'm not with you on that one." But she knows him. Oh yes, she knows him.

Silently he strolls back to his new home. He is peaceful. The King reigns. He will tell Vonny about their love; the time is right. They will need to meet at her house to release The Boat from dry-dock and regain the open seas. Until they know which tide to sail upon, they will need her blessing. And a new bed too—his weekend task. He sighs; the acceptance feels good. Reality at last. A cup of tea calls— and an honest chat with his landlady.

Peace descends as I write my tale of imagined mind-play. I know there is truth amongst the romantic idyll of jumbled words. But fairy tales don't happen in real life—or do they? She strokes Lord Swallow's beautiful face in her imagination. He sleeps at last, soothed and happy. "I love thee," she whispers in his ear. They kiss gently—not with fiery passion but with intimate care and relief. They are reunited with their beautiful vessel at last. "Let's sleep a while, My Love," he says. "We are both exhausted after our separate journeys. When we wake a new day will have begun; bright skies and a fresh wind shall greet us. We are ready to face the world."

"Come to me, my Love. Come to me as truth upon the morning hush. Come to me in all your richness and readiness. Come to me my bride, as lively water over rocks and sand. We shall begin our life together as we are destined—as The Angels have always intended. Come to me."

"You are staring at me;" The Go-Getter is arguing with his sister across the kitchen table this morning. "Ma, please tell Rinky to stop staring." Honestly, there's always something to argue about and when there's nothing left to start a fight the 'staring' card is played. "Hurry up; The Farmers' Market won't wait for ever. Get in the car; the dog can come too." I distract the children with my instruction. Children and hound scramble for the best places; the Bog-Brush always barges Rinky off the front seat. Peace at last, until Rinky chips in with another accusation. "Ma-*do* something; the dog's *staring* at me!" At which point the Go-Getter and I burst out laughing. "Did you see the new brood of baby chicks?" I ask, quickly changing the subject; The Minx is looking thunderous in the back seat. Don't ever laugh at your children, especially not in cahoots with a rival sibling. Oops—bad mother. "Are they the brood from The Shid?" Asks my giggling chappie. "Yes," I answer. "Can you *believe* the mother hen made them jump from the top of the fridge where she was sitting? I was about to put the nest on a lower shelf before they hatched. We'll call them the Fridge Jumpers."

Sunday 1st April 2007

It is exactly four months since Adrian and I dived into the waves at Maketu; four months since we signed our unwanted agreement. My eyes well up during the weekly service today, accompanying the tragedy of Holy Week. I cannot feel Adrian with me; cannot even sense him looking through the church fence. No, he has gone from me and I am desolate.

*A.m. Mouse: The beginning of Holy Week—Palm Sunday and the first reading of the Passion-**"My God, my God, why have you abandoned me? Why are you not there"**? In this Lenten solitude the tears form behind closed eyes, escaping nonetheless. He is not beside her on the pew today.*

We hunt for the newly hatched chick when we get back from church. Rejected by his 'Fridge Jumping' mother and supposedly contained in the basket under a warm light bulb he has escaped. Eventually we find him shivering under the sofa. He must feel the cruel hand of abandonment too. I tuck him into the warmth of my cleavage while overhearing a conversation the Go-Getter conducts with his visiting school friend: "Last night I dreamt us Class 5 boys were put in prison for smoking marijuana!" My eyebrows shoot up but I pretend not to listen. "We didn't mind though, cos they've got computers in prison." "Oh—cool," answers his friend Mat. "They get pocket money in prison too; sounds okay really."

We spend the day quietly on The Mountain. Unfortunately our visiting friend manages to chip a front tooth on the trampoline. I telephone his mother who sounds unconcerned by the incident. Cedric and I try to reintroduce the wee chick to his Fridge Jumping family. He can't keep up with the busy troop so we try again later. Cedric tucks him under his mother at bedtime.

P.m. Mouse: Again, she jerks him back to their private land. He is both excited by the signal from his phone and scared at the same time. He thought he had lost her—silence over many days an increasing sadness as well as a semi-relief. He does not want the burden of the Tidal Wave—and yet, she is his Lady—he cannot bear the thought of losing her forever. Does she understand this is why he does not make a clean break? That this is why he prefers the silence? In not responding he is not encouraging her to break her family ties. By keeping silent perhaps he will remain in her longing? Perhaps—but there again he may be driving home the nails in his own coffin to perfect love and union. Will she lose the respect she once had for him? He is risking the life of their spark, especially now that she is through The Castle Gates and his restrictions are lifted.

But can he trust her word? He has done so in the past, only to find a different story from The Laird. Oh, he does not believe she lies to him; just that she makes light of something deathly serious. And what of him? Well, he knows he cannot trust himself around her—their attraction is too strong; too perfectly aligned to resist, unless he hardens his heart to her, as he has done these past few months. Hmm—Dear Angels in Heaven—please help us this Easter. St. Michael, as you return to our autumn skies please rescue your stranded Warriors. Last year you befriended them with swords and song writing, valiant endeavour and passionate honour—perhaps you might again as this new, golden season reaches our shores. Amen.

Monday 2nd April 2007

A beautiful shore and warming sun welcomes us as we walk this morning. I am in Tui Park with the dog. We run, splashing into the familiarity of our favourite bay. The water is glassy still today. The heat scorches my shoulders. Shoals of tiny fish dart around us—swish, turn—this way, that way—between our doggie paws and feminine toes. The Bog-Brush and I enjoy our golden moments, knowing they won't last forever. Returning to the shade of the exotic trees I notice steam coming off the sands; the tide is receding and the ghosts of quandary disperse over seaweed ribbons and secretive mangrove; beautiful.

I see Adrian in the distance at school this afternoon. He doesn't look up. Was I too forward in my message last night? "*He can't bear the thought of losing her forever,*" was that too bold a statement? Maybe he *can* bear the thought. I hang another golden Easter egg above the seasonal table at school pick-up time; one every day during Holy Week. "I don't think we'll have time to *Beat the Bounds,*" says Little J—a European ritual which we considered introducing here. "Perhaps we should find a more culturally fitting event next year," I suggest. We agree and decide to dance 'Strip the Willow' instead. I would love to ask The Laird to lead the dance. I can't think of a more fitting way to celebrate Easter with this beloved community than over the hand-shaking agreement of my two men as they lead The School in celebration. Cordelia picks up her violin and plays a melody that could accompany the dance.

As the sun and music wash over me in this delightful environment my love for Adrian is confirmed. I am happy and accepting. Whatever happens, together or apart, nothing can steal the joy we share. I write up my diary while I wait for the children to gather their school bags. I smile as I think of

'Little Hopper', happy this morning with his chicken siblings in The Mountain sunshine at home. He is smaller than the others but seems to be holding his own.

Driving back up the hill I wonder if I should get the family home to England. Perhaps this has to happen before Adrian and I have a chance to be together. Is the path ahead impossible? Little Arthur's insistence taps the keys of hopeful melody. Are we being called to gift him life?

P.m. Mouse {Unsent}: *He made love to her twice last night. She felt him, strong and powerful beside her—inside her—insistent and commanding as Lord Swallow, celebrating their gift without shame. She overheard The Laird speaking with a close friend yesterday. His defences are down at last. She can hear the beginnings of acceptance and grief. Four months to the day and he is seeing the truth. I feel sad for him, but not sad enough to change direction. I know the path I tread is the right one; the right path for our future growth. Is this The Laird's chance to break away from his mother? Will this encourage our emotional freedom? Does he need to find someone or something new in his life, as I have done?*

P.m. Mouse: *Goodnight, My Distant Friend—sorry about Sunday's message. I shouldn't have presumed what you are thinking. It probably made you cross if none of it rang true. Forgive me—I just need to talk to you, that's all. How are you? How are the cows? I think of you on your evening milking session. I see your busy life taking off in the school newsletter. I find it sad that I am not part of you anymore, that I cannot share these things; orchards and farm, trolleys and archery, invention and creation as we had always planned. Everyday you grow more distant. Perhaps that is what you need? The last thing I want to be is an annoying burden—so—I ask you again—please send me a blank text now if you want me to stop sending messages. If I do not hear I shall continue to send the occasional text. I hope to go away for a short time over the holidays, to write and make decisions. Sleep well. M—X*

I receive no blank text.

Chapter 4 Now?

Tuesday 3rd April 2007

I rise at five a.m. The dog and I walk in the moonlight. A single More Pork Owl hoots in the pine trees below the cabins. Three Mamacou Fern stand as silhouettes above the gorse covered mountain. A few stars are visible above their branches. The ducks wake; their eerie quacks from the wetland below the drive echo along the gorge. Back home I switch on the computer and settle down to write. The story is reaching fever pitch—both the first Book and this current, second Book that I live each day. Passion and sensuality bounce off the screen, making my mouth dry and my heart beat unusually fast.

The Laird comes downstairs. His eyes are red—my poor darling—has he been crying? My heart goes out to him but I cannot change direction. I am undaunted by the journey ahead. He disappears to the top cabin to send an English friend a message. He needs his friends right now.

***Early P.m. {Unsent}:** We saw you today Sir—all smiles and checked shirt. Were you carrying something for the cows? Milking buckets or feed? "Adrian is becoming a farmer," I tell the children. Our trusty Minx pipes up and says; "Oh—couldn't you become his helper?" She never fails to supply some intuitive gem.*

Cedric's College friends are involved in a performance of the Musical 'Joseph'. As a family we went to see the show last night—spectacular! The Laird is upset his eldest son didn't follow his suggestion and leap on stage with his classmates. I sigh—the more he insists the children join in, the more they refuse. A tricky lesson for their showman father.

"Why don't you just go down and confront Adrian properly?" The Laird asked me last night. He knows the dilemma we face. "I have my pride—it's complicated," I say. "We are vaguely in touch. I wish you knew that my love for you remains the same."

Wednesday 4th April 2007

The end of lent approaches. It is Maundy Thursday tomorrow. The washing of feet; of service and unselfish acts. And here I am, thinking selfish thoughts of fulfilling my personal, private passion. Not a good thing. In fact, probably the worst thing I *could* think. So, we shall see what today brings. I will plan our holiday. I will organize some escape for myself; time away to

233

think and write. We shall make plans and move forward, I hope. Dear Lord, please help us.

Our festival group meeting goes well this afternoon, although we can't find the painted board that Adrian made last year. {He hasn't been part of the group this term.} The board works so well with the Easter poem I wrote. Little J. and I look everywhere. My tales of our Mountain life always amuse her. The 'Fridge Jumpers' make her giggle. "Have you and the dog been banished yet?" She asks playfully. "Almost," I reply; "along with the pig and my pet rooster; Wonky. I think we might be heading for an Elf-House at the bottom of the land before long."

ANTIPODEAN EASTER

A burning sky lends time a pause,
Stillness—waiting—sunset shores.
Look, the circling birds up high,
Seek shelter for the night time vigil,
And on the skyline a lone hare, watching for the moon,
When will his time come? Surely soon.

The world is waiting, bathed in reds and golds and flaming crimson,
Turning to night each note of the birdsong.
And in the distance the olive mountain beckons, forlorn.
The sad dance begins— {pause}
Knowing the sun will rise again, majestically on Easter morn.

P.m. Mouse: *Dear Friend—do you know where our Easter board for the Seasonal Table could have gone? The one with your sunset on one side and my St. Michael on the other? We looked everywhere today after our Festival Group meeting. No luck. Not in the kitchen by Class 1 or in the costume cupboard. Any ideas? We need it by tomorrow. Also need to ask you a couple of other things—business of course-M-X*

Adrian: *Hi, My Friend. I have no idea where board is—ask Marcie. It was behind organ. Wonder what else you wanted to speak to me about? Oh, Sienna will read the poem tomorrow. Thanks. I liked the little cow references in the last tale.*

The atmosphere at home is difficult. My poor Laird becomes more rattled as each day passes. What a Lenten journey for us this year; our reason for this Antipodean escape, I know. "How about this for an idea"? He asks. "If *you* agree to speak honestly with Simon then *I* will contact Adrian, letting him know he may meet with you. I can't wait for your decision any longer. I am unhappy you are not speaking to anyone, apart from your dubious Book. I need to know where I stand in all this chaos. And—I do want you to be happy." I thank him. Kissing my husband I climb the stairs to bed. We both know that we have been out of love for a long time.

Late P.m. Mouse: He happens to be in town, strolling along the waterfront. He will pass The Marina on his way home. It is tempting yet awkward to gaze through the railings. The wind is up again tonight. It blows his hair into his eyes, was even blowing the cows' tails into the milk as he worked this evening. The stars take his gaze heavenwards—perhaps she watches there too? He arrives at the boat-yard faster than he expected— but—what is this? Not only has the padlock been removed but the gates stand wide open. He is shocked, scared and excited all at the same time. What can it mean?

He dares to take a step inside, not even sure if he wants to go there again. But the need to be close to his Boat is greater than the urge to run away. Yes. Masterfully, as befits a newly crowned King, he strides openly towards 'The Celestial Sea'. Is someone watching from the office doorway? He senses he is not alone. As he expected his Lady has left him a note—she was ever one for notes. However, on closer inspection he discovers it is not his Lady's handwriting that greets his enquiring eye, but The Laird's.

Maundy Thursday 5th April 2007

The end of term; nearly the end of Lent and perhaps the end of 'Dry Dock' as Easter arrives. How strange that everything should come together at once, and at this poignant time of year; four months since we signed our unwelcome agreement on Maketu beach. And yes, the path is opening before us; wide and possible. Of course, it isn't strange that Easter takes our story's hand and opens the Marina Gates. I am used to the extraordinary timings that continue to hold our tale. Easter—a time of re-birth and new beginnings as we come towards our second Book's grand 'dénouement'.

I take the bull by the horns and telephone Simon, the Senior Marine Official. "Yes, I can see you today," he responds—"how about after school drop-off this morning?"

We duly meet and I am asked to sit in his 'office', {his car}, beside the school buildings. In the end, we sit in *my* 'office', to keep the Castle Hound from going too mad. She breaks any ice with her crazy, over-friendly antics anyway. I am surprisingly calm in the face of having to speak to someone about my connection with Adrian. The honourable truth of our union means I feel no guilt or embarrassment. I am aware that he knows a lot; that he has spoken to both The Laird and Lord Swallow at length, as well as to Big J. who informed him of our bond in the first place.

"I imagine things are not too easy between you and The Laird, right now", he begins. "I sit here, wearing many different hats. For a start, I am the Chairman of Governors and I am also a parent at School. Adrian is my son's adored teacher and he is a personal friend too. Now, I see my friend, The Laird, with whom I play squash having a very hard time and my heart goes out to him. He is worried that you are not talking to anyone. It is only in talking to others that you can get a sense of perspective. I have given him the details of some free counselling that the N.Z government offers. It's a really useful service, especially if you decide to part. It is always a painful process. They say there are thirteen levels to travel through. A difficult journey for all involved. If you go down that route then you would need this help to make it as painless as possible. You need to know it is never a case of ending 'happily ever after.' Someone is always the loser."

"Now, I'm not the one to say whether it is the right path for you to be following," Simon continues. "It may be right on a spiritual level but not on an everyday one. I pass no judgement or comment. That is for you to decide. I have spoken to Adrian and I understand that it is something extraordinary and sacred that you share. But he assured me it was over in January. He was sorry and knew he had made a mistake. I also have to consider the whole affair from the perspective of his job and his professional conduct."

Lord Swallow makes a dash from the top field towards the classrooms as we speak, probably cutting it fine for his Main Lesson teaching. I expect he has been tending his beloved cows. He must see us as he runs by. My charming Marine Official smiles ruefully—"should we beckon him over?" We continue with our conversation, concern for The Laird uppermost in Simon's mind. "Even if just for him, I think you should try the counselling," he suggests. "And have you noticed how everyone is treating this with the greatest respect and care? You know, The Laird understands your need for creativity and passion. The other day he spoke of a rose being plucked from its natural habitat; how it will bloom for a while in water but not forever. It thrives where it can grow." My caring husband; he knows me so well on one level yet not at all on another. I bless him. How can I even consider putting him through this agony?

And now it is my turn to speak. "I am not the kind of person who would normally consider an association like this; I need you to understand that. It is only because of the beauty and truth of this connection that I am considering following its path. I have a very strong need in me; have had for many years now, to reach much deeper levels of union than we, as a married couple, are capable of. Our union has always been about going out to others, about creating community and providing a base from which things can happen. This is a natural place for The Laird with his reliance on others for a sense of well-being. But I am more self-sufficient. I have needs for privacy and seclusion that he feels uncomfortable with. I need that now to be able to grow and he needs to grow too. I think I have been a replacement mother figure and it is now time to leave home and lean less on me and more on his growing, inner strength. I feel sure this is an important step. I cannot say I know in what form but I have never regretted my action or choices. If we had stayed in the U.K there is no way that our life-style, our family circle or cultural structures would have granted us this opportunity, however one might regard it."

He looks at me seriously and asks; "and have you told The Laird all this?" "Yes, we do not keep anything from each other. We talk in controlled conversation; never heated, although I suspect he is not feeling in control of the situation." "It sounds to me as if you are waiting for his permission to take some sort of step, and that his language for growth is different from yours; am I right?" "Yes, that is it", I agree. "Well, I don't think he is going to come up to your level; you will have to meet him halfway. And he would not run with your idea of living under the same roof, yet having freer ties; he is not that free, himself." "I know", I reply. "He will not give you the green light for a night of sexual romp either, of that I can assure you!" "It is not about sexual romp, I explain; "I won't deny it is there, but it is not the driving force."

Simon is a gentle, wise man. He listens and understands in a non-judgemental manner giving me comfort and reassurance. I feel confidant in the reality of the situation, in the meaning of its presence in our lives and I can tell that he respects my reasoning. "The Laird and I have been together for a quarter of a century", I continue. "We have reached a turning point and this is an important part of it." He asks me what he can do to help. "I need to know what Adrian is *really* feeling. I suspect he is not being totally truthful with himself and the rest of us. There are things that have passed between us that mean he could not truly mean the ambivalence he claims. For a move, in any direction, I need to know more from him. I cannot ask because he will not tell me, for lots of different reasons. He has been badly rattled by The Laird. Could you try and find out, without putting him under any pressure?" Simon agrees to do what he can. "I should have some answers by the end of the Easter weekend," he says. "Did you know that ambivalence is the beginning of change? I have just done a course on it."

"I can make decisions once I know Adrian's truth", I say. "It may well be that I choose the humility of self-sacrifice. I know that riches lie there. I am writing a Book about our unusual journey", I add. "Yes," he has heard. I tell Simon a little about the content; about our Boat, The Celestial Sea. I touch on the extraordinary magical happenings; such as the Angel light photo we took of ourselves on the Pa site when we crowned each other with swords and garlands, agreeing to keep to our own Kingdoms with a solemn vow. I mention the strange events around the Festival Archway in the dead of night and the picture The Laird brought back on his return from New Zealand two Februarys ago. "It was one of Adrian with a chalk-board drawing behind him; we put it up on the wall in my parents' kitchen. I have only just realized the significance. You can guess what the drawing was?" Simon looks at me and says; "a Boat, of course". "Yes, it was a Boat".

We chat a little more; we talk about The Boat being in dry-dock behind locked gates. "I suppose I am a henchman, or something?" he laughs. "No" I reply. "You are the Senior Marine Official; everyday, a new page of the story is written". He grins. "You shall have the first copy of The Book if it comes to anything," I decide. "Oh great, can I come on a fishing trip then?" He asks. "Oh, no Sir!" I reply. "It is not about fishing, most *definitely* not about fishing!" He leaves the car with a friendly chuckle and almost a wink. "Thank-you", I say. "You are a good friend to us all."

I wonder what Simon makes of our unusual situation as he walks back to his car; a mental health professional he must come across many different challenges in his working life, though possibly not anything involving mystical boats, school scandal and Angels.

Arriving safely in his classroom, Lord Swallow must have many thoughts swirling around in his mind: "So, his Lady is in the Senior Marine Official's office. He spies them as he runs down from checking his 'Ladies' in the meadow above the school, hoping not to be late for his Main Lesson. Why is she meeting him here? Easier than the boat-yard perhaps? The Bog-Brush is presiding over events, he can tell, sprawled over Simon's legs, dissolving any nerves. He wonders what bombshell she is dropping now. He is excited, yet horrified at the same time. What is he being called to do? To be? Is he ready? Oh, goodness—eyes down, dash past, hurry on with the tasks in hand. My word, but she sets a spanking pace. And he? Yes, he is still thrilled to be a part of the grand adventure."

So, the ever-loving Laird will let Lord Swallow know it is *sort* of acceptable for him to meet with his wife. The ultimate gift any man can give another. My, my. The dénouement approaches fast and for these unusual friends, their hearts beat in time; scared, excited and relieved that the end, or the beginning, is in sight.

* * * * * * *

This afternoon I help Sammy transport pupils from school to Camellia House; the After School Club that I mentioned earlier. Unfortunately we get stuck in a huge traffic snarl-up. The entire town is gridlocked. A couple of car accidents and a lorry load of spilled earth bring police cars and standstill traffic queues everywhere. I really don't need a vanload of stir-crazy children today, including the Bog-Brush. Luckily Josh produces a packet of chocolate muffins, which rescues the hour-long wait and interests the dog. Eventually we arrive at Camellia House and I help the children make Easter baskets. Sammy prepares a celebration barbecue and families spill into the garden with bottles of fizz and chatter.

Camellia House is celebrating the end of its first term. I talk to Sammy, whose company I always enjoy. She is launching an organic cookie business with her mother while her husband, Bruce, concentrates on the After School Programme. I like her dynamism and vitality. We share a similar optimism and I applaud her energy. We talk about filling our lives with overflowing initiative and commitment. "I suppose I have been in that space for the past few years," I say. "Coming to New Zealand has allowed me to go inwards; calming down my life somewhat. In fact, I'm writing a book," I tell her; "a romance." She looks up from turning the sausages; interested. "Based on anyone I know?" She asks. "I blush." "You're going red," she laughs, adding; "Oh, I keep meaning to say, I like the music you and Adrian wrote last term." I am surprised by her comment. Does she subconsciously understand the scenario? "There's a lot more where that came from," I reply.

Good Friday 6th April 2007

We walk on the beach before the three o'clock church service this afternoon. It is a hot, hot day. The Laird and I have run out of conversation. We walk in silence. The holiday atmosphere has returned, despite the arrival of autumn. Surfers tackle the waves, Maori girls in tight bikinis build sandcastles and a group of teenagers chat loudly as they walk along the sand dunes. We take a different beach access path today. I peer over smart fencing at expensive houses. The deluxe homes are modern and varied. I stop outside a dark blue building with extensive gardens running right down to the beach. Bougainvillea tumbles over the elevated deck and a woman hangs out laundry with a small dog at her feet. As I look out to sea I wonder what this weekend heralds. Are we running for the boat-yard, Lord Swallow? Are we getting ready to set sail, or do we gift The Celestial Sea to the Maritime museum and wave her goodbye?

Easter Saturday 7th April 2007

A.m. Mouse {Unsent}: Good morning, My Love. What is in your mind? What are you doing today? We have been busy—as usual. The Book is coming along nicely. You would have enjoyed my early morning walk; the clouds were pink and the stars still twinkly. The pig keeps chasing the baby chicks. We shut her on the deck yesterday but she barged her way into the house, shredding the recycling bag in her perpetual hunt for food.

I am happy this morning. When I delivered The Laird his morning cup of tea he noticed my twinkly eyes that match the stars. "You've been at that Book again, haven't you?" He accused. "Yes, I admitted with a big smile. "There are some funny parts, which you might enjoy." He was friendly for a while, but it didn't last. "I'm warning you—I am angry today." Oops—better run for the boat-yard. Are we ready to set sail, Lord Swallow?

"I shall be buying my ticket out of here before long," he added. And yesterday as I chopped onions he said: "you had better get used to crying." Oh dear—doom and gloom. How come I feel so light and happy all the time? I'd better assume a mature and serious attitude. And so, My Friend—how go the cows? How goes your heart? What do I sense is coming? Did you speak to Simon? Perhaps I might know soon. Blessings on this Easter Weekend—X

"Help Ma, Molly's in the larder; she's ripped a hole in the dog food sack!" Rinky yells from the kitchen, bringing the family running. I arrive to find her riding the pig out of the larder! The Dog and the Go-Getter throw themselves into the fracas, yelling, kicking, and barking above the pig squeals—crazy!

The cat watches from the draining board until our uninvited houseguest leaves the kitchen with a grunt. Luckily Cedric doesn't storm down the stairs to complain about the racket. He sleeps through the pandemonium; a miracle in the face of our family crisis this fine Easter Saturday morning.

Midday sees us enjoying the town's annual Jazz Festival. We join Clive and his family in a Turkish restaurant at lunchtime. We sit on cosy alcove benches with cushions piled high. Antique fabric panels catch my eye, and old harness too. I like the way the walls are painted in a Mediterranean blue wash and niches with rusty lanterns promise intimate, candlelit evenings. The Turkish patron supervises his young staff while overseeing the stone oven. A Russian waitress brings colourful platters of dips and oven-baked pita bread to our table. The Laird draws her into conversation and we discover she has recently moved from Scotland. She is a skilled artist, specializing in Celtic art. Kiwi life brings all sots of different nationalities together; you never know whom you might meet. She gives us the website details of her business venture, incorporating her artistic interests. Like his mother, The Laird never misses an opportunity to engage strangers in conversation. I have to admit, this often makes me cringe; my husband's constant flamboyance and often inappropriate behaviour increases each year.

With appetites satisfied, we push our way through the crowds that throng the harbour-side walkway. A variety of musical performances keep us entertained as we stroll through the town, eventually reaching the van. I bump into Simon as I open the vehicle's sliding door. "Thank-you for the other day", I say. "I have made some phone calls," he informs me. "You should hear something soon."

Easter Sunday 8th April 2007

Of course, the Grand Finale of our second Book has to be today; no other day would be fitting. I wake early and walk the dog, expecting my phone to light up, knowing the blessed hand of Angel-held destiny continues to direct events.

A.m. Mouse: The Good Friday service was sad and forlorn—their personal Crucifixion. The Laird and his Lady are on a roll; nothing can turn back the clock. They have crossed oceans for this minute opening; this whisper glimpse of possibility in their otherwise immoveable burden. They are being given a second chance; their quarter century done; their uphill struggle complete. An unorthodox, second chance. Ever keen for higher learning she sees it before he does. He is in pain. He cannot conceive of going against all he has ever believed. He teaches this code of practise for goodness sake! Why does she always challenge him? Always push him so? He works hard to join her impossible stance and she blesses his valiant striving. He knows, deep down, there is truth in what she seeks. Perhaps this is his chance to stand alone and self-empowered; knowing she is there, will

240

always be there, but allowing him his vocation and freedom.

The heavy rock in front of the Easter tomb needs to be moved and he is the one being called to shift it. These are the thoughts that nag the edges of his more conventional mind. She knows what she is doing. Why does she always know? Little Woman, born to rule; the meaning behind her name.

Meanwhile, Lord Swallow remains at the edge of the Forest, tending his cows with calm assurance that something is happening. He is surprised by his calm—yes—the last four months have prepared him well. His life is in order—his mind is in order—his strength assured. She would hardly recognize him today. But of course she would, she has known all along. After all, it was with her that he made a large part of the journey. He is grounded now and knows what he wants. A group of birds circle up high, 'seeking shelter for the night time vigil'. His eyes follow them as the calm observer.

The sad Friday leaves our shores for another year. We attend the Easter vigil as a family which in itself is quite a feat. The enthusiastic new Priest preaches on the heaviness of the rock in front of the Easter tomb-**"Are we willing to move the rocks in front of our own tombs to achieve deeper communion with Christ?"** I wonder what he would make of my reply. **"To lay down one's life for another is the greatest form of love,"** he continues. **"He bowed down his head and gave up the Spirit."**

I cannot sense Lord Swallow on the pew this evening, but, on glancing up I meet his honest eyes seeking mine. Walking out of the Forest at last to greet me I imagine him standing to one side of the altar in front of the celebrants and not more than two metres away. He is calm. He is centred. His hands lie still by his side. We gaze at each other while listening to the service, our eyes only closing when we bow our heads for God's blessing; for his guidance and love.

Midday, Adrian: *Resurrection—new life—fresh start—mighty power— life-giving power. Oh, Christ, your power floods the world with new hope; new strength. Holy Power, stir in our hearts an inner spring, though autumn leaves fall onto the cooling Earth outwardly may there be a spring within us. May the sap of our souls course through us. Inner Power—strengthening— surging—growing a new ring of strength—a new layer of wide, heart-wood— new branches of love and compassion—new roots of faith and courage.*

As I write, a new idea comes to me. I cannot deny the pleasure and ease you bring into my life. To have a companion who understands my thoughts and ways is rare, and you do. I know I can search my heart and write it and you will understand; a Companion of the Soul. So, my intention changes— softens—an idea springs. But first the background. This was a message to invite you to a meeting; a meeting where I would tell you clearly that the maelstrom I would not meet. The calm contentment of my cud-chewing cows gives me a new steadiness and foundation for clarity—a measuring stick. I will protect their harmony for it is graced. So, no Tidal Wave will I call into the fields and folds of their farm. You must make your choice without me in the picture. Your decision must be for you. I will not be a partner/husband to you. These were my thoughts and the ones I voiced to Simon who had suggested a facilitated meeting. But now—a new thought. Clear I stand by these words. My cows are the symbol of God's grace; the hand of destiny and I trust them. Harsh this sounds. Hmm—you have your children and family to consider. I have my cows and community. They temper my desires and longings, elevating them to more refined forms; to service and to work— touchstones for steadiness. Pressing my head into a warm flank, breathing their warm goodness and herding them back to their field—strong and steady I must be. And from here I say, "Dear heart—My Soul's Companion— work we have to do together but run to me you may not; it will startle the cows."

Mouse: Thank-you, Lord Swallow. An acknowledgement was all I needed. Our Easter guidance comes to us in a bovine message—a fitting simplicity. As always, I take your lead. Tread gently in the field. Perhaps wave to me from the shore as I sail our Boat alone; probably back to Northern Hemisphere waters.

My True Love and Soul Companion, there are rich blessings in selfless humility and abandonment of longing.

Take care—your Lady, always-X

Happy Easter

* * * * * * *